Meredith, Alone

Meredith, Alone

Claire Alexander

GRAND CENTRAL
PUBLISHING

New York   Boston

Grand Central Publishing
Hachette Book Group
1290 Avenue of the Americas, New York, NY 10104
grandcentralpublishing.com
twitter.com/grandcentralpub

First published in 2022 in the UK by Penguin Michael Joseph, a division of Penguin Random House UK, a Penguin Random House Company.
First Grand Central Publishing edition: November 2022

Grand Central Publishing is a division of Hachette Book Group, Inc. The Grand Central Publishing name and logo is a trademark of Hachette Book Group, Inc.

The publisher is not responsible for websites (or their content) that are not owned by the publisher.

The Hachette Speakers Bureau provides a wide range of authors for speaking events. To find out more, go to www.hachettespeakersbureau.com or call (866) 376-6591.

Library of Congress Control Number: 2022937915

ISBNs: 9781538709948 (hardcover), 9781538709962 (ebook)

Printed in the United States of America

LSC-C

Printing 1, 2022

For Benji, Elizabeth, and Alice.
The loves of my life.

I fear me this—is Loneliness—
The Maker of the soul
Its Caverns and its Corridors
Illuminate—or seal—

Emily Dickinson, "The Loneliness
One Dare Not Sound"

A journey of a thousand miles begins with a single step.

Lao Tzu (and Meredith's therapist, Diane)

Prologue

I've got six minutes to walk to the train station, plenty of time if I wear my flat boots. My trench coat is hanging on the hook by the front door, my red hat stuffed in its pocket. My bag on the kitchen table contains everything I need for a day at the office. My hair is freshly washed and straightened; my lips are glossed. They match my hat—by chance, but I like it.

Somewhere between the kitchen and the front door I become aware of a seed of doubt in my throat. I can't swallow it down or cough it up. My chest is tight, my palms hot. Tingles race up my arms, like tiny electric shocks. I keep my eyes on the floor, watching my feet slide across the wooden boards I'd sanded, so painstakingly, only a month earlier. It's as if they belong to someone else.

I slump onto the stairs, sit on the third step from the bottom, and try to swallow. I'm still staring at my feet, encased in the thick socks I always wear with my flat boots because I tend to be between sizes and I'd opted to go up a half in them. The boots stand tall and proud beneath my coat at the end of the hall. I know they're there, but I can't reach them.

All I have to do is walk to the door. Slide my feet into my boots and pull the zippers. Put on my coat and my red hat. Hook my bag over my shoulder and lock the door behind me. A simple sequence that takes less than a minute of my day. If I leave now, I can still make my train. I can still get to work on time.

But the seed in my throat is swelling. I gulp for air. There's nobody here to help me and I can't help myself because my arms and legs are on fire.

When I can finally take my phone out of my bag, three hours have passed, I've missed twelve calls, and I'm still sitting on the third step from the bottom.

Day 1,214

Wednesday, November 14, 2018

My name is Meredith Maggs and I haven't left my home for 1,214 days.

Day 1,215

Thursday, November 15, 2018

I'm tidying the living room when he arrives. First, he pulls up outside my house in a gray car. Next, he walks up my path. He has a slim folder tucked under one arm and long legs. It only takes him three strides to reach the door.

At 10:57 a.m. the tall man rings my doorbell.

I like it when people are punctual. I don't get many visitors—my best friend, Sadie, and her kids, James and Matilda, and the grocery deliveryman are my only regulars. Sadie is often late and frazzled, but I let her off because she's a single mum with a busy job—a cardiac nurse at the biggest hospital in Glasgow. The grocery deliveryman is always right on time.

I take deep breaths, watch my feet walk to the door in their blue Converse. Look at my right hand as it reaches for the handle, grips, pushes, pulls. I draw the door toward me, slowly, and do a quick scan. Checked shirt, buttoned right up to the neck, under a navy duffel coat. A few years younger than me, I think. Or maybe just someone who benefits from fresh air and sunshine. He has dark hair, short at the sides and longer on top. A friendly face—open eyes and an easy smile, not forced.

I don't get a lot of visitors. But this one seems OK, on first impression.

He offers a hand. "Meredith? I'm Tom McDermott from Holding Hands, the befriending charity. I've been looking forward to meeting you."

I wish I could say the same, but of all the things I have to

4

look forward to—and it's a short list admittedly—this isn't one of them. Meeting new people has never been a joy. Especially people who visit solely to make sure I'm not neglecting my personal care, or wasting away, or drinking vodka for breakfast. When the boxes have been ticked and the forms have been filled out, I'm really rather boring.

I shake Tom McDermott's hand, because it's the polite thing to do. He's the first man to come to my house since Gavin—lovely, sweet Gavin, who was no match for my nightmares—but I don't feel threatened. I don't find Tom McDermott intimidating, in his checked shirt and duffel coat, standing on my doorstep.

Still, I don't let him in. Not yet. Even though I invited him here, grudgingly, after Sadie left the leaflet on my kitchen table under a box of Tunnock's Teacakes and I went through the motions. The same leaflet that Tom McDermott has just fished out of his folder and is holding up in front of me. I interlink my fingers behind my back in response to the large black capital letters: "WE'RE HERE TO HOLD YOUR HAND." An act of defiance that only I'm aware of.

I look at the two people on the front of the leaflet. I know their faces well—I've seen them several times a day because they're attached to the front of my fridge with a magnet in the shape of a heart. One is a middle-aged woman, the other a man who looks old enough to be her grandfather. He has cloudy eyes and a tuft of white hair on either side of his head, and looks tiny in his armchair, shoulders hunched up around his ears. They're smiling at each other and—right on brand—holding hands.

"I always thought befriending was for old people," I tell Tom McDermott, ready to label the leaflet as Exhibit A.

"Actually, we try to reach out to anyone who might need a friend. Elderly people, teenagers, anyone in between."

"I have friends," I tell him, stretching the truth.

"Maybe you have room for another one?"

I think about this, about the way my tiny circle might not pass for a circle at all—unless cats count—and I'm not really concentrating on what he's saying about training and risk assessments and codes of conduct. But I decide I'm curious enough to let him into my house.

I couldn't move my almost-completed jigsaw of Gustav Klimt's *The Kiss* from the coffee table in the living room, so I'd carefully pushed it against the wall. If Tom McDermott needs a table, we can move through to the kitchen.

I leave him there and go to make us tea. ("No sugar—I'm sweet enough," he tells me with a wink, and somehow it comes across as quite endearing, not sleazy.) When I return, he's kneeling down, looking at *The Kiss*.

"How long did this take you?" he asks.

"A few days, just doing the odd half hour here and there," I say, setting the tea tray on the floor. I've added a plate of chocolate cookies, despite Tom McDermott claiming he's sweet enough.

"Amazing," he says, and I *think* he's talking about the jigsaw, not the biscuits, but he reaches for a cookie and takes a bite. He stays on the floor, his long legs crossed, and washes his cookie down with a gulp of tea. For a total stranger, he's making himself very comfortable in my living room. I perch on the end of the couch, my mug sending heat into my palms.

"Meredith, it's really good to meet you. Before we start chatting, let me give you some information about the charity. It was set up in 1988, right here in Glasgow, by a woman called Ada Swinney, whose mother was housebound due to dementia. Our mission today is exactly the same as Ada's was back then—to offer company, friendship, and support to anyone who needs it."

I don't know what to say, so I sip my tea.

"The most important thing, at all times, is that you feel comfortable and safe. At any time, if you don't, you can tell me to leave and I will—no questions asked!" He takes some forms out of his folder. "Shall we get the boring stuff out of the way first?"

I answer all his questions and nod in all the right places until the forms are back where they belong.

"You're clearly a bit of a star at jigsaw puzzles," he says. "What else do you like to do with your time?"

After a few long seconds of Tom McDermott smiling—he has, I concede, kind eyes—and me looking blankly back at him, I say, "I read a lot."

"Well, I can see that!" He gestures at the books lining an entire wall of the room, then jumps to his feet in one surprisingly smooth motion for someone with those legs. "Quite a variety you have here, Meredith. Plenty of classics…history… art…do you have an all-time favorite?"

"It's actually a poetry collection. Emily Dickinson." I join him at the shelves and reach for a slim orange book, its spine soft and creased from decades of use, from the touch of fingers much older than mine. I bought it in my favorite secondhand bookshop; it has *For Violet, ever yours* handwritten on the inside cover. I've often wondered who Violet was, and why a book given to her with so much commitment ended up being available to me for two pounds. Whatever its story, I feel safe with it in my hand.

"Dickinson. She felt a funeral in her brain, didn't she? Genius."

"You can borrow it, if you like." I surprise myself by offering him the book.

"I would love to. Thank you, Meredith. I'll take very good care of it, and give it back to you the next time I see you."

I'm a little taken aback. I expected him to say—politely, kindly—that he couldn't possibly take my favorite book. But by the time I've taken my seat back on the couch, he's tucked it into his folder and has helped himself to another chocolate cookie.

"Meredith, I know you haven't left your house for a very long time," he says.

"One thousand two hundred and fifteen days," I tell him.

"A very long time," he says again.

"Well, it's flown by."

"You count the days?"

I shrug, feeling stupid. "I guess I have nothing to count down to, so I count up."

I fold my arms across my body, well aware of the message that sends.

"We don't have to talk about that, if you don't want to." He keeps his voice soft, a contrast to my sharpness. "I'm here to get to know you. I'm interested to learn about your life, what you like and don't like, how you pass your time. And...well, maybe we can figure out a way to help you get back into the world?"

"I am in the world," I say defiantly.

"Yes, of course you are. But—"

"And I have a cat. Fred."

"Fred? Astaire, Savage?" He grins.

I don't. "Just Fred."

"I love cats," he says. I'm beginning to think that Tom McDermott will agree with me no matter what I say. He thinks my jigsaw is amazing. He loves Emily Dickinson and cats. I'm also beginning to regret giving him my most treasured poetry collection. I might never see him—or that beloved, faded orange cover—again. I wonder if I could ask for it back. Maybe he'll go to the bathroom and I could slip it out of his folder and put it back on the second shelf from the top, where it belongs.

But he shows no sign of going to the bathroom and wants to keep talking about cats.

"What happens if Fred gets sick?" he asks.

Tom McDermott has underestimated me. I've been asked all these questions before.

"Fred has never been sick," I say proudly. "But I have a very good friend, Sadie. Sadie would take Fred to the vet."

"Ah. That's good. What else does Sadie do for you?"

"She picks up my prescription once a month. That's it. She's my friend, not my carer." My shoulders feel tense. They've been frozen in place—somewhere near my ears—since I gave him my book. "I don't need anything else."

"And you work...full-time?"

"I'm a freelance writer, so it varies. But I'm kept busy."

"A writer? That sounds exciting."

"It's not really. I don't have bylines in the *New York Times* or anything. It's just web content for businesses."

"Believe me, it's exciting compared to what I used to do." He pulls a face. "I got made redundant from my job in finance last year. So I'm taking a bit of time out, trying to figure out what to do next."

I nod. I've never been good at small talk.

"What about your family, Meredith? Do they visit often?"

My stomach clenches. I take a gulp of my tea.

"It's complicated," I tell him.

"I'm pretty good with complicated," he says, and his voice is gentle. "But we don't have to go there, Meredith."

"I have a mother. And a sister. Fiona. Fee. She's eighteen months older than me." I rush the words out of my mouth.

"What's your sister like?" It's a natural question, out of his.

"Different from me. But I don't know anything about her anymore. We haven't spoken for a long time. I don't see her or my mother at all, actually."

"It *is* complicated," Tom says softly. Then he waits, and the fact that he's giving me space makes me wonder if I can say more. But I can't find the right words, so I go back into the kitchen for more cookies.

Half an hour later, I stand at my front door and wait patiently for Tom McDermott to leave, to take three strides down my garden path and get into his gray car and drive away. I'm exhausted from all the talking, all the questions, all the worrying about my book, all the pretending my life is a ten when the truth is that most days barely scratch the underside of a six.

He's taking his time to go. He's already thanked me profusely for my hospitality, looking straight into my eyes and telling me he'll be back to see me next week, if that's OK with me. Fred watches us from his favorite place, the comfy chair on the upstairs landing. It's the first man in the house for him too; I wonder if cats pick up on things like that. Part of me is pleased that he didn't come down to welcome Tom.

"Remember, there's no obligation on your part," Tom says. "If you hate my jokes, or can't afford all the cookies I eat, you can tell me to go away at any time. No hard feelings, I promise."

"You've got my favorite book, so I suppose I'll need to see you again."

"Very true." He smiles. "And I'm looking forward to seeing what jigsaw you're working on next."

"A mosaic tile design," I tell him. "It's intricate."

"Well, I can't wait to see it. Until then, Meredith."

I raise my hand to bid him farewell, but he pauses on the doorstep.

"One more thing, Meredith...if you don't mind? I'm curious—there must be something you used to do that you miss? One thing you can't do at home?"

It's started to rain heavily. Tom McDermott buttons up his duffel coat. Behind his head, the dense, gray clouds of the late-afternoon sky move toward me. I'm aware of them, without looking directly at them. I inch backward, away from the open door.

"Swimming. I love swimming," I say softly.

"I'm a terrible swimmer," he says. "I can do doggy paddle, and that's about it. Anyway..." He pulls the collar of his coat tighter round his neck and shakes a raindrop off the tip of his nose. "I'll be swimming home at this rate. Goodbye, Meredith. You take care."

"You too, Tom McDermott," I whisper as I close the front door.

That night, I dream I'm doing doggy paddle in a huge lake with Emily Dickinson. Tom McDermott and the old man from the leaflet are sitting on the side, watching and waving and eating chocolate biscuits.

Day 1,219

Monday, November 19, 2018

I check the clock: 8:19 a.m. Almost right on schedule. Plenty of time to exercise before putting my eggs on to boil at 8:54 a.m. Two eggs, five minutes, for the perfect runny yolk. It took me three days to master it and it was worth the trial and error.

But before perfect eggs, twenty minutes of cardio. What a revelation it was, the discovery that a twenty-minute workout each day—with a rest day of choice—is all I need to stay fit. I have a few favorite YouTube workouts, but I mix it up now and then, just for fun. And the beauty of doing it at home, alone, is that nobody sees how out of breath I get after six rounds of burpees.

I always follow cardio with relaxation: stretching, deep breathing, and positive affirmations. "I accept myself unconditionally" is one of the recent additions to my repertoire. This morning, yet again, I struggle to get on board with it; it doesn't quite roll off the tongue. Diane, my therapist, tells me to stick with it, that it has to become a habit to have an impact. I told her that I didn't think affirmations were supposed to be lies, which led to a long conversation about self-sabotaging behaviors.

Morning workout done, and with my eggs simmering, I drop two slices of sunflower-seed bread into the toaster until they turn golden brown. I give them a light spread of butter, slice them neatly, and pop them onto a plate. Next, the eggs go into their spotted cups, and I crack the tops (the best part) and sit down at the table with tea in my favorite mug, the one that matches my egg cups. It's 8:59 a.m. Perfect. I get a kick out of these little achievements.

I do a few hours of work offline, have a cheese and pickle sandwich for lunch, then log on. I try to limit my time online because I know how easy it is to get stuck there. A digital hour is like ten seconds in the real world. I wrote a schedule once, but quickly realized it didn't allow for those spontaneous Google moments that pop up on a regular basis, like when you need to know how to make a béchamel sauce or can't remember the name of Henry VIII's fifth wife (he popped into my head when I was thinking about misogyny one day, and I always get the Catherines mixed up).

I know some people think the internet is the root of all evil, but I couldn't survive without it. Literally. I can get anything I want delivered to my house, often within twenty-four hours. Fresh milk and tampons and batteries and books. I don't even have to answer the door, if I don't feel like seeing anyone that day. I have a box attached to the front of it, big enough for parcels. I fitted it myself, I'm proud to say.

Luckily I found a clever app that records the time I spend online and disconnects me when I reach my daily limit of eight hours. Up to six of those are spent working, depending on how many projects I have on the go, which leaves two hours for misogynistic kings and everything else. Even after all these months, it still surprises me when I hit the limit. But it makes me use my time.

After catching up with the news (it's International Men's Day, which leads me down a rabbit hole of opinion pieces about toxic masculinity), I sign into StrengthInNumbers, the online support group I joined after Sadie emailed me a link with "CHECK THIS OUT!!!" in the subject line. That was just one of her bright ideas. She has a lot of those, sending me links to new books or articles she hopes will give me the push I need to become a Normal Person again. She emails me reviews of new restaurants, texts me with Groupon deals for spa weekends and afternoon tea deals. Just in case, she writes. I delete them without reading them. I know Sadie means well, but I don't want to spend my free time reading research papers on social anxiety disorder or books about agoraphobia by people with a string of random letters after their names.

For the record I don't have either of those things.

I have to admit that StrengthInNumbers was one of Sadie's better ideas. I like the anonymity of making connections online, and it's comforting to know I'm not the craziest person in the country. Today, ninety-eight people are active—about normal for a Monday morning. Evenings and weekends are much busier, for obvious reasons. I'm lucky to be able to work from home and set my own hours, so I'm not tied to the nine-to-five grind. That's one thing I definitely don't miss. I often work late—I like being awake when the city sleeps.

I check in with a few of the regulars and ask about their weekends. Janice (WEEJAN) had a difficult time with her wayward teenage daughter, but she managed to resist eating all the chocolates in the Quality Street tin (she only had eight, and didn't make herself sick afterward). Gary (RESCUEMEPLZ) says he went on a bender—despite his best intentions—but what else can he do while he's on an eighteen-month waiting list for a counselor? I tell him it took twelve months for me to get my therapist, Diane, who's not exactly my favorite person in the world but I certainly never feel any worse after talking to her. Janice says he could get a private therapist for fifty pounds an hour. Gary says times are tough and he can't afford to pay fifty pounds an hour. Janice points out that he probably spends that on beer and vodka in a week, which doesn't go down well. I leave them to argue about the dangers of self-medicating and the strengths and weaknesses of the National Health Service. They'll go around in circles, as usual. I'm just about to log off when a private chat window opens on my screen.

CATLADY29: Hello?

I hover my cursor over the profile picture—a fluffy white cat, which makes me smile. I check her details: female, 29, Glasgow.

JIGSAWGIRL: Hi! ☺

CATLADY29: I'm not sure if I'm doing the right thing. It's my first time here…I just need someone to talk to…☹

JIGSAWGIRL: Hey, that's OK. I'm Meredith.

CATLADY29: Hi, Meredith. I'm Celeste.

JIGSAWGIRL: Hi, Celeste. I see you're in Glasgow? It's always nice to meet a fellow Weegie.

CATLADY29: You're in Glasgow too? Oh, that makes me feel like I'm talking to a real person. Whereabouts do you live?

JIGSAWGIRL: I'm definitely real. ☺ I live in the East End.

CATLADY29: I've just moved into a new place in the city center. Near the art school?

JIGSAWGIRL: Seriously? That's my old stomping ground. Good times!

CATLADY29: I'm on Sanderson Street.

JIGSAWGIRL: No way! That's where I lived. Number 48. Flat A.

CATLADY29: Meredith, you won't believe this. I'm in 48D.

JIGSAWGIRL: OMG! How crazy is that? The flat above!

CATLADY29: I know, right? When did you live there?

JIGSAWGIRL: I moved out about five years ago. Decided it was time to take the plunge and buy my own place. Do you like it there?

CATLADY29: I love the location. Tiny flat, though. Hardly big enough to swing a cat.

JIGSAWGIRL: LOL! I remember. Speaking of cats...who is the cutie in your profile picture?

CATLADY29: Ah, that's my mum's cat. Lucy. No pets allowed here, unfortunately ☹

JIGSAWGIRL: I have a cat. He's called Fred.

CATLADY29: Aww...you're so lucky! You'll need to put him on your profile picture so I can see him!

JIGSAWGIRL: I will! He deserves to be shown off ☺

CATLADY29: It's nice to meet you, Meredith. What brings you here?

My fingers move quickly over the keyboard, giving my stock answer.

JIGSAWGIRL: Friendship and support. I have some mental health issues.

CATLADY29: I hope that wasn't prying?

JIGSAWGIRL: Not at all. ☺

CATLADY29: ☺ So, how does it work on here?

JIGSAWGIRL: Well, there are different channels for different things. Depression, addiction, PTSD...everything really. Those are monitored and moderated by volunteers. There are lots of advice pages as well, with links to professional helplines and resources. And you can also chat privately to people, individually or in groups. Like we are now.

CATLADY29: It's quite daunting, to be honest.

JIGSAWGIRL: Hey, it's OK. I can't promise to help, but I can definitely listen, if you want to talk about anything.

I imagine her looking at her screen, wondering whether to confide in a stranger. Trying to decide whether sharing whatever it is that's been occupying her thoughts or giving her nightmares will make her feel better or worse. That's something I can't give an answer to. After almost two years, I still haven't fully opened up to Janice or Gary.

CATLADY29: Actually, I think I'd just like to chat about cats for a while, if that's OK?

JIGSAWGIRL: I can't think of anything I'd rather do. ☺

We end up chatting for ages, not just about our mutual love of cats but about Liza, who still lives in 48B and hangs her wet underwear over her windowsill to dry. I tell Celeste I'd have thought she'd have learned her lesson after a gust of wind blew her black-lace thong into the path of the number 60 bus, circa 2002. Celeste tells me she doesn't think Liza wears black-lace thongs anymore and sends me multiple laughing-face emojis, and I laugh out loud at the memory.

I realize that Sadie will be here soon—she texted me last night to say she'd pop in after picking James up from school. Before I sign off, I tell Celeste it's been really nice to chat to her, and I'm not just being polite.

Sadie arrived halfway through the first year of secondary school, a head taller than all the boys and with an attitude as bold as her hairstyle. So blonde it was almost white, she wore it close to her head, shaped around her ears. The other girls in our class looked at her disdainfully from behind their permed curtains, but she reminded me of the models in Mama's Freemans catalog. I didn't have the bouncy curls or Sadie's cool crop;

Mama refused to pay for such luxuries. My hair was long and curly, the same boring color it had always been.

Mr. Brookes sat Sadie next to me in English, and after a quick grilling (yes, I watched *Twin Peaks*, I definitely preferred *Home and Away* to *Neighbours*, my favorite New Kid on the Block was Donnie, but Jordan was a close second), we were friends.

"You passed the test," she told me a few years later.

"You failed mine, but I felt sorry for you," I deadpanned.

"We're like salt and pepper," she said. "Totally different, but we come as a pair."

She visits me as often as she can, sometimes with the kids in tow. James and Matilda divide their time between Sadie and her ex-husband, Steve, who's a guitarist in a Led Zeppelin tribute band and left her for a fan six months after Matilda was born. Sadie is feisty. Her response to Steve when he announced his imminent departure over cereal one Saturday morning was: "You actually have a fan?" After he left with his battered suitcase, Sadie marched into the garage and drenched his prized Gibson Les Paul in pastel pink paint. She snapped a selfie with the guitar in one hand, middle finger raised just in case he didn't quite sense the tone, along with the caption "This will remind you of your daughter. It's the same color as her nursery walls."

That was about a year ago and things are as amicable as they can be when adultery and abandonment form part of the bigger picture. Steve's fan left him only a few weeks after falling for his riffing skills, and he went back to the family home to beg Sadie's forgiveness, but she'd already changed the locks. He tried to serenade her through the letter box, and she blasted Red Hot Chili Peppers on Spotify, screaming, "John Frusciante—now, he's a guitarist!"

Sadie has one weekend a month without the kids and she tries to cram in as much as possible. She popped in to see me once between her third and fourth dates of the day (lunch and dinner; breakfast and brunch were done and dusted). "I have a very narrow dating window," she told my raised eyebrows. "Stop judging, stick the kettle on, and I'll tell you all about Larry who still lives with his mother."

I don't judge Sadie, not really. Not any more than everybody judges everybody else. If anything, I'm fascinated by her dating life. It's been so long since I went on a date, it feels like a lifetime ago. "You should join an app," Sadie told me once. "Just for a laugh. You never know—you might meet someone who will make you burst through that front door. I'll come over to see you and find a Meredith-shaped hole in it."

I laughed awkwardly. We both knew that it would take more than that for me to leave the house.

The thought of staying at home for three days, let alone three years, is so alien to Sadie that she didn't quite believe it for the first month. Until she turned up one evening and I was lying under the kitchen table. At that point she took it pretty seriously.

Equally difficult for Sadie to accept is that I'm happy like this. Or at least, I'm happier than I was during the whole lying-under-the-table phase. It could be worse than scratching the underside of a six. I think she's got the message, but we still go through the motions now and then.

"What about people?" she says.

"What people?" I say.

"Other people! People you meet when you're out. Random people who make your life more interesting."

"Random people have never made my life interesting."

"Remember that night…when we met that guy who read our palms?"

"The guy who said you were going to become a chef?"

"It could still happen!"

"Well, I don't think I'm going to have six kids."

"You never know."

"I know that much."

"OK, so he was a terrible fortune-teller. But don't you miss those nights? Meeting ridiculous, interesting, crazy people?"

"Sadie, I don't remember half of them. And they really weren't all that interesting."

Her face falls, and I feel bad. The people we met were only part of the story. We always created our own fun, Sadie and I, going from bar to bar, laughing and dancing and mapping out our lives.

"Don't you miss eye contact?" She says it quietly, as if she's scared I'm going to cry.

"I'm having that with you, now," I tell her gently.

"Yes, but you must be sick of my eyes."

"Never. Your eyes are beautiful. They change color depending on your mood."

She goes cross-eyed and sticks out her tongue. "Are they beautiful now?"

I smile at her, my funny friend who'd do anything for me.

Like a dog with a bone, she's not finished. "What about fresh air?"

"I have my windows open all the time, and I often stick my head out the back door for a nice big gulp of Glasgow's finest."

"Meredith, don't joke."

"I'm not."

And so it goes, until one of us gets bored and we start talking about other things.

"I hate seeing you like this," she said to me last Christmas Eve, after we exchanged gifts, toasted friendship, and shared a tight hug. She was going to pick James and Matilda up from Steve's and go home to start preparing for lunch with her family the next day.

I stepped back from her and sighed. "Like what?"

"Like...alone."

"I'm not alone, Sadie. I have Fred." Ever supportive, he mewed loudly from the kitchen. "And I'm not lonely or miserable. I have been, but I'm not right now."

"Nobody should be alone on Christmas Day," she told me in the cross voice she uses to hide more complicated emotions.

"I have Fred," I said again. "I'm going to watch *Some Like It Hot* and start my new jigsaw. I can't wait."

"You and your jigsaws!" Her voice was less cross. She punched me lightly on the arm before closing the front door behind her. I stood there for a while, my hand pressed against my side of the frame. Sometimes when she leaves, it feels as if all the life has been sucked out of the house.

Today, James has a cold, Matilda has a new tooth, and Sadie has a hangover. "We won't stay long," she promises as they discard hats and coats and boots all over my hall. Fred has no time for children; he's hiding under my bed.

"What have you been up to?" I ask her. "You look worn-out," I add, the way only lifelong friends can. "Actually..." I look at her closely. "You also look *amazing*. Your eyes are shining."

"I've met someone," she whispers, unable to stop the smile that spreads across her face. She gives me the look that tells me this isn't a conversation for little ears. By the time she's emptied a bag of toys on the living room floor and unwrapped a cookie for each of the kids, I've made us tea and piled my favorite vintage plate—one of my best eBay wins—with grown-up treats.

"I can't eat a thing," Sadie says between gulps of her tea. "Ooh, these do look good, though. Maybe just one." She takes a bite of chocolate and peanut butter brownie. "Mer, this is incredible."

"Yes, but tell me about your someone," I say.

"Colin," she says, and I swear her cheeks flush and her eyes sparkle when she says his name. "We met online, two weeks ago. We've had three dates. I've never met anyone like him." She reaches across the table and grabs my hand. "I'm so happy, Mer."

Over two cups of tea, she tells me that Colin is forty-two, a craftsman, divorced, has no kids, but is absolutely fine with dating a single mother ("Unlike most of the idiots I meet," she adds). He's generous, he's funny, he's self-deprecating, he's tall, and he doesn't give two shits about the Old Firm, Glasgow's two rival football clubs. Basically he's Sadie's ideal man. "He's completely different from Steve," she says. "Mer, I think I could really fall for him. Can you believe it?"

I return her grin; it's contagious. And yet her excitement reminds me of how deprived I am of such a chunk of the spectrum of normal human emotion. When I think about Gavin, I remember what it was like to be in a relationship, but not how it *felt*. As if it happened to someone else who told me about it at the time. My life is divided into before and after, and the before remains out of my grasp.

Matilda toddles into the kitchen, chocolate smeared across her face. She launches herself at me, buries her head in my lap.

"Oh God, you're covered in chocolate!" Sadie jumps up. "Let me grab some wipes and get you cleaned up. Tilly, come here, you wee rascal."

"Sadie, it's fine," I tell her, ruffling the curls that are now tickling my chin. Nobody has been this close to me for a long time. I wrap my arms loosely round Matilda's wriggling body, savor her biscuity little-girl scent. I know she'll have moved on to something else in a minute. While Sadie rummages through her collection of bags in the hall, I look at Matilda's tiny feet, encased in striped tights, her chocolate-tipped fingers. I tickle her rounded belly and she giggles. I laugh too, and she looks up at me.

"Let me see your teeth," I say, and she opens her mouth wide, throws her head back to give me a better look.

"Wow! You have lots of big teeth!" She nods enthusiastically, her mouth still wide open. Her blue eyes fix on mine, and she stays surprisingly still, holding my gaze until Sadie barrels into the room.

"Aw, look at you two, having a moment!" she coos, but the next thing I know she's swept Matilda up into her own arms, transferred her into the living room, and the moment is over. I feel cold suddenly, without her warm body next to mine. I pull the sleeves of my sweater down over my hands and cross my arms over my abdomen, trying to give myself the heat I never get from anyone else. I sit like that, cold and serious with a painful lump in my throat, until Sadie is back in the room.

An hour later, when Sadie and the kids have gone, I follow their trail around my home, sweeping up crumbs, wiping chocolate fingerprints from surfaces, putting things back in their rightful place. I know Sadie finds it hard to relax when she's here with the kids. I think she thinks the mess they make bugs me, but it doesn't. "Your place is immaculate!" she always says, and sometimes it sounds like an accusation.

It's true, but what does she expect? It's only me here, with a very particular ginger cat who has fastidious toilet habits and cleans himself several times a day. One plate and one fork in the sink does not take long to wash. It takes me days to fill the laundry basket. I create very little waste. And in any case, I like things to be in order. I feel out of sorts if I'm living in clutter.

But the kids' mess is different. It reminds me that I have people in my life who care. Who'll keep coming back into my home for as long as I'm here and leave a trace of themselves behind. Tidying up after them gives me a taste of what it would be like to be a mother. To have small people relying on me to keep them clean, warm, happy, and safe. It hurts to think about that too much.

I clean the kitchen table, think about Sadie curled up on her couch, grinning at her phone. At those early relationship texts that cause your heart to leap. I don't know if my heart will ever leap again.

As I'm returning the dustpan and brush to the cupboard under the sink, I spot Matilda's yellow sippy cup in the big plant pot in the corner of the kitchen. I wonder why she chose that spot to hide it. I think about leaving it there for her to discover the next time she visits. Instead, I take it into the living room and put it in the center of my bookshelf. I want to be able to see it, when I'm sitting there at night, doing a jigsaw or reading a book. It looks out of place in the room and perfectly at home at the same time.

Day 1,222

Thursday, November 22, 2018

Tom, his big smile, and his duffel coat are back.

"I'm so sorry, Meredith," he says as he sits down on my couch. "I forgot your Emily Dickinson book."

My heart sinks. I would have canceled today, if it hadn't been for my book. I like Tom, but I worked late last night and I'm not in the mood to chat.

"Oh, don't worry," I say woodenly. "I'll make tea."

While I'm waiting for the kettle to boil, I stare at my reflection in the oven door. Do oven doors make you look older? I have no idea, but there's definitely the burden of something on my face today that I've not seen before. I'll be forty in a few months. The only man in my life is here because he makes friends with complete strangers while he figures out what he wants to do for a real job.

I pour the tea, pile the biscuits on a plate, and trudge back through to the living room, where I find Fred lying on Tom's lap, legs akimbo, purring loudly. I stare at him. Clearly he's now more than happy to welcome Tom into our home.

"Doesn't he love getting his belly rubbed?" Tom grins at me.

Fred glances in my direction as I put the tea tray on the coffee table, then turns his attention back to his new best friend.

Judas, I think.

"How's your week been, Meredith?"

I shrug. "Same as usual."

Tom reaches for his tea, and Fred jumps off his lap. He does

25

a figure eight round my ankles, and I reach down to rub his head, letting him know I forgive his minor indiscretion.

"You know what I'd love to do? A jigsaw. I haven't done one since I was a kid, and I don't know how good I was at them then, but I'd like to give it a go. Are you up for it?"

I realize that I am, actually, up for it. I've finished *The Kiss* but not started on the mosaic tile design yet. And at the very least, a jigsaw might distract Tom from asking any more tricky questions. "Do you want to pick one?" I point to the boxes on the lower shelves of my bookcase.

He chooses quickly, instinctively—Santa Maria del Fiore, Florence's magnificent cathedral, in a thousand pieces. "That's a tough one," I tell him. "So much detail."

"I like a challenge," he tells me. "Anyway, my teammate is a pro."

I move the tea tray onto the floor and spread the jigsaw pieces across the table. "Always start with the edges," I tell him. "But first we separate the colors. It makes it so much easier."

We work in silence for a few minutes, creating order from the tiny parts of the Florentine landmark. He collects the light colors; I gather up the dark.

"It took more than a hundred and thirty years to build," I tell him. "The huge dome was always part of the plan, but it took them a while to figure out how to do it, so it was left exposed for years."

"Wow. The view from the top must be amazing."

"Let's look for edges now," I tell him, but I'm thinking of myself walking the hundreds of small, narrow steps to the top of the cathedral. Of how tiny I would be, compared to the Florentine skyline, but how big it would feel when I finally reached the summit. Like being on the huge roller coaster at the Camelot Theme Park when we were kids. Our bare legs dangling at the highest point, Fee liked to point out what she could see on the ground, laughing at how tiny everybody was. All I wanted to look at was the sky.

We lose track of time, and Tom ends up staying longer than an hour. "I'm sorry, Meredith. You must have things to be getting on with."

"It's OK. Time flies when you're trying to build a cathedral." I look down at our work, edges complete, the cloudy sky beginning to take shape.

He laughs loudly, an unfamiliar sound in my quiet little house. "Meredith, you're funny."

I fuss with the tea tray, feeling embarrassed. "Nobody has ever said that to me before."

"Sometimes people don't point out the obvious. But it's one of my best qualities." He winks at me. "I'm sorry again about your book. I can pop it through your door tomorrow when I'm passing."

I think about it. "Don't worry. Just bring it next week."

Day 1,225

Sunday, November 25, 2018

A question I get asked a lot is, doesn't time drag? I swear, it doesn't. At least, no more than I imagine it does for anyone else. Some days and weeks and months slip through my fingers like sand. I have the same number of hours in the day as everyone and I don't have a partner or children to whittle away at them. I spend around three minutes a day getting to work, not three hours like some people. But I still sometimes get to the end of the week and I haven't cleaned the wooden slatted blinds in the living room, or removed the chipped polish from my toenails, or opened the pile of mail growing on the windowsill. There are always things I never get around to doing, like replacing the seal around the bath and organizing my wardrobe by season. Living a solitary life with minimal interruptions doesn't necessarily make me more productive than anyone else. Some days, I don't even take a shower.

Sunday is the hardest day, but I do what I can to fill the empty space. I get the papers delivered, separate the sections, and spread them across the kitchen table. I bake half a dozen scones and fill the teapot, even though it's just me. Scones and plates and knives and napkins, and it can pass for a family table. Hands grabbing to get the sports section or the glossy supplement. Passing the butter dish and leaving crumbs in the raspberry jam. Chatter and laughter over the low hum of the radio. I wonder what Fee's doing today, whether she's thinking of me.

Maybe she and Lucas and Mama are eating scones and drinking tea together. Or heading to the pub for Sunday lunch with all the trimmings. I don't want to be there, but I do want Fee here. The old Fee, at least. The Fee I shared a bedroom—and sometimes a bed—with for more than half my life. The Fee I walked down the aisle. The Fee who made me feel safe, until she didn't. Briefly I want her here so much my chest hurts. Then I remember why she's not, and my scone turns to stone in my mouth.

1993

"Why don't we have any photographs of us as babies?" I asked Fiona.

"We do," she said.

"We do?"

"Mama has a box in her wardrobe. It has some old stuff in it. Polaroids. There's one of you and me in the bath. You were a fat baby."

"I want to see it," I said, ignoring the dig.

I was fourteen, had my first serious boyfriend, and spending time with his family had made me look closer at my own. Normal was chatting at the breakfast table. Normal was telling the truth, even when it hurt. Normal was family pictures.

Jamie's mum had pictures everywhere: on the mantelpiece, attached to the fridge door with magnets, lovingly presented in albums and pulled out at every opportunity to embarrass the kids. She'd created a gallery on the staircase wall, where all the professional photographs (family portraits, graduations, and weddings) were displayed, carefully arranged in matching silver frames. I'd see her make minuscule adjustments to them whenever she went up or down the stairs—a little house-keeping en route to the bathroom. It was the professional portraits that fascinated me the most. It had never occurred to me that people would actually pay other people to take photographs of them in their best clothes, with freshly styled hair, in front of pastel-colored backgrounds. The photograph of Jamie the toddler on his dad's knee, sitting next to his mum and big sister, gave me a glimpse into another type of family. Their faces were shiny with joy. No empty eyes. No simmering resentment.

I stayed with Jamie longer than I should have, because being around his family made me happy. When we split up, I missed his mum more than I missed him. Sometimes, I'd take a detour to my part-time job at the fish-and-chip shop so I could pass their house. Even when the living room curtains were drawn, I could feel the warmth from inside. I craved it.

"Tell me more about the photographs," I demanded, switching the TV off.

Fiona sighed but turned to face me on the couch, her arms crossed. "Why? They're just ancient pictures." But I could see through the blasé act. She was pleased she knew something I didn't. We didn't have many secrets, not yet. We'd shared a room for as long as I could remember. I knew she wore her best bra on a Friday (purple, lacy). I knew she sometimes cried in bed when she thought I was asleep.

I shrugged. Two could play that game. "Whatever. I'll just go and find them, see for myself."

My sister jumped to her feet. "I'll show you," she said.

We crept upstairs. I don't know why, as Mama was at bingo and wouldn't be back for hours. Even so, her presence was felt. She was every creak on the staircase, every rattle of the window frame. She was nowhere and everywhere, all at once.

I hadn't been in her bedroom for months. It smelled like nail polish and cigarettes; the dressing-table mirror was dusty. I turned away from it. It felt strange to see myself in her space. This was not somewhere I'd ever felt welcome. It was Fiona I had gone to when I wet my bed or had a nightmare.

"Come on," Fiona said impatiently, pulling me toward the wardrobe. She stood on her tiptoes to reach the top shelf and grabbed an old shoebox.

I expected to have time to go carefully through its contents, but my sister had other ideas. She took the lid off the box and upended it, sending scraps of paper and photographs scattering across the floor.

"What did you do that for?" I cried, kneeling to gather them up.

Fiona laughed. "Here, look." She held a photograph in front of my face. "It's a fat baby in the bath."

I snatched it from her fingers, looked at two little girls in our avocado-green 1980s bathroom. I was sitting in the bath, my chubby toddler arms and rounded belly glistening with water. I wasn't looking at the person behind the camera; my eyes were on my sister, and I was laughing. Fiona was in the bath too, but she was standing up with her arms in the air, performing for the photographer. I was short and chubby; she was tall and thin. A memory: the two of us sitting in front of an electric fire, wrapped in warm towels, drinking something sweet from mugs. Then, when we were dry, Fiona dropping her towel and dancing on the spot, demanding, "Count my ribs! Count my ribs!" I can't remember if it was me she was talking to, or someone else. I don't remember anyone else being there, but we were too young to make hot chocolate for ourselves. Someone must have warmed the towels and swaddled them round our damp bodies, turning us into human burritos. That part is a blank.

I didn't want to ask Fiona if she remembered the hot sweet drinks and the electric fire. "Do you remember this being taken?" I said instead.

"Nope." Fiona was bored now, playing with the makeup on Mama's dressing table. She twisted a red lipstick to its highest point and applied it slowly, her eyes peering at herself in the mirror.

I set the bath photo aside. I was going to take it, I decided. I couldn't imagine Mama ever looking at these reminders of the past, let alone noticing if one was missing. I felt my cheeks getting hot; I was angry. Photographs shouldn't be stuffed in an old shoebox and hidden at the back of a wardrobe. They should be displayed in frames on mantelpieces or on fridge doors or in albums that are within reach at all times. I wondered why she'd even kept them. Was she behind the camera? I don't remember her coaxing us to give her our best smiles or instructing "Say cheese!" in a singsong voice. I don't remember us huddling over the Polaroids, watching our faces and bodies take shape. I don't remember us doing anything that warranted immortalizing as an important memory. Or even just a normal day that was sweet and special in all the small ways that matter, in the end.

I turned back to the photographs. There were lots of black-and-white ones, of people I didn't know. On the backs of some of them were names and dates, the shaky, spidery script faded. There was a beautiful woman in a shiny wedding dress, on the arm of a tall man with a beaming face. On the back, it simply said "1948." I did a quick calculation. Mama was born in 1957.

"I think I've found our grandparents."

Fiona stopped preening and kneeled beside me, smelling of Mama's Shalimar. I hated the smell; it made me gag.

"She was called Maria," Fiona said, tracing the bride's curves with her finger.

"Really? How do you know?" It pissed me off that Fiona knew stuff I didn't. She knew about the photographs; she knew our grandmother's name. What else did she know?

"I heard Mama talk about her once," she said. Then she shrugged. "Maybe I dreamed it."

I wanted to get annoyed at her for not taking this as seriously as I was, but I couldn't. I understood. My own memories were obscure and inaccessible. I didn't know what was real and what wasn't.

"Do you remember having hot drinks when we were wrapped in towels, sitting in front of an electric fire?"

Fiona turned to me with a strange look on her face. "Yes. Yes, I do," she said. "Hot chocolate, I think." And something about the way her eyes were slightly out of focus told me she was telling me the truth.

I grinned at her. "I just remembered it now," I said.

"We always did that, after our bath," Fiona said. "We sat in front of the fire to stay warm. It wasn't all bad, you know."

I didn't say anything, because I didn't know. But I let myself luxuriate in my sister's memory of caring hands lifting us out of the bathtub, drawing us close, wrapping us up, stirring hot water into powdered chocolate, switching on the fire. I closed my eyes and tried to draw Mama into my own memory, but all I could recall was my sister's bony knee resting on my thigh, her long toes wriggling next to my smaller ones as the soles of our feet soaked up the heat of the glowing bars.

Over the next few weeks, whenever Mama was at bingo or in the pub with Auntie Linda, I'd sneak into her bedroom and look through the box of photos. There were only a handful of Fiona and me, always together, apart from two photos of Mama holding newborn babies, which I assumed were us. In one, she stood in front of a rosebush in an unfamiliar garden. It could have been any baby—you couldn't even make out its face, with only a tiny foot visible, sticking out of a fold in the blanket. Mama wore kitten heels and large sunglasses, and she was thin, and she had a cigarette in her hand. She was half smiling.

In the other, she was sitting on a brown couch, leaning against orange cushions. You could see the baby's face more clearly in this one, red and scrunched up. Mama was looking up to the side, her face pale, her hair tousled. She looked tired. I don't think she wanted her photograph taken.

I didn't know which baby was me and which was Fiona. We were born only eighteen months apart, so Mama wouldn't have aged much in that time. I guessed that she was holding Fiona in the happy, smiling, smoking picture, and me in the pale-faced, tired one. She's always said I was a difficult baby, so it would make sense that the red scrunched-up face belonged to me.

One night, I crept into Mama's room while Fiona was watching *Top of the Pops*. As soon as I opened the wardrobe door, I knew something was different. Things had been rearranged; it was tidier. And the box was gone. Luckily I had the photograph of Fiona and me in the bath. I'd slipped it under my mattress. I still had a little piece of our childhood. A little piece of happiness.

Day 1,227

I have a sign on my front door that says "NO COLD CALLERS."

"Does this only apply in the winter?" Sadie asked me the first time she saw it, her eyebrows raised.

I ignored her.

"It's very...shouty," she muttered as I walked away from her.

It's the doorbell I hate. Every time it goes, it reminds me that there's a world out there I'm no longer part of. Sadie knows never to turn up unannounced, and in any case, she doesn't ring the bell. She does a loud, extended *rat-a-tat-tat* on the door with her knuckles, so I know it's her.

My shouty sign works, most of the time. But now and then, the doorbell rings when I'm not expecting a delivery that needs a signature or won't fit in my parcel box. And after I get over the initial shock, I can't ignore it, because it might be someone I care about. Or used to care about.

Today, it's not. But it's not someone trying to sell me double glazing either. It's a boy with a gap in his teeth and a large bucket swinging from his fingers. He looks vaguely familiar.

"Hi, lady." He grins at me. "I live across the street. Can I wash your car for a fiver?"

I focus on his freckled face, force the background of my street to fade away. "Well, thanks for the offer...but I don't have a car."

His green eyes widen. "You don't have a car?"

"Nope." I lean against the doorframe.

"For real?" He looks around, like he's trying to spot a car hiding somewhere, to catch me.

I smile. "For real. No car."

"Wow. So how do you get places? Like, work and stuff?"

"I work from home."

"Really?"

"Oh, come on—you must have heard of the internet."

"Of course. But my mum turns the Wi-Fi off when my brother and I get too addicted to our screens."

He laughs. And in that moment, there's something about his happy freckled face that makes me want to tell him the truth—that it's been years since I went places, that all the walking I do is within the confines of my house. But I can't tell him that, because then I'll forever be known as the weird lady from across the street who never goes anywhere. I'd much rather that this little kid thinks I walk to the train station and wait on the platform, like all the other normal people do. Like I used to do, without thinking twice about it.

"So you live across the street?"

"Yeah." He points to the house with the cherry blossom tree in the garden.

"Oh, I love your tree," I tell him. "It's so pretty. When it flowers, I know spring is here. I sometimes sit in my living room and look at it."

"You do?" He screws up his face.

"Sure. You know…when I'm not working and stuff. Anyway, why are you washing cars? Are you saving up for something?"

"It's my mum's birthday next week. I want to buy her a necklace. With a heart on it. And a little blue stone. She saw it on the internet."

I can picture it—elegant and delicate, resting against the skin of a woman with her arms round her sons. "That sounds beautiful. What a lovely thing to do for your mum."

He shrugs. "It's expensive. So I need to wash a lot of cars. I'd better go. Bye, lady."

"You can call me Meredith."

"That's a funny name."

I laugh. "You think so? What's yours?"

"Jacob Alastair Montgomery." He puffs up his chest. "I'm ten years old."

"OK, Jacob Alastair Montgomery. Listen, I don't have a car, but how about you clean the front of my door and my step instead?"

"Um…OK. Sure."

"Take your stuff out of your bucket and I'll go and fill it up for you. Deal?"

"Deal."

I leave him to work with his warm water and dish soap and sponge. I sit at the window and pick up my book, but my eyes keep going back to the cherry blossom tree in Jacob's garden. It's disrobed for winter, but it won't be too long before spring is here again, and it will burst into bloom. It always takes me by surprise, how one day it's naked, and the next it's covered in catkins.

He rings the bell ten minutes later. I take my time to inspect the door and kneel down to look at the step.

"Good job, Jacob. I'm impressed."

"I cleaned that thing as well." He gestured at the parcel box. "It had bird poo on it."

"Well, thank you so much. I had no idea my door was so disgusting. I'm very pleased you stopped by." I take a five-pound note out of the back pocket of my jeans and hold it out to him.

"Thanks." He grins up at me. "That's my first fiver."

"You came here first?"

"No, I tried the next-door people first, but they didn't answer."

"Maybe they were out? Or didn't hear the bell?"

"Maybe. Or maybe they're just rude."

"Want me to wash your bucket out before you go?"

"Thanks, Meredith."

Day 1,229

Having returned my Emily Dickinson book intact and sweet-
ened me with a very enjoyable debate about the relative merits
of Sylvia Plath and Ted Hughes over our Florentine jigsaw project, Tom ruins what was shaping up to be a very pleasant
Thursday.

"Is your father around, Meredith?"

I look down into my tea, while he waits patiently.

"I have no idea where he is. He left when I was five—I haven't
seen him since."

"Oh God, I'm sorry."

"It's OK. I barely remember him."

If Tom's uncomfortable, he's not showing it. "It must be
hard, not having family support."

I shrug. "I survive."

Tom looks at me until I look back at him. "Shall we have
another cup of tea?" he asks.

"Yes." I start to stand up, but he puts a hand out to stop me.

"Let me make it for a change. A splash of milk, no sugar,
right?"

I bite my lip and nod. Nobody has made me a cup of tea for
the longest time. I rest my head against the back of the couch
and listen to Tom rummaging around in my kitchen. As unfamiliar as this is to me, I know he's safe in there, searching for the
teabags and the sugar. It's the rummaging around in my mind
I'm not so comfortable with.

"My parents are dead. Car crash." He says it as soon as he comes back into the room.

I stare at him, at the mugs in his hands. Neither of them have been used for years—one has a faded floral pattern; the other bears the slogan "Glasgow's Miles Better." He wasn't to know I always stick to the same mug, of course.

He hands me the one with the slogan. "It was a long time ago. I was only ten. I moved in with my grandparents. They were kind, but old...obviously. Old-fashioned too. My teenage years were kind of difficult. No brothers or sisters, just me and my grandparents. I was a bit of a loner."

"Tom, I'm so sorry."

"I don't know if I should have told you that. Do you mind?"

"Not at all," I tell him, and I mean it.

We sit in silence on the couch, drinking our tea, Tom's revelation an unexpected but not unwelcome presence between us. I don't think we'll be going back to the Santa Maria del Fiore today.

"It's not always been this way, with my sister," I say. My shoulders relax a little when I realize it doesn't feel like a bad thing to let the words out of my mouth. "Fee...we used to be inseparable. We shared a room until I moved out. But now it's...well, it's them. And me."

"Them?"

I look down and pull at a loose thread on my jeans. Now it does feel like a bad thing, because I have nothing to follow it up with. Just awkwardness and anxiety and heartache. I stick to the logistics. "They don't live far away. Fee and her husband, Lucas. Just outside the city. And Mama's still in the house we grew up in, on the other side of the park. She'll never leave it."

"But there's no contact? None at all?"

I shake my head.

"Have you ever tried to find your dad?"

"I've thought about it. I'm not sure he'd want to see me. If he did...he'd have looked for me before now, surely."

"Maybe he has."

I screw up my face. "It wouldn't be hard for him to find me. My mother has never moved. And you can find anyone online these days."

"True. But you hear crazy stories, don't you? Of siblings who were separated at birth and live three streets apart for decades but have no idea."

I twist my hair round my finger until the tip of it goes numb. "I guess it's easier to live with the fantasy of him than risk the reality of him being a big fat disappointment." *Or me being a disappointment to him*, a voice says in my head.

"What's he like, in your fantasy?"

"He's a good man. But maybe that's wishful thinking. Fee felt differently. Or at least, she pretended to. She always said we didn't need him. That we were just fine without him. What a crock of shit that turned out to be."

"We all have different recollections of the past."

"I think I'd know if he wasn't a good man," I say defensively. "I was young, but...I'd know. Because the bad stuff sticks in our minds, right? There's no bad stuff, not with him."

"If you want to look for your dad...well, I could help. If you like."

I try to imagine a reunion, but I can't even find a starting point. Nothing about it feels natural, even in a meeting-a-stranger kind of way.

"I'll think about it," I tell him, then I look at my watch. I don't want to be rude to this sweet, kind, patient man, but I'm exhausted. I want to watch television with Fred on my lap and no one else in my house.

"What are you having for lunch?" he asks me, and it's such an obvious change of subject that I can't help but laugh.

He laughs too, as he reaches for his coat. "I've just realized how hungry I am. And I've seen your impressive collection of recipe books. I'm sure you're rustling up more than fish fingers."

"I'm having spaghetti puttanesca. It's my favorite. Anchovies, olives, capers, tomatoes, garlic, and lots of Parmesan. I've always wanted to go to Italy, do a cooking course. Learn from the best."

"Maybe you will, one day. See that cathedral for yourself."

I don't tell him that I almost did. Gavin and I talked about going to Tuscany, in the early days of our relationship when I believed my life would follow a normal path—not perfect, certainly not perfect, but normal.

Before he leaves, Tom spends a few minutes playing with Fred in the hall, rubbing him underneath his chin until he's purring like crazy.

"Wait there," I say to him. I go into the kitchen and rummage through the freezer, find what I'm looking for.

"Puttanesca sauce." I feel a little embarrassed as I hand him the small plastic tub, but his grin is natural, spontaneous.

"Thank you, Meredith! That's my dinner sorted. You're a star."

I smile back at him, thinking about how whenever I fry onions, or boil water in my large pan, or feel the weight of wet pasta in the sieve, I picture my father's large hands, slicing and stirring and shooing me away from the heat. I want to share this memory with Tom, tell him that whenever I suck spaghetti through my teeth I'm five years old again, with tomato sauce smeared around my mouth, enjoying the sound of my father's laughter. But I don't say anything, because I don't know if it's my only memory of my father, or if it was just a dream.

1986

It was almost too quiet. I couldn't even hear Fiona breathing. I could only see a mound under the duvet, the slight curve of her hip, a crop of fair hair sticking out the top. I always envied her hair. It was the color of straw most of the time, but in the summer it turned a beautiful sunny blonde. Mine was brown and sludgy by comparison.

"Like horse poop," Fiona said once, and I agreed wholeheartedly.

I couldn't quite reach my sister's hair, or I'd have stroked it just to make sure she stirred. I had to fall asleep before Mama came in, because I was rubbish at pretending. I screwed my face up too tight and looked like I was constipated. So Fiona said. I tried to count sheep, but I lost track of my numbers and had to go back to the beginning.

I got to thirty-three when I heard the creak on the stairs. The footsteps got louder. I didn't think counting was going to work this time.

I saw her hands first, her white fingers gripping the outer edge of the door. Her nails were a different color than they had been earlier that night—she must have painted them after she sent us upstairs. The bright pink almost glowed in the low light of our bedroom.

"Why aren't you asleep yet?" She wagged a finger at me as she came into the room. I glanced over at Fiona's still body.

"You should be sleeping." Mama kneeled on the floor between the two narrow beds. "Little girls need their sleep."

I didn't know what to say—Fiona would have known what to say—so I smiled.

Mama looked at me, her mouth a tight line. Then she smiled back. "Let's get you tucked in."

I lay still, watching her pink fingernails move as she fussed with my duvet, smoothing it down over my torso. "It's really important that you go to sleep, angelface. You've got school tomorrow. How will you learn if you're falling asleep at your desk? You want to get good grades, don't you? Make something of yourself?"

"I guess."

"You guess?" She raised her eyebrows. "Guessing won't get you far in life, angelface. Determination and hard work, that's what you need. What do you want to be when you grow up?"

I shrugged. "I've not really thought about it. I like writing stories."

"Writing stories?" She laughed. "That's not a proper job."

"What did you want to be when you were little?"

"Lift your head up." She wasn't looking at me, but something flashed in her eyes as she plumped up my pillow. "Meredith, let me tell you something. I had lots of dreams when I was your age. I worked hard at school. But I met your father, and Fiona was born. Then you. Don't do what I did. Don't let children get in the way of your dreams before you're old enough to see them through."

"OK. I...I think I can sleep now." I was jealous of Fiona, who was probably dreaming about all sorts of wonderful things.

My mother stared at me for a few seconds, then stood up and walked out of the room.

Day 1,231

Celeste and I have been chatting on the forum nearly every day, sometimes only for a few minutes, sometimes longer. She's a hairdresser at a busy, trendy city-center salon and entertains me with tales of women who tell her all their marriage troubles and the minor celebrity who's always disappointed when the regular folks don't recognize her at the basins. She tells me she feels a bit like a therapist, that she asks her clients what their holiday plans are and an hour later she finds out they're sleeping with their neighbor.

I tell her about a project I've been working on for a new high-end furniture retailer. I was up late last night trying to write five hundred words about a chaise longue and another four hundred about velvet lampshades, which is harder than it sounds. She tells me she's a bit jealous of me, being my own boss. I don't often think of it that way, and it feels nice to see myself from her perspective, even though she's only getting a fraction of my story. Nobody on the forum knows the extent of my isolation. They know I live a fairly solitary life, but I've never felt able to reveal the truth. The more I talk to Celeste, the more I want to open up, but the harder it gets. Our budding friendship is like no other relationship in my life because there's a complete absence of sympathy and obligation. Sadie is my best friend, but I know she feels guilty if she hasn't had time to visit, or if she's too tired at the end of the day for more than a couple of text messages. And as lovely as Tom is, it's part of his contract to be on my couch at the same time every week.

I know I'll need to fully open up to Celeste at some point, but I push the thought to the back of my mind. She doesn't have the same qualms about sharing.

CATLADY 29: Meredith, I was sexually assaulted. Oh my god. I've said it. You're the first person I've told.

My mouth goes dry.

JIGSAWGIRL: Oh my god. When?

CATLADY 29: A few weeks ago.

JIGSAWGIRL: Oh, Celeste. Are you OK? Sorry, that's such a stupid question…

CATLADY 29: I'm all right. It could have been a lot worse. I managed to get away from him.

JIGSAWGIRL: You haven't been to the police?

CATLADY 29: No. I haven't told anyone. Just you.

JIGSAWGIRL: You're so brave, Celeste.

CATLADY 29: I don't feel brave. I feel lost, Meredith. I think about it all the time. I cry about it all the time.

I swallow around the lump in my throat.

JIGSAWGIRL: However you're feeling is natural, Celeste. I'm so sorry this happened to you, I really am. What are you going to do? Will you report it?

CATLADY 29: I have no idea. I just wanted to tell someone. It feels like a huge step. Thank you for listening, Meredith. For being there.

JIGSAWGIRL: I'm always here, Celeste. I mean that. I wish I could do more to help. Is there anything I can do?

CATLADY 29: Honestly, having you to chat to makes me feel so much better. So just keep being you, I guess ☺

JIGSAWGIRL: I'll try ☺

CATLADY 29: I need to go now. I'm getting some new furniture delivered.

JIGSAWGIRL: Not a chaise longue? I know where you can get one of those...

CATLADY 29: ☺☺☺ I still can't believe you used to live in the downstairs flat. It makes me feel like this was meant to be.

I log off, make a cup of tea, and sit with Fred on the couch, thinking about Celeste, about how much braver she is than me.

I can picture her clearly, because I know every inch of her flat. I wonder if she has her bed right under the window, like I did. I used to love reading under the covers on rainy mornings, listening to the water drumming against the glass. Hopefully her bedroom window is more airtight than mine was. When the rain was really heavy, a tiny trickle of water would gather where the glass met the wood.

Despite its flaws, I loved 48A. I stayed there for fourteen years, not entirely through choice but because that's how long it took me to save a deposit for a place of my own—this house, the final one Fee and I saw at the end of a long day of disappointment.

"It smells musty," Fee hissed as soon as we stepped inside. "The doorframe is falling apart."

I gave the real estate agent an apologetic smile. "It's a steal," I muttered under my breath. "You have to see the bigger picture."

"Look at the state of that wall. There must be twelve layers of paper."

I ignored her and started opening doors. "There's a window seat in the living room!"

She rolled her eyes. "Total old-lady house."

I sat on the old-lady window seat tucked inside the bay window, letting the sun warm my back. I didn't have to look anywhere else. I was home.

Fiona was wrong. There weren't twelve layers of wallpaper in the hall. But there were four, which was more than enough. It took me ten Sundays to remove every last trace, clean the walls, and paint them a color that looks blue or lavender, depending on the time of day.

I did the opposite in the living room, where the tired, grubby walls had once been cream. I chose a wallpaper with a vivid pattern—abstract swirls in shades of blue and delicate copper shapes that sometimes looked like flowers, sometimes like mysterious creatures from the depths of the ocean. I wasn't entirely sure if I loved it, but it was like nothing I'd ever seen before, and that was enough. I'm not great at wallpapering, but luckily the first wall I tackled would be largely hidden behind my books. By the time I reached wall number two, I had hit my stride. I wallpapered in the evenings, after work, until my arms were too tired to carry on.

How lucky I felt, to have a room filled with books. I trimmed the loose threads from the deep cushions of the window seat, covered the faded spots with a sheepskin rug.

The previous owners left behind an old kitchen table on wobbly legs and two benches, which was a huge boost to my budget as it meant I could buy a couch straightaway. I could only afford a basic one, but I loaded it with velvet cushions, piling soft throws for cold nights into a large basket.

I didn't put too much thought into colors or styles; I just went with my gut. I ended up with a home that offered me both light and shade, equal amounts of space and protection.

It was perfect, with its imperfect wallpaper and wobbly table legs.

James was only a year old when I moved in. He wriggled out of Sadie's arms and crawled up the creaky stairs. We followed him, laughing at his speedy little legs.

"He's wild," Sadie told me. "I'm exhausted."

I showed her around the upstairs: my spacious bedroom, primed to be painted a dusky pink; the bathroom with the lime-green mosaic tiles that I'd have to live with until my bank balance recovered; the tiny second bedroom that was the designated dumping ground for my redecoration efforts, filled with empty paint cans and scraps of wallpaper.

"Perfect size for a nursery," Sadie said, nudging me, steering James away from a discarded paint roller.

I made a face at her. I'd been seeing Gavin for a few months, and he was a nice guy, but we were a long way from marriage, or babies, or marriage and babies. I met him the old-fashioned way, at a bar, one Friday during impromptu after-work drinks. I'd only intended to stay for one glass of wine, but I decided I'd rather bask in the warmth of Gavin's easy smile than go home to my laundry basket and microwave meal for one. We talked for hours about conspiracy theories and true crime documentaries and the awful stories we'd heard about internet dating, and we'd been seeing each other twice a week ever since.

Sadie was right—the room was the perfect size for a nursery.

"Or an office," I pointed out.

"Meredith, I need more friends with children. All the women I meet at the baby groups are just so earnest and good. Their kids only eat organic and they never, ever watch TV. At least, that's what they say. They're lying, of course."

"They sound fun," I laughed. "I don't think I'm ready to have a kid yet."

"You're almost thirty-five," she said. "Time to get a move on maybe?"

I tickled James under the chin until he giggled. "Come on. I want to show you the living room."

An hour later, I sat on my window seat and watched Sadie strap her tiny son into his car seat. She said something to him, and he looked toward my house and waved. Sadie beamed at me, proud of his latest achievement. I waved back enthusiastically. After she drove away, I sat there for a while, thinking about any future children I might have. I'd never made a provisional list of baby names or tried to form an image of my kids in my mind the way some people do. I was aware of the relentless march of time, but I still wasn't sure I had what it takes.

I thought I still had plenty of time to make my mind up.

But things are a little different now. It seems like only yesterday Sadie and I were standing in the room that could be a nursery, figuring out where a crib would go.

Sometimes, when I'm lying in bed, alone, I long for someone else's skin against mine. But it's not a man's body I crave—it's that of a baby, tucked into the crook of my arm, its easy breath warming my chest. Giving me a reason to live.

2014

We watched the parade from Gavin's window, a bird's-eye view of the plumed headdresses, oversized masks, saxophones, and drums. The street had become a sea of people, dancing and clapping and cheering.

"Come on." He held up my denim jacket, ready for me to slip my arms into. "Let's go and join the fun."

"I've never seen Glasgow like this," I said as we weaved down Byres Road. Despite the crowds, I felt safe with Gavin's arm looped round my shoulders. He was tall; I was just the right height to tuck under his arm. I watched our feet—my blue Converse and his scuffed leather lace-up boots—hit the pavement in sync. Like his boots, he was dependable, comfortable, built to last.

It took us three times as long as it should have to reach our favorite part of the neighborhood—a cobbled lane lined with cafés and bars. We browsed the market stalls; he bought me a bracelet beaded with tiny moonstones and silver stars when I wasn't looking. I slipped it on; it felt cool against my wrist.

"I love it." I kissed him on the cheek, and wondered if now was the time to say that I loved him too, even more than the beautiful bracelet.

We'd never said those words, in the six months we'd been together. Sometimes, after sex, or when we walked hand in hand through the Botanic Gardens at dusk, I felt the weight of expectation press down on my chest. So I'd roll away from him, or go and put the kettle on, or start talking about something ridiculous that had happened at work.

"Shall we get a drink?" I said instead.

"Perfect timing." Gavin nudged me toward a tiny empty table in the corner of the bar. "I'll get the beers in."

My phone vibrated in my jacket pocket.

Where ru guys? We'll come and join you! Fxx

My fingers hovered over the keypad. I typed out a bunch of half-hearted responses, then deleted every one.

"Everything OK?" Gavin sat down and handed me a bottle of beer.

I took a grateful sip. "It's just Fee. She and Lucas want to join us."

"Cool. Where are they?"

I took another swig from my bottle, avoiding his eyes.

"I don't really want to meet up with them," I admitted.

"What's the story with Lucas?"

I hadn't wanted to introduce him to Lucas, but he and Fee came as a package, and she was excited to double-date. "Never again," I'd said to Gavin afterward, relishing the cool evening air on my face after two hours in the crowded restaurant wearing a forced smile, pretend-laughing at Lucas's jokes. "You're so sensitive, Meredith!" he'd said, more than once, and Fee had jumped in: "She's always been like that!"

"He's a bit of a weird one" was all I said.

"But your sister is cool."

I smiled at him. "Yeah, she is. I feel bad, but…"

"Hey." He reached for my hand and gave it a squeeze. "Don't."

I shrugged and took another gulp of beer.

"I haven't spoken to my brother in over a year," he reminded me.

"Yes, but he's in Hong Kong. It's a little different. Were you ever close?"

He shook his head. "Not really. Everything's fine when we do speak. It's not like there was a big fallout or anything."

"Well, there's the difference," I said. "Fee and I *are* close. If I don't text her back, she'll worry about me."

"Meredith, you're thirty-five," he said gently.

My first thought was how much I loved the way he made my name sound—it was almost musical. "I know that." I laughed. "She'll still worry." But I turned my phone off, and we chatted and drank, my leg staying close to his under the table.

"I wish I could help you," he said out of nowhere.

"With what?" I asked him, surprised.

"All your family stuff. I know it's a weight on your shoulders. I just want you to know . . . well, I'm here. For whatever."

I felt brave in the moment. Maybe it was the beer. Or his brown eyes, never straying from mine even when I glanced down at the table, where my fingers shredded a beer mat and fiddled with the moonstones and tiny silver stars.

"Remember I told you about my dad? How he left when I was really young?"

"Sure." He reached for my hand across the table, the way good men do.

I put my hand inside his and let him wrap his fingers round it. His skin was warm. I knew, then, that he was good for me.

"My mother used to tell me he left because of me. I asked her what I did to make him leave, and she said I didn't do anything. She said he just left because I wasn't enough to make him stay."

"Fuck." He stared at me. "For real?"

I nodded. "I can't remember how old I was when she first said it. I don't even know where or when it happened. But it did. More than once. I can hear her voice saying the words. Like it was yesterday."

He rubbed the top of his head. "Shit. I'm sorry." Finally he broke eye contact, and I wondered if I'd ruined it. If I'd lost him, because even the little I'd told him was just too much. But then he looked back at me, squeezed my hand even tighter. "I can't believe your mum said that, Meredith."

"Her voice—the voice…it's not even her voice anymore—it's always in my head. Telling me I'm not good enough. I try to silence it, but I can't."

"You know it's not true, though? You're more than good enough. I wish you could see yourself the way I see you."

I leaned over the table and kissed him.

In the early hours of the next morning, as we wandered hand in hand back to his flat through the carnival debris, exchanging smiles with other lingering revelers, I nearly told him I loved him.

Day 1,240

Monday, December 10, 2018

CATLADY29: Meredith, I think I'm going to go to the police.

JIGSAWGIRL: OK…that's a good thing, right? How do you feel?

CATLADY29: I know it's been a few weeks since it happened, but I just feel like I need to do it. I've been thinking that he's out there, probably preying on other women…if I can do anything to stop that, I feel like I should.

JIGSAWGIRL: I'm so proud of you. I really am.

CATLADY29: Thank you, Meredith. I've written out a statement to take to the police station. I know I'll have to go through it all again, but I wanted to get it all clear in my mind. Can I ask you a favor? Can I send it to you? I want to make sure it makes sense, that it's not too jumbled.

I agree, because how could I not? I give her my email address, and within a minute a ping notifies me that her message has arrived. I open it straightaway, my heart filling my mouth.

She was walking home from a bar. She'd been with her friends but had to walk the last few minutes to her flat alone. She was two minutes from her front door when he came up behind her and put his hand over her mouth—he had thick gloves on and she couldn't breathe. She just froze. He dragged her down an alleyway beside a shop and started grabbing at her, squeezing her breasts, and rubbing her crotch. Finally something kicked in and she fought back, and she kicked him as hard as she could. He slapped her face, hard, then put his hand back over her mouth. He stuck his other hand down the front of her jeans. Time stood still. Then she heard a car on the street, and voices getting louder, and he pushed her to the ground and ran off. She could feel wetness in her mouth and realized it was blood coming from her nose. She lay on the ground for a while, then got up and ran home—she doesn't really remember getting there. That's it. That's all she can say. She thinks he had dark hair and eyes, and he had broad shoulders and big hands, but that's not enough to pick him out of a lineup, is it? But she's willing to try. She doesn't know what else to say to me, and she hopes this isn't all too much to put on someone she hardly knows, but she's really, really grateful.

I don't realize I'm crying until Fred jumps onto my lap and rubs his nose against my thigh. For the rest of the day images of Celeste invade my thoughts. I see her recoiling from his slap. I see her on the ground, her face smeared red. I see her running home, desperate for a safe place. Lying in my bed, my eyes tightly closed, I'm right there with her. Then I am her. It's my breath fighting against his glove. It's my breast he's squeezing; it's my body being groped by his cold, rough hand. It's my blood in my mouth. It's me, it's me, it's me.

Day 1,243

Thursday, December 13, 2018

Tom McDermott is observant, I'll give him that.

"You pull at your cuffs a lot," he tells me over ginger beer (bought by him) and Viennese whirls (baked by me).

I'm aware that one of the cuffs of my sweater is indeed stretched over my hand, so there's no point denying it. Instead, I shrug. "Bad habit."

Tom laughs. "I can think of worse. Like biting your toenails."

I laugh too, despite myself. "Yuck."

"Actually, you'd have to be pretty flexible to be able to do that. Quite a skill, don't you think?"

I put the last of my Viennese whirl in my mouth, let the buttercream and jam soak into the shortbread. I'm pleased with my efforts—I've been honing my dough technique, and this batch is just the right level of crumbliness.

We talk about random things—Scottish independence, what we're both watching on TV, why exactly someone would want to bite their toenails. He's got his friend's wedding coming up, and he's nervous about his best man's speech. I tell him he can practice it on me; that I'll be entirely objective and tell him if any of his jokes aren't funny.

"How do you feel about marriage, Meredith?"

"I don't know what marriage is supposed to look like," I tell him, tucking my feet underneath me on the couch. "I didn't spend a lot of time with other families growing up. I guess Sadie's parents were the closest thing to a normal couple. I mean, they got divorced as soon as Sadie went to college. But I guess that's normal too? Waiting until the kids move out before going your separate ways?"

Bob and Sylvia's breakup came as a shock to Sadie, but it happened quickly. They ripped off the bandage and within twenty-four hours Bob had moved into a flat in a neighboring suburb and Sylvia had repainted the master bedroom purple. It was as if they'd been planning it for years.

"At the risk of sounding cynical, I think my parents died before their marriage had a chance to fall apart. My grandparents… they always seemed happy. Celebrated their golden wedding anniversary the year before they died."

"Fifty years…wow. I don't think I have enough life left to be married for fifty years."

Tom laughs. "Me neither. Although…I do have a confession to make."

"Have you lied about your age?"

He smiles. "No. I haven't lied about anything. But I am married."

I stare at him. "You're married?" My eyes automatically go to his left hand.

"I don't wear my ring, although I did until recently. We separated six months ago."

"What's her name?"

"Laura."

"That's a nice name. Is she a nice person?"

He rubs the bridge of his nose. I've noticed him do this, now and again. I think it's a stress thing. Whether Laura is a nice person or not, something about thinking about her puts him on edge.

"She's a very nice person."

I wait, sensing that we're about to cross a line—a line we've been dancing along for weeks. I remind myself that the reason

Tom is here is to be a friend to me, since I'm the one running low in the friendship quota. I want to be a friend to him too, but I'm very aware that he probably already has several people in his life who fill that role.

"We've been married for three years. We were together for five before that. So when the big day was done and dusted, we didn't want to waste any time. We started trying for a baby right away."

I picture Tom with a baby in a carrier nestled against his chest, his face beaming with pride. He'd be a great father.

"It happened really quickly. A honeymoon baby. We felt so lucky. Then we went for the first scan, and there was no heartbeat."

"Tom, I'm so sorry."

"As soon as we got the green light to try again, we did. And we got pregnant quickly. But we lost that baby too. A lot later, this time." He lowers his voice, looks at the floor. "Laura had to give birth to him. A little boy. Christopher."

"Tom, you don't have to tell me this," I whisper. I feel as if I've picked the lock on his diary.

"We lost four babies in two years."

I don't know what to say. I put my hand on his knee, even though I'm not sure if I should or not. I don't think it was a bad thing to do, because Tom puts his hand on top of mine and keeps it there.

"Hardest thing I've ever had to go through, Meredith. But I always thought Laura and I would get through it. What doesn't kill you makes you stronger, right?"

"So I've heard."

"She had lots of tests, but the doctors couldn't figure out why it kept happening. There just didn't seem to be a reason. So we decided to try one more time. Actually, Laura did. I wanted to stop. I couldn't bear to see her go through losing another baby."

I find myself hoping for a happy ending to this story even though I know that's not an option. If it was, Tom would be walking in the park right now, with his child strapped to his chest and his arm round his wife, not sitting on my couch with tears in his eyes.

"The nursery was ready. We had the stroller in the box in the loft. We had a box of knitted baby clothes from Laura's auntie. We were prepared. We just needed some luck."

"Do you want a cup of tea? Something stronger? I have some brandy in the kitchen, I think."

He shakes his head. "One day I came home from work, and she'd gone. Left me a note. Told me she couldn't bear to look at me anymore. That when she did, all she saw were four dead babies."

I gasp. "That's awful."

"I know. It was. I've hardly spoken to her since. She's living in Manchester with her sister. But she's not a bad person. She just couldn't handle my grief on top of her own."

"Could you handle hers?"

"I'm not sure. I was willing to try."

I squeeze his knee then slide my hand out from under his. "I'm going to make us a pot of tea and look for that brandy. I'll be right back."

"OK, Meredith."

While the kettle is boiling, I sob and I pull the cuffs of my sweater down over my hands. The fabric is so taut over my shoulders it almost hurts.

Day 1,244

Diane has long red hair that she wears piled on top of her head in a neat bun, sometimes with a pencil stuck through the middle of it. Milky-white skin and a terrible internet connection. She lives on the other side of the city but it feels like a world away when we're trying to have a conversation and her screen keeps freezing. It's our third video call and I still have serious doubts, but I waited twelve months for this and promised Sadie I would give it a chance, so here we are, trying to fix me.

Diane already knows more about me than I ever intended to share. I was hoping to get away with providing a sketchy outline of my past and present mental health, but Diane is a woman on a mission, determined to fill in the blanks.

"I want you to try some mindfulness techniques, Meredith," she says.

"OK," I say, because what choice do I have? Plus, I want to wrap this up and get on with my baking. I'm making savory scones with black olives, feta cheese, and sun-dried tomatoes.

"I'm going to give you two exercises, and I'd like you to practice them every day. You might find one of them works better than the other—that's absolutely fine. It's also normal to feel a little silly to start with, but just go with the flow. These techniques can be really good for grounding the mind in the present moment and reducing feelings of anxiety or panic."

"OK."

"The first thing I want you to do is yawn and stretch every hour, for ten seconds."

"What if I don't need to yawn?"

Diane laughs. "I thought you might say that. Just fake it! That often triggers a real yawn anyway. Let me show you." She opens her mouth wide and says "ahh" for what seems like a really long time. Then she stretches her arms high above her head. She does it really slowly—it's actually quite mesmerizing.

"You're probably wondering, what's the point of this?" Diane says when her face is back to normal and her arms are in their usual place.

I don't say anything, but think, *You're spot on, Diane.*

"Well, the idea is that the yawn interrupts your thoughts and feelings. It brings you into the present. During the stretch, let yourself notice any tightness in your body. If you do, you could say 'relax' or even 'hello.'"

"Hello?"

"It's all about noticing without judgment. Take another twenty seconds to notice the tightness, then get back to whatever you were doing—cooking, reading, eating, doing a jigsaw."

"Right."

"The second exercise is called raisin meditation."

I can't help myself—I burst out laughing. "I like raisins."

She smiles. "Well, that's a good start. Again, it's really simple. You just take a raisin and try to eat it in a mindful way. I'd suggest sitting down somewhere quiet, with no distractions. Put the raisin in your mouth and eat it really slowly. Try to use all your senses—smell, touch, taste. What's its texture? How does it feel in your mouth? How does it taste? Don't be in a rush to swallow it—let it linger in your mouth. After you swallow it, smile."

"Smile?"

"Trust me, Meredith."

*

Sometimes, it just hits me. Actually, that's the wrong verb. It grips me.

It starts in my throat: a cold vise round my neck that gets tighter and tighter and tighter until I can't catch my breath. When it's really bad, it feels like I'm choking.

Then the pressure moves down my body. My chest next. My heart races like it's trying to hammer a hole in my breastbone. Within seconds I'm coated with sweat. So hot I want to rip my clothes off. I would if my arms and hands weren't numb. In the meantime, my mind is whirring. The physical sensations are familiar and my memory tells me they won't last forever but I still think, *This time I'm going to die.* Beyond that, I can't think of anything. My heart continues to thump; I desperately try to catch a breath. Finally I see stars, like when I closed my eyes as a kid and pressed the heels of my hands down on my eyelids. My legs and feet tingle until they can't support me. If all goes well, I'll collapse onto a soft surface.

This is it—you're going to die, says a voice in my head. It's not my voice, but it might be my mother's. *And you're going to die alone.*

I can't say how long it is before I can steady myself—thirty seconds, thirty minutes, an hour. When I'm able to move, I crawl to bed and sleep for a long, long time.

I really can't see how Diane and her raisins can help me with this.

1990

"How do I look?" She twirled into the living room.

Fiona gave her a cursory glance, turned back to the television. "Stunning," she said flatly.

"Meredith? Does your mama look beautiful?"

"You do. I love your dress."

"This old thing?" She slid a hand down either side of her body, cocked a hip, and pouted at me, as if I was a man she was trying to seduce. Feeling uncomfortable, I shifted my position on the floor.

"Where are you going tonight?" Fiona asked, even though she couldn't care less. I waited for Mama to tell her to mind her own fucking business, but she was in too good a mood.

"Pub with Auntie Linda, then who knows? Wherever the night takes us." She strutted across the room, inspected her reflection in the mirror above the mantelpiece as if she was about to walk the red carpet with a Hollywood hunk, not drag her heels down Duke Street with Auntie Linda, who wasn't actually our auntie or any relation at all but had been around forever and sometimes slipped me a pound note when Mama wasn't looking.

Her left leg was inches away from my shoulder; I could see a crop of short hairs under her knee where the razor had missed its mark. Her skin was so pale it was almost blue. I looked up and watched her fluff her hair, then rummage in her handbag, checking for her cigarettes. The bag was silver, to match her shoes.

She'd made an effort, and I knew it wasn't for Auntie Linda.

The truth is, I hated her dress. It looked like it was made of thin plastic, pulled taut over the sharp angles of her body. I imagined her hip bones piercing the fabric, pointing at Auntie Linda and the rest of the pub.

She applied a lipstick I didn't recognize, a departure from her usual bright red or pink. The new nude shade didn't suit her. But she seemed happy with the result, giving her hair one last fluff.

"Don't wait up!" she trilled over her shoulder as she left the room.

"Have fun," I told her.

"That's my plan, angelface, that's my plan!"

"Do you hate her?" Fiona asked as soon as the front door slammed shut behind our mother in her plastic dress.

"Fiona!" I turned to her, shocked, but her eyes were still glued to the television screen, her mouth set in a firm line.

"What? Don't play innocent with me, Meredith. We both know she's a bitch. She hates us back anyway."

"Do you really think so?" I was more curious than upset by my sister's words.

Fiona shrugged. "There's no love in that woman's heart," she said matter-of-factly.

"Of course she loves us," I said. "Doesn't it happen automatically when you have a baby?" I was too young to know anything about the mechanics of giving birth, but I'd seen women cooing over their infants at the park and watched enough grown-up television to know that there's generally believed to be something magical about the transition to motherhood.

"Maybe she loved me in the beginning, a bit," Fiona said. "By the time you came along, her life was really shit."

I stared at her until she looked back. "I'm kidding! Jeez, Meredith, don't cry. She told me I ripped her apart when I was born and that she'd never forgive me. She thought I'd killed her."

"Has she ever told you anything about when I was born?"

"No. But I remember it."

"Liar. You weren't even two. Nobody remembers anything from that age."

"Well, I do. She didn't make it to the hospital in time so she pushed you out on the kitchen floor. It was a bloodbath. You screamed for days."

"I don't believe you." I sulked, angry at her for ruining my entrance into the world.

We sat in silence for a few minutes. She watched television and I stared at the screen, not following the action, not interested in a bunch of doctors talking in urgent voices over someone lying on a hospital bed.

"She loves us," I said stubbornly.

Fiona sighed. "Who cares? As soon as we're old enough, we're leaving. I'll get a job. We might get a house of our own if we say we're homeless. We'll tell them she kicked us out, then ran away."

I hadn't realized how much I wanted that. My tummy clenched: fear and excitement. Hope, even. "I can come with you?"

She stared at me. "Of course you can, you nutcase. How could I leave you? We're a team."

I grinned. "When? When can we do that?"

"When I'm sixteen."

"That's ages away," I grumbled, the balloon of excitement inside me slowly deflating.

"Be patient," Fiona said firmly.

"Do you promise?" I asked her. "Promise we'll get our own place?"

"I promise." I'd never seen my sister look so serious, so I decided I had no choice but to believe her.

Day 1,245

CATLADY29: I heard back from the police.

JIGSAWGIRL: And?

CATLADY29: Not a lot, really. They don't have much to go on, do they? A random man I didn't even get a good look at, no witnesses. They said they're looking into it and they'll keep me updated.

JIGSAWGIRL: Are you feeling OK? I've been thinking about you.

CATLADY29: Better, I think.

JIGSAWGIRL: I'm glad. I know I've said it before, but you're so brave.

CATLADY29: Thank you, Meredith. How was your therapy session yesterday?

JIGSAWGIRL: It was OK. My homework is to fake yawn and eat raisins.

CATLADY29: That sounds interesting! Everything is worth a try, I guess!

JIGSAWGIRL: I guess... ☺

CATLADY29: I feel like a teenager asking my crush out on a date, but do you want to swap numbers?

JIGSAWGIRL: ☺ Of course.

I type my number carefully and hit send. Within minutes of logging off, my phone buzzes.

Hello, Meredith! This is your new friend Celeste.

I smile. I have a new friend, Celeste. And then I do something that takes me by surprise.

Hello, new friend Celeste! Would you like to come over for coffee/ tea and cake? Tomorrow? Meredith x

I read it a few times, my finger hovering above the little arrow waiting to send my invitation. I read it again, then delete it. I put my phone down on the table and go in search of Fred. He's lying on my bed, curled up so tightly it takes me a moment to work out where his head is. I crouch down on the floor and stare at him. If he wakes up, I'll send the text.

He doesn't wake up, but I remind myself that cats are contrary, and I really can't let Fred make all my decisions. One of Diane's beloved affirmations—"Choose faith over fear"— pops into my head, and I take it as a sign to go downstairs and finish what I've started.

Hello, new friend Celeste! Would you like to come over for coffee/ tea and cake? Tomorrow? Mer x

I hit the arrow before I can talk myself out of it. I don't have time to get nervous, because she replies straightaway.

I would LOVE to. Text me your address and I'll be there. It's a date. X

Day 1,246

Sunday, December 16, 2018

I wake up early so I can get all my Sunday chores done before Celeste arrives. I change Fred's litter tray—he stares at me unblinkingly from his spot on the kitchen windowsill the entire time—then sweep and mop the floors, scrub the bathroom from top to bottom (I've surprised myself by growing rather fond of the lime-green tiles), and change my bedsheets. I open every window in the house, enjoying the cold air on my skin. Since I've already worked up a bit of a sweat, I decide to work out now instead of this evening. I run up and down the stairs fifty times, but I'm seven seconds slower than my personal best: nine minutes, twenty-three seconds.

I flop onto the floor, wait for my heart rate to return to normal, and do some stretches. Fred joins me, elongating his limbs as he rolls around next to me on the carpet.

Even after all that activity, my mind is still restless. I've never tried internet dating, but getting ready to meet Celeste in real life feels a little like how I imagine that to be. I remember when Sadie met a guy she'd been chatting to online for two months. "I feel like I'm actually a little bit in love with him," she told me the night before their date, and she practically had love hearts leaping out of her eyes, like you see in old cartoons. She worked out they'd spent more than two hundred hours getting to know each other, with texts and phone calls late into the night when the kids were asleep. "That's like, fifty dates, with a few over-nighters thrown in," she said, winking.

But when Sadie and Jason (or Justin, Julian, something like that) finally set eyes on each other, there were no cartoon love hearts.

"Nothing!" she wailed, her body slumped over my kitchen table. She was properly crying, like someone had died.

"Nothing at all? Not even a tiny flutter?"

"Nothing. It was like being on a date with my grandma's next-door neighbor." She started rummaging in her bag. "I need to smoke. Do you mind?"

I frowned at her but opened the back door wide. "Blow it away from me. And what's wrong with your grandma's next-door neighbor?"

"Nothing at all." She clutched the inside of the doorframe and exhaled dramatically into the late-afternoon half light, like a soap opera character on the verge of a long-overdue breakdown. "He was nice. Just a perfectly normal guy. But I don't want nice or perfectly normal, Mer. I want butterflies. I thought I'd found them. But as soon as he started talking, they died. Or flew away, or something."

I'm standing in the same place now as Sadie and I were that day. I open the back door slowly, until I can feel the fresh air on my face. Celeste will be here in two hours, and I don't want to be her grandma's next-door neighbor. I don't want to be perfectly normal. I want to be amazing, because that's what she deserves.

She'll be here in two hours, and I'm not ready. I've showered, but I'm back in my dressing gown, my damp hair creating a cold cape. What do you wear to meet someone you've chatted to, more or less on a daily basis, for weeks, but wouldn't recognize if you passed them on the street? I know everything, and nothing, about her.

Scanning the contents of my wardrobe, I rule out my usual

uniform of leggings and a sweater—too casual. There's nothing special about leggings and a sweater. But I don't want to look like I've made too much of an effort either, like an old lady in her Sunday best. I don't buy many clothes—what's the point?— and Sadie took three bags of old stuff and bad memories to the charity shop for me two years ago. I find a denim shirt on a hanger underneath a chunky cardigan I've had forever and never wear but couldn't bear to part with. Leggings and a denim shirt—it's the best I can do. Maybe if it goes well with Celeste— if she's not put off by the jigsaws—and she comes to see me again, I'll order something new. Like one of those cute swingy dresses with large stiff collars.

She'll be here in an hour, and I still need to dry and straighten my hair. I kneel on the floor of my room in front of the tall mirror, peer at my pale skin and tired eyes. I'm fastidious about taking my vitamin D supplements, but it's not the same as feeling sunshine on your cheeks. Celeste is twenty-nine and not a recluse. She's been through something horrific, but she's not hiding away. She will have radiant skin, I'm sure of it.

Something is clawing in the pit of my belly as I go through the motions with my hair straightener. I deliberately don't make eye contact with myself, but I already know. I know what I'm going to do.

I go back downstairs with only half my hair straight, and text Celeste.

Celeste, I'm so sorry! I'm not feeling well. Can we rearrange?

The three little dots that tell me she's replying appear immediately. I feel like I'm going to be sick. That's what I deserve, for lying to her.

Oh, Mer, I'm sorry to hear that! Don't worry about it at all! Of course we can rearrange. Let me know if you need anything at all. Lots of love xxx

I want to tell her how sweet she is and how sorry I am, but I'm too overwhelmed with guilt to continue the conversation. I turn my phone off and lie on the couch. Within seconds Fred is curled inside the crook of my arm. He stares at me; I touch him gently on the nose. I still feel sick. I pull the throw over us both and wait for the day to be over.

Day 1,255

Tuesday, December 25, 2018

It's Christmas, and I've done everything everybody else does. More, perhaps. I sent cards to remind a handful of people I'm still alive. My own cards form a small but special collection, the highlights being a handmade one from James with an angel that he claims is me at the top of a tinsel tree and a huge "To the One I Love at Christmas" from Sadie, because she thinks she's hilarious. I got a real tree delivered and decorated it with multi-colored lights and a big shiny star because I love the smell, even though Fred paws at the needles so much the bottom third is sparse within days. Between the tree and the frankincense-and-myrrh-scented candle and the mulled wine, my olfactory nerves are subjected to a festive overload.

I made mulled wine in my big copper-based pot. After stirring it gently and trying to be mindful, I sipped it from a mug while I wrapped presents. I buy so few that I could easily wrap them all in an hour. But I spread the task out over the whole night. I used brown kraft paper because it's recyclable and the shiny/glittery stuff isn't, but I made it less boring with red-and-white twine and the recipient's name in careful looping script with my Sharpie. Maria from *The Sound of Music* was right about brown-paper packages tied up with string. When my wrapping was finished, I watched *Miracle on 34th Street* (both versions) and *The Polar Express* and *It's a Wonderful Life*. My movie snacks were hot chocolate with whipped cream and marshmallows and ginger-bread cookies and dark sea salt caramel truffles. I made the gingerbread cookies, but I bought the truffles, in a posh pink tin, from a fancy website. Everybody needs to taste dark sea salt caramel truffles at least once in their life. I also made a spicy, boozy Christmas pudding, not because I particularly like it but because it's a Christmassy thing to do and the prep can take a couple of hours, which filled an empty Saturday morning nicely. I don't have church services and school nativities and outdoor ice rinks and busy supermarkets to go to, so it's important that I fill my time. 'Tis the season to be busy. Sadie sent me lots of pictures of James's nativity, in which he was a camel and didn't look too happy about it. Over FaceTime I told him he did a great job because camels are famous for being grumpy, and who wants to be a wise man anyway? I told him that most wise men aren't as wise as they think they are. He giggled, then Matilda grabbed the phone and held it up to her crusty nostrils while she sang "Jingle Bells" to me.

Tom turned up yesterday—unannounced, but I forgave him, because he was wearing a Santa hat with a jingly bell on the end of it. "I'm just visiting all my favorite people!" he said. He stayed for a big slice of pudding and said it was the best he'd ever tasted. I'd bought him a gift—a soft scarf in a subtle tartan—and wrapped it and hidden it in the TV unit. Just in case he got me one. And he did, which was lovely, but also embarrassing because he gave it to me in the living room so I had to get his parcel out from the TV unit and explain why it wasn't under the tree with the others. But he laughed and agreed that he didn't know whether I would get him a gift either and isn't Christmas gift etiquette a strange thing? I didn't ask if he bought all his befriendees a gift; I didn't want to know.

I unwrap my gifts as soon as I wake up because that's what everyone does on Christmas morning and it helps to distinguish it from just another Tuesday. Tom's is a journal with thick creamy pages and a smooth leather cover in rich tan, with my intials embossed on the front. I adore it.

Sadie comes over for chocolate croissants, straight off a night shift at the hospital. She's wearing Christmas-tree earrings and has tinsel wrapped round her stethoscope. She gives me a huge bottle of the perfume I wore when I was twenty-one, which I spray immediately and liberally. For the rest of the day I feel like I'm in Sadie's bedroom getting ready for a night out. It's nice to have a break from twenty-four days of frankincense and myrrh. It triggers good memories; we talk about the places we used to go and the people we used to see until Sadie has to leave to get the kids from Steve's place.

"They'll be desperate to get back and play with all their Santa toys," she says apologetically.

"Of course they will," I reassure her, knowing she would be delighted if I grabbed my jacket and told her to hang on, I'd just come with her. Instead, I press the kids' gifts into her hands—a box of wild animal figurines for James because he wants to be a zookeeper when he grows up, and an oversized unicorn puppet for Matilda that I know she'll get a kick out of. Then I kiss her on the cheek and wish her a merry Christmas.

The rich fragrance lingers in the air all day, long after Sadie has left. It's so much sweeter and stronger than anything I would wear nowadays, and she knows that. She's bought me nostalgia in a tall, slim bottle.

I unwrap Fred's gift for him, a stuffed mouse filled with catnip, which makes him go crazy for half an hour before he conks out on the couch and sleeps for the rest of the day. I sit next to him and eat a big helping of curry I made earlier in the week, carefully balancing the plate on my knee. I don't like turkey—I never want to eat it any other day of the year, so why today?

I exchange a few texts with Celeste, who moans that her stepdad is snoring so loudly on the couch that she and her mum can't hear the television; I tell her that Fred is doing the same next to me. Then she tells me that she's finally told her mum and stepdad about the assault, and that her mum cried a lot, but they're being really supportive.

I curl up with Fred and watch James Stewart figure out the meaning of life. I eat cheese and crackers and then finish off the Christmas pudding, even though I'm not hungry. I open the bottle of sparkling wine Sadie brought over and drink the whole thing far too quickly. I think about my sister, and I close my eyes, and the phone wakes me up at five minutes to midnight.

It's Mama, her voice dull. She asks me what I've done all day, why I didn't get her a gift. Yes, she got my card. No, she hasn't sent any this year. Waste of bloody time. She has something for me under the tree and I'll get it when I've pulled myself together and am brave enough to show my face. Fiona and Lucas have just left, she says, and my stomach flips. They were there all day, she says. Lucas carved the turkey and ate two portions of trifle. I wish her merry Christmas and hang up before she's finished talking. I turn my phone off. On Boxing Day, I have a panic attack.

1998

He first came into our lives on a miserable Sunday afternoon, as the incessant Glasgow rain drove against the living room window like a persistent, unwanted guest. Mama and I were watching a black-and-white film, although I wasn't paying much attention. I longed for color.

"Hey!" Fee's voice rang through the hall, and it sounded different. I couldn't hear what she said next; I realized she was speaking to someone else. I heard the sounds of jackets and shoes being discarded, muffled laughter. I looked at Mama, but her eyes were fixed on the television screen, where a young woman with anguish in her eyes was clinging to the arm of a frozen-faced older man.

We rarely brought people home. Sadie, now and again, although she usually just hovered in the hall for the short time it took me to grab my jacket and shove my shoes on. Never any boys. But here was one, in our living room, possibly the tallest person to have entered our space. He loomed over us until Fee hissed at him to sit down.

"This is Lucas," she said.

I mumbled a hello; Mama muted the television and looked him up and down.

"It's nice to meet you," Lucas said. "I've heard a lot about you."

Mama smiled. "Really? Like what?"

We all waited, but not for long. He and Fiona were well prepared.

"Well, I know you make a great fish pie," Lucas said.

I always made the fish pie. But Mama took the compliment.

"I think there's one in the freezer," she said. "Would you like to stay for dinner?"

Fiona beamed, and Lucas nodded enthusiastically. "Yes, please, Mrs. Maggs. That would be lovely."

"I'll go and get started then." Mama handed Fee the remote control on her way out of the room.

We sat in silence until MTV broke it.

"What have you been up to?" Fee asked me, sitting next to Lucas on the small couch. As if I would actually have something interesting to tell her. I watched her hand slide into his; his grip tightened.

"Not much. I did some baking. Sticky toffee pudding. We can have it after the fish."

"Amazing." She nudged his arm.

"Sounds good," he said obligingly. I look at his feet in their grubby white sports socks. They looked enormous next to Fee's.

"We're a proper couple now," Fee told me. "Lucas asked me to be his girlfriend in the car on the way here."

"Congratulations," I said. And to him: "You're a brave man."

Fee and I laughed, and he smiled. I noticed that it didn't reach his eyes.

We watched MTV until Mama called us for dinner. It was strange to have a fourth place set at the table. You'd think it would give the small wooden rectangle balance, but it didn't. I don't know if it was his size, or his unfamiliar young man smell, or the way he reached his long arm in front of me to grab the salt, or the awkwardness I felt when I accidentally brushed my foot against his under the table. Maybe it was all of it. Or maybe I was just jealous, as Mama said later. "You might get a boyfriend one day," she remarked after the front door closed behind Fee and Lucas.

"Maybe," I muttered. I knew my sister was only saying goodbye to him in the garden, but my heart didn't stop racing until she was back in the house, alone.

Lucas was a regular Sunday-dinner guest, after that. Mama heated up something I'd cooked earlier that day. She passed it off as her own and Fee and I played along. I always offered to set the table, so I could make sure the salt, pepper, and ketchup were right next to Lucas's place. He never had to reach over me again.

Day 1,257

It turns out that Tom is better at jigsaws than either of us expected, and our own miniature version of Santa Maria del Fiore is almost half-complete.

"We should enter a jigsaw competition," he tells me. "I've heard you can win big money."

I chuckle. "That could be your new career. What did you want to be when you grew up?"

"A private detective," he tells me in all seriousness.

I laughed. "And you ended up in finance? Or were you an undercover cop trying to lift the lid on corporate fraud?"

"Ah...well, that would be a lot more exciting. But...no. Just boring old investments and pensions, sadly. What about you? What was your childhood dream?"

"Something creative. More creative than what I do now. I always liked the idea of being a chef, or a reporter. In fact, I worked for a newspaper before...you know. This. It wasn't exactly hard-hitting journalism. But I was getting somewhere maybe. Slowly."

"And you had to leave, obviously?"

I nod. "My boss was really kind. But it's difficult to report for a local newspaper if you never go anywhere."

I find the piece of herringbone brick I've been searching for, and triumphantly press it into place in the center of the cathedral dome. We fall into a comfortable silence, building the scene piece by piece.

"What's it like, sharing a jigsaw with me? A complete novice?"

I laugh. "It's fine. But you do know I do other jigsaws, when you're not here?"

"I wouldn't expect anything less," he says.

"I actually don't mind having you here," I say awkwardly.

"I like being here," he replies.

"Maybe I'm not as much of a loner as I thought I was."

"Being a loner is nothing to be ashamed of, Meredith. I think enjoying your own company, having that inner strength, is something to be proud of."

"Maybe." I finally meet his eyes. "I don't feel very strong, most of the time."

"Meredith, you're one of the strongest people I know."

"Do you really mean that?"

"Of course I do. I wouldn't say it otherwise."

"I think I want to be stronger."

He looks out of my bay window. "There's a big world out there, Meredith. It's waiting for you."

2001

I spotted Bill's tiny advert on the library's public noticeboard:

```
PR assistant wanted.
No experience required.
Flexible hours.
```

"I wanted someone who likes to read," he told me when I asked him why he advertised in a library of all places. The only other applicant was a woman who actually worked in the library, but luckily Bill decided it was fairer to give the job to someone who didn't already have one.

The interview was short, because I didn't really have much to tell him. I had an A in Higher English and had worked in a call center until two weeks ago, when the company folded. Bill nodded, made a few notes, then told me the job was mine if I could start on Monday.

He was a one-man band, before I came along, in an office half the size of Mama's living room. He had to cram a desk into a dusty old cupboard for me. I sneezed all day, and my eczema flared up. I didn't have a contract; he paid me in cash every Friday and warned me I'd be out of a job if the work dried up. But there was plenty of work. I loved the challenge of turning an everyday product or service into an exciting press release local newspapers would take notice of. Sometimes they did, sometimes they didn't. Dog-grooming products and Italian restaurants weren't exactly front-page news.

There was a whole other side to Bill's work that I wasn't part of. I was new to the PR world, but I knew writing press releases for local businesses didn't pay enough to cover rent and my wages as well as whatever expenses Bill had in the big house in one of the poshest suburbs of Glasgow with his wife and two kids.

People used to come to his office, but they'd quickly leave together, usually under the guise of going for lunch. One day, I was reading the paper and a familiar face appeared in front of me. It was a woman who'd gone for lunch with Bill a few days before. She was a nurse at a big city hospital, and she wanted the world to know that staff shortages and unfair working conditions had led to a patient's death.

After that, I paid a little more attention to anyone who turned up at the office.

Bill wasn't really into giving feedback. But one day, after I'd been there for about six months, a press release I'd written about a hair salon that had extended their premises to include a nursery for clients' kids made page five of the paper. When I arrived at work, it was lying open on my desk. It had someone else's byline, of course, but it was basically all my words, with a few tweaks.

"You're a great writer," Bill said without looking away from his computer screen. "Better than me."

I blushed and mumbled a thank-you, feeling the weight of his compliment.

"You should go to university. Or take a journalism course at college."

"I'd love to. But I can't afford it."

"Of course you can. Move back in with your mother. Apply for a grant or get a student loan. You can work here when you don't have lectures. Plenty of people with less means than you make it through further education."

"Thanks, but I'm happy working here."

The next morning, college brochures were stacked high beside my keyboard. I stared at the back of Bill's head. "What the hell is this?"

"No harm in taking a look, right?" He said it without turning round.

"I guess not." But I put the brochures on the floor and didn't give them a single glance until I got home.

I read them all, cover to cover. I looked at photographs of wholesome, smiling young adults with clear skin and white teeth. None of them looked stressed or overworked or strapped for cash. I let myself imagine what it would be like to sit in a huge lecture theater, day after day, and learn about something I was interested in.

The next morning, before work, I put all the brochures but one in my recycling box. Every now and then, I leafed through it, wondering what it would be like to look up at the University of Glasgow's gothic bell tower as a student and not as an outsider. To study in the Round Reading Room, to walk through the cloisters with my friends like the people on page nineteen. Then I'd slide it back under my bed.

I never applied to the University of Glasgow or any other university, college, or night school. I carried on working for Bill, until he had a heart attack on the way to the office one morning and dropped dead on Sauchiehall Street. I got a job in another call center, asking people if they were satisfied with their home energy providers.

Day 1,269

Tuesday, January 8, 2019

I know there's something wrong with Celeste as soon as I answer the phone, before she's said a word. Her breathing is heavy.

"I think I just saw him," she says between gulps of air. "In the supermarket."

"What? Who?"

"The man who attacked me. Maybe. I don't know. I'm pretty sure it was him. He looked at me, Meredith."

"Oh, Celeste." I sink onto the couch. "That must have been horrific."

She sniffs loudly. "I know it probably wasn't him. But for that split second it was. And...oh my God, is this going to happen forever? Am I going to abandon my shopping cart every time I catch the eye of a tall man with dark hair?"

"No," I tell her. "But it's early days. It's understandable. What did you have in your shopping cart?"

"What?"

"Tell me what you had in your shopping cart."

"I can't remember...sweet potatoes...broccoli...pineapple juice. That's all, I think. I'd only just got there."

"OK. What else was on your list?"

"Um...cheese. Eggs. Milk. Bread. Cereal. Yogurts. It was a big shop."

"My therapist tells me to list things when I'm feeling anxious," I explain. "Like the contents of my wardrobe or the last ten

86

books I've read. Five foods beginning with 'A.' It helps, I think."

"I think it's just talking to you that makes me feel better. Thank you, Meredith. You always know what to say."

"Really? I feel like I'm completely clueless most of the time."

"You're definitely not clueless. You should be a counselor."

I laugh. "I'm sorry you had to abandon your shopping cart."

"Me too," she moans. "I have absolutely nothing in the fridge."

When she phoned, I was just about to make soup. Apple and parsnip, with crusty bread on the side. Celeste sounds like she could do with soup. I hesitate, then take the plunge.

"Why don't you come over? Have some lunch."

"That's really sweet of you, Mer. Thanks so much for the offer. But I just don't feel like going anywhere."

"I can relate to that."

"I feel better for talking to you, Mer."

"I wish I could do more to help." I mean it. As soon as one of us disconnects the line, I suspect she'll start crying again.

"It's my thirtieth in June. My mum thinks I should have a party. I don't really feel like celebrating it, but I have to, I think. Mum says she'll do all the organizing—I just have to turn up."

"Sadie threw me a surprise party at the local pub for my thirtieth," I tell her. I don't mention that it was the first birthday party I'd ever had. "I thought it was just Sadie, my sister, and me going for a drink."

"Ooh, that's lovely."

"It was. Up to a point. My mother turned up and made a bit of a scene. It's...easier to relax when she's not around."

The night wasn't a complete disaster. After the pub, we went back to Mama's and when she went to bed Fiona and I had an after-party for two in the kitchen. We ate bowls of oven fries with melted cheese on top, drank vodka, and danced to the radio.

"It's nice of your mum to want to throw you a party," I say.

"I know. She's a sweetheart. She just worries about me too much."

In the brief silence I think about what it would be like to have a mother like Celeste's, who throws birthday parties and cries at the thought of her daughter being assaulted.

"I'm sure your party will be lots of fun," I tell her.

"If I go ahead with it, would you like me to send you an invitation?"

I hesitate, then: "Yes. I like getting things through the post."

She laughs. "I'd love you to come to my party, Mer."

"I'd love that too." That much is true. I just don't know how to make it happen.

The idea pops into my head a few minutes after we say our goodbyes. If our roles were reversed, and I had been the one crying on the phone, I have no doubt that Celeste would be sitting next to me right now, offering a shoulder to cry on, which is definitely one step up from an ear pressed against the telephone, two miles across town. If I was a good friend, I'd do the same for her. She needs me. If that isn't a good enough reason to leave my house, what is?

I spend the next hour wondering if I can actually do it. What would it take to get to Celeste's? Phoning a taxi. Getting into the taxi. Making small talk with the driver for as long as it takes to get to her flat (I checked Google Maps and it's estimating an eight-minute journey by car at this time of day). Paying the fare, getting out of the car, walking to Celeste's front door.

I pace around my living room. I stare out of the window, looking for a sign—like two magpies or a flying pig. I lie on my back on the floor, breathing from my diaphragm. Then I get up off the floor and decide to take it one step at a time. I empty my bladder, floss my teeth, brush my hair. It rained earlier, so I spend fifteen minutes looking for an umbrella before giving up. I put on my jacket and Converse. I retrieve my handbag from the hall cupboard, then decide I won't need it and put it back. I take fifty pounds from my takeout fund—Sadie goes to the ATM for me whenever I'm running low. I'll forgo my Thai curry this weekend—Celeste is worth it.

There are no more steps apart from the big ones. Starting with phoning a taxi. It's easier than I thought it would be. It's not as if I don't speak on the phone to people on a fairly regular basis—Sadie, Celeste, the Thai restaurant, those annoying tele-marketer people who call at least three times a week.

I've barely hung up on the taxi company when my phone buzzes. A text: my driver is en route, and I now know the make and model of the car, plus the registration number. I'm impressed by how much technology has advanced since I last did this. Then it hits me that in a few minutes a car will be parked outside my house, waiting for me, its meter ticking with expectation.

This time it feels as if something very small has exploded deep inside my brain. I briefly lose control of my senses—all I can see are shadows, the silence is deafening. I put my hands out in front of me until they make contact with something solid. It's the wall. I push my fingertips against it until I can feel pressure moving up my arms, then let my body fold onto the floor. Now that I can't fall, I'm safe to tear off my jacket. I can feel sweat pooling under my arms, at the base of my spine, on the soles of my feet. I can't get my Converse off; I've temporar-ily lost my fine motor skills and the double knots I so carefully formed just minutes ago are beyond my capabilities.

It takes me a while to realize that the persistent buzzing noise isn't coming from inside my head but the pocket of my jacket. I fumble for my phone, swipe at it aimlessly.

"Taxi for Maggs? It's waiting outside your property."

I gasp. "I ... I'm sorry. I need to cancel."

"Bloody hell. It's a bit late for that."

"Sorry. Sorry."

"Are you OK, miss? Do you need help?"

"I'm fine. I'm sorry." I hang up and let the phone slip from my fingers.

Day 1,271

Thursday, January 10, 2019

"What does your depression feel like, Meredith?" Tom asks. It's raining—we're sitting in the living room, watching the water trickle down the bay windows, eating biscotti bought by Tom to celebrate our completion of Santa Maria del Fiore.

The truth is, I'm not really in the mood for celebrating after my failed attempt to visit Celeste. I haven't told Tom, embarrassed that I entertained the thought of it when I can't even cross the front door. The shame is bearing down on me, and I'm not sure I have the energy to hide it for the next hour.

"Like a weight. A constant weight," I say flatly.

"It never lifts?"

"OK. Maybe not constant. It's not so heavy when I'm doing a jigsaw with Fred on my lap. Or when I'm reading on the couch with candles lit."

"What about when other people are here? Like Sadie, or me."

"It depends."

"On what?"

"Oh, I don't know. The time of the month. Whether you ask stupid questions. You're not my therapist, Tom." I'm getting irritable.

"You're right, I'm not. I'm just someone with depression, talking to another person with depression."

"You have depression?" I'm surprised, then not so surprised. I've noticed, now and then, a shadow briefly darken his face. A slightly-too-long pause before a smile. With hindsight, just a few

91

of those minuscule details most people are too preoccupied to notice. But I have all the time in the world to pick up on such things, and I also live a life filled with dark shadows and slightly-too-long pauses.

"I do. I have, for a long time. It comes and goes. So I can relate to what you're saying about the weight. I often describe it as a feeling of doom. Always feeling as if something bad is going to happen, even though my rational brain tells me that's unlikely to be the case."

"Yes, I get that," I say softly. I want to reach out to him, or at least to shrink the space between us on the couch, but I don't think we're quite there yet. Tom is my friend, I realize. I look forward to his visits, even if some of his questions push me toward the edge of my comfort zone. He's someone I care about. I don't want him to be depressed; the thought creates a lump in my throat. I want better for him.

"OK, let's try something. I'll go first."

"OK," I say warily.

"I first felt depressed when I was twenty."

"I was seven. I couldn't get out of bed; it was like my body was made of stone. I told Mama I had a sore throat and she let me stay out of school for three days. She left me under my duvet the whole time. I remember Fee bringing me juice cartons and packets of chips."

If he's shocked, he's doing a good job of hiding it. "I got my diagnosis when I was twenty-five."

"I was eighteen."

"The first person I told was my girlfriend at the time. She tried to be supportive, but she didn't really understand."

"I told Sadie. She was upset. Angry I hadn't told her sooner."

"Do you think she had the right to be angry?"

I shrug. "Anger is always about something else, isn't it? Like rejection, or fear, or grief. I think she felt all those things. She took it personally that I hadn't asked her for help. I guess she was scared because she didn't understand what it meant, and sad because I wasn't the same person to her. I mean, I was—I am—but we all put people into boxes, don't we? With labels on them. So-and-so is such-and-such a person…"

"Whereas people are much more complicated than that."

"Well, yes. If they let themselves be."

"What do you mean?"

"I think some people just don't want to feel anything too deeply. It's too difficult. My mother and sister think depression is just my excuse for everything."

"How long have you been taking antidepressants for?"

"Twenty years, on and off," I tell him.

"That's a long time. What else do you do to manage your depression?"

I tell him the truth. "I stay home."

1997

"How can I help you today?" Dr. Frost asked, sliding a box of tissues across the table to me. He was a wiry old man with a no-nonsense approach. I knew we were on the clock, but I couldn't stop crying and on that day, of all days, a little kindness would have gone a long way.

It was my first time in the doctor's office for years. Mama didn't trust doctors; she was a better judge of our health. But I was eighteen, so I could do this without her. I hadn't been at work for a week, mumbling about period pains and curling up under my duvet.

"I think I'm depressed," I told Dr. Frost in a shaky voice.

He handed me a questionnaire and a pen. "Just be honest."

Have you found little pleasure or interest in doing things?
Have you found yourself feeling down or hopeless?
Have you had trouble falling or staying asleep, or sleeping too much?
Have you felt that you're a failure or let yourself or your family down?

And so on.

I worked my way through the list. Yes, yes, yes to everything. But "yes" wasn't an option. I had to choose between:

No, not at all.
On some days.
On more than half the days.
Nearly every day.

I paused at the final question.

Have you had thoughts that you would be better off dead, or thoughts of hurting yourself in some way?

Fee and Sadie called me Mer, but I had once watched a film where a character called Meredith was nicknamed Death. On more than one occasion, it's occurred to me that it's the more appropriate option. My pen hovered between *On more than half the days* and *Nearly every day*. But I decided to lie. What did it matter? I'd racked up enough points on the other eight questions.

I passed the questionnaire back to Dr. Frost and waited while he read through it.

"Have I passed?"

"There are no right or wrong answers," he said, peering at me over the top of his glasses.

"Right," I said, feeling like I was in the headmaster's office.

"Miss Maggs, the results of the test indicate that you have depression."

"OK." This was the least surprising news I'd ever been given. "What now?"

"Now I give you a prescription." Dr. Frost scribbled on his pad. "One pill a day—come back and see me in six weeks. It could take that long for you to feel the effects of the medication, so don't worry."

"I worry all the time." My laugh sounded forced and hollow.

His eyes shifted to his clock before they settled back on my face. My seven minutes were up. "Try the pills, Miss Maggs. We'll take it from there."

"OK," I said again. I would take the pills. I'd go through the motions. I'd keep hoping for light. I'd strive to be Mer, and not Death.

*

"Where have you been?" Mama was in the hall when I stepped into the house. She was wearing her coat and carrying her handbag; I didn't know if she was just back or about to leave. I hoped it was the latter, but she followed me into the kitchen and watched me as I dropped the white paper bag from the pharmacist onto the table.

"What do you have there?"

I sighed. There was no point in lying. She always found out what she wanted to know. "It's medicine." I picked the bag back up and crammed it into the pocket of my denim jacket.

Her eyes flashed. She held her hand out, palm facing upward. "Let Mama see—there's a good girl. Families shouldn't have secrets."

"It's no secret, Mama. I told you—it's medicine."

"What kind of medicine? You don't look sick to me." She moved closer, her arm still stretched out toward me. I looked at the deep lines on her palm.

"Antidepressants."

"Stop muttering, Meredith. You're not a child."

"Antidepressants," I said louder.

My mother laughed. "What do you have to be depressed about?"

I stared at her. "It's complicated."

"Meredith, you are the opposite of complicated. Is this you trying to be more interesting?" She was right in front of me now, close enough to tickle the soft skin under my chin with her long nail. "You don't need happy pills; you just need to get a life. Hand them over."

"No."

"*No?*" Her eyes flashed again.

"They're my pills."

She finally dropped her arm and brought her face inches from mine. I could smell cigarette smoke and see foundation settled in the fine lines around her mouth.

"Let me see them."

"I'm not going to." I could feel the adrenaline rushing through my body. I tried to focus on keeping both feet firmly on the floor and wondered when Fiona would be home from work at the salon. I could have done with her barreling into the kitchen, complaining loudly about clogged-up sinks and old ladies with spongy scalps.

Taking my attention away from Mama, if only for a few seconds, was a bad idea. I wasn't prepared for the slap. The force of her palm against my cheek made my head spin.

I hate you. The voice was inside my head, but the words were directed at her. I held my tears back until she left the room, my hand still gripping the box of pills inside the white paper bag in my pocket.

Day 1,279

Friday, January 18, 2019

Diane always wears something green—a silky blouse, a hairband, a sparkly brooch. I think someone must have told her once how much the color complements her auburn hair and matches her eyes and she decided she'd never wear anything else. It's true—it's her color. Today, she's got an olive-green turtleneck on. I hate turtlenecks—they make me feel claustrophobic.

I tell her about trying to leave my house, and she makes reassuring noises.

"You've taken a huge step, Meredith, even if you don't see it that way."

I shrug.

"You've not mentioned Celeste before," she says.

"She's a new friend. We met online. She had a bad experience, and she confided in me. I wanted to be there for her."

"Hold on to that," she says. "It's real progress. Can you do something for me? Whenever you catch yourself thinking about failure in a negative way, switch it around in your mind. Think of it as a lesson. We can learn from our failures, and do things differently next time for a better outcome."

"I'll try."

"Great. And how are you getting on with your mindfulness techniques?"

"I'm doing them," I tell her. I don't add that what I'm most mindful about is not letting Fred eat any raisins, because they're toxic to cats.

"OK," Diane says. "Remember, we're working at your pace. Keep going with them. And don't forget about your breathing exercises. But I'd like you to add something else to your daily routine. Have you heard of cognitive behavioral therapy? CBT?"

Her green eyes penetrate my laptop screen. I manage not to look away and nod.

"CBT is a type of therapy that targets how our thinking processes affect our feelings. I think this might work for you because structure is a big part of your life, and this is a highly structured approach."

"Right."

"I'm going to give you some homework for next week."

"OK." I'm not surprised. Diane loves homework almost as much as she loves diaphragmatic breathing.

"I want you to get a notebook and pen, and sit down in a quiet, comfortable place. Then think about leaving your house, and write down how you feel about that. Write down everything that comes into your mind, even if you think it's ridiculous, or that it doesn't make sense. Bring the notebook to our next session, and we'll talk about it. Does that sound OK?"

"That sounds great, Diane."

Day 1,284

If you google "how to cut your own hair," you get about 1,320,000,000 results. But like most things in life, it's best to keep it simple.

I lay out a comb, a ponytail band, and styling shears in front of the bathroom mirror. I've known from a young age that kitchen scissors should go nowhere near hair. I told Mama I wanted a fringe once, but she wouldn't take me to the salon.

"I can do it just as well," she declared, rummaging in the junk drawer under the sink until she found a huge pair of orange-handled scissors. I looked at them, aghast, then back at her. She was smiling. Fiona stayed on the other side of the room, near the door, ready to bolt if Mama decided she wanted another guinea pig.

I look at myself in the mirror as I brush my hair flat against my back. I haven't trimmed it for a few months, and the ends reach my bra strap. By the time I was nine I could almost sit on it. Every day, since I'd started school, Mama had pulled it into two long plaits on either side of my head, so tight I would have a headache by lunchtime. One morning, when the teacher briefly left the classroom, I ripped the bands out in a rare act of defiance, letting the curly lengths billow around my shoulders.

"You look like a princess," one of my classmates told me. "I want hair like yours." I felt like I was walking on a cloud for the rest of the day. Fiona dragged me back down to earth on the bus on the way home. "You'd better fix your hair," she said. "Mama will go mental."

"Help me then." I pushed the ponytail bands into her hands. "I can't do it."

Between us, we fashioned two slightly uneven plaits, our small hands fumbling with the strands, working against the movement of the bus.

"Let me go in first," Fiona muttered as we walked up the garden path to the front door. "I'll try to distract her."

She could be a good big sister, when she tried.

Our efforts were pointless. Mama knew straightaway that I'd messed with her handiwork. "Don't you like your plaits?" she asked me.

I might have got off lightly if I'd kept my mouth shut. But being a princess for a few short hours had ignited a fire in my belly.

"No," I said. "They give me a headache. I can't concentrate at school."

"You should have told me," she said, pulling me toward her in a tight embrace. My arms hanging loose at my sides, I peered round her and caught Fiona's eye. She shrugged, as taken aback as I was. Mama definitely wasn't the cuddling type.

Just as quickly as she'd put her arms round me, she let me go.

"Wait there," she said, walking into the kitchen.

I caught Fiona's eye again; we exchanged a nervous, hopeful look. Back then, we still had hope.

Mama came back into the hall, but she didn't have a chocolate biscuit or something else to make up for two years of daily plait-induced headaches. I saw a flash of orange; she was spinning the handle of the clunky scissors round her pointed index finger.

"I think it's time for a haircut—it's getting far too long." She took one of my plaits in her hand, rubbed her fingers against the ends. She put her hands on my shoulders and turned me slowly to face the long mirror on the wall.

"Right, Mama's salon is open." I caught her eye in the mirror and smiled through my nerves. She didn't smile back; she had the same look on her face as when she did something important, like sewing on a button or writing checks to pay the bills. Fee hovered behind us, watching intently.

"Yes, it's far too long," Mama said. "No wonder you're getting headaches, angelface. What a weight to be carrying around on your head."

I was confused—my hair didn't feel heavy. But Mama knew best, so I didn't say anything.

"I saw a hairdresser do this on the TV once," she told me as she lifted one of my plaits and opened the scissors wide. Fee's eyes and mouth were wide too, in the glass.

My plait hit the floor—and it *did* sound heavy.

"Right, time for the other one! We don't want you to be lopsided." Mama laughed.

I couldn't speak; my throat felt blocked, as if my heart had turned to stone and was trying to escape out of my mouth, like an enormous rock jammed in the opening of a cave.

Mama didn't notice my silent tears trickling down my cheeks. Her forehead was wrinkled as she concentrated on making sure the ends were even. My new hair barely reached my chin. Finally she stepped back to scrutinize her efforts.

"Not bad at all, for an amateur."

"It's ... short," I croaked.

She smiled, finally catching my eye in the mirror. "It'll grow back."

"It's not so bad," Fiona told me later, kneeling behind me on our bedroom floor, gently brushing my shorn locks. Crying silently, I couldn't bear to look in the mirror again. I knew she was lying.

"I look like a boy," I sobbed. "I can't go to school like this."

"We'll fix it," Fiona said firmly. She grabbed a copy of *Smash Hits* from under her bed and started flicking through it. "Look!" She held it open. "In a few months it'll be a cute bob. Like Winona Ryder."

I was too young to know who Winona Ryder was, and it took a lot longer than a few months for my hair to resemble anything close to a cute bob. The Alice band I wore to school the next day did nothing to detract from the lack of length. My new hair was the talk of the playground. Fiona stayed by my side during break time and lunch, ready to pounce on anyone who dared poke fun. But nobody did. Boys sniggered. Girls stared at me from a distance, wide-eyed and wary, like I was some sort of wild animal.

I think of my nine-year-old self now, of her courage, as I divide my long hair into two sections and pull each one over the front of my shoulder to hang down over my breasts. I pick up my shears. They're cool against the palm of my hand, and another memory—a much more recent one—flashes into my mind: blood and water pooling at my feet and swirling around the plug hole, my body sliding down the slippery shower door. Goose bumps on my skin as I come to, my limbs aching, the open blade glistening in the small rectangle of afternoon sunlight flooding through the bathroom window.

Day 1,294

Saturday, February 2, 2019

Celeste is coming over today, a spontaneous arrangement we made last night, and I'm so nervous I can't sit still. I can't cancel on her again, because that would just make me seem like a complete flake. If Mama taught me anything, it was that what other people think is of paramount importance. I pace around the house, analyzing every nook and cranny, trying to see it through her eyes, to identify something that screams "This is a woman who never goes anywhere."

Maybe today will be the day I tell her the full story.

She's right on time, and I swing the door open with what I hope is a relaxed smile on my face, not the tight expression of someone who's been alternating between unnecessary cleaning, deep breathing, and the obsessive eating of raisins to try to quiet her mind.

As it turns out, it doesn't matter. Her face is hidden by a bunch of flowers—beautiful large fresh petals in bursts of orange and yellow and pink that I can't help but beam at.

"Hello," she says, revealing her face. It's a sweet one, with a sleek bob haircut, freckles on her nose, and a gap between her two front teeth.

"Hello." I smile back and accept the flowers from her outstretched hands. "Wow. Celeste, thank you so much. These are beautiful."

"It's so lovely to see your face at last," she says.

"It's so lovely to see yours," I say. I mean it, which surprises me a little.

I arrange the flowers in a vase from the dusty depths of one of my kitchen cupboards, and it feels like a novelty, because nobody has bought me flowers since Gavin. I take my time, enjoying the sensation of the velvet petals on my fingers. While Celeste is distracted by Fred, I lower my face and inhale deeply—a sweet tanginess that not even the most expensive scented candle can replicate. I give the flowers pride of place on the living room windowsill as Celeste runs her fingers along the spines of my books, marveling, "Have you really read all these?"

I give her a quick tour of my house, and she makes all the right noises, laughing at Fred following us into every room. She admires my framed vintage posters of Capri and Sicily on the wall on the upstairs landing and tells me her uncle is Italian.

"Really? Wow." I imagine childhood summers under a hot sun, a tiny Celeste skipping down cobbled streets.

"He's lived in Paisley his whole life," she says, as if she's reading my mind. "Runs a takeout place on the high street."

We both laugh.

"I'm trying to learn Italian," I tell her.

"Meredith, you're so sophisticated!"

Back in the kitchen, I make a pot of tea and slice the pecan and walnut cake while Celeste looks at the 1,000 pieces of Salvador Dalí's *Christ of Saint John of the Cross* spread all over the kitchen table. I'd hoped to finish it last night, but my session with Diane wiped me out, and I fell asleep on the couch after dinner. I woke up at midnight, hot and confused, with a sore neck. I couldn't get back to sleep, so I baked.

"This is amazing, Meredith." Celeste is still studying the jigsaw.

"I just have to finish some of the sky," I tell her. "Have you seen the real thing? It's here in Glasgow."

"Really?"

"Yeah. It's been in the Kelvingrove since 1952. I was blown away when I saw it." I feel a pang of longing deep in my chest.

Celeste takes a sip of her tea. "I'm so ashamed to say this, but I haven't been in the Kelvingrove since we went there with the school. I'm a bit clueless when it comes to art. Not like you."

I wave away her compliment, but feel a blush on my cheeks.

"Hey, maybe we could go together sometime? You could give me a guided tour."

Here it is—the chance for the truth. I look down at my hands, out of the window, back at the stupid jigsaw. Anywhere but into her eager eyes. I feel ridiculous, showing off my paperboard version of a great work of art (with a huge gaping hole in it, no less, underneath Jesus Christ's left armpit) when the real thing is less than three miles away.

"I don't get out much" is all I can say.

"Then let's go out. Get your coat—we'll leave right now. We can go anywhere you like."

I look at her enthusiastic face and screw up my own. *Tell her now*, my inner voice demands.

"Does being on the forum help with the loneliness?"

Tell her now.

"There's a bit more to it than that," I say, willing her to join the dots that are currently on different planets.

Instead, she reaches for my hand and squeezes it gently. "You have so much going for you, Meredith. I wish you could see what I see."

"That's what Gavin used to say."

"Gavin?"

"He was my . . . someone I used to know."

"Well, Gavin was right. Seriously, Meredith. You're so incredibly kind and sweet. And quirky."

I know she means well, but I'm embarrassed. I wasn't fishing for compliments. "Don't people say 'quirky' when they mean 'crazy'?" I joke.

"Oh, not at all! Quirky is good."

"OK, let's reclaim 'quirky.' And I'm great at jigsaws. Don't forget that."

"You're bloody amazing at jigsaws. And you're a cat person. We cat people have to stick together."

As if on cue, Fred pads into the room. He jumps onto the kitchen bench beside Celeste and paws at her elbow. She laughs and scoops him into her arms. "See what I mean?" She pushes her phone across the table to me. "Take a photograph of me with this gorgeous boy, Mer. Actually, come here. Let's get a selfie."

"I've never taken a selfie," I admit as I sit next to her.

"Well, I'm honored to be in your first selfie." She holds the phone at arm's length, tilting her hand until our upper bodies are framed on the screen. Fred doesn't cooperate. He starts licking his paw and cleaning his ear, so when we check the photo, he's just a fuzzy orange blob on Celeste's lap. Celeste is fresh-faced and beaming, all white teeth and shiny hair. My smile is lopsided, and I'm not looking directly at the camera.

"I love it," Celeste declares. She loops her arm round my back and squeezes my shoulder. It's an unfamiliar experience, but not in a bad way. Luckily Celeste is accustomed to these prosaic forms of human connection and doesn't show any sign of being aware of my awkwardness. She swings her legs over the bench and gets to her feet in one easy movement, saving me from trying to work out how to disconnect from her, like an ill-fitting jigsaw piece that's been forced into the wrong space.

After Celeste leaves, Fred sits on the window seat, his nose almost touching the glass. I wonder if he's going to eat my new flowers, but he only sniffs them for a second, then resumes his staring. The scene has all the ingredients for a still life—in fact, it reminds me of a website I came across once dedicated to doctored Van Gogh paintings. *Sunflowers* had a large black cat with destructive eyes chewing on one of its stalks. Fred doesn't have any malicious tendencies, thankfully, so I think the flowers will remain intact. I consider googling "How long do flowers last?" but decide I'd rather just hope they live for a long time.

I lie on the couch and admire the bouquet for a few minutes— I might need to invest in a flower jigsaw, although I think the demonic black cat has ruined *Sunflowers* for me—while Fred sits on the window seat pining for Celeste. He probably prefers her to me, and I can hardly blame him. I prefer her to me too.

She's already emailed me our selfie. (Subject: Happy days!) I set it as my phone's wallpaper, even though I look like a startled meerkat. I look at it for a moment, then I change it back to my favorite picture of Fred as a kitten, curled up on the end of my bed.

My phone tells me it's 4:48. Normally, by this time on a Saturday, I'd have done my laundry, prepared my dinner ingredients, practiced my Italian, and ordered my grocery delivery for next week. I haven't done any of those things, and I can't find the motivation to get started.

I look around the room: at the hundreds of books in alphabetical order, the neat stacks of jigsaws. I think of Dalí's painting, incomplete on my kitchen table. My eyes scan the other boxes. The Grand Canyon at sunset in vivid colors. Rome's historic skyline. *The Raft of the Medusa* by Théodore Géricault. *Salisbury Cathedral from the Meadows* by John Constable. I've been collecting boxes filled with places I'll never go—works of art I'll never see.

1993

"If you could go anywhere in the world, where would you choose?" Sadie looped her arm through mine. We were on our way back to her place after school to paint our nails and watch *The Chart Show* she'd taped last Sunday.

"Kelvingrove Art Gallery," I said without hesitation.

"Meredith Maggs." She stopped abruptly but maintained her grip on my arm, so I jerked backward, my backpack thumping against my shoulders.

"What?" I stared back at her.

"Of all the places in the world? That's where you would go?"

"Right now, yes."

"The big old museum near the university?"

"Yes."

"Not Paris, or Australia, or New York, or the Amazon rain forest?"

"Nope."

"Why the fuck would you go there?"

I swallowed. "Because I've been asking for years, and she's never taken me."

"Your mum?"

I hesitated, then nodded. Our friendship was still in its infancy, and I was desperate to protect it from Mama and the realities of life at home.

Sadie checked her watch. "Come on." She grinned, tugging my arm back toward the school. "I'm pretty sure there's a bus into town from the other side of the park."

"Where are we going?"

"Where do you think? *Kelvingrove fucking Art Gallery.*"

There was a bus from the other side of the park, but it didn't go into town—or at least, not the part of town we wanted to be. I sat on the low wall surrounding a large parking lot while Sadie quizzed the bus driver.

"We need to get the 38," she said, dropping her backpack at her feet and squatting beside me. "There's one due in seven minutes apparently."

"Have you got enough money?"

She patted her jacket pocket. "I've got my bank card. I'll withdraw some more when we get there."

"You've got a bank card?"

"You don't?"

"No," I admitted. I'd just started working in the local fish-and-chip shop at weekends. Mama took half my wages; the rest I stashed in an old shoebox under my bed.

"Go to the Clydesdale," she told me. "You get two free movie tickets when you open an account."

I wanted to tell her how lucky I was to be her friend, this statuesque young girl who carried herself like an adult and knew everything girls our age should know. Instead, I nodded. "Movie tickets. Cool."

The 38 arrived seventeen minutes late and was jam-packed. We squeezed into our own pocket of space, clutching onto the overhead rail to keep our balance. Still, whenever the bus turned a corner or came to a stop, our bodies swayed in unpredictable directions. At one point Sadie ended up with her nose under a tall man's armpit; she made a silent gagging face and my laughter rang down the length of the bus. I had so much fun, I almost forgot where we were going. But the wave of slow-moving city traffic finally carried us to our destination, and there it was in front of me: the red sandstone palace with the steepled roof.

Only an hour before closing, the museum was quiet. "Look!" Sadie pointed above us at the Spitfire hanging from the ceiling. My head spun in all directions as I tried to look at everything— the huge stained-glass window, the enormous stuffed elephant, the ancient costumes standing proud in glass boxes. We stared at the paintings, not understanding why we were drawn to some more than others.

"I wish we had a camera," I told her.

"Next time," she said. "We'll make a day of it. Bring a picnic for the grass outside."

I squeezed her hand.

We stuck our heads into every room, explored every corridor, feeling grown-up, until we stumbled across the treasure we didn't know we were looking for.

Christ of Saint John of the Cross. Salvador Dalí, 1951, said the small card. I looked up, and my jaw dropped.

Day 1,299

Thursday, February 7, 2019

I can't stop scratching. The tiny patch of eczema on the pad of my thumb, the one that never completely goes away, has spread across my entire palm.

"I've had it for as long as I can remember," I tell Tom. "I shouldn't scratch, but it's hard not to."

"Do you need something from the doctor? Or can I get you something from the pharmacist?"

"I'll put my cream on after my bath tonight. But…thanks." Somehow, we've reached a stage where I'm letting him do things for me, like bringing me organic chicken breasts when they're missing from my grocery delivery or holding Fred on his lap with steady hands while I trim his claws, and it doesn't make me feel useless.

"Mama used to tell me she'd tie my hand to the table leg to stop me from scratching," I say casually, pouring his tea and putting a fruit scone on his plate. I don't ask him anymore if he wants whatever I've baked that week. He always says yes, eating everything I put in front of him.

"Are you kidding?" The shock in his eyes is a stark reminder of how different our points of reference are.

"Nope. I scratched so much in my sleep I had blood on my sheets in the morning."

He winces. "Ouch."

I'd begged Mama for something from the doctor when the itch got so bad I didn't care how weak she thought I was.

"You're such a drama queen," she told me. "Leave it alone and it will sort itself out."

But the more I scratched, the bigger the patch seemed to get. Within a few weeks it covered the entire back of my hand and the top of my wrist. I was scared to look down when I lay in the bath, imagining it spreading up my arms, across my back, over my chest. Taking over my body.

"You're driving me crazy," Mama said one morning when I couldn't stop crying, but she grabbed my hand and looked at it.

"I think it's eczema," Fiona piped up. "A boy in my class has it. He needs to put a really smelly cream on it twice a day and he can't go swimming because the pool water makes it worse."

I sobbed, not caring if I was being a drama queen. My swimming lessons with Auntie Linda every Thursday after school were the highlight of my week. After my lesson, she came in the pool with me, bobbing around in the shallow end because she didn't want to get her hair wet. I practiced holding my breath under the water, twisting and turning my body like a mermaid. Afterward, she gently brushed the tangles out of my hair while I ate salt-and-vinegar chips from the vending machine and she let me keep the silver coin from my locker. I had an old shortbread tin under my bed that I kept them in, my secret stash.

"Nonsense." Mama's nose wrinkled in disgust and she dropped my hand. "That isn't eczema."

"It's not?" I felt a glimmer of hope. I might be able to keep swimming after all.

"Definitely not."

"What is it then?" Fiona demanded. "Is she allergic to something?"

"She has faulty genes, that's all," Mama said smoothly. She pulled a cigarette out of the packet with her teeth and flipped open her heavy silver lighter with her initials engraved on the side.

"I don't understand," I said, rubbing the itch behind my back with the thumb of my other hand.

"Of course you don't." Mama tipped her head back and blew a smoke ring high in the air. I watched it float, disperse, then dissolve into nothing.

"You come from bad stock, Meredith," she said eventually. "Your skin will get worse as you get older, so you might as well accept it now. One day, you'll wake up and you'll be covered in crust from head to toe. Nobody will want to go near you. What a shame. But that's the luck of the draw."

I stared at her, my mouth open. "What do you mean 'bad stock'?"

"Your father, angelface, had terrible skin. It used to shed all over the place, like a snake. I think yours will be even worse. We'll need to get you a vacuum cleaner to keep under your bed." She laughed, expelling a cloud of smoke.

"What about Fiona?" I asked. "Why doesn't she have it?"

"Ah, she's the lucky one. She has my good skin. Like I said, angelface, it's the luck of the draw."

I ran to my room, slammed the door, and held my breath under my duvet while I waited for her to storm after me. But she didn't come. I think I fell asleep, because when I became aware of someone sitting on my bed my head was hot and it took a moment to figure out where I was.

"I'll make a doctor's appointment for you," Fiona whispered. "I'll phone tomorrow—I'll pretend I'm her. We'll try to get one straight after school and be as quick as we can."

"Thanks," I croaked. The red skin on my hand pulsed.

"It's not true, about our dad."

"How do you know?"

"Do you remember him shedding his skin like a snake?"

"No," I said. The truth was, I didn't remember anything about him. In the few years since he'd left, the features on his face had lost their shape. When I closed my eyes and tried to picture him, it was like searching for someone at the bottom of a murky pond.

Did he have my eyes, which could be blue or green or gray depending on the light and what I wore? Was he fair-haired like Fiona, or dark like me? Sometimes, when I was strong enough to pull him out of the pond, his features always swarmed around just above his head—I was never able to pin them down. Even in my dreams he was faceless, simply a presence who moved through our lives, elusive and fleeting. But he didn't have crusty skin in my dreams. I was sure I would remember that.

I sighed and pulled the duvet over my head. I knew Mama was only trying to get one over on me. It was always a competition, and she never let me win.

Fiona pulled my duvet back down and we locked eyes in a hard stare until I blinked. I never won with her either.

"Do you remember him?" I demanded.

"Yes," she said.

"Tell me about him."

"I remember them arguing, not long before he left. It was a warm day. They were in the kitchen... As soon as I walked in, Mama screamed at me to go upstairs."

"What did he look like? What color was his hair?"

"Light brown."

My heart felt heavy, like I had a weight pressing against my chest. "Why didn't he take us with him?"

She shrugged. "I guess he didn't want us."

I didn't want to believe her. I scratched at my palm.

"Anyway, the important thing is, he wasn't all crusty, Meredith. I remember his skin. It was smooth. Smooth like a normal person's."

This was no comfort to me. "That just means I'm the only faulty one in the family." I lay back down, turned away from my sister. I pulled my duvet over my head again and dreamed of a time when I could leave.

"I scratched until I had blood under my fingernails," I tell Tom.

Sometimes, I just can't deal with the kindness in his eyes. I pick up our plates, brush the crumbs from our scones into the garbage, and move around the kitchen doing things that don't need to be done. He lets me.

1999

She helped me pack, not even pretending to be happy for me.

"*Fee.*"

"Are you taking these?" She waved hair curlers at me. Neither of us had used them for years.

"You can keep them," I told her. "I'm trying to pack light. Don't have much storage space in the new place."

My sister rolled her eyes, making no effort to hide it from me.

"Will you come over this weekend, for dinner?" I stacked the last of my books into a box and taped up twenty years of escapism.

"Not sure. Might be busy." She opened my wardrobe and started riffling through it.

"Doing what?" I demanded.

"I have plans with Lucas. Not that it's any of your business."

I bit my lip and tried not to react. She always knew how to push my buttons. "Well, you can bring him, I suppose. I'll get takeout. Your choice. Pizza? Curry? Special fried rice?"

She mumbled something I couldn't hear.

I left her to her huff and started squashing my duvet and pillows into a garbage bag. I needed new ones—I'd had them since I was a kid. But purchases like that would have to wait. I'd been working in the call center for a year, saving like mad for enough money to pay my deposit and my first month's rent and bills and build up an emergency fund. I saw on a TV program that it's important to have an emergency fund. It seemed like a grown-up thing to do.

Most people would think my new place was nothing special.

Distinctly un-special, in fact. But maybe most people grew up dreaming of a big house with a garden and a fancy kitchen and a huge television. A bath with fancy clawed feet. A hot tub outside. A shiny car in the driveway. Maybe two cars in a double driveway. My dream had always been a little simpler. I was moving into a tiny ground-floor flat with peeling wallpaper. There was no bath, just a narrow shower with a door that didn't close all the way. I didn't even have a television. I'd deliberately not bought any new stuff before I moved in. Mama always warned us not to tempt fate. She said she knows from experience that life has a habit of blowing up when you least expect it to.

"Hey, this is mine." Fiona detached a blue hooded top from the tangled bundle of clothes she'd dumped on the floor.

I looked up. "It's got a cigarette burn on the cuff."

"It's still mine."

"Take it then. And piss off if you're going to be in a stinking mood. I can do this myself."

She glared at me, pulled the blue top over her head, and stuffed her arms into the sleeves. But she didn't piss off; she just sat and looked at me. I looked back at her. It had been a hot summer; her freckles had multiplied across her cheeks, her blonde hair was almost white in some places. I pictured her sitting in this room in ten years' time, wearing the same top with the burn on the sleeve. Same top, same room, same life.

"Fee." I crawled across to her, reached out for her hand. She pulled away, but I grabbed it and held on tight.

"Ouch. You're hurting me."

"I don't care. Talk to me." I wanted to hear her say it. I wanted her to say she didn't want me to go. That she didn't want to be left behind. And maybe part of me wanted her to admit that she was jealous that I was leaving. That after all those years of her being the leader, the decision-maker, I was the one who was making a bid for freedom.

"I just hate it when you take my stuff without asking."

Before I could launch my counterattack—without a shadow of a doubt she was the one who was most guilty of that particular offense—she squeezed my fingers. We both burst out laughing at the same time.

"I know this is hard for you. But it's time. Actually, it's way past time. We had a deal, remember?"

"Meredith, we were, like, ten when we made that deal. There's no way we could actually have moved out when I was sixteen."

I shrugged. "OK, but I waited another six years. And I asked you to come with me. Don't forget that. You still could—it's not too late. You and me. Just the two of us."

She shrugged. "I'll probably move in with Lucas."

That wasn't what I wanted to hear. Lucas had hung around, like a bad smell, longer than I'd hoped he would. He made my skin crawl, always looking at me for a second too long, with narrowed eyes, and brushing against me when he walked past, even when there was plenty of space.

I tossed more clothes into a garbage bag. "Well, you can't stay here forever."

"I know, I know. Maybe she'll die soon. Have you heard her cough? Then I can have this place to myself. Start over."

"That's a terrible thing to say," I murmured.

"Yeah, whatever. Don't tell me you haven't thought about it yourself: how much better it would be if she wasn't here."

"We'd have so much fun together, Fee. You and me in the city center."

"It won't really change anything, you know."

"You promised me, remember?" I tried to keep my voice steady. "All those years...I believed you."

"I wasn't lying! I believed it too."

"So what changed? Come on, Fee. We can start over together."

She sighed. "Meredith, you're moving to a one-bed flat."

"So? Haven't we always shared a room here?" I shifted my position on the floor to stop my feet cramping, still clutching her hand. "If you don't want to share, we could find somewhere bigger. I can ask if I can transfer my deposit."

"Oh, I'm looking forward to having this room to myself," she said breezily. "And I can't be arsed to pack. Moving is one of the most stressful things you can do in life, did you know that?"

"Can't be more stressful than staying here."

She laughed. "Maybe."

"You're almost twenty-two. You have a job."

"In a *supermarket*."

"It's still a job. She can't keep you here. I don't understand why you want to stay." It was my turn to get angry. I wanted to slap her. I settled for digging my nail into the soft pad of skin at the base of her thumb. She didn't even flinch.

"I don't want to stay."

"Why then?" I was begging. I didn't care. "I don't understand."

"You will, one day." My sister let go of my hand.

I didn't have a lot of stuff, but getting it all into Sadie's car was like trying to solve a puzzle. It took us a few attempts (and several cigarette breaks) until we squashed the last bag into the back seat. Fiona came out to sit on the wall and laugh at us; she didn't do much to help.

"I can't see out of my back window, but I think we're OK." Sadie flicked her cigarette butt onto the road. "It's not too long a journey."

"I just need to grab my jacket." I gestured toward the house, where my sister was now lurking at the doorway.

"Want me to come in?"

"I'm good. I'll only be two minutes. Thanks, though."

Fiona had my denim jacket over her arm. She squeezed it

against her belly when I reached for it. "This is so weird," she whispered.

"I'm not going far." I wrestled my jacket from her and put it on before she could hold it hostage.

"I know, but…"

"I know." We'd never spent twenty-four hours apart. Neither of us had any idea what life would be like from now on. For me it felt exciting and terrifying in equal measure. For her I couldn't see what there was to get excited about.

"This is ridiculous." Fiona looked up at the ceiling, the way she did when she was trying to stop herself from crying. "I need to go and get ready for work. My shift starts at two. Come here, you big idiot." She hugged me tightly, then turned and ran upstairs.

"I'll phone you tonight," I said to her back. She gave me the V-sign without turning round.

I looked around the hall, at the jar of coins on the console table next to the phone and the bowl of dusty potpourri that had been there forever. It was time to go. I took a deep breath and walked into the living room.

She was still in her dressing gown, watching *Supermarket Sweep*. Her hair was in rollers, her skin shiny.

"Mama, I'm leaving now."

She whipped her head round, a big smile plastered on her face. "Come and have a chat with your mother, watch some TV. I can turn this off, put my *Taggart* video on."

"I hate *Taggart*," I told her.

"Really?" She stared at me, like I was a stranger who'd just walked into her house, uninvited. I stared back.

"There's been a *murdah*," she growled. She was trying to be funny, and it broke my heart a little.

"I can't stay long. The car's packed. Sadie's waiting."

"Sadie Schmadie. Suit yourself. Party pooper."

"Yep, that's me. So. I'll see you then. Soon."

She lit a cigarette and took a long draw. "Maybe you'll invite us over sometime?"

"Sure...once I'm settled. Need to make it nice for you. The wallpaper's terrible."

"I'll miss you, angelface."

"Will you?"

She looked at me, surprised, her cigarette halfway to her lips. "What a thing to ask. You're my daughter."

I searched for something—anything—behind her glassy eyes. "You'll take care, yeah? Go easy on those things."

"What, these things?" She waved her cigarette at me. "Oh, you know me, angelface. I can resist everything—"

"But temptation," we said in unison. I gave her a small smile.

She pushed herself off the couch. Only forty-three but could easily be mistaken for a woman ten years older. The cigarettes didn't help, of course, but it was more than dull skin and discolored teeth and wrinkles that had accelerated the aging process. She'd given up on life a long time ago; my biggest fear was ending up like her.

I was taller but not by much. We stood eye to eye in the middle of the living room until she wrapped her arms round me. I let her for a few seconds. I patted her softly on the back; she felt frail beneath my hands.

"I need to go," I said. "Lots to do."

She took a step backward and folded her arms under her chest. "Bugger off then." Her eyes were already back on the screen.

I closed the living room door behind me. Before I reached the front door, I could hear her laughing.

"I've been calling you all night, where have you been?"

Fiona hiccupped. "I was at the pub with Mama."

"You never go to the pub with her." I turned onto my side and pulled the duvet up to my chin, looking up at the bare walls. I hadn't found the energy to put any pictures up.

"Well, I did tonight," she said. "Better than sitting in the house on my own watching crap TV."

"Where was Lucas? You said you were seeing him tonight."

"He had to go into work. *Again.*" Lucas worked nights in a meat factory. He stayed in Mama's good books with steaks he said he got for free, but I had my doubts about that.

"You could have come here."

"Hmm. Next time. You don't even have a TV yet."

My duvet still smelled like our old bedroom: Impulse and incense and a trace of cigarette smoke. I breathed it in deeply.

Fiona's breath sounded shallower. I concentrated on the other noises at her end. A door closing, water running.

"Are you having a bath?"

She laughed. "I'm making coffee."

"Oh God, Fee. Don't drink coffee at this time. You'll be up all night."

"Och, who cares? You can stay up and talk to me."

I wiggled my toes. They were still cold, but the three-bar electric heater and duvet were starting to help.

"Where's Mama?"

"Still at the pub." The kettle whistled; I heard running water again, the chink of metal against ceramic. I closed my eyes and saw my sister in the kitchen. She was perched on the counter with her legs stretched out, her toes resting on the table. She slurped loudly in my ear just as I saw the mug reach her mouth.

"I wish I was there with you," I whispered.

"Och, no, you don't. You're all set in your fancy flat."

"It's the opposite of a fancy flat, Fee." Apart from having no central heating, the bolt on the front door was shaky, the carpet was threadbare, and the fridge was the size of a shoebox. I didn't see all those things when I first saw it. I just saw freedom.

She took another slurp of coffee. "This tastes like shit."

"What happened at the pub?"

"Nothing exciting. Auntie Linda was there, and Bruce and Kenny. When I left they were doing tequila shots at the bar."

"Jesus. She'll be in some state when she gets back. You should get to bed."

"She might not make it back. Kenny was all over her, the wee leech. I reckon they'll go back to his—he only lives down the road from the pub."

"Gadz."

"I know. Auntie Linda was asking after you."

"I miss you," I said loudly, knowing whispers are often lost on drunk people.

"You'd better not call me every night to tell me that," she said airily. "I'll have to block your number."

I waited, hoping she'd fill the quiet with something softer. But it was Fiona, so she didn't.

"I'm not sure I've done the right thing, moving out."

"Of course you have, you big idiot. The sky's your oyster now."

"The world is your oyster, you mean."

"Yeah, whatever."

I moved onto my back. "I thought you didn't want me to leave."

"Well, you did leave. So we just have to deal with it."

"I guess we do. There's a big crack on my ceiling. I didn't notice it before."

"Nice. What else?"

I looked around the tiny room, at the patchy walls and the bedsheet pinned over the window.

"There's not much to report. It's basic. It'll be fine when I've painted, got some curtains."

"I'll bring a plant over. That's what people give for a house-warming, right?"

"I have no idea." I laughed. "It sounds very grown-up. And I'm not sure this counts as a house."

"Well, you're all grown-up now."

"You next."

"Hmm. We'll see. Hold on. I'm putting the phone down for a second. Just getting my jammies on."

I closed my eyes and saw her in our—her—bedroom. It was a mess—even messier than it was when I was there. Fiona could make the mess of a dozen people. She'd leave her clothes in a pile on the floor beside her bed and step over them when she got up in the morning. She wouldn't take her makeup off before she went to bed.

"Can't be arsed brushing my teeth just now," she said, as if she was reading my mind.

"What jammies are you wearing?"

"The ancient purple spotty ones. The ones you hate."

"I don't hate them. They just give me a bit of a headache."

"Well, you're not here to see them, are you?"

"That's a silver lining, I suppose."

"Cheeky. Hang on. Just getting comfy."

I listened to muffled sounds, saw her smooth out her pillow, making sure her toes weren't sticking out the bottom of her duvet. I heard a click as she turned her bedside light off. I did the same, pressed my nose against the top of my duvet and listened to my sister breathing. I could almost be back at home with her.

"I miss you too, Meredith," she said sleepily. I listened to her breathing grow deeper and turn into soft snores before I ended the call. I'd always envied her ability to drop off within seconds. I lay awake for hours, staring into the darkness of the unfamiliar room until my tired eyes put random shapes together to form my sister's face.

Day 1,307

Friday, February 15, 2019

I'm not normally nervous before my sessions with Diane. But today, with my notebook on my lap, I'm fidgety and tense. I'm also five minutes early. I sit in front of my open laptop and take a few deep breaths, hearing her voice in my head. *In through the nose, out through the mouth.* All that's missing is plinky-plonky music.

Her face appears on my screen. She's curled her hair in the style of an old-fashioned movie star. I can see her gliding across a dance floor in a satin gown on the arm of a dapper gent.

"Meredith, hello!" She smiles. "How are you today?"

"I'm not sure," I admit. I wave my notebook at her. "I don't think I've done very well with my homework."

I left it to the last minute, like a rebellious schoolkid. Finally, late last night, I curled up on the couch beside Fred and thought about leaving my house.

It's a brand-new notebook, bought from my favorite online stationery shop for this purpose. It has a shiny blue cover printed with dancing horses. I wrote my name inside the front, like I really am at school: *Meredith Maggs*. And on the first fresh page there's a single word.

Panic.

Before Diane asks, I show her the page. "That's it. That's all I wrote. I'm a writer, and I only managed one word." I close the notebook and slump back in my chair. I'm so tired. I just want to watch TV and cuddle Fred.

"Meredith." Her voice is soft. Comforting. "What you've done is fine. There's no right or wrong here. Like I always tell you, all in your own time. You're in a safe place—let's explore your word together."

"OK."

"We'll get there, Meredith," she says. "Just by showing up here, once a month, you're making big changes."

For the next forty minutes we talk about all the things I couldn't write down. How I feel like my heart is going to jump out of my chest. How my throat closes up and I can't catch my breath. How I think I'm going die.

Afterward, she asks me, "How do you feel?"

"Tired. But OK."

"I'm proud of you, Meredith," she says. "And I think you're ready for some more homework. We're going to start exposure therapy, to help you gradually move out of your house until your anxiety levels have reduced."

"I love homework," I say drily. When Diane laughs, she opens her mouth wide to show neat white teeth and no fillings. One time, the screen froze when she was mid-laugh. She looked like a beautiful wildcat. I stared at her for a while, waiting for her to come back to life, imagining her face smashing through my laptop screen, her teeth clamping down on my neck until she drew blood.

"*Meredith.*"

"Sorry. What did you say?"

"I want you to take five steps out of your house."

After our session, I sit on the couch for a long time, still holding my notebook. Maybe I'll write more in it later. I look out of the bay window, at the gray clouds swirling. I don't know if they're creeping closer or moving farther away. I've noticed, in the last couple of weeks, glimpses of divine sunlight between spells of winter gloom. It makes me think of the hopeful ending to Shelley's "Ode to the West Wind": *If winter comes, can spring be far behind?* In the early afternoon, when I bend over my jigsaw at the bay window, the sun casts a glow on my cheeks.

If I lived on a farm, lambing season would be getting underway. I don't live on a farm, of course, but who knows? Maybe someday I will. My future will come round, like another season. But all in my own time.

Day 1,324

Subject: SAVE THE DATE!

The notification pops up on my computer screen during a boring morning of admin. I stare at the white box until it disappears. It seems to take longer to do that today.

I go back to my invoices, but I can't concentrate, knowing that the email is there. Waiting for me to open it. Forcing me to confront the impossible.

Celeste's party is thirteen weeks on Saturday. More than three months away. A lot can happen in three months. But also, nothing can happen. Even now, I'm surprised by how quickly time passes in isolation. You don't need to have a morning commute and work in an office and meet friends for dinner or take your kids to after-school activities to know what it's like to get to the end of a day and realize you haven't done a lot of the things you should have done.

I have a choice, I realize. I can let the next three months pass as normal, safe in my comfort zone, and go nowhere. Or I can push myself much further—for Celeste, because she's worth it, but mainly for myself.

I could do it, I think, my belly clenching. I could continue Diane's exposure therapy. I could choose faith over fear. I imagine myself turning up at Scottside Bowling Club, the look on Celeste's face when she sees me. I'll wear my black asymmetric dress, I decide. It's been hanging in my wardrobe for four years, spurned every day in favor of leggings and sweaters. I'll curl my hair and put on bronzer. I'll make an effort.

What's stopping me from going?

I'm stopping me from going, I tell myself crossly.

Well—what are you going to do about it? I retaliate.

Leave it with me, I reply.

I open the email.

Day 1,327

I'm not sure if I can make it to Celeste's party, but I can cook her dinner. I still feel nervous about her being here, but it's not from a lack of belief in my cooking skills. (I'm no Mary Berry, but I keep my knives sharp, know how to season, and taste my food as I go.) What I'm worried about—what I'm always worried about—is that my truth will come out, and that she'll leave before she's even tasted my food. We've established that she likes quirky, but I'm not sure that's an entirely accurate description of my situation.

When I answer the door to her, I'm reminded that she's not a stranger. She's been here before, and we had fun, and she likes me enough to come back. And I like having her here—my house seems a little brighter when she's in it.

I think it's her mouth, which always seems to be on the verge of a smile. I'm the opposite—mine naturally turns downward. I'm going to try to smile more often, and coax the corners of my mouth toward the sky.

I wonder how she can be so cheerful, given what she's been through.

"I've started self-defense classes," she tells me. "Our instructor is a fifty-year-old woman from Govan. Hard as nails, she is. She's amazing. We learned how to do the heel palm strike this week. Right under the chin. Pow!"

"You're doing all the right things," I tell her, which reminds me that I'm not.

"This is delicious, Mer," she enthuses between mouthfuls of chili. "I'm a terrible cook." She takes a swig of wine and grins at me. "When you come to mine, you'll get a grilled cheese and ham, at a push."

"Well, it's lucky I like cooking for you," I tell her, hoping my voice sounds natural. "You'll just have to keep coming here."

"Did your mum teach you to cook?"

"No. We never got home-cooked meals growing up. Everything came from the freezer aisle in the supermarket."

As soon as we were teenagers, we were deemed old enough to take responsibility for the shopping and the cooking. Mama was more than happy with this arrangement, as long as we got the necessities. She gave us a list, with the most important items written in precise capitals. WHITE WINE. CIGARETTES. HAIRSPRAY. We didn't dare forget any of those things, but beyond that we had free rein. Mama's need for control didn't extend as far as the kitchen. So we loaded our shopping basket with our favorites from the frozen aisles: pizza, Findus Crispy Pancakes, those little smiling faces made of potato, huge bags of chips, Viennetta. Occasionally I'd chuck in some frozen peas to add some color.

Sometimes, Mama sat on the window seat in the kitchen, a glass of wine in one hand, a cigarette in the other, watching us heat up our frozen delights. Early evening, she was always at her least critical. She had that third-glass-of-wine buzz, a full pack of cigarettes, and both daughters right where she could see them. By the time dinner was over the wine bottle was empty, scorn had replaced her silent observance, and we'd be willing her to fall asleep. I'd do the dishes, Fiona would empty the ashtray, and we'd turn off the lights and scuttle off to bed like mice afraid to wake the sleeping cat.

"Did you have a hard childhood, Mer?" Celeste asks softly.

"I'm not sure," I reply honestly. "I don't really know what other people's were like."

She squeezes my hand gently but doesn't let go. And so we chat. I give her glimpses of my life with Mama, about tiptoeing past her bedroom so as not to wake her, about sitting in the bath for an hour, long after the water was cold, because it was the only room with a lock on the door, about leaving, at age twenty, and feeling that my life could finally begin. It feels right to let her in, but only part of the way. I don't want to spoil it.

2001

"Oh. It's you." Mama looked me up and down. "Did you bring anything?" Her eyes landed on the bottle of wine tucked under my arm.

I sighed and handed it to her. "Nice to see you too, Mama."

"Your sister's out the back," she said over her shoulder as she walked away. I followed her, closing the front door behind me. I'd been carving out a new life for myself and hadn't been in her house for months. But it looked and smelled no different; it never would. Unopened envelopes were piled on the hall table, a jumble of shoes and jackets on the floor. Cigarette smoke and carpet cleaner. I pushed the swell of disquiet down to the pit of my stomach and reminded myself that I was here for Fee. We spoke every day on the phone, but I hadn't seen her for a couple of weeks.

She was in the kitchen, spreading butter on burger buns. "Mer!" She bounced across the room and planted a kiss on my cheek. "It's barbecue time!"

"So I believe," I said. "Didn't even know we had a barbecue."

"Lucas borrowed it from his dad," she said.

I shrugged my jacket off and looked out of the window. "Lucas's dad is here?" I watched a thin man in jeans and a red tracksuit top fiddle with the knobs on the front of an enormous shiny barbecue. It took up half of Mama's tiny garden, which couldn't be described as a garden really—just a dozen or so dirty concrete slabs and a few wilting plants in cracked terra-cotta pots.

Lucas stood beside his dad, squinting in the sun and drinking from a can of lager.

"And his mum." Fee pointed the butter knife in the direction of a middle-aged woman with a neat bob and sunglasses. She appeared to be listening intently to Auntie Linda, who was chatting her ear off as usual.

I looked back at Lucas and his dad. "That's what he'll look like in twenty-five years. Did you know hair loss is genetic?"

"Oi, stop it. Make yourself useful and slice some cheese."

She was uncharacteristically quiet as we buttered and sliced. "What's the big occasion?" I asked. "It's not like her to have people over." Mama had joined Auntie Linda and Lucas's mum outside, laughing at something one of them had said. I could see the black fillings in her bottom teeth. She caught me watching her and I looked back at the cheese quickly.

"She's actually got quite friendly with Lucas's parents," Fee told me. "She goes to bingo with his mum sometimes. They're called Karen and George."

"Karen and George," I murmured.

My sister moved around the kitchen, collecting paper plates, lettuce, tomato ketchup, mayonnaise. I helped her arrange everything on the small table.

"I think Lucas is going to dump me," she said.

"What?" I stared at her. "What makes you think that?"

"He's been moody this week, like he's stressed-out. He won't talk to me about it."

"I'm sure it's nothing," I told her, when what I wanted to say was "Get in there first. Dump him before he dumps you. Because you deserve so much better." I felt a fizz of anticipation at the thought of her ending their relationship, which was quickly replaced by guilt.

"Yeah, hopefully," she said. "I'll go and see if the burgers are ready."

"Fee."

She stopped and looked at me expectantly. "What?"

"Just…are you happy?"

"Of course I'm happy, Meredith. I'm also bloody starving."

I bit my lip. "It's just…"

"Mer, spit it out." She was impatient now.

"I'm starving too," I told her.

"Great." She grinned. "Then let's eat."

We ate George's slightly overcooked burgers and sausages—"Better burnt than food poisoning," he joked—and made small talk until the sun started to go down.

"You're cold, pet," Auntie Linda said, rubbing her dry, warm hands up and down my arms. "Here, take my cardigan. I'm like a furnace these days. Bloody menopause." She hushed my protests and draped it over my shoulders. "You could do with some more meat on your bones, now that I think about it."

"I eat plenty," I tell her truthfully.

"Nervous energy, just like your mama," she replied, as I knew she would. We'd been having the same conversation since I was a teenager. Back then, it was mildly irritating; now it was as comforting as her soft decades-old purple cardigan with frayed cuffs. Nobody else had ever worried unnecessarily about my weight or insisted I wear their clothes to stay warm.

I didn't know what to say, so I pulled Auntie Linda toward me and gave her a squeeze. I was aware of Mama's eyes on me, sensed her dark presence in my peripheral vision. I pulled Auntie Linda closer. It was at that moment that my sister started shrieking, and everybody else stopped talking and stared at Lucas, who had one knee on the concrete slab and was offering up a ring box.

I watched Fee burst into tears, grab his hands, and pull him to his feet. I watched her jump into his arms and wrap her legs round his body. She buried her face in his neck as he spun her round. Everybody held back and gave them their moment—a polite delayed reaction. Then Mama shouted, "This calls for champagne!" I looked at her, and I realized she knew this was going to happen, of course she did, because good boys asked for permission first and Mama never had people over. I stared at her face, and she stared back, and as hard as I tried I couldn't make myself feel as happy as she looked.

Day 1,329

Saturday, March 9, 2019

I've eaten enough raisins. I'm pretty damn good at diaphragmatic breathing. I've even been doing my affirmations.

It's time, I wrote in an email to Diane yesterday. I'm going to leave my house.

That's wonderful, she replied. Let's make a plan.

Obviously I won't be venturing far, but I want to be prepared.

Think about what will help you to feel safe, Diane said. A coat? Comfortable shoes? Something in your hands?

I put on my coziest hooded top and my Converse, and grab a handbag from the hook in the downstairs cupboard. It's empty, apart from my bus pass (long expired), an almost-depleted tube of hand cream, some loose change, and a hairband. It feels too light looped over my body.

I look around the hall for something I can use to weigh me down. I end up back in the kitchen, grab the pepper mill from the table, and pop it inside. It's the perfect shape and size, filling the main compartment of the bag nicely.

I'm stalling.

This is a very big deal.

I have my fingers on the door handle. Diane and I decided that I would count backward from twenty. When I reach five, I'll open the door. By the count of one, I'll have both feet on my front doorstep. I'll take five steps down my path, then I'll go back inside, put the kettle on, and have a licorice tea.

It feels good to have a plan. *Twenty...nineteen...eighteen... seventeen...* I count in my head. At fifteen a loud thud on the other side of the door makes me jump. I stuff my hands in my pockets and take a step backward. It's the postman, I realize, delivering the books I ordered from Amazon yesterday, a cultural history of Italy and the latest must-read crime thriller. They're waiting for me in the box and the postman will be at another house by now. But the moment has gone.

I discard my bag and my shoes. I'll try again tomorrow.

WEEJAN: I had the worst date last night. THE WORST ☹

JIGSAWGIRL: What happened?

RESCUEMEPLZ: Ooh do tell

WEEJAN: It was a blind date. My friend Edie told me he was six feet tall, built like a rugby player. Well, guess what? He barely came up to my shoulder and he'd slip through a floorboard if he turned sideways!!

RESCUEMEPLZ: LOL THAT'S HILARIOUS ☺

CATLADY 29: Awwww, Janice! Your friend Edie clearly needs glasses! What did you do?

WEEJAN: Well, I'd been to get my hair done and my mouth was shaped for a Chardonnay, so I decided I might as well make the most of it.

RESCUEMEPLZ: Well, they say beauty is more than skin deep!

WEEJAN: Hmm, that's what I hoped. But this guy was a right tosser. First of all, he told me he'd just ordered his pint so if I could get my own drink, he'd buy the next round. I mean, I'm more than happy to buy my own drink but he didn't have to tell me he was a tight sod! So I bought myself a LARGE glass of white wine and you'll never guess what he said?

JIGSAWGIRL: ??

WEEJAN: He said, "A moment on the lips, a lifetime on the hips"! Can you bloody believe it?

JIGSAWGIRL: What a cheek!

RESCUEMEPLZ: LOL

CATLADY29: I hope you threw your wine in his face!

WEEJAN: I didn't. I downed it, put my empty glass on the bar, and turned round and walked out.

JIGSAWGIRL: Good for you ☺

CATLADY29: Woohoo!

WEEJAN: Then I got the bus home and ate an entire box of chocolates ☹

JIGSAWGIRL: ☹

CATLADY29: ☹

RESCUEMEPLZ: I hope you didn't throw up afterward?

WEEJAN: I thought about it, but I didn't.

JIGSAWGIRL: Well done, Janice. You're doing really well.

WEEJAN: I haven't thrown up for six weeks.

RESCUEMEPLZ: I can't believe you ate the coconut ones. They suck.

CATLADY29: I love the coconut ones! But my favorite is the caramel swirl.

RESCUEMEPLZ: Green triangle all the way.

JIGSAWGIRL: The Purple One for me.

WEEJAN: Well, I like them all. Obviously.

JIGSAWGIRL: Oh, Janice. How do you feel today?

WEEJAN: I feel all right, hen. No more blind dates for a while, though. And no more chocolates.

CATLADY29: Well, you never know—Prince Charming might be just round the corner.

WEEJAN: Ha! I'll believe it when I see it.

CATLADY29: He'd be lucky to have you.

WEEJAN: Awww, you guys.

RESCUEMEPLZ: *yawns*

WEEJAN: LOL

RESCUEMEPLZ: Guys like that give us decent blokes a bad name.

CATLADY29: Are you in a relationship @RESCUEMEPLZ?

WEEJAN: Oh, don't get him started, hen.

RESCUEMEPLZ: I'm weighing up my options ☺

WEEJAN: Lol that's one way of putting it.

CATLADY29: Are we all single then?

JIGSAWGIRL: I guess we are!

CATLADY29: I used to think it was the be-all and end-all to be in a relationship. I'm not so sure anymore.

WEEJAN: You're right there, hen.

RESCUEMEPLZ: Gotta love yourself first.

CATLADY29: I'm trying!

JIGSAWGIRL: Easier said than done.

WEEJAN: But we're on the right track, hen ☺

2002

When I turned up, Mama was sitting on her doorstep smoking. "You're late," she said.

"My bus was late," I told her, stuffing my hands into my jacket pockets. "Hello to you too."

The smoke left her nostrils in a long blast of resentment. We looked at each other in silence. She was like a wild animal, daring me to come closer with large, dark, unpredictable eyes.

Fee broke our standoff, stomping past Mama with a bulging garbage bag in each hand. Her eyes lit up when she saw me. "You're here! We're just chucking everything in the back of the van." She headed toward the white transit van parked outside the house, yelling over her shoulder, "Go upstairs and grab whatever you can. Lucas is up there taking the wardrobe apart."

"She's taking all my bloody furniture with her," Mama grumbled, grinding her cigarette butt into the step. "I'll be left with an empty house. All on my own. Who'll know if I fall and break my leg? I could starve to death."

"I'm sure you'll be fine. You're forty-five, not eighty-five."

"I feel eighty-five," she muttered.

I edged past her, leaving her smoking and moaning about aging, the irony completely lost on her. Walking upstairs, I was a young girl again, trying to find refuge from harsh words and loaded silences. I pushed the bedroom door open slowly.

"Meredith. You've decided to grace us with your presence." Lucas sounded like a little boy reading from a grown-up script.

"My bus was late," I said, hating myself for being so quick to offer an excuse. My default position—giving people less reason to be annoyed at me when no such reason existed in the first place.

"Give us a hand, will you?"

I took a deep breath. "Sure. What do you want me to do?"

There was a beat before he answered; I could feel his eyes on me. I kept mine anywhere else—the Blu-Tack reminding me where our teenage-girl posters used to be, the faded pink curtain that had dangled limply in the window for as long as I could remember, the half-dismantled wardrobe where my clothes once hung.

"Support this while I get the screws out," he said.

I held on to the side of the wardrobe with both hands. I'd never been so close to him; I could almost taste his aftershave. I tried to focus on what was going on below us, willing Fee to run upstairs. But there were no approaching footsteps, only faint voices.

"We're practically family now, Meredith," Lucas said in a low voice. I looked at him, reluctantly. He had blackheads on his nose, five-day stubble on his chin. "This time next year, I'll be your brother."

"Brother-in-law," I told him quickly.

"Are you looking forward to it too?"

"What the hell are you talking about?" I gripped the cheap wood.

He laughed, giving me a flash of metal fillings. "Come on, Meredith. Don't play shy with me. I've seen the way you look at me."

I wanted to spit in his face. I imagined doing it, watching a fat glob of phlegm slide down his cheek. I wouldn't have done it, of course. I was too nice. Instead, I froze. He kept looking at me, and I didn't let my breath out of my body until Fee charged into the room demanding to know why it was taking so bloody long to take apart a piece-of-crap wardrobe.

*

We sat on Mama's doorstep drinking tea out of chipped mugs, watching Lucas drive off in the transit van.

"You're finally moving out," I said, nudging her shoulder with mine.

She nudged me back. "Only a few years later than planned."

"I know we couldn't actually have left when you were sixteen," I told her quietly. I could hear Mama moving around in the kitchen, but she had a habit of sneaking up unannounced. "It would have been too much for you, looking after us both. You did enough of that here."

She shrugged. "I tried my best."

"You did good," I told her.

"I'm getting married next year." She said it matter-of-factly, like she was still trying to convince herself.

I drank my tea and looked up into the sky for courage. Now was the time to tell her about what Lucas had said upstairs, about all the times he'd made me feel the opposite of how the man who loved my sister should make me feel. I played the scene out in my mind, but no words seemed to fit, no outcome was a happy one for everybody. I wondered if I'd misheard him, if I'd imagined things, if it was ever possible to outgrow the person you'd been raised to believe you were. Or if I was stuck with her forever.

Fee and I sat on the doorstep, holding the empty mugs, until the white transit van came back.

Day 1,330

Sunday, March 10, 2019

After yesterday's failed attempt, my new plan is simple. Get out—and back in—as quickly as possible. And I don't need a handbag to walk down my path.

I emailed Diane last night, telling her I hadn't been successful but that I was going to try again today.

That's the spirit, she replied. Remember—it's not a failure. It's a lesson.

I open the door slowly. It's a bright day but cold. I can feel the sharpness on the tip of my nose. My street seems unusually quiet for a Sunday afternoon. I look at Jacob's cherry blossom tree, its coppery bark still bare. I saw Jacob and his mum a few days ago from my window seat. They walked toward their house with bags of shopping, chatting animatedly. His freckled face looked up at hers, and he said something that made her laugh. I watched until their front door closed behind them.

I have a new plan today, and it doesn't involve counting. "I'll step out after the next car passes," I tell myself. I used to make deals like this with myself all the time.

I'll get out of bed after I've said the alphabet forward and backward.

I'll ask Mama if I can go to Sadie's tonight after the bird on the fence chirps.

I'll get out of the bath when the last bubble collapses.

Buying myself time.

Today, it's not long before a red Mini meanders past. *I'll step*

145

out when I can't see it anymore, I vow. I keep my eyes on it until it's the size of a toy car, then watch as it disappears round the distant bend of the road.

I take a deep breath, and I step forward.

I've never been so aware of my body—of *having* a body. I can feel every part of it. My belly clenching, my heart thumping, my skin hot and itchy on my palms. A noise explodes in my ears—a white vehicle flashes past. I think of Diane's words, reminding me to breathe. "It doesn't have to be fight or flight, Meredith. Center your body. Bring the air in through your nose—one, two, three, four. Then let it go through your mouth—one, two, three, four, five, six. You're right here. You're OK."

I'm OK. I'm on my front doorstep, and I don't think I'm going to die.

Move your feet, whispers a voice in my head. Go on. *You can do it. Just one more step.*

And so I do. I take five slow, shaky steps, and I breathe.

I celebrate by baking a triple-layer berry Victoria sponge, and I think it's my best yet. Maybe I'll offer to bake Celeste's birthday cake. I've left my house—is it such a stretch to think I could make it to her party? I dance around my kitchen, licking buttercream off the back of the spoon.

I email Diane: I did my homework.

She writes back: You're a star.

2003

Fee's bachelorette party was like any Friday night at the Bonnie Bairn, but with plastic tiaras, sashes, and flashing badges. The eight of us—Fee's oldest school friend, Jayne, her workmates Shirley and Lisa, Sadie, Mama, Auntie Linda, me, and the bride-to-be—squeezed into a booth and took it in turns to go to the bar.

"This is fun." Fee nudged me with her elbow. Her eyes shone with excitement and white wine spritzers. I grinned at her as we clinked our glasses together. I wanted to be as happy as she was. But I couldn't forget why we were there, knocking back mouthfuls of green liquid from sticky shot glasses and cajoling every man who walked past us to pay a pound to kiss the bride. We had seventeen dirty gold coins so far—our goal was to fill a pint glass. "The bride takes home the money at the end of the night," Auntie Linda told us, although I suspected Shirley had other ideas. Fee always moaned that she never chipped in for birthday presents at work.

"Let's play a game," Jayne suggested. She started rooting around in her bag, pulled out a spiral notebook and pen with a fluffy pink pom-pom on the end of it. "It's called 'Mr. and Mrs.' I've got Lucas's answers, so let's get yours, Fee, and we'll see how you match up!"

Fee groaned. "Oh my God, Jayne. OK... but I need another shot first. Whose turn is it to get them in?"

"It's mine." Sadie stood up and gave a little shimmy as she tugged her denim miniskirt toward her knees and grabbed the kitty envelope. "Tell you what, I'll get two rounds in. Keep us going for a while. Mer, give us a hand, will you?"

I followed her to the bar, snaking between the crowds of after-work drinkers and hard-core regulars. It seemed hazier than the last time we were in—I wondered if people were lighting up even more than usual as a last-ditch attempt to stick their middle finger up at the imminent smoking ban. It was a point of great soreness for Mama, who had taken to telling us about the good old days, when freedom of choice was protected and people could smoke on buses, in schools, even in other people's faces if they felt like it.

Right on cue, Sadie lit up a cigarette. "I thought you might need a break," she said. "Although your mother is behaving remarkably well tonight."

"She's always easier when she's with Auntie Linda." I looked back at our booth. Mama and her only friend were deep in conversation, while the others laughed uproariously at something on Lisa's phone. My mother's face was all sharp angles and deep-set lines—the result of a half lifetime of frowning and smoking, I guessed. By comparison, my sister's face was glowing with happiness. If you plucked her out of the tired pub in the East End of Glasgow and dropped her onto the pages of a bridal magazine, she actually would pass for one of those women brimming with anticipation for the best day of their lives.

"I'm never getting married," I said.

"And so speaks the chief bridesmaid, ladies and gentlemen." Sadie laughed. "It's a good thing you're not making a speech."

"God, can you imagine? Still, what harm would it do? By the time we get to speeches, she'll have married the sleazebag." I laughed, but Sadie didn't.

"Is that really how you feel, Mer?" She took a deep draw of her cigarette, narrowing her eyes.

"Come on, Sadie. You know he's hardly my favorite person."

"Does Fee know?"

"That he's a sleazebag?"

She raised her eyebrows.

I sighed, letting my shoulders slump under the weight I'd been carrying for months.

"She knows Lucas and I aren't exactly best friends. But I think she's OK with that really. She likes to keep that part of her life separate. She doesn't want her crappy family to taint married life. Can't say I blame her."

"You'll always be the most important person to her, Mer," Sadie said gently.

I shook my head. "That's not what happens, Sadie. When you get married, your life revolves around your spouse. That's just how it is. Or how it should be, in an ideal world. And Fee wants the ideal world. I want it for her too."

"Maybe you should talk to her about this, Mer." Sadie linked her arm with mine and eased me gently to the bar.

"What, tonight? At her bachelorette party? Don't be ridiculous. It's too late. She's getting married in a week. Anyway, it'll be fine. He loves her, and that's what counts. I'll just miss her, that's all. She's always been...there."

"She'll still be there."

"Yeah, but he will be too."

We returned to the booth with two trays of drinks, to find they'd started the quiz without us ("Because you were taking so fucking long," Mama hissed). We hadn't missed much. So far, Fee had scored zero points because she and Lucas didn't agree on the following: who said "I love you" first, who wanted more kids, who wears the trousers in the relationship, and who is the better dancer, singer, driver, and chef. Fee and her friends thought it was hilarious that the groom knew nothing about the bride. I caught Sadie's eye and downed my shot.

The day Fee married Lucas was supposed to be wet and windy, but the weatherman was wrong.

"It's sunny!" Fee jerked open the flimsy pink curtain, like a little girl waking up on Christmas morning and hoping for snow. It felt strange to be waking up in my old bed, with the scratchy covers and the remaining curly-cornered posters on the wall.

"I can't spend the night here alone," Fee had pleaded. "And it's bad luck for Lucas and me to see each other the morning of the wedding." So we'd stayed together in our room, talking softly over the bedside table that still bore the marks of our childhood sticker obsession, just like we did when we were six, eight, ten, sixteen. Wondering about what the wedding would be like, both of us still trying to come to terms with the idea of one of us being someone's wife.

"Don't forget about me," I'd whispered in the darkness, when I was sure she was asleep.

I'd slept badly, waking frequently out of disturbing dreams.

"Come on, we need to get ready." Fee was already on her feet, pulling on her dressing gown with *Bride* on the back. "Meredith, get your gown on!"

I followed her downstairs, feeling the weight of *Bridesmaid* on my back. The smell of bacon wafted up to meet us. Mama had promised a full English breakfast on Fee's special day. Maybe today wouldn't be so bad.

For once, Fee didn't complain about the brittle bacon or rubbery eggs. In fact, she barely ate anything. "I'm too stressed!" she shrieked, turning down Mama's offer of toast with an outstretched hand, like she was a diva on the set of a Hollywood movie. But she was smiling, her eyes shining. I knew she wasn't all that stressed. She had an idea in her head of how a bride should behave on the morning of her wedding, and she was hitting every note.

For someone who'd never been preoccupied with her appearance, she was spending a lot of time finding the exact shade of nail polish to complement her bouquet and the ratio of hair up vs. hair down. I wasn't being much help, so she ordered me to get my dress on or we'd never make it to the church on time.

"I'm going to fine you every time you say that," I told her over my shoulder as I stomped into our bedroom. She laughed, pleased that I was playing along.

We couldn't find a bridesmaid's dress with long sleeves, and our budget didn't stretch to bespoke, so we agreed—in hushed voices, while Mama was questioning the price of the tiaras—that I'd wear a matching lilac pashmina.

"You can wear it any way you want," Fee said, squeezing my elbow.

"What's that?" Mama demanded when we went to pay.

"A pashmina," Fee told her sharply.

"A scarf? For a June wedding?" Mama stared at me.

"Well, we live in Scotland. It'll probably be as cold as a witch's tit." Fee winked at me and put her hand over the pashmina. She knew Mama wouldn't make a scene in the bridal shop.

The pashmina was soft against my skin. It was perhaps the best twenty quid Mama had ever spent on me, and she had no idea why. I still wasn't convinced lilac was my color, but it was the best of a bad pastel bunch. As Fee pointed out, bridesmaids couldn't wear black. It was the rule.

"Mer! I need you!"

She looked beautiful. "You're radiant," I said. "Everyone says that about brides, but you really are."

"Really?" She grinned at me. "Shit, Mer. I'm a bride." She grabbed my hands. "I'm a fucking bride!"

I grinned back at her. "I know. How the hell did this happen?"

"I need you to zip me up. What time is it? Do you think I should arrive late? Just a little? That's what brides do, don't they?"

I turned her round to face the mirror. "I'm sure five minutes wouldn't do any harm. Keep him on his toes, yeah?" I tugged at the zip gently, taking care not to catch her skin. "There you go. Perfect."

"Thanks, Mer."

We looked at each other—and ourselves—in the mirror.

"Do you hate him?" Her eyes locked onto mine.

"No," I told her.

"Good. Because he loves me, Mer. He really does, you know?"

"I know," I said softly. I kissed the back of her head. "Come on. We've got a wedding to go to."

She spun round and grabbed my hands again. "I'm never going to sleep in this bedroom again. Let's say a proper goodbye." I let her pull me onto her bed, and we bounced and laughed until we were out of breath and Mama shouted from downstairs for us to stop making a racket and hurry the hell up.

We were five minutes late, but Lucas was later.

"I can't believe this," Fee hissed. "It's my wedding day and I'm standing in a bloody cupboard."

"It's not a cupboard," Mama said. "We're just waiting here until Lucas arrives. He can't see you, remember? It's bad luck. Calm down, Fiona. Your cheeks are getting red. You'll sweat your makeup off if you get all riled up. Think of your photographs."

I watched my sister pace from one side of the small room to the other. "Let's just get out of here," she said.

"Really?" I rushed to speak before Mama. "You're not going to go through with it?"

Fee looked at me strangely. "Of course I am. Don't be stupid, Meredith. I mean, get out of this room. It's making me claustrophobic."

"Yeah, I know," I muttered. "I'll open the window."

"Don't go messing with things, Meredith," Mama said sharply. She looked at her watch. "He's thirteen minutes late, Fiona. Maybe he's changed his mind. How long shall we give him?"

"Phone him, Meredith!" Fee pleaded. "Find out what the hell is going on. *Please*."

"I don't have his number," I said helplessly.

"Oh my God…This is awful. My life is over," Fee moaned. Mama sighed.

Four minutes later, Lucas turned up, looking slightly disheveled but otherwise ready and willing to take my sister as his wife. Fee was straight back in action, dusting powder over her nose and chin, straightening her tiara, offering a cheek for Mama to peck before she went to take her seat.

We linked arms to walk down the aisle. "He's probably just hungover," she whispered. "He was drinking with the boys last night."

"That's wise, the night before your wedding." I couldn't help myself.

She sighed. "I know."

The double doors into the body of the church formed the final obstacle. I stopped walking.

"What?" she demanded impatiently.

"I just want you to be sure."

"I *am*. Come *on*."

"It's a big thing, getting married. And you're only young."

"Meredith, stop. I'm getting married. If my stupid fiancé had been here on time, I'd be married already."

"OK, OK. Listen, I'm sorry. I'm sorry our dad's not here to walk you down the aisle."

"Even if he was, I'd still want you to do it."

I stroked her cheek. "You really are beautiful. I'm not sure he deserves you."

"Nobody does." She winked at me. "Now, come *on*."

Day 1,333

Wednesday, March 13, 2019

I'm sitting in the kitchen, just about to start my 1,000-piece jigsaw of Belgium's Antwerpen-Centraal railway station, when the doorbell rings. I prepare myself for small talk with the grocery delivery guy—who happens to be fifteen minutes early, which is highly unusual.

It's not the grocery delivery guy.

"Your hair is so long" is the first thing my sister says to me, the first thing she's said to me for three years.

I grip the doorframe. Random, unwanted memories and harsh words jostle for space in my mind. I inhale through my nose, then let the breath escape, slowly and audibly, through my mouth. I stare at her, holding my body in place, just breathing, unable to form words.

Fee looks back at me, waits. She doesn't know how I'm going to react, and I don't know either. Finally I blurt out, "I thought you were the grocery delivery guy," because it's the only thing I know to be true right now. This is the moment I haven't ever let myself imagine, because it's just too huge, so the only way to make it bearable is to think about my shopping.

She looks different. Her hair is shorter, peppered with gray, and I don't recognize her glasses. She's wearing a padded parka with an enormous furry hood, her supermarket-branded polo shirt, jeans, lace-up ankle boots. Her cheeks are flushed; I can't tell if it's from nerves or the biting wind. Her hands are in her pockets, and she's not carrying a bag.

154

It's just her. My sister. Standing on my doorstep.

I stare, forcing her to break the silence. "I...I'm sorry...I didn't know..." She clears her throat. "I didn't know what to do. I didn't even know I was coming, actually. I just woke up this morning and thought it was time. I came straight from work."

Still I say nothing. But I open the door and step back to let her in.

We're both silent as we walk into the kitchen, neither of us brave enough to attempt small talk. I switch the kettle on and put a teabag in the pot. I have my back to her, but her presence in the room is intense. I go back to my breathing, trying to exhale three years of hurt.

"I've left him," she says finally.

I tighten my grip on the teapot, waiting a few seconds before I remove the lid and fill it with boiling water. Doing things I know how to do, things I can't mess up. I get two mugs from the cupboard, milk from the fridge, sugar, teaspoons. "Do you still take it?" I ask, glancing at her.

"What?" She looks at me blankly.

"Sugar?" As if how she takes her tea is more important than the fact that she has just left her husband of sixteen years.

"One sugar," Fee says.

When I hand her the mug, I notice she's still wearing her wedding ring.

"You're still wearing your wedding ring," I say, and it comes out like an accusation.

"I'm not ready to take it off yet," she says in a small voice. "But I have left him. I moved out a week ago."

"Why?" I ask. "Why, after all this time? Why now? Why not back then?"

A memory barrels into my mind: my hip bones pressed painfully against the sink; the smell of stale beer; discordant piano notes from another part of the house. I make a tight fist and press my fingernails into the palm of my hand to bring me back to the present.

Fiona takes a sip of her tea but it's still too hot and she winces. I think she's waiting for me to lead the way to the kitchen table. Before, she would have sat down without thinking about it; a sibling doesn't need to stand on ceremony. But any familiarity we once had is long gone. And I don't want to sit down. I feel strangely in control, standing in the middle of my kitchen in my slippers, waiting for my sister to make eye contact. Waiting for her to speak.

She's saved by the bell.

"That's the grocery delivery guy," she says.

"Why?" I ask, again, after my shopping is spread over the kitchen counters. I keep myself busy by putting it away, but not with the care I normally take. I cram a whole chicken into an already crowded freezer drawer; shove tins haphazardly onto the wrong shelf.

"He's a bully," she says.

"*Really.*" I mutter it under my breath.

"It took me far too long to see his true colors. I'm so sorry, Meredith. I…I can't explain it. It's like…he controlled me, you know? He had such a hold over me, and it took me years to see it. I'm sorry."

I've waited a long time to hear it. Two words that can mean everything or nothing. I don't know what I expected to happen, what I thought I would feel. Everything is just the same. Fred rubs against my ankle, purring. I feel the softness of his tail brush my bare skin as he slips away. I want to scoop him up, go into the living room, and watch an old film I've seen a thousand times before. I want Fee to leave, to take "I'm sorry" with her.

"I'm sorry," she says again.

"Sit," I tell her, grabbing the pieces of Antwerpen-Centraal railway station, stuffing them back into their box. I push the lid down, slide it to the other side of the table, away from us.

We sit opposite each other, waiting, drinking our tea. Whenever I look at her, I have to look away again before the pain crackles through my body like a zip line.

"Meredith, I'm sorry."

"Stop saying that."

"I don't know what else to say. If it makes any difference, my life is a mess."

"This isn't just about you, Fiona," I snap. She looks wounded, but I don't care. I want my words to sting the way her silence has.

"I didn't want to believe you," she says. "It was easier to believe him. I don't know how I can make it up to you. I mean, do you even want me to?"

"I don't know," I say honestly. I look down at my fingers, long and slim, holding my mug. "I still don't understand why you're here. What's changed?"

When I finally look up at her, tears are streaming down her cheeks. "I lost another baby."

"Oh, Fee," I whisper, and I'm shocked by the pang of love I feel for her, amidst all the hurt.

We were twenty-four and twenty-five and we thought we were so grown-up. But we were babies.

It was the longest time I'd spent on my own with Lucas, sitting in the sterile hospital waiting room while my sister bled down the corridor. She was my sister, that day, first and foremost, before she was his wife.

"Tell me again what happened," I demanded.

He looked up from his phone, his eyes cold gray stones. "She was just bleeding. I told you." Like he couldn't be bothered.

"When you got back from the pub?"

"Yeah. I thought she was asleep. I made cheese on toast, took it up to bed. She was in the bathroom. Lying on the floor."

"She'd passed out." It wasn't a question.

"Aye." His phone buzzed; he glanced at it. "She'd passed out."

"And what did you do?"

"I ate my cheese on toast."

"You ate your cheese on toast."

"*I ate my cheese on toast.*"

I clenched my fists. He was mocking me. A nurse bustled past and gave us a quick smile. I hoped she didn't think we were a couple, having a casual chat about cheese on toast to temper our excitement and nerves while we waited to have our scan, to see our baby taking shape for the first time. The thought made me feel sick.

"Meredith, I thought she was drunk. I was drunk. It was two o'clock in the morning."

"She wasn't drunk." I glared at him. "She was having a miscarriage."

"Well, I didn't know that, did I? Didn't even know she was pregnant. Neither did you, come to think of it."

I folded my arms and tried to quell the anger. Fee had been in the room down the corridor for a long time. "I'm going to find out what's going on."

He shrugged, pulled the collar of his jacket up toward his ears, and looked back at his phone.

It was another ten minutes before I was allowed in to see her. "We've got lots of emergencies today," a nurse said apologetically, leading me toward Fee's room. "Another wee while and you can take her home."

"So soon?"

"Sure. Unless she takes a turn for the worse. She's best at home in her own bed. You can always call if you have any concerns."

Fee looked like a child, her pale face tiny against the pillow. "I'm wearing a diaper," she told me, and we both started crying.

I sat on the cold plastic chair and held her hand.

"Does Mama know?" she asked.

"I haven't called her yet," I admitted. "I wanted to see you first."

"I'll call her when I get home. No point in her coming here. She hates hospitals."

"Who doesn't? I really don't think you should be on this ward, you know. There are babies here. It's totally insensitive."

"Where else would I go?" she said quietly. "Anyway, it's fine. These things happen."

"Did you know?" I thought of Lucas's barb, wondered why she hadn't shared something so life changing.

She nodded. "My period was late. It's never late. And my boobs were rock hard. I was going to tell you. I was going to phone you today, ask you how you felt about being Auntie Meredith."

"Oh, Fee."

"It wasn't planned. Lucas...he's not ready. Where is he, by the way?"

"On his phone in the waiting room."

"He'll be texting his mum and his sister, letting them know what's happened."

"He's a dick, Fee. Do you really want to have a baby with this guy?"

She pulled her hand away. "Meredith, he's my husband. Of course I want to have a baby with him."

"Really?"

"Yes, really. I love him."

"He doesn't deserve you."

She sighed. "You'd say that about anybody."

"No, I wouldn't. He ate cheese on toast while you were passed out on the bathroom floor. There are lots of guys out there who wouldn't do that."

"Well, you marry one of those guys," she huffed.

"I'm not getting married. It's a crock of shit."

"Whatever."

"I mean it." I reached for her hand again, and she let me hold it. "If you have a baby, I'll be the best Auntie Meredith," I told her.

"I know you will." She squeezed my fingers. "I love you, Mer."

"I love you too."

"Can you ask Lucas to come in?"

I sat on my own in the waiting room, looking at the pages of an old magazine, not reading the words. I sat until Fee and Lucas walked out of the room, hand in hand. Her eyes were pink and puffy, his were still cold gray stones.

I'm sitting on the floor, my back against the radiator. There's a tiny lump in the linoleum that I can't get rid of no matter how hard I press. I rub it with my thumb. Back and forward, forward and back. My eyes drift over my kitchen. I'd be cooking a stew, if she wasn't here. This annoys me. I look at her back, still hunched over the table.

"Where are you staying, if you've left him?"

Her body tenses. I know the answer. But I want to hear her say it.

"Where do you think?"

"With her?"

She turns to face me, her eyes torn. "Meredith, where else can I go?"

"Does she know you're here?"

She shakes her head, doesn't look at me.

"I should be making a stew," I tell her.

"I'm sorry," she says for the fortieth time.

I contemplate getting on with my stew, leaving her to feel awkward at my table. But I stay where I am, my backside growing numb on the floor. I rub, rub, rub at the tiny lump.

"Do you remember that time we went to stay at Auntie Linda's? I was only about eight... You'd have been six?"

"A little," I say warily.

"She came to collect us from school and picked us up in her big red car. Told us we were having a special sleepover. We were so excited."

"I don't remember the red car. But I remember being happy at Auntie Linda's. I didn't want to go home."

"Me neither. Do you know why we stayed there so long? We were there about a week, I think."

"I don't know, Fiona, and I don't care. I have no interest in reminiscing about a visit to Auntie Linda's. What's this got to do with anything?"

She swivels round on the bench and looks at me. Her eyes are desperate. "Mama tried to kill herself, and it nearly worked."

A chill runs through me even though the radiator is warm against my back. "How the hell do you know that?"

"I overheard a conversation between Auntie Linda and a social worker. They were talking about Mama going into the mental hospital. The social worker asked Auntie Linda if we could stay with her until they found a foster home for us."

"And you're only just telling me now?"

"When should I have told you?" There's an edge to Fiona's voice now. "When you were eight? Nine? Ten? What kind of big sister would I have been if I'd told you our mother was so unhappy, she wanted to leave us forever?"

"Fiona, I wish she had left us forever."

Her breathing is rapid. She's rubbing the side of her jaw like she does when she's anxious.

"I'm not telling you this to make you feel sorry for her."

"So why are you telling me?"

"Meredith, a lot happened you don't know about."

"I'm sure it did. But a lot happened that I *did* know about. That I'll never be able to forget, no matter how much fucking therapy I have."

"I'm trying, Meredith." My sister's voice is shaky; she's holding back tears. I think I've seen her cry twice in all the years I've known her.

I remember what she's been through and soften a little. "I know you are. But maybe it's too late."

"Maybe it is. But I want to try."

I press my thumb against the lump on the floor until it hurts. "You can try."

"I know you got the worst of it. I do know that. But she took it out on me too."

"What did she take out on us, Fiona? Being a mother? Being lonely? Having lousy taste in men?"

"I don't think she had a happy childhood either."

"Don't make excuses for her."

"I'm not," my sister says quickly. "I'm just trying to figure it all out."

"I stopped trying to do that a long time ago."

"I think you're a few years ahead of me there."

"You'll get there. If you want to."

"Could we...get there together?"

"Like you said, I'm a few years ahead of you."

"That's true. Listen, Meredith..."

I wait, feeling years of tension stretch between us.

"I believe you. About Lucas. I believe you. I'm sorry I didn't say this earlier." Her voice is desperate now.

"Why now? After all this time? What's changed?"

More fat tears roll down her cheeks. I ignore my instinct to comfort her and wait.

"I've finally seen him for who he is, Mer," she whispers.

I know she's holding back, that there's so much more she could tell me. I don't want to know, not yet.

"Meredith, I'm so sorry. Please give me a chance to make it up to you."

I feel numb, as if I've exhausted a lifetime of emotions in the last hour. My stomach growls; I'm hungry.

"I need to make my lunch," I say. "I think you should go."

But I don't make my lunch after the front door closes behind her. I sit on the kitchen floor for a long time. Finally I run a hot bath, light lavender-scented candles, and lie in the water until I'm shivering. I let the tears flow, crying noisily for two little girls, for the time they'll never get back, and for the mother who wanted to die.

2015

I was washing wineglasses when Lucas came into the kitchen. He leaned against the counter, took a long swig from his beer bottle, and looked me up and down in that way of his.

"You know something, Meredith? We've never really had a chance to get to know each other."

We'd had plenty of chances. Christmases, birthdays, Sunday dinners. It doesn't take too much to get to know someone a little bit. A question is a good starting point. "How's your week been, Meredith?" "What's going on with you, Meredith?" "Seen any good films lately, Meredith?"

"What do you want to know?" I said to him, trying to keep my voice light. Light and breezy, like Fiona's. I focused on Mama's wineglasses again. One of them had a smudge of dark lipstick on its rim; I gently scraped it off with my thumbnail.

Lucas had moved closer to me. "You have bubbles on your elbow," he said lazily.

I laughed nervously.

"Here—let me." Before I could do anything about it, he was rubbing my arm with Mama's dish towel. It felt so wrong it almost hurt, even though he was barely touching me and it was over in seconds.

"Please don't do that," I said quietly.

He laughed, raised his hands, and let the dish towel slip from his fingers. He was mocking me. "Is that the most action you've had in a while, Meredith? What is it with you and men? What do you do that repulses them so much?"

"Leave me alone, Lucas."

He persisted. "Fiona says you haven't been on a date since...
What was his name? Gary?"

I didn't look at him and tried to concentrate on Mama's wineglasses, but I knew he was smiling—and not in a good way. I
could hear it in his voice.

"Gavin," I said. "And I have been on a date actually." I'd been
for dinner with Toby, one of the designers at work, a month
before. It was nothing to write home about, but I told Mama
and Fiona about it, knowing that this kind of thing impressed
them. Partaking in vacuous conversation over pizza and cheap
red wine was a more acceptable thing to do on a Friday night
than watch a true crime documentary (alone) or doodle with
top-quality pens (alone) or knit (alone; even though I was fash-
ioning a lilac cardigan to give to Louise at work, who was
expecting a baby girl).

"Are you calling your sister a liar?"

"No," I said quickly.

He moved closer to me until I could smell the distinct sweet
odor of beer on his breath. I fought my instinct to recoil and
kept my feet clamped to the kitchen floor. I looked for shapes in
the froth in the sink water, like I used to do in the clouds when
I was a girl, lying on my back, squinting into the sky, convinced
that I was looking at an old man's hooked nose, or a strawberry,
or a whale. Maybe even a heart, if I was lucky.

I saw no such shapes in the water, but the distraction helped
slow the tension I felt building in my body. It started in my belly
and rose upward through my chest, filling my lungs and coming to an abrupt stop in my throat, where it stayed, hard and
thick and immovable, like an iron doorstop.

Lucas put his arm round my shoulders, and at this point I did
recoil, but it was too late. He has long arms and a tight grip and

I'm thin. I dragged my voice from the back of my throat and told him to stop, but the word disappeared before it was fully formed. The last thing I remember thinking, before he pushed my upper body toward the sink and pulled up my skirt, is that he was surprisingly strong for a man who drinks so much and never works out.

Day 1,334

Thursday, March 14, 2019

"You look tired."

"I'm OK." He's right; I am tired, but not too tired to hold up my barriers. I don't feel like letting Tom in today.

"I'm not sure I believe you."

"I'm not sure I care." I look into his kind eyes and try to harden my own. It's not easy faced with his relentless concern. I don't know how he does it.

"Did you do any baking yesterday? I'm starving."

"No," I lie. I have seventy-two cheese scones encased in a Tupperware tower on the kitchen counter—the product of my sleepless night. He must have noticed; a tower of plastic is hard to miss. I want to see what he does when he catches me.

"That's not like you," he replies evenly. I imagine the tower falling, scattering scones across the floor. I have no idea what I'll do with seventy-two scones. If he has noticed them, he's not giving anything away.

"You think you know me so well."

"Don't you think we know each other pretty well by now? I see you more often than I see most of my friends."

I look at him through narrowed eyes. "Indeed." I have a funny feeling deep in my belly.

"Meredith, I'm sorry…that came out wrong. My *other* friends, I mean."

"Whatever."

"Meredith, of course I think of you as a friend."

"Really?"

"Why does that surprise you?"

"Oh, I don't know. Why don't you tell me, since you know me so well?"

Tom sighs. "Would you like a cup of tea?"

"No, thanks. I've had five already this morning. I've been up since 4 a.m. Help yourself, though. You know where everything is."

"So you are tired. You don't have to put on an act for me." Tom looks behind my spotty mug for one that I don't generally use myself. I appreciate the fact that he knows, by now, that I have my favorite things. That I've never had to tell him.

"I'm not," I say to his back.

"Meredith, is anything else bothering you?" He turns round and leans against the counter, his long legs crossed at the ankle. "You can talk to me. I want to help."

"I don't think you can, Tom. Anyway, that's not your job, is it? You're not my therapist. You're not here to fix me. You're just here to make sure I'm still alive. Not lying dead on the couch, being eaten by Fred."

I'm only half joking. It's something I've thought about, now and again. What would happen to me if I died? It could be days before someone realizes. I'm fit and healthy right now, but I could have a heart attack or a brain aneurysm and be gone in a second.

"Well, that too. Although I don't think Fred would eat you, unless you smelled of tuna."

"Ha ha."

"Anyway, I know I'm not here to fix you. I'm here to drink your tea and eat your cookies."

I laugh in spite of myself.

"Let me just have my tea and then I'll get out of your way, all right?"

"All right. Actually...Oh, go on—I will have a cup. Since you're making it anyway."

"Good stuff."

"It's not that I don't want to talk to you, Tom. It's just…"

"It's difficult. I completely understand."

"Until you came along, I didn't really tell anyone anything. I mean, I speak to Sadie, but she's known me forever, she knows what things were like…before. She knows Fiona, she knows… stuff."

"She's part of your history."

"Exactly. With you…there's just so much to explain. My head hurts thinking about it."

"Well, maybe you don't have to tell me everything? Just the parts you think it might help you to talk about?"

"Maybe…" I have a lump in my throat. I take a gulp of tea and it hurts. I'm not sure if that's what makes the tears come, but here they are, sliding down my cheeks.

"Meredith…" His voice is soft, which makes me cry more.

"I'm sorry, I'm being ridiculous."

"Don't apologize, OK? Drink your tea." He fetches a clean handkerchief from his pocket and places it in front of me. He's the only man I've ever met who carries proper posh handkerchiefs around in his jeans pocket.

"What jigsaw are you doing this week?"

"Antwerpen-Centraal railway station."

"Wow. Tricky. So…listen…what do you do when you can't find that jigsaw piece? Part of the sunset, say. Do you take it all to bits?"

"Of course not. Never. I…I take a break, I guess. Water my plants. Read a book. Phone Sadie. Bake."

"And when you go back to the jigsaw, do you normally find the piece?"

"I suppose so. I always find it eventually. Or I work on another part."

"That's what we're doing here, Meredith."

"Trying to piece me back together?"

Tom laughs. "We're taking our time. Trying different things. There's no rush."

"Very clever of you to use a jigsaw analogy, Tom."

"Thank you. Do you get my point, though? Friendships take time. Everything takes time."

"I saw my sister yesterday. She just turned up."

"Wow. How did it go?"

"I'm still trying to process it, Tom. I don't know how to feel."

"I bet."

"Her husband raped me."

As soon as I say the words, I wonder if I actually did say them, or if I said something else, like "Would you like a cheese scone? I'm sorry I lied to you before. I did bake yesterday. Actually, it was this morning. I baked seventy-two cheese scones at 4 a.m. because I couldn't sleep and if I'd laid in bed thinking about my life for a single second longer, I would probably have taken the sharpest knife in the kitchen drawer and sliced down my ulnar artery."

It appears that I did say the words, because Tom is staring at me like I have two heads or something.

"Your sister's husband?"

I nod. "In my mother's kitchen. She and Fiona were in the living room. Fiona didn't believe me at the time, but she says she does now. I haven't seen my mother since that night."

The color has drained from Tom's face. "Meredith...wow. I'm so sorry that happened to you. What a..."

"Nightmare."

"Well...yes, a nightmare. I mean...I can't even find the words. I'm sorry, I...I wasn't prepared for that."

"I wasn't prepared for it either."

"What do you think will happen now, between you and your sister?"

"I have no idea."

"What do you *want* to happen?"

"I have no idea," I say again, feeling helpless. "She's left him. She wants to make things better."

Fee texted me last night: I'm here for you. Whenever, wherever, however you need me. Let me help you, Mer.

That's what I needed from you back then, I thought. But after dancing around different responses, I simply wrote back: I need time.

She replied immediately: Of course. Love you too

You don't have the right to say that to me, I thought, slamming my phone into the drawer of my bedside table. I picked up the nearest book—something Sadie lent me about emotional detox—and read the same paragraph four times before opening the drawer again.

Love you too, I wrote, because I do, despite it all.

"I'm glad you're here," I tell Tom. "I think it would have been really hard to be alone today."

He looks at me with his kind, concerned eyes, always giving me space to make sure the next move is one I'm comfortable with.

"Could we just sit here, and do nothing much?" I ask him.

He reaches for the remote. "That's exactly what we'll do."

2015

I walked home from Mama's that night the way I always did. Door to door, it took twenty-seven minutes. Fiona and Lucas got in their car at the same time. I saw one of my sister's hands raised in a wave as they drove past, but my own stayed deep in my coat pockets, clenched in tight fists.

I stared at their car until it turned off the street, making its way toward their two-bedroom new build on the outskirts of the city. I wondered what they were talking about. Comparing our takeout chow mein and special fried rice to the place they usually ordered from. Laughing at the memory of Mama's attempt to play "Ode to Joy" on the piano, her sunken eyes peering at the yellowed song book, her top teeth chewing the corner of her bottom lip as her skinny fingers stretched over the keys. Wondering why Meredith wasn't married, why Meredith didn't just lighten up and have a drink, why Meredith had such an attitude problem.

They'd stopped offering me a lift a long time ago, because I always said no. I liked to walk. It took about ten minutes to shed the skin of artifice and amenability, all the while thinking about the sweet relief of screaming into a pillow when I got home.

"Meredith!" Her voice cracked the stillness around me. I stopped walking.

Mama was barefoot and wore an old trench coat over her sequin dress. It swamped her frame, almost long enough to scrape the pavement. The belt was missing; she crossed her arms to stop it from flapping open. I'd never seen this coat before. I wondered briefly where she'd got it, then decided I didn't want to know.

For better or for worse, life can change in a matter of seconds. People take their first and last breaths. Cars crash, planes plunge into oceans. The healing process after decades of hurt can begin with a simple gesture.

Or a question: "Are you all right?"

Anything like that, from her on this night, would have gone some way to easing the pain. To giving me a glimmer of hope that it might, someday, be possible to recover from what Lucas had just done.

But this was not one of those moments.

"I need some money." She had an aggrieved look on her face, as if I was the one asking for a favor when she just wanted to get home and scream into a pillow.

I breathed deeply. "What for?"

She shrugged. "This and that. Help your old mama out, will you?"

"I don't have any cash on me. I'll transfer some into your account when I get home."

"You're a good girl, angelface." Somehow, she made it sound like an insult, like I was good in the absence of other, more interesting qualities. "Why don't you come back in and have a drink with me? A wee nightcap. Just the two of us."

"No, thanks, Mama." I started backing away. "I'm tired. Thanks for dinner. I'll sort your money. Fifty quid. Don't ask again."

"Yes, ma'am." She brought her hand up to her temple in a mock salute.

I turned and walked, and I didn't look back until I'd passed a few more houses. She was still standing on the pavement, looking like a little girl dressed up in her mother's clothes. I couldn't read her expression.

I wasn't held down.
I wasn't drugged.

I wasn't attacked in a dark alleyway in the middle of the night.
He didn't tape my mouth up.
He didn't tie my hands behind my back.
He didn't rip my underwear off.

The temperature dropped over the course of my short journey. I picked up the pace and distracted myself from the cold by picking out houses I recognized from the streets of my childhood. Some had changed since then, with extensions and new windows and fancier cars in their driveways. Others, like Mama's, had stayed the same, just grown older and more neglected with their weather-beaten walls and thin curtains and tired lawns. Mr. Lindsay, my old math teacher, who had an affair with Mrs. MacGowan, head of English. I wondered who lived in his bungalow with the gray door now.

Julianne Adair, a girl in my primary-school class, lived four doors down from poor Mr. Lindsay. The house still belongs to her parents, although it sits empty all summer when they stay in their camper on Loch Lomond. Mama doesn't speak highly of the Adairs, says they got above their station after they won twenty-four thousand pounds in the lottery. Mama doesn't like it when people get above their station. She seems to take someone else's good luck or just reward as a personal affront.

I thought about Julianne Adair the rest of the way home. I hadn't seen her for years; I had no idea where she was now or whether she joined her parents in their camper on Loch Lomond during their extended summer break. I remembered she got picked on for having a lazy eye, then in middle school had corrective eye surgery and turned into the bully. I had a vague recollection of a school bathroom altercation with Sadie—I'd need to ask her about it. She remembers things like that better than I do.

Keeping my mind on Julianne Adair, a girl who meant

nothing to me then and means nothing to me now, a woman I might never see again for the rest of my life, is what helped me get home.

I didn't try to get away.
I didn't fight back.
I didn't break my nails or get his skin beneath my fingernails.
I didn't bleed.
I didn't cry.

Day 1,341

Thursday, March 21, 2019

It's surprisingly hot for this time of year. Spring is here, but it feels more like summer. Over the last few days Jacob's cherry blossom tree has produced an abundance of flowers, like an enormous cotton candy cloud. I texted a picture of it to Celeste and pointed it out to Tom when he arrived this morning.

"They'll drop in a couple of weeks," I said. "The pavement will be a fluffy pink carpet."

"A short life," he mused. "Like ours."

I stared at him. "Yes, but they bloom every year. They come back to life."

He looked at the tree for a moment. "We should pay more attention to our own lives," he said.

"You're being weird," I told him, and left him on the doorstep.

I've opened all the windows, filling the rooms with swathes of light and sparkly dust clouds and the faraway voices of kids playing in their gardens. I prop the back door open, and Tom and I drag our kitchen chairs closer to my tiny patch of concrete that barely passes for a back garden. But the walls round it are high, and the sky is blue.

I take the big plant out of its pot and turn the pot upside down—a makeshift table between our chairs. We're not drinking tea today, for a change. We agree that neither of us eats enough fruit, so I make us smoothies with my new smoothie maker, which is very smooth itself, standing on my kitchen worktop all modern and shiny.

"Gorgeous day." I stretch my legs out in front of me until my toes hang over the doorway. My feet are bare and I admire the pedicure I gave myself last night. My toenails are a deep, rich burgundy. They looked almost black last night, but in the bright light, they shine bloodred. I'm pretty pleased with my efforts.

I think about inviting Tom to take off his shoes and socks but change my mind. I don't think we're quite at the stage where it's not weird for him to wander around my house in his bare feet. Next to his trainers, my feet look tiny. I wiggle my toes and enjoy the sensation.

Apart from telling me several times how amazing I am to have reached the end of my path, Tom's not saying much, which isn't like him. He's normally Mr. Chatty.

"Hey, are you OK?" I try to keep my voice casual.

"Fine and dandy," he says, but he doesn't look my way. His eyes are focused on some far-off place beyond the rear wall of my garden.

"I don't believe you," I tell him, thinking about the cherry blossom.

He sighs. "Just one of those days."

"Those days suck."

He nods. "They sure do."

"How's the smoothie? I keep getting raspberry seeds stuck in my teeth; it's driving me crazy. Rookie mistake."

"Oh, it's delicious. Just what the doctor ordered."

We sit in silence for a moment. I watch a bird land on the fence, then take off again. I wonder where it's been, and where it's going. What it must be like, to be able to go wherever you like, whenever you like. To be so small that you can balance on the skinniest branch of a tree, a delicate perch from which to view the world.

"If you had to be an animal, what would you be?"

He laughs. "You ask the best questions, Meredith Maggs. I must admit that's something I've never given much thought to. I mean, I love cats."

He gestures to Fred, who's lying on the concrete slab nearest the back door. He's definitely a homebody, never ventures any farther.

"But would you want to be a cat?"

Tom studies Fred, my feline best friend. "Hmm. I'm not sure. Maybe a monkey. I've always wanted to be more acrobatic. I like the idea of swinging through the jungle with my monkey pals."

I laugh, sending a mouthful of smoothie down my sweater. The image of Tom hanging upside down from a tree by his tail is too much.

"Crap," I groan, looking around for something to clean up my mess. The dish towel is hanging over the oven handle at the other end of the kitchen. "What am I like, eh? You can't take me anywhere!" I laugh. I roll up the bottom of my sweater and quickly pull it over my head.

And then we're not laughing. Tom stares at my arms, the part of my body I never expose to anyone.

"Meredith..."

"Don't, Tom. Just don't." I stand up quickly, so quickly I trigger a chain of events that makes getting away from him, away from his shocked, questioning eyes, harder than it should be. I tip my chair backward; one of the legs catches the plant pot turned table and Tom's smoothie goes flying. The glass smashes, Fred startles and jumps in the air. I burst into tears and run out of the kitchen.

I've been in the bathroom for half an hour when I hear the front door close. I wonder how long it took Tom to realize I wasn't going to come out.

I let out my breath.

The lighting in the bathroom is soft—I don't like harsh light anywhere—but not soft enough to obscure the multiple silver ridges, so agonizingly precise, running the length of my inner arms. They form a background for the fresher, bright red lines. So fresh that they're not even scars yet. So ugly that Tom was unable to stop staring, the way people look at roadkill or smashed-up cars on the highway.

I never got to tell Tom what animal I would be. I close my eyes and imagine myself as a dolphin in a vast ocean, water running off my smooth, ridge-free body as I propel myself forward for miles and miles. I grab my dressing gown from the hook on the bathroom door, slide my arms into it, and knot the cord tightly round my waist.

2015

4 a.m. I was hot and cold and exhausted and on high alert. People—parents, mainly—talk about being pulled in a million different directions. That was what my body felt like.

I'd been lying on my bed, fully clothed, since I got back from Mama's. I didn't remember locking my front door. I might have boiled the kettle but didn't remember drinking tea. I hadn't transferred money into her account; I'd get an angry phone call tomorrow.

I felt grubby. I pulled at my skirt, felt it rise and fall against the bare skin of my legs. I had goose bumps down my shins. I wanted to rip my clothes off, but they formed a shield I wasn't ready to get rid of. I turned over onto my front and squeezed my eyes shut.

5 a.m. My eyes felt sore in their sockets. I summoned all my energy to turn onto my side, curled up in the fetal position. I imagined myself as a child in protective arms, warm and sleepy. I wondered what it was like to feel so safe that you believed nothing bad would happen to you, ever.

6 a.m. I heard my next-door neighbor's door close, the soft pad of footsteps, a car engine shuddering to life. Saira was an accident and emergency doctor and often worked Sundays. Our paths rarely crossed; she did long shifts, often through the night, but I knew she also lived alone. When we did see each other, we waved and smiled, asked, "How are you?" and replied,

"Fine, thanks." I wondered if she could give me a pill to help me sleep.

7 a.m. I was cold. I folded myself up in my duvet like a burrito, trying to move my body as little as possible in the process. I closed my eyes again.

I heard a young Fiona's voice in my head: *Think about something nice.* Easier said than done. Someone once asked me what my favorite childhood summer holiday memory was. I lied and said something about going to the beach and finding a crab and scaring my sister with it so much she dropped her ice-cream cone in the sand. But we never went to the beach.

I thought about the time Fiona and I lay on towels on the grass in the back garden and covered ourselves in cooking oil because we'd heard it would give us a great tan. We read magazines, pointing out clothes we liked and makeup looks she'd try out on me the next time Mama was at the pub and we had unrestricted access to her dressing table. We sucked lemonade ice pops that left our chins sticky and squinted at the sun through cheap sunglasses. We burned with all the oil and woke up the next morning in skin that flamed red and was hot to touch.

I thought about the time Fiona and I sneaked out of the house one warm July night and walked to the fish-and-chip shop in our pajamas and flip-flops. I couldn't remember why we'd gone to bed without dinner. We'd doused our fries in vinegar and ate them on the swings in the park, washed down with soda. We stayed there, swinging and eating and not talking about anything too much, until we had empty bags and greasy hands.

It was dark. Everything in my bedroom formed an unfamiliar shape. My wardrobe loomed at me, the leaves of my big plant reached out like grabbing hands.

My thirst overcame my reluctance to move. I sat up gingerly and winced at the dull pain in my head. I lay back down.

9 a.m. I woke with a start. I'd arranged to have lunch with Sadie today. I called her; we had a brief exchange in groggy voices. I don't know what I said, but she was in my bedroom within half an hour. I let her hold me.

6 p.m. I'd slept all day but felt worse than I did before. I turned my bedside lamp on and squinted in the sudden light. Gradually things went back to normal. My wardrobe was just a wardrobe; my plant meant no harm.

In the bathroom I held my head under the tap and let cold water run down my throat for what seemed like hours. It trickled down my neck and dampened the neck of my T-shirt. I didn't care.

I decided I might as well do what I normally did on a Sunday night. I ironed my work clothes for the next day, hooked the dress on its hanger over my wardrobe door. I wiped down my kitchen worktops—there wasn't much else to clean, as I hadn't cooked or eaten anything all day. I was aware of the empty pit of my stomach, but I couldn't face food. I watered my plants and dragged my cardboard recycling bin to the edge of the pavement. I lowered blinds, closed curtains, transferred a tub of frozen ratatouille into the fridge for another night's dinner.

Then I took a bath. I peeled off my top, my long skirt, my underwear. I would never wear them again. I used my toes to push them tightly into the corner of the bathroom. I filled the tub with water that was as hot as I could bear and sank down. I scrubbed myself with a flannel until my skin was pink, like a salmon fillet. The discomfort felt good. I washed my hair, then washed it again. I drained the water, then blasted cold from the shower head. The shock made me catch my breath, but I forced myself to sit under it until my skin was so numb it didn't feel part of me.

My teeth were chattering as I wrapped myself in a towel and left wet footprints on my way to the bedroom.

I dried my hair, because if I didn't it would frizz during the night and look terrible in the morning. I did it roughly, quickly, with my back to the mirror. I passed the time by counting the books in my bookcase. It took a few attempts, but I seemed to have one hundred and twelve.

Finally I brushed my teeth and crawled back into bed. I left my lamp on, but I closed my eyes and tried to think of something nice.

Day 1,342

It's not difficult to keep my arms hidden. I'm normally alone, and even then I rarely wear short sleeves. I don't like to look at my scored skin more than I have to. In fact, I can go weeks without catching a glimpse of my bare arms, if I'm careful. I close my eyes in the shower and keep the lights dim during baths. It's not often that it's so warm in Glasgow that I can't bear long sleeves, and if I can't, I open all the windows. It's not rocket science.

It wasn't too warm yesterday with Tom in my kitchen. It was just right. My toenails looked great, and I was feeling OK until I asked a stupid question and took a gulp of smoothie at the wrong time, and the day turned sour.

It's after lunchtime—I managed half a bowl of tomato soup and left the rest on the floor for Fred—and I've had six missed calls from Tom already. I wonder when he'll give up. I glance at my phone on the couch beside me. He's texted too. It's not normal for me to have thirteen messages. I haven't read any of them because I have no idea what to say in response.

I need to keep busy. I turn the radio on—loud—and start organizing my kitchen cupboards. It requires just enough concentration to demand focus, but not too much for my sleep-deprived brain to handle. Last night was rough. I worked on my Eiffel Tower jigsaw for hours, vowing to stay up until I completed the top third. I finally admitted defeat at around 3 a.m., and it took another hour to fall asleep. I woke several times between then and 9 a.m., dragging myself out of bizarre, inexplicable dreams that were full of slow-moving shapes and faceless adversaries. Even Fred stayed away, his usual spot at the bottom right of my bed empty.

Hours later, my eyes are still puffy, my pupils black pin-holes. I have a patch of eczema on my chin and my cheeks are flushed red. It's not a good look. But it's fine for organizing cupboards.

I fill a deep bowl with warm water and liquid soap. I might as well clean while I'm at it. I have seven cupboards—this will take me hours. I feel some of the tension leave my shoulders. A whole day stretching ahead of me with no way to fill it is my personal hell. That problem, at least, I have solved.

I move Fred's bowl of tomato soup onto the worktop to make room for the contents of my first cupboard. I notice that it's untouched.

He's not on the purple chair in the living room, or on the comfy chair on the upstairs landing, or under my bed. I do a sweep of the house, three times, checking all his usual lounging spots as well as places he couldn't get into if he tried, like my wardrobe and the bathroom cabinet, because that's what people do when they're desperate. I call his name until I'm sobbing so hard I can't speak.

He's not in the house. I open the back door wide and scan my tiny outdoor space. I have a bistro table with chairs that started out bright blue but have faded and gone rusty. A few empty plant pots that collect rainwater; the little birds like to drink from them. I have a locked storage box with a random collection of tools, which hasn't been opened for years. There's nowhere for Fred to hide, nowhere for him to become trapped. He could have jumped over the wall. I've never seen him jump that high, but I know cats can do it. He could have jumped over the wall and he could be anywhere by now.

Slumped at the kitchen table with my head in my hands, I try to remember when I last saw him. I work backward, like a movie in reverse, forcing myself to relive the pain. He was sleeping on the warm concrete when Tom and I were sitting at the back door. When Tom's glass smashed on the floor, he woke up. He ran, but not into the house. When I eventually came back downstairs, Tom was gone, every piece of glass had been picked up and taken away, and the back door was closed.

I need to call Tom. I don't want to, but he's the only person who might be able to help.

He picks up on the second ring. "Meredith?"

"I'm not phoning to talk about yesterday," I say quickly. "Fred is gone. Did you see him before you left here?"

"I'm not sure. Are you OK? I've been so worried."

"Tom, please. I've lost Fred. That's the only reason I'm calling."

"OK. Did I see him? I don't think I did, no. Not in the house anyway. Wasn't he lying outside? I don't remember him coming in after that. Shit...I shut the back door. I'm sorry, Meredith. I didn't think."

"Could he have slipped past you, without you noticing?" I don't know why I'm asking. Fred isn't in the house.

"I guess so, yeah. Could he be hiding somewhere?"

"I've looked everywhere."

"Meredith, I'm sorry. For everything."

I have no idea what to say to him. I stare out of the kitchen window, chewing my lip. The thought of life without Fred is unbearable.

"I'll go out and look for Fred."

"Thank you," I whisper.

Two hours later, I've experimented with three different kitchen layouts and still can't decide whether the mugs should be on the far left above the kettle or the far right beside the plates and bowls. A dull ache has settled behind my eyes, and I have no idea what time it is. I can't eat anything; I think my stomach has shrunk to the size of a pea. I can't bring myself to get rid of Fred's soup, and a crinkly skin has formed on its surface.

I run to the front door when the bell rings. I've braced myself for bad news, but my heart still sinks when I see Tom's empty arms.

"I'm so sorry, Meredith. I've been up and down the whole street and the next four and there's no sign of him. But I'm sure he'll come back. He's a house cat."

"Thanks for trying." I scan the street behind him for a flash of orange. My voice sounds strange; I don't know how to behave around Tom, not now.

"I left my number at every house. But listen, I really do think he'll come back. He might have taken a wrong turn, but he's smart—he'll work it out. He'll miss you and want to get back to you."

"That makes me feel even worse," I mutter.

"Sorry." Tom looks like he's going to cry.

"Stop apologizing, Tom. None of this is your fault." I pull the sleeves of my sweater farther down over my hands. It's colder now—not a day for bare toes wiggling in the sunshine.

"Can I come in for a few minutes?"

"I'm tired. I can't...it's Fred, all I can think about is Fred."

"I get it. Let's make a plan. We'll put up some posters—do you have a photo of him?"

I nod. "He's all I take photos of."

"Right. Email me a recent photo and I'll print it off, make some posters. I'll come back tomorrow, widen the search. Knock on more doors. We'll get him back, Meredith."

"You're a good person, Tom."

He shrugs. "I really think he'll come back. He might be sitting at your back door now."

"I should go and check."

"Yes, but…don't sit in the kitchen all night, OK? Get some sleep. You look exhausted."

"I look like crap."

"You look exhausted. Listen, you know you can talk to me? About anything. Tell me to piss off and mind my own business if you like. I can take it. I'd never forgive myself if something happened to you that I might have been able to help prevent."

"Like if I killed myself, you mean?" I cross my arms, slide my right thumb inside my left cuff. Rub the raised skin.

"Is that something you think about?" Tom's eyes stay on mine, steadfast. He runs his hands through his hair. "Jesus, Meredith. I can't believe we're talking about this on your doorstep."

I stare back at him. Keep rubbing.

"Is it?"

"Sometimes," I whisper.

"Meredith." He reaches out to me, but I shrink back. I mouth "sorry" to him and look into his sad brown eyes until the door closes. I turn the lock, slide the chain over, walk slowly into the kitchen to wait for Fred.

2015

I heard something click. Footsteps. Then Sadie was on her knees, her face inches from mine. I'd never seen her look so serious. Her mouth moved, but I couldn't hear any words. I tried to smile at her, but my lips felt strange, like they'd been stretched out of shape and wouldn't go back to normal again. But then nothing felt normal anymore. Not since last month, since my life shattered in my mother's kitchen.

Sadie's palm was warm against my forehead, her hands strong but gentle on my shoulders as they guided me toward the floor. Then her fingers gripped under my armpits and she pulled me slowly out from under the kitchen table.

Why was I under there? I wanted to ask her, but I was too tired to try to talk. I wasn't sure what she was doing, but I felt warmer than I had before she was here. There was something soft under my head and round my legs.

Time passed; it could have been seconds or hours. I stared at her serious face the entire time. She made eye contact now and then, her mouth still moving. I wished I could hear her.

She put plastic gloves on, the kind you wore when you dyed your hair, and took things out of a large green bag I didn't remember seeing before. I'd never seen her in nurse mode. I wanted to tell her how proud I was of her for devoting her life to helping others. But I couldn't talk. She was talking but into her phone—not to me. I felt something sting somewhere, and she squeezed my shoulder. She brought a straw to my mouth, and I sipped, then gulped, feeling the water dribble down my chin at the same time as it trickled down my throat. She talked into her phone again.

"I'll be right back," she said, and this time I could hear her.

"OK," I croaked, and I could talk. My body felt heavier than it had before. Some parts of it hurt—I wasn't exactly sure where—but at least it all felt like it belonged to me.

I stared at the ceiling until Sadie got back. Her arms were full—my dressing gown, although she put it on me back to front, which made me want to laugh, my pillow, more soft things over my legs and feet.

"Are you warm?" She pulled her gloves off and placed her palm against my forehead again.

I nodded. "What happened to me?"

"You don't remember?"

I thought about it for a second.

"He raped me."

"I know, sweetheart." Her hand was warm against my skin. "But do you remember what happened last night?"

A memory danced around the edge of my mind and disappeared before I could catch it. I shook my head.

"You don't remember cutting your arms?"

I see the glint of the knife, feel the heat on my skin. I squeezed my eyes shut as the safety and warmth slipped away from me.

Sadie brought it back to me and cupped my face between her hands. "Mer, you're OK. You'll be OK," she whispered. "I promise. I promise you'll be OK."

She said it over and over, with her warm hands holding me together. I wanted to believe her. But also, I was lying on my kitchen floor, with my dressing gown on back to front, and my best friend kneeling beside me with tears in her eyes. I was clearly a long way from OK.

Day 1,343

He won't leave me alone.

"Meredith, I'm in a difficult position here."

"My heart bleeds for you." My phone is pressed tightly against my ear.

"Please don't be like that."

"You're my friend, Tom. Don't do this."

"I'm worried about you."

"Stop saying that. I don't want you to be worried. I want you to be on my side."

"It's not about taking sides."

"Clearly. If it was, you'd be on mine."

"Of course I'm on your side, Meredith."

"I thought it wasn't about taking sides, Tom."

He sighs heavily. I know I'm acting like a baby. I can't help it. He's unleashed a beast.

"I need to do this. Please try to see things from my side. Wouldn't you do the same if roles were reversed?"

"I hate it when people say that," I tell him, crossly. "I can't even begin to imagine what it's like to be you. And don't dare tell me you have any idea what it's like to be me."

"Wow."

"What does that mean?"

"I think I have a little more self-awareness than you're giving me credit for. I know our lives are very different. But we have more in common than you realize."

"Liking cats and cake isn't what I'm talking about, Tom."

"Well, we both like books... I've got you to thank for my newfound appreciation of Margaret Atwood."

"I'm not a one-woman lending library, Tom."

He's silent. I've hurt his feelings. But right now, in this moment, I don't care.

"I'm feeling out of my depth here, Meredith. I need some help. Your arms... that's recent. And if I don't follow the protocol, I might not be able to see you anymore."

As angry as I am with Tom, the thought of never seeing him again makes me feel sick. Like he's my lover and I've caught him cheating on me.

"You're cheating on me," I tell him.

"What? What are you talking about?"

"You're cheating on me with social services."

He laughs, and it's a sad laugh, but it makes me even angrier. I squeeze the bridge of my nose until my eyes water.

"Meredith, the last thing I want to do is betray you. That's why we're having this conversation. I'm telling you what I need to do because I won't go behind your back. But that doesn't change the fact that I need to do it. I need to make sure I'm doing everything I can to help keep you safe."

"I'm perfectly safe."

"I'm not sure that you are."

"Tom, if I was going to kill myself, I'd have done it by now."

"Are you telling me that you won't harm yourself again?"

"Yes."

"I don't believe you, Meredith. And that's the problem."

"Tom, don't make me beg," I beg.

"Look, they might not even turn up. They might just call you. They're overworked, right? Would that be OK? Could you speak to them on the phone?"

"What good would that do?"

"Help me out here, Meredith. I'm trying."

"I was happy before you came along. You've ruined everything."

"I don't think you mean that. Any of it."

"I was fine without you," I mutter.

"Your arms don't look fine."

His words are like a slap. I take a deep breath.

"Meredith, I'm sorry. That was out of order."

"Save it. Go and call your friends at social services. I don't care." I end the call and hold the button on the side of my phone until the screen goes dark, gripping it until my fingers start to ache. If social services call, they can leave me a message.

2015

Sadie was there, but she was in the kitchen, pretending to be busy. I was in the living room, staring at my books. I'd seen pretty pictures online of people's color-coordinated book-shelves. I fancied doing it too, but from what I could see there were a few colors I was short on. I needed more green and purple books, and how would I even go about getting those? Who phoned a bookshop and asked them to send out a selection of books with green and purple spines? If they didn't already think I was crazy, they would after that.

"I'll get it," Sadie yelled when the bell rang, as if there was any chance I'd go to the door. I was hardly going to run away—I hadn't stepped foot outside my house for four weeks.

I was still counting green and purple books when a woman came into the room. "Hi, Meredith, I'm Amelia," she said in a chirpy voice. I glanced at her. She had a cheerful face to go with the voice—rosy cheeks and eyeliner and bouncy curls. I couldn't work out if she was twenty-five or forty-five; she was one of those people who looked the same their entire lives.

"This is a lovely room," Amelia said. "Let me just sort myself out, then we can have a chat." I watched her take off her scarf and her jacket, blow her nose, and rummage in her bag—a soft, slouchy briefcase-type thing in olive green—for a note-book and pen. I heard the pen click and tugged the sleeves of my top farther down my hands until only my fingers were peeking out.

"Meredith, I don't want you to be nervous or scared about

this." Amelia looked at me intently. "It really is just a chat to help us figure out how we can help you."

I nodded, because it's what she wanted me to do.

An hour later, Amelia said goodbye. I'd answered a million questions—most of them truthfully—and I was exhausted. I'd told her that I hadn't stopped taking my antidepressants and I definitely wouldn't do that without speaking to my doctor first. I told her that my boss had given me another few weeks off work and, no, it wasn't stressing me out at all. I told her that I'd leave my house soon, as soon as I was ready, but I just wasn't there yet. I told her that I had a strong support network, although I didn't mention that the entirety of it was currently in my kitchen. I told her that I hadn't really meant to harm myself and I had no intention of doing it again and, yes, I would call the Samaritans if I had suicidal thoughts and I was going to read all the information she'd given me and think about therapy and maybe even an online support group because, yes, I knew I wasn't alone.

A few minutes after I heard the welcome sound of the front door clicking shut, Sadie brought me a cup of tea and a packet of cookies I didn't remember buying. Things kept appearing in my kitchen—every time I opened the fridge, I wasn't sure what I was going to find.

"You've survived," she said. "Was it awful?"

"Not really. I don't think I'll be in a straitjacket anytime soon."

Sadie smiled but it was a sympathy smile. I looked away and drank my tea.

"I can stay over. The kids are at my mum's."

"I'm fine. Honestly. I'd rather be alone."

"You're like Greta Garbo. 'I vont to be alone...'"

"She didn't actually say that, you know. Well, she did in the movie…in *Grand Hotel*. But in real life she said, 'I want to be let alone.' There's a big difference."

"I stand corrected. Do you want to be let alone?"

"*Yes, please,*" I said to her in my most dramatic movie-star voice, looking at her over my mug. We both laughed.

"OK, Garbo. I'll call you in the morning? Let me know if you need anything, though. Tea, biscuits, black-and-white movies…"

Tears sprang to my eyes. I thought about asking her to stay, then changed my mind. Before I could say anything, she grabbed me and pulled me tight against her. I rested my head on her shoulder and looped my arms round her waist. The sleeves of my top had ridden up, and I could see that the bandages Sadie had carefully changed only yesterday were already a little grubby.

Day 1,344

Sunday, March 24, 2019

Fred is still missing.

Sadie arrives just as the afternoon is slipping into evening. Time is going so slowly I feel like it's going backward. I barely look at the clock as it is, relying on the position of the sun to inform my scant routine. If it's high in the sky, I should have brushed my teeth by now. If it's teasing the roof of the red-brick house behind mine, it's well past dinnertime. If it's starting its ascent on the left of my kitchen-window view, I've either stayed up too late or woken too early.

I do know that I haven't seen Fred for three days. That my face has taken on angles it didn't used to have and that no amount of food will fill the gap, so there's no point trying. I've taken the week off work and told my clients I have the flu.

I'm not sure I have the energy to deal with Sadie, but it would probably require slightly more effort to cancel her and deal with the fallout. So I'm ready. I've raised the blinds, I've returned my duvet and pillow to my bedroom, I've scrubbed the mugs congregating in the sink. The effort required to wash my hair is beyond me, but I sit in a hot bath until my face flushes pink, then put on a clean sweater and jeans.

I shouldn't have bothered.

"You look lousy," Sadie says.

"I know. I miss Fred." I burst into tears.

"Oh, sweetheart." She drops her bag and pulls me toward her. I let her hold me, breathe in her familiar scent. A faint biscuity trace of fake tan. The sweet chocolate notes of the Thierry Mugler perfume she's worn since we were teenagers. In all the years I've known her, Sadie hasn't changed. Meanwhile, I've changed so much I don't recognize myself.

"He'll be back; I know he will." She whispers the words into my ear and squeezes me tightly. "Sit down. I'll look after you."

I watch Sadie as she moves around my kitchen, looking in the wrong places for everything.

"I rearranged," I say weakly.

"It's better." She finds the mugs and holds two in the air triumphantly. "I'm making you a cup of sweet tea. None of that wishy-washy herbal nonsense."

I roll my eyes at her back but let myself smile.

"Do you remember how grown-up we thought we were, when we started drinking tea? Grab my bag, will you? I brought treats." She heads to the living room, a mug in each hand. "Four teabags in one pot."

She winks at me as we sit on the couch.

I laugh for the first time in days. "I thought everybody needed their own teabag."

"And we let them sit in the pot for so long. It was as bitter as hell." Sadie rummaged in her bag and pulled out a pack of cookies and a box of muffins. "Dig in. Let's get some meat back on your bones, Maggs."

I break off a piece of cookie. "What else do you remember about being a teenager?"

"A bad perm and terrible eyebrows. Remember how thin we plucked them? It's a miracle we have any left."

"I didn't have a perm. But I loved those temporary colors, the ones that washed out after a week."

"Ooh, yes! I never knew what color you were going to be on a Saturday night. The purple...that was a winner."

"Mama hated it. That's partly why I did it. A mini rebellion every Saturday morning."

We eat, drink tea, and talk about how bad our hair was.

"How are the kids? And Colin?" Now that I've settled into Sadie's company, I don't want to lose the momentum. Hearing about her cute, funny kids and her perfect boyfriend isn't going to make me feel envious or solitary right now. It's the perfect distraction, a glimpse of normal life to help keep me on an even keel. Plus, the more she talks, the less I have to.

"The kids are great. Steve's taking them to Center Parcs this week. Center Parcs! He can hardly cope at soft play for an hour, so I don't know how he expects to survive five days at Center Parcs. They'll be in a right state when they come back to me after mainlining sugar for a hundred and twenty hours, but whatever."

I take another bite of cookie and lean against the back of the couch, listening to Sadie talk about how she's willing to give Steve more time with the kids—just this once—because she knows the kids will love it and—let's be honest—it gives her some time to herself, even though she's working every day and doesn't have anything exciting planned in the evenings and definitely not with Colin because he's working away in bloody Blackpool with his stupid bloody brother, and I'm listening and nodding and making appropriate noises until I can't keep my eyes open and I'm vaguely aware of Sadie lifting my feet onto the couch and covering me with a blanket and kissing me on the forehead and a door, somewhere, softly closing.

When I wake up, the sun is high in the sky and I have no idea what day it is.

According to scientists—or the internet, at least—owning a cat yields multiple health benefits, like lowering the risk of heart disease, improving sleep, and reducing anxiety and stress.

I don't know about any of that, although I do find it comforting to have Fred lying at the foot of my bed, and running my hand down his back always makes my breath a little steadier. But it's the little things I miss about him. I remember Auntie Linda telling me that what she missed most about her husband were the things that made no sense to anyone else. How he started on the back page of the newspaper and read to the front. How he separated his food on his plate so his peas weren't touching his mashed potato. How he never, in twenty years of marriage, passed a pair of magpies without saying "two for joy."

I miss the way Fred lies on top of the washing machine when it's on a spin cycle. The way he pushes a Q-tip around the floor with his nose. The way he stares at me whenever I eat soup. I don't have a husband of twenty years and probably never will. Fred may well be the love of my life.

2016

I'd been expecting Sadie and pizza, but the noise at my front door definitely didn't sound like her. I opened it cautiously. She was wearing a big smile and holding a box, and I didn't think it had pizza in it. Pizza doesn't purr.

I stepped aside and let her in and she didn't waste any time, setting the box down on the floor of my hall and lifting the lid with a flourish. The furry creature looked at me with large gold eyes. I stared back at it.

"Sadie..."

"Wait—hear me out. He's only six months old. He's neutered, and he's an absolute dream. The folks at the animal shelter said cats like this don't come along too often. Look at him—he's pure ginger!"

"I can see that. But I don't want a cat. Ginger or otherwise."

"You'll want this one, sweetheart. Watch." She scooped him out of the box with one hand, his tiny body snuggling neatly in her palm. His legs and tail dangled aimlessly. He was still looking at me. He might have been asking for help.

I blinked. "How did you...? What...?"

"I had my name on a waiting list at the shelter." Sadie put the cat on the wooden floor and he finally broke eye contact to look down at his paws, inspecting the new surface. Then he sat down, yawning widely.

"So you want a cat?"

"Well, I did. I thought it might be nice to have a pet. For James, you know? And cats are so much easier than dogs. More independent, cleaner, no need to walk them. But then... well, I'm pregnant."

"You're what?"

She shrugged. "I'm pregnant. So I can't get a cat. Newborn baby and all that. Can't have a cat jumping into the stroller, rolling around in the crib."

"Sadie, how long have you known?" I grabbed her arms and pulled her toward me. "Are you happy?" She'd been talking about leaving Steve-who-can't-keep-it-in-his-pants since James was a newborn.

She let me hug her—briefly—before she wriggled away, as she does.

"Only a week. I wanted to tell you face-to-face. So here I am, with my face."

"And a cat," I said pointedly.

"And a cat! And yes, of course I'm happy. Nothing cuter than a baby. Except maybe a kitten?" She looked at me from under her lashes.

"Don't try to turn the charm on me, Sadie Jess," I told her, but I was smiling.

"Stick the kettle on, will you? I'll just grab Ginger's bits and pieces from the car and get him settled into his new home."

I watched her skip down my garden path toward her battered blue car. "I'm not calling him Ginger!"

The cat stretched out on the floor, pushed a paw against my foot.

"And I'm not promising anything," I whispered at him.

He closed his eyes.

I had no idea cats needed so much stuff. A litter tray. ("He could be an outdoor cat, of course," Sadie said. "But you don't want to be worrying about him if he stays out all night.") Some kind of squishy tartan thing she claimed was a bed. A box of medicines that are apparently essential for optimal feline health.

A tiny brush and comb. And dozens of shiny pouches of cat food. ("Enough to last at least a month," she said, stuffing them into my cupboard.) Turkey, trout, duck, game, tuna.

"The only thing he doesn't have is a cat tree."

"A cat tree? What the…"

"I'll show you. You won't believe what you can get online." She pulled her phone out of her back pocket and started tapping the screen.

"Sadie…" I took her hand. "Enough about Ging—the cat. Talk to me. What's going on? What's Steve saying about the baby?"

"I told him it wasn't his. I was joking obviously. Just wanted to see what he'd say."

"And?" It had been a while since I'd been in a relationship, but I didn't think this was how things were supposed to go.

"He laughed at me." Sadie sipped her tea and watched the cat pad around the living room, sniffing things. "He laughed at me because he's an asshole and he doesn't think another man would look twice at me."

"He is an asshole," I agreed. "You don't have to stay with him, just because you're pregnant."

"I know. But I can only think about one thing at a time. And I don't want to be a homeless pregnant single mum."

"At least you're not a sad old cat lady."

We both laughed at the same time.

"You're the new, young, hot face of old cat lady-ness. Does that mean you're keeping him?"

"I don't think I have much choice, do I?" I nodded at the cat, who was now curled up on the purple chair in the living room. My favorite spot. I was clearly going to have to share.

"You won't regret it, Mer."

I looked at her. "What if he needs to go to the vet?"

"That's where Auntie Sadie comes in. Don't worry, sweetheart. We've got this."

I watched my best friend of twenty-five years walk to her car, a spring in her step despite the weight I knew was bearing on her shoulders. Nobody else ever saw it but me. She'd go back to her asshole boyfriend and sweet toddler, and I'd try to make friends with a ginger cat. I waved as she drove away; she blew me a kiss.

I was still standing at the front door when I felt a softness against my ankles. The cat pressed harder against my leg, and I could feel the vibration of his purr. He didn't seem interested in going outside. That, at least, we had in common. I closed the door firmly and we walked, together, back into the living room, where we both curled up on the purple chair and kept each other warm.

Day 1,347

I'm chopping vegetables when I hear the scratching. It's so faint the radio would have drowned it out, but I'm not in the mood for background noise tonight, even the classical stuff that's supposed to be relaxing.

So I hear him right away, and I drop my knife and my carrot, and I turn round slowly because I think it really is too good to be true. But he's there; he's definitely there. He's skinnier than he was the last time I saw him but it's Fred and he's looking right at me, impatient as ever, waiting for me to let him in.

He eats an entire bowl of cooked chicken, makes a figure eight round my legs a dozen times, then curls up in the corner of the couch and promptly falls asleep. I stare at him for a while, wondering where he's been. I stroke him, aware of his prominent ribs under my hand, but he doesn't seem to have come to any harm. Both eyes and ears intact, no obvious injuries. Maybe he's more streetwise than I thought.

I call Tom, the first and the last person I want to talk to.

"He's back."

"Oh, I'm so glad. Meredith, you have no idea." Except I do—I can hear the relief in his voice. "How is he doing? All in one piece?"

"He seems to be. He's in a chicken-induced coma."

Tom laughs. "Thanks for letting me know. I've been thinking about him. Well…about you mainly."

"I'm OK. I've been through worse."

"I know you have. Of course you have. But still—it's Fred."

"Yes, it's Fred. And he's back. No more sunbathing on the concrete."

"Indeed."

"Anyway, I wanted to let you know. Thanks for looking. And for the posters and...everything. Thanks for caring."

"I do care."

"I know."

"Meredith..."

"Yes?"

"Have social services been in touch?"

"You called them?"

"Well...yes. I told you I was going to."

"Goodbye, Tom."

"Wait...I'll see you tomorrow?"

"Let's leave it this week, Tom."

Day 1,352

Monday, April 1, 2019

It slips through my letter box: gray and glossy, my full name on the front in cursive script. My breath catches in my throat. I know what's inside.

Now that it's here, I'm wondering whether I want it after all.

I read *Celeste is 30!* in bold sparkly letters along the top of the card. I run my fingers across them and feel the glitter scratch the surface of my skin. The necessary time and place details are followed by *No gifts please! But if you'd like to make a donation to Rape Crisis Scotland on my behalf, that would be amazing.*

Love, Celeste is handwritten in the bottom right corner.

I hold the card in my hands and look at it for a while, before using a shamrock magnet Sadie and the kids brought me back from Dublin to fix it to the front of my fridge, next to Tom's Holding Hands leaflet. I look at it, then I slip it out from under the shamrock and slide it over the leaflet. I've looked at those faces for long enough.

How can I possibly tell Celeste I can't go? I have no plausible excuse. It needs to be the truth. I mindlessly eat a raisin from the jar on the kitchen table, then dial her number before I can talk myself out of it.

"Meredith, what a lovely surprise!" Her voice is like sunshine. I feel like a dark cloud, about to unleash a rain shower on her morning.

"Hi! Thanks for the invitation." I try to sound happy and carefree.

"Oh, you got it? Amazing! You know, I'm quite looking forward to it now. I'm so glad you'll be there to celebrate with me, Meredith."

I close my eyes and press the phone against my ear. *Celeste, I can't come to your party. I'm so sorry.* But even though it's the truth, the words sound false in my mind, and I can't make them a reality.

"Me too," I say instead.

"Can I tell you something?"

"Of course." I sit on my window seat, look at Jacob's cherry blossoms, still holding firm. It's a relief to let Celeste take the reins of the conversation. Unknowingly, she's momentarily let me off the hook.

"I haven't been out at night since the assault. I'm just...a little scared, I guess. I mean, I'd never go out on my own, or anything. Not now. But it's still daunting...you know?"

"Absolutely," I tell her.

"The girls in the salon go out every Saturday night straight from work, for dinner and drinks. I never go with them anymore. The thought of it makes me feel so anxious."

"Celeste, I completely understand." *More than you can imagine.*

"I knew you would, Mer."

"Don't be too hard on yourself. Just take it at your own pace. You'll get there, I promise."

"At this rate my party will be my first night out in six months."

"Well, why not? You'll be surrounded by people who care about you, people you know you can trust."

"You're absolutely right, Mer. You're a superstar, you know that?"

I'm the opposite of a superstar, I want to say. *I might lose Tom, because he knows the truth, and I might lose you, because I can't tell you the truth.* Instead, I make an excuse about having to get scones out of the oven and spend the next ten minutes rubbing my fingers against those glittery letters.

Day 1,354

I've been searching for a piece of red for ten minutes when the doorbell rings. I'm trying a new kind of jigsaw—a departure from my usual landmarks and artworks. It's very modern, very abstract—basically just a swirling mass of colors—and very, very hard.

Sadie knows by now not to turn up unannounced, and I haven't ordered anything online that requires a signature. I always make a note of that on the chalkboard in the kitchen, so I'm mentally prepared for the small talk. Today's not a grocery delivery day. I quickly go through the options in my mind, pausing in the hallway, waiting to see if they go away. It might be Tom—I texted him last night to tell him to stay away this week too. I tell myself it's a Jehovah's Witness or someone trying to sell double glazing. That I can handle.

"Miss Maggs? Can you hear me?" She has an English accent and sounds official. I know then that the day I've been dreading is here.

"Who is it?" I try to make my voice sound more assured than I feel.

"Miss Maggs, hello. My name is Sophie Bamford. I'm from social services. Could I come in and have a chat with you, please?"

Sophie Bamford is the fifth social worker to visit me in three years. There was Amelia, in the beginning, then Theo, who came twice, but he was new and way out of his depth and ended up being signed off with stress. I hope it wasn't just from seeing me—we had quite a nice cup of tea and a chat and we got on quite well, I think. I can't remember who came next, but Colette (or maybe Colleen) turned up about a year ago, and she didn't have the best bedside manner. She said "hmmm" a lot when I answered her questions, which made me feel like she didn't quite believe what I was saying. A month after Colette/Colleen I got a letter saying they were going to close my file, with a list of numbers to call if I ever needed help. I used it to test my new mini paper shredder.

"It's not convenient right now. Could you come back next week? I wasn't expecting you."

"I'm sorry about that, Miss Maggs. I understand your... situation. Please will you just open the door, and we can chat properly?"

I get the feeling that Sophie Bamford isn't going to go anywhere. I take a deep breath and walk a few steps closer to the door. Fred appears at my side and wraps his tail round my ankles. I scoop him up and hold him close. He settles into my body and lets me cuddle him. In many ways he's the most uncatlike cat ever.

"Someone has raised a concern, Miss Maggs. I'm just here to make sure you're OK. But I need to see you and speak to you face-to-face to do that. Please can you—?"

"I'm absolutely fine."

"You don't sound absolutely fine, Miss Maggs. You sound a little... agitated."

"Of course I'm agitated. I was having a nice morning and now you're here making demands of me. Is it a crime to be agitated?"

"Absolutely not." Her voice is softer. "I'm sorry. I promise I'm just here to make sure you're OK. Mr. McDermott is concerned that—"

"Mr. McDermott doesn't know what he's talking about."

"Miss Maggs, I'm sure you can understand why I don't want to have this conversation on your doorstep."

I take the chain off the door and yank it open. Sophie Bamford is short, barely up to my shoulder. She has a neat brown bob, a striped scarf round her neck, and glasses that remind me of Harry Potter. I don't care that she's here, that she's going to sit in my kitchen and ask me all sorts of invasive questions. I've been here before, and I can go through the motions again. I don't care about any of that.

What I care about, more than I've cared about anything for a long time, is the fact that my friend Tom has betrayed me.

I'll give Sophie Bamford her due; she's certainly prepared. She seems to have memorized everything there is to know about me—all the bad stuff, at least—and rarely has to look at my file. She must be new. She's far too keen.

She's also very thorough in her questioning. I've always found this kind of thing more bearable if I turn it into a game. I'm not going to get any prizes for answering correctly—beyond my freedom, of course—so I pretend I'm on the clock. No pauses, no "um" or "ah." I answer as quickly as I can. Next. Next. *Next.* I give myself extra points for maintaining eye contact with my interrogator. It's a little difficult, because she's looking down at her notebook a lot. Her handwriting is large, with low loops on her "g's" and "y's." I expected her writing to be small and neat, like her.

I can make out a few of the words from the other side of the table—"risk," "coherent," "schedule"—but I don't want her to catch me staring at her notes. I'll find out what her assessment of me is at some point anyway. I know my rights.

As always, the best is saved for last.

"Meredith, have you tried to harm yourself recently?"

"No," I lie. Her use of my first name doesn't fool me. We're not friends.

"Mr. McDermott believed he saw recent evidence of self-harm during his last visit with you. He was concerned enough to make a referral to our department. Do you remember the visit in question? It was on the…"—she flicks through her paperwork—"…twenty-first of March."

"I remember."

"Do you remember telling Mr. McDermott something that might have caused him concern?"

"No."

Sophie Bamford looks at me through her little round glasses. I can't read her expression. She should be a detective, not a social worker. "Are you sure, Meredith?"

"Positive. Thanks for your concern, but I'm fine. Really. No plans to kill myself anytime soon."

She raises her eyebrow; it forms a neat arch while the other one stays perfectly straight. I think about telling her that only about a third of people have the ability to raise one eyebrow, but I don't know how she'd take it.

"Sorry," I say. "That was a bad joke. I have no plans to kill myself. Ever."

"Right," she says finally. "Thanks for your time, Meredith. You know where we are if you need us."

I nod and watch her button up her coat, wrap her striped scarf round her neck, place her paperwork neatly back into the file, and snap her briefcase closed. She pauses and looks at me before she leaves the kitchen.

"What's life like for you, Meredith?"

I don't know why she bothers. I'm not about to spill my guts to her just because her briefcase is closed and her scarf is on. There's no off the record with these people.

"Life is great, Sophie."

Day 1,362

Thursday, April 11, 2019

The purple "T" on the calendar—taking up today's entire square, because what else would happen today that's worthy of a calendar mention?—makes me feel nervous. For the first time since our last disastrous meeting I haven't told Tom not to come. It's not because I want to see him, just that I haven't had the energy to deal with any life admin. Apathy has settled over me like a veil, but I can still feel the pressure of my hurt and anger. I've heard nothing else from Sophie Bamford, but I can't shake off the sense of betrayal. Before Tom came into my life, I was doing just fine. I spent Thursday mornings with my sewing machine or my food processor, not with an opinionated man who seems to think it's his calling to save me.

It's possible that I'm still angry. My throat feels like it closes over every time I try to swallow my granola, and my oat milk tastes funny. I abandon my half-eaten breakfast in the sink. I don't know what to do with myself and the noise in my head, so I go back to bed, even though Tom might be here in half an hour.

I'm way behind schedule this morning. Getting out of bed has turned into an arduous task. I haven't exercised for five days, and the apples in the fruit bowl are turning brown.

I lie on my bed and pick up my book. I don't plan to sleep, but it's inevitable. I read barely a page before my eyelids start to feel heavy.

When I wake up, Fred is stretched across my feet and my head aches. I'm overwhelmed by a sense of unease. Of all the rooms in my house, my bedroom is my favorite. I've worked really hard to create a calm, relaxing space. A sanctuary. No busy prints, no bright colors, no clutter. I took weeks to plan every detail, from the off-white floorboards to the family of pillar candles in wrought-iron lanterns in the corner of the room. I painted the walls a soft blue and hung clusters of my favorite prints. I catch the eye of Chaïm Soutine's *Woman with Arms Folded*. What is her impenetrable gaze telling me today?

Get your act together.

I turn away from her and squeeze my eyes shut. Today, even the muted shades and soft light grate my nerves.

At first I think the pounding is inside my head. It feels like a tiny person is beating against my skull with angry fists. As I come to, I realize there's nobody inside my head, but there's definitely someone banging on my front door.

Tom.

I nudge Fred, who seems oblivious to the banging, off my feet and slide my legs from the bed. My whole body aches, like it does when you get over the initial shock of a beating. The soles of my feet feel strange and heavy on the floor. I crouch gingerly and grab my slippers from beneath the bed.

By the time I'm making shuffling old-lady movements down the stairs, the banging has stopped. I pause, gripping the banister, and contemplate turning round and retracing my steps. Then it starts again, and I hear his voice for the first time.

"Meredith, can you hear me? Please let me know you're OK."

There's something else underpinning his words. Something I can't turn my back on. I open my mouth, but I have no voice. I haven't spoken for more than a week. I've been screening my calls, waiting an appropriate number of minutes (not so few that it seems suspicious, not so many that they begin to worry and call the police or something stupid like that) before sending an apology text with a conversation starter. It works in my favor that these days it's normal for relationships to be kept alive by a keypad.

I stand on the safe side of the door and squint into the spyhole. Tom's standing close to the door, so his head looks enormous, too big for the rest of his body. I pull back and take a deep breath. I've never figured out if my spyhole is a two-way thing. I'm not comfortable with being watched at the best of times, and I certainly don't want Tom to see me like this, in my grubby pajamas with furry teeth and matted hair.

"Meredith? Please just let me know you're OK. I'm worried about you."

I open my mouth, experiment with sound. Whatever I'm trying to say, it comes out like a croak. I clear my throat, swallow hard.

I knock on my side of the door.

"Meredith, thank God! Are you OK?"

I knock again.

"OK, OK, I hear you. Jesus. Are you sure you're all right? Knock once for yes, twice for no."

Knock.

"Right. That's good. Have you eaten today?"

I think of my bowl of granola in the sink. It will be soggy by now. *Knock.*

"Have you taken your medication?"

Knock. Knock.

"Did you take it yesterday?"

Knock.

"OK. OK. Do you think you can open the door?"

Knock. Knock.

"OK. That's OK, Meredith."

I lean my head against the door and wonder if I knock three times, he'll know it means "I'm sorry."

"Listen, I have an idea. I'm going to go and get a coffee, stretch my legs. Will you go and take your medication and drink a glass of water?"

Knock.

"Then maybe we can chat? Do you think you might be able to do that? Or I'll chat, and you can listen? You know I like the sound of my own voice."

Despite myself, despite everything, I smile. *Knock.*

By the time Tom gets back I've swallowed my pill, downed a glass of water, and resumed my position on the floor, on the safe side of the front door. I feel guilty that Tom has had to go and buy a takeout coffee, so I've wrapped a couple of bourbon biscuits in tinfoil. I'll pass them through the letter box when he gets back.

"Meredith? Are you there?" There's no banging this time, just a polite knock.

I find my voice, although it's still a little croaky. "Hi, Tom. I'm here."

"Great. It's so good to hear your voice."

"I've got something for you." I hold the letter box open, push the biscuits through.

Tom laughs. "Amazing. Thank you, Meredith. I'm going to sit right here on your doorstep and dunk my biscuits in my coffee."

"Just watch they don't fall in."

He laughs again. "I'll try."

I shuffle my body round so my back is against the door. I'm probably sitting just as close to Tom as I normally do on my couch. Maybe even closer. We just happen to have a door between us this time.

"I'm sorry, Tom. I should be making you coffee. You should be drinking it in my kitchen. I'm just not feeling like visitors right now."

"Meredith, I get it. Really. I have days like that too."

"Really?"

"For sure. Doesn't everyone?"

I think about it. I'm not convinced everyone has days when they can only talk to their friends through a closed door, when they push biscuits wrapped in tinfoil through a letter box instead of presenting them on a nice plate. I don't really believe that everyone doesn't speak for an entire week or hobbles around their house like a person twice their age. But I appreciate his efforts to make me feel less of a nutcase.

"What have you been up to, Tom?" I don't want to talk about myself; I want him to tell me something that will take me out of this hallway, out of this house, out of my head.

Like when Fiona and I were kids and I asked her to tell me a story when my thoughts kept me awake at night. Neither of us wanted to hear fairy stories, so she told me stories about kids at our school, kids who skipped in the playground and always had treats in their lunchboxes and whose parents were in the PTA.

Maybe the stories weren't entirely true, but I didn't care. They were enough to take me somewhere else.

"Well, I've been working a lot. But you don't want to hear about office politics and IT issues. Hey, here's something cool. Do you remember Sunday night—that amazing sunset?"

I don't say anything. I can't bring myself to tell him that I don't remember the amazing sunset or any sunset because I've barely looked out of my windows for days.

"I was walking back from the gym, over the bridge, just as the sun was going down. It stopped me in my tracks. This huge streak of red across the sky. It reminded me of a poem—'Out of the Sunset's Red,' by William Stanley Braithwaite. Do you know it?"

"I don't," I admit.

"I'll send you a copy. Anyway, the sunset wasn't even the best part. I walked past this couple—they were seventy, maybe older—holding hands, just watching the sun go down. It was—I don't know—it was a moment. I've been thinking about that couple all week. It's made me realize how much I want that. I want to be standing on a bridge when I'm seventy, hand in hand with someone I love, watching the sun go down. Someone to enjoy those little things with."

My eyes are closed. I'm on the bridge too, wrapped up warm. I see the old couple and notice their interlaced fingers. I feel the love radiating from them.

"Well, I guess you have to put yourself out there. When did you last go on a date?"

"It's been a long time. I don't have much luck with dating apps. All that swipe-left-or-swipe-right business feels kind of brutal to me."

"You're an old-fashioned sort, Tom McDermott."

"I suppose I am, Meredith Maggs. I don't suppose you have any more cookies, do you? They went down a treat."

Day 1,363

Friday, April 12, 2019

Fee calls just as I'm finishing work and wondering what to do with the rest of my evening. I feel weirdly unsettled, like I've forgotten to do something important. I wonder if it's the silent, sparkly pressure of Celeste's party invitation stuck to the front of my fridge.

"Are you OK?" she asks.

"Yeah," I say. "I think so."

"Mer, I've been thinking about what it was like when we were kids. How we dealt with stuff. How you dealt with stuff. I didn't know how to help you. I told Mama once."

I know the answer, but I ask it anyway. "What did she say?"

"That you were doing it for attention. That if I told anyone else, you'd be taken away from us. I didn't know what to do, Mer. I'm sorry."

"I'm so sick of you apologizing to me."

"Me too." She laughs.

"I want to stop," I say again. "I'm going to tell my therapist about it. I'm going to tell her everything."

"Yes, do that. Also, I have an idea," Fee says. "If you ever feel like you're going to do it…you want to do it…text me, and I'll call you right away. If I'm at work, I'll tell them it's a family emergency. This is what we created our code word for, Mer."

"I guess you're right," I say. "OK."

"I'm here for you, little sister."

1990

We were baking, because we were bored and trying to stay out of Mama's way. Fee was being kind, letting me mash the butter and icing sugar together with a fork, the part we both liked best.

"We should have a code word," she said as she scraped eggshells into the garbage.

"What?" I was only half listening to her, enjoying the way the fork slid through the butter. I made a criss-cross pattern, then long slices, then pierced it over and over.

"A code word. You know, like the Secret Service."

"What do we need a code word for?" I switched to a wooden spoon and gave my mixture a smooth surface again.

"Emergencies." Fee rummaged in the cupboard and pushed the tub of cocoa powder across the worktop to me. "Five tablespoons, no more."

"I know," I huffed. "We've made this cake a million times. What are you going on about anyway? What sort of emergencies would we need a code word for?"

"Serious ones."

"Aren't all emergencies serious?"

She grabbed the cocoa powder from me and started adding it to my mixture. "You'll have a serious emergency in a minute if you don't stop being cheeky."

"I'm allowed to be cheeky to you," I told her. "You're not the boss of me."

She raised her eyebrows. "You're getting brave, little sister. I've taught you well."

We worked in silence for a few minutes, pouring the chocolate we melted earlier over the butter and sugar and cocoa powder, adding a splash of milk, then mixing and mixing until it was smooth.

"Chocolate cake," I said as we took turns to spread the buttercream on the first of our sponge layers.

"Yes, Meredith—this is chocolate cake," Fiona mocked me.

"No—that can be our code word. Code *words*."

"That's rubbish. Every time I ask you if you want to bake a chocolate cake, you'll think I've got an emergency."

"No, I won't—I'm not stupid. I'll know the difference."

She picked up the second sponge layer and placed it carefully on top. I pressed it down a little, until the filling oozed out. We both ran a finger round it and licked off the gooey sweetness.

"OK," Fiona said. "Chocolate cake it is."

Day 1,370

Friday, April 19, 2019

I wake up on my fortieth birthday with a buzzing in my ears and Fred lying across my chest. I gently push him to one side of my body; he squeaks at me in irritation. "It's my birthday," I tell him, tickling his belly. He rolls away from me into a ball, nonplussed.

I realize that the buzzing is coming from my phone. "Happy birthday!" Sadie sings in a loud, weird whisper. I laugh. "Thanks. I'm still in bed."

"I know you are," she says. "I'm in your kitchen. Get your forty-year-old ass down here, Meredith Maggs. And make sure you're decent. I'm taking photos."

"What are you like?" I sit up and reach for my dressing gown at the end of the bed. "Do I have time for a shower?"

"Sorry, that'll have to wait. I'm really struggling to keep Matilda's fingers out of your cake."

A bedsheet stretches across my kitchen wall, with "Happy 40th Mer! We love you!" scrawled across it in bright pink letters. The ceiling has turned into a pink-and-gold balloon sky, and the biggest cake I've ever seen sits in the middle of the table, surrounded by cards and presents. I look at it all, then at Sadie's, James's, and Matilda's shiny, eager faces, and I burst into tears.

"Come here, you big softie." Sadie opens her arms and pulls me into their group. We hug for ages, then Matilda starts jumping up and down, and we all do the same, bouncing and laughing in our circle around the kitchen.

"Cake time!" James shouts.

"Yes, cake time," says Sadie. She leads me to the table. "I'll get the candles; start opening your presents. We only have an hour before I need to get these two to school and nursery—I'm on day shift today."

"I can't believe you've done this," I tell her. "You're the best."

"I know," she says, putting a cup of tea in front of me. "But you are too. And now you're forty! How do you feel?"

I shrug. "Thirty-eight?" I unwrap a beautiful soy wax candle in a ceramic pot, a pale blue cashmere sweater, a delicate silver chain bearing a tiny crescent-moon charm.

"And this." Sadie slides a large box toward me. "You might need these at some point. Hopefully." Her face is serious all of a sudden. "Go on," she says gently.

I take the paper off slowly and remove the lid from the box. They're shiny and solid, built to last for years, to withstand the toughest of terrains. And they have bright orange laces.

"Hiking boots," I say, running my fingertips over the warm, grainy surface. I look up at Sadie. "Thank you," I mouth, because I have a lump in my throat. She grins at me, and we clink our mugs of tea together.

After I blow my candles out to enthusiastic cheers and we eat huge slices of chocolate cake ("For the love of God, don't tell your teachers you had birthday cake for breakfast," Sadie mutters as she wipes the telltale smears from around the kids' mouths), I try my new boots on for size.

"They feel good," I tell Sadie. "I'll need to break them in, though, before I attempt Ben Nevis."

"Just you get stomping up and down that garden path," she tells me, giving me another hug before she inspects the kids' clothes for crumbs, then bundles them into their jackets. I stand at the front door in my new boots to wave them off.

I still have cards to open—a small pile that Sadie's left neatly at the end of the table. There's one from Tom, with an illustrated cat on the front wearing a party hat and a "40" badge, staring at a birthday cake with startled eyes. It makes me laugh.

Inside Celeste's card—it says, "You're 40 and Fabulous!" on the front—is a gift voucher for her salon. "Come for a pamper...you deserve it!"

I'll try, I think.

Auntie Linda's has an enormous vase of flowers and an even bigger "40" on the front. Her message—"Many happy returns, Meredith. I think of you often. Love Auntie Linda"—gives me a little belly flip that I don't quite know what to do with. I touch the glittery petals—they remind me of the eyeshadow Mama and Auntie Linda wore when they went out dancing in the eighties.

I haven't had a birthday card from Mama or Fee since I turned thirty-six, but I recognize their handwriting straightaway. Fee's script is small and neat, while Mama's capitals shout "MEREDITH!" at me from the front of the envelope. I reach for hers first, tearing it open before I change my mind. Her card has flowers on it too, but no "40," no glitter. Not even any words printed inside, apart from hers, underneath a ten-pound note: "Meredith, I hope you have a nice 40th birthday. Mama. (Treat yourself to something when you leave the house.)" I turn it over; it still has the price sticker on the back: 99p.

I make another cup of tea before I open Fee's card, trying to work out if I'm happy she's made the effort, beyond the daily text messages she's been sending. Sometimes I reply, sometimes I don't—it still feels awkward and strange. I canceled today's session with Diane, partly because I don't want to do CBT on my birthday, but also because I'm not sure I have the energy to update her on what's happened. That my world fell apart when my cat escaped. That I've alienated one of my only friends because he caught the smallest glimpse of the part of me I'm most ashamed of. That I've lost all motivation to open my front door, despite the progress we'd made.

I decide I can't spend my birthday being angry, and especially not in a room filled with pink and gold balloons and my very own handmade banner. So I open Fee's card. It's one of those personalized ones I see ads for all the time on television. The photograph on the front is one I haven't seen before. Fee and me as kids, blowing out birthday cake candles. We always used to do that—blow the candles out together. We didn't have parties, or balloons, or banners adorning the walls. But we always got a cake with candles, and the excitement was too much not to share.

You'll never be as old as me!!!

She used to say it to me all the time—showing off, relishing the year and a half of maturity and wisdom she had over me. At what point does it switch, and we wish we could turn the clock back instead of propel its hands forward?

Beneath the printed "HAPPY BIRTHDAY!" her words tell me "I miss you."

1993

I knew there was something wrong as soon as I set foot in the house. It was too quiet for a Sunday evening. Normally when I got back from the fish-and-chip shop Fee was clattering around in the kitchen, the radio blaring. Mama was either watching TV or getting ready to go out. But the kitchen door opened into emptiness and the silence from upstairs was heavy.

I ditched my jacket and backpack in the hall. As usual, my hands stank of fish and vinegar and my hair was stuck to my scalp after hours over the fryer with a stupid net over my head. I needed a shower before I could do anything else.

"You're late."

I jumped. She was sitting at the top of the stairs, smoking.

"We were busy. It's the summer holidays." I wasn't in the mood. "You'll get ash all over the carpet."

"Fuck the carpet. Where's your sister?"

I stared at her. "I've got no idea. I've been at work all day. Where's your daughter?"

"Did you bring me anything? I haven't eaten all day."

"You didn't ask for anything." I did get a free bag of fries, but I was so hungry I ate them on the walk back.

Ash was gathered perilously at the end of the cigarette. The slightest twitch of her hand, and it would disperse all over the stairs. I wanted to grab it and ram the butt up one of her nostrils. I definitely wasn't in the mood. "Do you really not know where Fiona is?"

"No, I really don't know where Fiona is," she snapped.

"I need to have a shower." I waited for her to move, but she didn't. I took a deep breath and pushed past her.

"You stink." Her words punched me from behind before I reached my bedroom door.

I looked at my sister's mess. Toast crusts on a plate and the dark dregs of coffee in a mug. The contents of her spotted makeup bag strewn across her unmade bed. A tangle of clothes discarded on the floor. All the bits and pieces I walked past and stepped over and regularly swept off my bed, moaning that they didn't belong there and why couldn't she ever keep her stuff on her own side of the room? A tightness started to spread in my chest. I wanted her back there, among the clutter. I wanted to nag her about it like I had that morning as I rushed to get to work on time.

I opened the wardrobe doors, letting my breath out when I saw her scruffy green sweater, her camouflage jacket with patches on the arms, her denim backpack. Wherever she'd gone, she hadn't gone far.

"What did you do?" I folded my arms over my crumpled T-shirt.

She was drinking red wine, watching television with the sound down low.

"What did you do?" I forced my voice to be louder—it didn't come naturally to me.

She looked at me out of the corner of her eye. "I did nothing. Your sister's just crazy. I thought you were the crazy one, but I'm not so sure now."

"You're a liar."

I ducked just in time, seconds before the wineglass smashed on the wall behind my head. "I'm not scared of you," I told her, and she laughed at me.

I slammed the front door behind me and walked quickly, with

no idea of where I was going. Round the block, along past the school, behind the shop, then I turned back and retraced my pointless steps. An hour later, I ended up at the park. It was empty, apart from someone in the distance, moving slowly on the swing. As soon as all the pieces fitted together—the poker-straight blonde hair, the slim thighs, the narrow shoulders, the jeans with rips at the knees—I ran.

She looked up, watched me race toward her. I waved, tried to do a comedy run to make her laugh, bringing my knees up as high as I could. She just looked at me. Her face looked different. It wasn't until I was a few feet away from her that I realized it was red and blotchy. She looked away.

I stopped right in front of her. "Fiona Maggs, what's going on?"

She shrugged. "Nothing much."

"It doesn't look like nothing much." I reached out for her hand. She took it, curling her fingers round mine, but stayed on the swing. We stood like that, not speaking, until she turned her blotchy face back toward me.

"Fee."

"Don't, Meredith. Just...don't."

"What are you doing here?"

"I don't know. I just needed a breather."

I'd never seen my sister so morose. She was the strong one. The brave one. The couldn't-care-less one. She wasn't the one to sit on a park swing on her own. That was the sort of thing I did.

"Did something happen?"

She shrugged.

"OK, something happened. You don't need to tell me if you don't want to. Just come home. Please. You've got toast crusts to clean up."

She laughed but said, "Not yet."

"OK." I looked around. "I'll sit over there. I'll wait for you."

I felt her watch me step onto a tiny kids' merry-go-round. It moved a little when I sat down, and I remembered the feeling I got when I was a kid and Fiona spun me round and round until I screamed for her to stop.

A few minutes later, she joined me. I shuffled over to make room for her.

We lay on our backs, letting our legs hang over the edge, and pushed our feet against the ground until we were spinning. Holding hands, we let ourselves feel dizzy.

"I'm sorry," she gasped out, when the merry-go-round finally slowed.

I clutched my stomach until it stopped churning. "What for?"

"For not being there when you got home. I'm your big sister. It's my job to look after you."

"No, it's not," I told her. "We look after each other."

We left the vast park behind and walked back to the small house, to our small lives. Wrapped in a comfortable silence, I watched our feet step in sync and felt my hands brush against hers as our arms swung between us. We reached our front door just as the sun set on the city.

Day 1,371

Saturday, April 20, 2019

I'm wearing my new boots from Sadie, the ones designed for hiking on muddy trails and clambering up hills. My feet feel safe, even if the rest of me is a little shaky. I go to the front door and take a deep breath before stepping outside. "I'm forty, and I'm wearing hiking boots," I tell myself firmly. "I can walk to the end of my garden path." Celeste's birthday party—now only six weeks away—looms large in my mind.

I see the fair-haired one first; she's on the inside of the pavement, closest to my window. She looks around twelve but might be younger. It's hard to tell these days. She's arm in arm with another girl—slightly smaller, she has darker hair. They walk in sync, the way people who know each other well do. The way sisters do.

I can still see them from my doorstep, their ponytails swinging, the arms that aren't linked hanging by their sides. Carefree. I wonder if people used to watch Fee and me walk down the street together and smile to themselves, thinking we didn't have a care in the world.

The two girls have disappeared. I take tentative steps down my path until I can see them again. The farther they go, the more I move toward the pavement. At the end of my path, I have a clear view of them until they disappear around the corner of the street. I decide that they are sisters, that they're walking back to a happy home.

I'm not sure how long I stand at the end of my path for. I

know I can't go any farther, but that's OK. I'm there long enough to watch an elderly woman I've never seen before inch past me. I'm looking at her, ready to smile and maybe exchange a few pleasantries, but she doesn't give me that chance. She's completely focused on her task, her eyes peering ahead through thick glasses, her depleted frame curving toward the ground.

I watch her make her long, laborious trek to a house a few doors along from mine, where she's swallowed up by a brown door that shuts with a slam. She was once a young girl too, and maybe her white hair was the color of sunshine and swung in a ponytail when she skipped down the street with her sister.

That evening, when I'm curled up on the couch with Fred, my new birthday candle filling the room with vanilla and ylang-ylang, I text my sister, because it feels like something I want to do.

I'm forty, but I'll never be as old as you, I write.

Day 1,372

Sunday, April 21, 2019

I travel in my dreams—to indeterminate foreign places, like vast oceans with colossal waves you'd never see on the Scottish coast. I'm fearless, running into them, watching the water swell over my head. But just as quickly I'm home, rinsing the salt off my body in my lime-green bathroom.

Last night, I could hear the waves crashing in the distance, but I was in a foul-smelling cave. I didn't have a torch, so I couldn't see anything. The backpack on my back was so heavy it scored thick welts across my bare shoulders. No matter how hard I tried, I couldn't take it off. Swaying under the weight of it, in the darkness, I tried not to breathe through my nose. The burden got too much, and just as I felt my knees buckle, a man's arms picked me up and carefully removed the backpack.

I woke up before I could see his face.

Day 1,377

I'm drinking a cup of tea at the bay window, killing time before I start work, when I see his head and shoulders moving past—much quicker than I'd expect them to, even for a ten-year-old. Then they disappear from sight. I bang my hand against the glass. When he doesn't reappear, I put down my tea and run to open the front door.

"Jacob, are you OK?"

He replies, but I can't make out what he says from behind the wall. I look around me. There's nobody else in sight. I take a deep breath and stuff my feet into my trainers. I went outside six days ago, so I can do it now.

I'm halfway down the path when he pops his head over the wall. "Hey, Meredith. How are you? Just fell off my skateboard there."

"Are you hurt?" I meet him at the end of the path.

"Nah. It's just a minor injury." He gestures to the blood trickling from his elbow.

I try not to smile. "You're a brave boy. How about I clean it up a bit, put a bandage on it?"

He considers my offer. "I think I'll be OK."

"You sure? Think a cookie might fix it?"

"Yeah, maybe. What kind?"

"Double chocolate chip."

He grins. "All right then."

"I'll be back in two minutes."

By the time I get back outside with the tin of cookies and my first-aid kit, he's sitting on my garden wall, inspecting his knees. "I've found more blood," he tells me.

"Well, it's a good thing I come with supplies." I pass him the tin. "Here, you take these. Let me know how they taste."

He munches while I wipe his elbow and knees. "Nice. Chewy."

"The right amount of chewy? Not too much?"

He thinks about it. "Maybe I should have another one, just to make sure."

"That sounds like a good idea." I rummage in the kit for a bandage. "So is this a new skateboard?"

"My cousin outgrew it," he tells me through a mouthful of cookie. "My mum will be raging. She told me to wear my knee-pads. But they're not cool at all."

"Well, they help to keep you safe." I gently press a bandage over the graze on his knee. "But like you say, they're only minor injuries. You'll be healed in no time."

"Thanks, Meredith. You're a good nurse." He jumps off the wall. "Want to see a trick?"

"Sure." I grab a cookie, sit on the wall like he had. I can't remember when I last sat on a wall, legs dangling, a sugary treat in my hand. Maybe never. I watch him bend his knees and jump, making one end of the board rise into the air.

"That's called an ollie," he says. "The pros jump really high. But I'm just a beginner, obviously."

"You'll be a pro in no time, Jacob."

He shrugs.

"Listen, I need to go in and start work. But...do you want to take the cookies? For you and your brother? I'll leave them here on the wall, until you're ready to go home?"

His eyes light up. "Yes, please. But my brother's not getting any. He's a pig. I'll just keep them under my bed."

I laugh. "Promise me you'll give them to your mum."

He rolls his eyes. "Promise."

"It was nice to see you, Jacob."

"You too, Meredith."

"Any more minor injuries, you know where I am."

"Yep."

I do need to start work. But I like sitting on the wall, my legs dangling. I stay a few more minutes, watching Jacob work his way up and down the street, practicing tricks with varying levels of success. He looks my way occasionally, and I give him a thumbs-up. I shuffle my body toward the edge of the wall, realize I can touch the pavement with my toes. In one move I could be standing on it, a surface no different from my own path. But I decide that today's not the day, not in front of Jacob, and I swing my legs back to the safe side of the wall. I go back into my house, leaving the tin of cookies behind me.

Day 1,385

I'm working on a particularly tricky section of sky above Ponte Vecchio, scanning the table for a piece that's just the right shade of blue with a touch of lilac, when the phone rings.

"Hello, angelface."

I take a deep breath. "Hello, Mama. How are you?"

"Well, I've been better. I've been sitting here thinking, where did it all go wrong? How in God's name did I end up like this? All alone on a Saturday night. If it wasn't for your sister, I'd have nobody. Nobody!"

I keep looking for my missing Italian sky.

"Did you hear me, Meredith?"

"Yes, Mama."

"Well, don't you care? Don't you give the tiniest shit about your poor mother?"

I sigh. "What would you like me to do about it, Mama?"

I hear her take a deep drag of a cigarette and loudly expel the smoke. I can picture her pursed lips, her fingertips yellow around too-long nails, her hair in a stiff peroxide helmet. She was a beautiful woman once—on the outside, at least.

"I don't expect you'll be paying me a visit anytime soon?"

"No, Mama. Sorry."

"Ha! Spare me your apologies. Just you stay locked up in your sad little house, Meredith, with your sad little puzzles and your sad little cat. Do you know how much shame you've brought to this family?"

No, but I'm sure you'll tell me all about it, I think. I feel wired, like I've just drunk four espressos. I close my eyes and try to visualize myself on the real Ponte Vecchio, marveling at the beauty of the sunlight hitting the waters of the Arno.

It doesn't work. My phone feels heavy in my hand. I sit it on the table next to my almost-finished jigsaw and press the speakerphone key.

"Thank God for your sister." My mother's voice is harsh and unwelcome in my kitchen. "If it wasn't for her, I don't think I'd even be here. I'd die of loneliness and nobody would know."

"Don't you see Auntie Linda?"

"She's not your auntie, you stupid girl. And no, I haven't seen her for months. She spends half her life in Spain now that she's in tow with that idiot Tony from the bookies."

"Good for her," I mutter. I can't help myself.

"Your sister was here yesterday actually. With Lucas."

The heat sweeps over my body like a wave. "With Lucas?"

"Yes, Meredith. With Lucas. Her husband, Lucas." Her voice is smug. She takes a drag. "Oh, didn't you know? They're back together. It was all a big misunderstanding." Faux sweetness coats her words. I'm familiar with her tricks, but they never fail to cut to my core.

"Right."

"It's great news, isn't it? I'm so happy for them. And proud. One of my daughters is in a relationship, holding down a job, making something of herself."

I can't work out if she's lying; I never could. I don't know what's worse: Fiona getting back with Lucas, or my mother finding such obvious pleasure in breaking the news, whether it's true or not. Pressure builds along my jaw, around my temples, between my eyes. The jigsaw pieces are out of focus.

"I have a job, Mama." I try to bring my focus back to what I know.

"Ah, yes…your little writing hobby. I keep forgetting. Won any awards recently?"

My silence riles her.

"Oh, for fuck's sake, Meredith! Can't you take a joke? I'm trying to lighten the mood here. You never did have a sense of humor, did you? Couldn't we both do with a laugh? Don't you think it's ridiculous, us both sitting alone on a Saturday night? We could be sitting together, talking about the good old days."

"Like the day Fiona's husband raped me in your kitchen, you mean?"

"You need to stop telling these tales, angelface."

"He *raped* me." My voice is shaking.

"Oh, Meredith. Why would you try to ruin his life?"

People often say, "I'm speechless," and then spew forth a torrent of words to convey how shocked/upset/excited they are. At this moment I have actually lost the ability to speak. I clench my fists, welcoming the sharp sensation of my nails digging into my palms. A brief distraction from the pain in my psyche.

My mother's voice continues, but the words don't make sense. I lift the phone from the table and hurl it across the room.

Day 1,386

I tell myself all day that Mama is lying, but I can't shake off the niggling doubt at the back of my mind. Because I desperately need to think about something else, I order a new outfit for Celeste's party, because it's my first party in years and that deserves something special. Scrolling through pages of dresses turns out to be a pretty good distraction, both from the niggling doubt and from the voice whispering in my ear, telling me it's completely preposterous to think for a second that I'll get to the party. *But I want to go*, I hiss back at it, as if wanting was all that mattered. *I want doesn't get*, Mama used to say.

I'm buying an outfit anyway. I decide against a dress and go for a jumpsuit, something I've never worn before but have seen on TV and the internet in various iterations.

My only concern is going to the toilet, but I'm sure I'll figure it out. Maybe Celeste can come with me and hold on to the sleeves to stop them from trailing on the floor. Are we at the point of squeezing into a toilet stall together yet? I think we might be after a few glasses of wine. Sadie and I used to do it all the time in various pubs around Glasgow. It saved us a few minutes of lining up and meant one of us could keep out intruders if the lock on the stall door was broken. They were always a laugh, those nights with Sadie in another lifetime.

I still haven't told Sadie about the party. It just feels like too much extra pressure. It'll be bad enough to let Celeste down if I don't make it without feeling like a disappointment to Sadie as well. Diane knows, but I pay her fifty pounds an hour for that honor now that my funded sessions have stopped. She questioned my decision not to tell my best friend the last time we spoke.

"Sadie is your strongest supporter," she pointed out. "I think she could help you with this in lots of different ways—whether you go or not. Maybe she could even go with you."

I nodded and changed the subject. Diane is good, but she doesn't understand everything. I haven't introduced Sadie to Celeste or Tom because I haven't quite figured out how to bring my before and after together in a way that doesn't bring me out in a cold sweat.

After I've ordered my jumpsuit, strappy sandals, and a cute little clutch bag, I dial Fee's number. She doesn't answer. I dial it eleven more times, like a stalker, and she still doesn't answer.

I've just put my book down and turned my bedside light off when my phone vibrates.

"Meredith." Her voice is a whisper. "I've been wanting to call you."

"Well, I wasn't stopping you," I say crossly.

"I know."

"Are you back with Lucas?"

"Meredith..."

"*Are you back with Lucas?*"

"No... not really."

"Not really? What the fuck does that mean? You either are or you're not. And if you are, this is the last conversation we'll ever have, I swear."

She doesn't say anything. I can hear some muffled background noise, someone else's voice.

"I need to go," she says. "I'll bring the chocolate cake over tomorrow."

The line goes dead. *Chocolate cake.*

I swallow my panic and turn on my bedside light. I call her back. It cuts straight to her voicemail, inviting me to leave a message.

My fingers fumble across the keypad: Is he hurting you?

I pace around the room for the next four minutes, until she replies: Not right now.

Where is he?
He's crashed out.
Fee, get out of there.
And go where?
Here. Come here.
Are you sure?
Of course I'm sure. Phone a taxi. Do it now. xx
OK. xx

Nobody has stayed overnight in my house for over a year, since the time Sadie drank too much gin and spent all night throwing up in the bathroom. I pull down the sofa bed in the room that could be a nursery or an office but has never progressed from a place to store random pieces of furniture. I open the window to let some air in, wipe dust from the windowsill with the sleeve of my pajama top. Fee doesn't care about stuff like that, but I do. I go downstairs, fill up the kettle, then sit on the window seat, my knees hugged to my chest, and wait.

The taxi's lights are bright as it pulls up outside my house. I don't wait for her to knock; I'm already holding the door open when she reaches the bottom of the garden path. She's got the hood of her jacket pulled up, even though it's not raining. When she's a few feet away from me, I can make out the shadows across one side of her face. The closer she gets, the more they take shape.

"Oh, Fee. What has he done to you?"

She doesn't say anything. I open my arms, and she falls against my body and cries.

It's not a new bruise, so there's not much I can do for her.

"It won't look so bad when I've got makeup on," she says, drinking her tea.

"Do you want to tell me what happened?"

She shrugs. "The usual. Too much beer. I answered back. Can't even remember what it was about."

"How long…?" I can't take my eyes away from the discoloration around her left eye. It's the darkest shades of purple and green and red, like an oil spill. It's such a perfect version of a black eye, it almost looks fake.

"The physical stuff…a couple of years. The rest…a long time."

I reach for her hand. "You must be exhausted. Get to bed— we can talk more in the morning."

She's brought her toothbrush, but no pajamas. I give her my favorite pair—warm red-and-white-checked ones, and a pair of slouchy white socks.

"Do you still get cold feet at night?"

"Yeah, sometimes."

I hover outside the bathroom until she comes out, thinking that I might have some new things to learn about this woman, but I still know exactly who she is, at her core.

Once she's settled and I've checked that the front and back doors are locked, I go up to bed. At 4 a.m., I'm still awake. I grab my duvet and pillow and creep into the spare room. I create a makeshift bed on the floor, and we both sleep until noon.

Day 1,387

"Meredith, I can't stay here forever."

I carry on washing the lunch dishes. "I know that. But you can't go back to him either."

"I won't."

"Has he been in touch?"

"Eight missed calls."

"Turn your phone off, and stay another night," I tell her. "We'll figure out what to do."

"I want to call the police," she says. "And not just for me."

"Don't do it for me. I'm not going back to that night." I place the final bowl on the draining rack and squeeze out the sponge.

"Mer." She touches my arm. "Why didn't you? Why didn't you call the police?"

I turn on the tap, letting cold water trickle over my hands, welcoming the numbness. Her hands on my arms take me by surprise. She turns me gently round to face her. I look at her and all I can see is the bruise. "I can't believe you're even asking me that." My voice catches in my throat as I imagine his hand striking her cheekbone, the same hand that left five purple stamps round my shoulder.

"I'm sorry." Her voice catches too. "Meredith, I'm so sorry."

I shrug her apology away. "Do you realize what it means, telling the police? It's a big step. Are you sure you're ready for that?"

"Yes," she says without hesitation. "Yes, I'm sure."

*

I lie on my bed, stroking Fred's soft belly. I've never been so tired. Now and then I hear my sister moving around downstairs. I don't understand how I can crave my own space and want to be right by her side at the same time. I imagine myself being split in two—a jagged line right down the center of my body. An imperfect jigsaw piece.

When I venture downstairs, she's slumped on the couch, scrolling through the TV channels.

"I don't want to talk about it," I say quietly. "But do you want to watch a film?"

Her eyes light up.

"You choose," I say, sitting at the opposite end of the couch, hugging a velvet cushion to my belly.

She scrolls until she reaches *The Wizard of Oz*.

"Seriously?"

"Yeah." Suddenly I'm ten and we're watching Dorothy click her heels on the worn-out VHS.

"Remember that time you made me be Toto for Halloween?"

She laughs. "Well, I needed a dog."

We watch the film from opposite ends of the couch. Fred jumps onto my lap; I stroke his head until he falls asleep. By the time Dorothy Gale reaches the Emerald City, Fee's asleep too. I cover her with a blanket, taking care not to wake her, then I watch the rest of the film. My couch has never been so warm.

Day 1,388

Two police officers arrive, a man and a woman with sincere, serious faces. I show them into the living room. "Do you want me to...?" I whisper to Fee.

"No, I'm fine." She shakes her head and closes the door behind them.

Two hours later, the front door clicks shut. I keep stirring the soup until I hear her voice.

"It's done. They're going to arrest him now."

"Are they going to charge him?"

"I think so. They seem pretty sure they have enough evidence."

I stare at her. "Well, all the evidence they need is on your face."

She drops her eyes. "Not just my face."

I watch her wrap her arms tightly around her belly, and it falls into place.

"Oh, Fee...the baby?" I can't bear to say the words louder than a whisper, but they still seem to echo through the house.

She bites her lip. "It happened so quickly."

"Talk to me." I pull her toward me. "Or not. Whatever you want. I'm here. Always."

"Thanks," she mumbles into my shoulder. "Fuck. What a mess."

"We'll get through it," I tell her, and for the first time I actually believe it.

"Someone is going to get in touch later, to let me know what's happening. Whether it's safe to go home."

I feel a sudden urge to swallow, and it takes more effort than it should. I go back to stirring the soup, slowly, watching the bubbles form. I turn down the heat, trying to ignore the fire starting in my chest.

"Why didn't you want me in there with you?"

"I didn't want you to hear what he does...did to me."

I can see my face reflected in the kitchen window, a dark shape moving behind me. I close my eyes, try to breathe through the pain.

"Do you want some soup?"

"Meredith." She puts her hand on my shoulder, and I flinch. Like I'd forgotten she was there.

I drop the wooden spoon on the floor, leaving a splatter of soup down my jeans.

With every thrust, he grunts. Tightens his grip round my shoulders. I'm terrified—of everything. That someone will come in. That someone won't come in. I tuck my head down, draw my elbows close to my sides. Anything to make myself smaller.

I open my mouth, but nothing comes out. My hands are trembling. "I'm having a panic attack," I tell myself, or maybe my sister. "I'm having a panic attack. I feel like I'm going to die, but I won't."

I press my toes against the floor and run my hands up and down my thighs. The floor is hard, the denim is strong and smooth. I take slow, deep breaths in and slow, deep breaths out.

When I'm back in the room, I let my sister hold me for a long time.

*

The female police officer comes back. She's short, with pale, freckled skin and brown hair in a neat bun at the nape of her neck. She tells us that Lucas has been arrested and charged with aggravated assault. He's been interviewed under caution, will be kept at the police station overnight and appear in court tomorrow. He's likely to plead not guilty and get bail, she says, but if he goes anywhere near Fee, he'll be taken back into custody until his trial.

"What if he comes for us?" I whisper.

"You must call 999 if he gets in touch with you," she says. "Even if it's just a text. Or call me. You have my number."

"When will the trial be?" Fee asks, her face white beneath the bruising. Some of the darkness has given way to lighter shades of yellow and brown.

"It could be six months away," the police officer says. She has wide, kind eyes; I wonder what horrors they've seen across our city.

"What will happen to him?" I ask her.

"I can't tell you that," she says apologetically. "A fine probably. Maybe a few months in prison as well. It depends on how he behaves between now and then."

Before she goes she hands Fee a stack of leaflets. "I wish we could offer all victims the aftercare they need," she says apologetically. "But here are some local services that help people who've been in abusive relationships."

"Don't go back there," I say as we watch the police officer drive away. "Stay here. With me."

"I need to go back for my things, Meredith. Before he gets out. I don't trust him to stay away."

"Me neither," I say. I go to make tea, return to find her crying quietly on the window seat.

"I should have done it years ago," she sobs.

"Never say that. Never say 'should.'"

She squeezes my arm. "You're stronger than you think, Mer."

I touch her wounded face with light fingertips. "He won't hurt us again."

She texts me: I'm here. I'm at Shirley's.

I call her as soon as her text comes through, like an overprotective parent.

"Just making sure," I say. "Did you get everything you need?"

"I didn't take much. But I did rip the flatscreen TV off the living-room wall. I bought it for him, so I figure I deserve it. Apart from that, just my clothes and some personal stuff. I don't need a lot. Fresh start and all that."

I know she's not feeling as brave as she's trying to make her voice sound.

"I'm exhausted," she admits. "I've just crawled into Shirley's spare bed, next to my flatscreen TV."

"I miss you," I tell her.

"I know," she says. "But this is the right decision. If I'd stayed with you, I might never have moved out. And I'd drive you crazy. I'm still a messy cow."

I know that's not the reason she left. She's treading carefully, aware that I need time to adjust. I also suspect that she's protecting me from Lucas. If she's not here, he's got no reason to be here either. For years he'd been a repugnant memory but not a conceivable threat. Now he's real again.

"Has Shirley locked the front door? And the back?"

"Yes. She also has a 210-pound husband who works at Barlinnie. I've basically got my own personal bodyguard."

My chest relaxes a little. "Good."

"Please don't worry," she says.

"Telling me not to worry is like telling me not to breathe."

"I know. Try to worry less then. It's not good for you."

"Hold on," I tell her. "I'm going to put you on speakerphone, get my pajamas on, and brush my teeth."

She yawns. "Hurry up. I'm exhausted."

Three minutes later, I'm in bed. I lay my phone on the other pillow and turn off my light.

"Fee?"

"Uh-huh?"

"Thank you."

"What the hell for?"

"For coming back to me."

"Well, thanks for having me," she murmurs.

I do my diaphragmatic breathing, moving the air in through my nose and out through my mouth, with one hand on my chest and the other on my stomach.

"What a racket," Fee says.

"Do it with me," I tell her. "It's relaxing."

"Jeezo. You'll be getting me to chant next."

I laugh. "Lie on your back and put one hand on your upper chest. Put your other hand just under your rib cage. Breathe in slowly through your nose but use your stomach. Your chest shouldn't really move at all. Try it. Breathe slowly, remember." I do it myself, feeling my belly gently push against the palm of my hand. "Then tighten your tummy muscles as you breathe out through your mouth. Do that slowly as well."

"That's a lot to remember," she mutters.

"Just keep doing it. It gets easier."

I imagine that Fee and I are breathing in sync, our bellies rising and falling together. I don't know how much time passes, as we settle into blackness—it's the time of night when minutes and hours play tricks on us.

"I miss you too, Meredith," Fee says, just as I think she's fallen asleep.

Day 1,392

Saturday, May 11, 2019

"Mer, I think I'm ready to move on." Celeste and I are working on the Manhattan skyline in 1,500 pieces. She's terrible at jigsaws—far too impatient—but I appreciate her attempt to share one of my passions. I tried to steer her toward one of my easier ones, but she was determined to transport us to the Big Apple.

"I'll get something different? Or do you want to just chat?"

She laughs. "I mean move on from being single."

"Really? You want to date?"

"I think maybe I do." Her cheeks are pink; she looks like an excited little girl.

"You need to get on a dating app." I find a piece with an edge and place it on the mat, roughly where I expect it to end up.

"Good idea! Think I'll find someone in three months? A date for my party?"

I laugh but keep my eyes on the jigsaw. I feel like my dream of being at her party is slipping away from me.

"We could do it together."

"Ha! Who would want to date me?"

"Meredith Maggs, what are you talking about?" She leans across the jigsaw pieces, her arms obstacles to my search. "You're a catch."

"That's sweet of you, Celeste, but I don't think so."

"For an intelligent woman you don't have a clue about some stuff, Meredith."

"You're probably right, Celeste."

"So...shall we do it? Take the plunge into the dating world?"

"I don't think I'm ready."

"When was your last relationship?"

"Oh...a while ago. I'm just old and set in my ways," I say breezily.

She doesn't say anything, just looks at me. "You are not."

"I'm an old stick-in-the-mud. I never go anywhere," I tell her, and it's the closest to the truth as we've ever got.

"Well, maybe you should."

"Maybe I should," I admit.

"What was his name? Your last boyfriend."

"Gavin." I stand up abruptly. "I'm going to get us some drinks."

When I come back, she's scrolling on her phone. "I've found the perfect app for us," she announces. "Totally user-friendly and free for a month! Come on, Mer—it'll be a laugh if nothing else. We can compare notes on the worst pickup lines."

"I'll help you," I tell her. "Let's see if your Prince Charming exists."

"Oh, he doesn't. I just want a decent lad."

For the next two hours we make imaginary and real wish lists: kind, tall, independent, must love cats (me); good sense of humor, loyal, easygoing, must want kids (Celeste). We check out some dating apps and narrow it down to two, then upload Celeste's profile picture, a headshot I take of her laughing in which she looks like the beautiful girl next door. I don't need a profile picture, but she insists on taking one of me anyway.

She makes me change into a nice top and pose in front of the living room wall. It feels ridiculous to start with, but then she tells me a joke and fluffs up the punchline and I laugh and she manages to get a photo of me looking like a normal, fun-loving forty-year-old woman who might not be living her best life but is trying her hardest.

2014

He was handsome even when he slept. Even when he had his mouth open and drool running down his chin. He was handsome, and he was really, really sweet and kind and patient, and there was absolutely nothing wrong with him.

But I had to break up with him. I did it in the middle of the night, before he woke up all sweet and handsome and made me breakfast and I changed my mind.

"Gavin." I turned my bedside lamp on and shook his shoulder.

He grunted and rolled over. "Sorry."

"What?"

"Sorry. Was I snoring?"

"No, you weren't snoring. I need to talk to you."

He rolled back toward me and squinted through sleepy eyes. "What's up? What time is it? Are you OK?"

"Yeah. Well... kind of. Not really."

"What's going on, Meredith?" He sat up and positioned the pillow behind his head.

"I need to tell you something."

He yawned. "Sorry. I'm exhausted. I'm listening."

I felt nauseous. He was looking at me, waiting for me to talk.

I hugged my legs to my chest. I didn't want him to touch me, but I had to give him something.

"Meredith, what's up?" He was a gentle man. He didn't even get angry when another driver pulled out in front of him without indicating, or a phone rang in the movie theater.

"Nothing. Sorry. Forget it."

"No, tell me. Really."

I turned my head away from him and stared at the light until my eyes hurt.

"Meredith, I know you find it hard to let people in."

"Well, that's a given."

I turned back to him and we looked at each other, across the bed that felt wider than usual. He wanted to comfort me—I knew he did. I moved in the opposite direction. Barely an inch, but he noticed and sighed.

"You have barriers like Hadrian's Wall."

"You're a strong guy. Surely you could climb over Hadrian's Wall." My attempt to meet him in a more lighthearted place fell flat.

"That's not the point. You don't want me to try."

I thought about it for a second. "I guess you're right. But it's not really about you. That's such a cliché, I know. It's not you; it's me. But I really do mean that. I mean, you're perfect."

"Is this about your mum?"

"Sort of."

He reached across the bed slowly. He squeezed my hand, then retreated again.

"I'm sorry, Gavin."

"Don't be sorry. You've got nothing to be sorry about. I want to help. What can I do to help?"

"You can leave." I said it softly, but it didn't lessen the blow. He looked at me as if I'd just told him I'd killed a puppy.

"You want me to go now?" He fumbled down the side of the bed for his phone. "At…half past one in the morning? Are you being serious?" The gentleness in his eyes had been replaced by confusion.

"I'm sorry. It's just…having you here, it makes everything harder."

"I didn't realize I was such a burden." He let go of my hand, and I knew he'd never touch me again.

I watched him get dressed, crossly but self-consciously. *That's the last thing you are*, I think. *It's just easier to be alone.* But I don't want to say it out loud, to admit that I'm simply not like other people.

"So...let me get this straight." He was facing away from me, sitting at the edge of the bed to pull his socks on. "You want me to leave because your dad left and your mum said it was your fault?"

I let his anger hit me; it was what I deserved. It was only a fraction of the truth, but it was all I could give him.

"Pretty much," I told the back of his head. He had soft, wavy hair—he'd been going on about needing a haircut for weeks. It curled around the nape of his neck, like a child's.

"Do you want me to come back?"

I shook my head.

"Never?"

"I don't think so," I whispered.

"Meredith, I don't get it."

"Me neither."

"Don't do that." He stood up and yanked his sweater over his head.

"Don't do what?"

"Act all passive. Feel sorry for yourself. You're the one doing this. This isn't me."

"I know that."

This was my chance to say I'm sorry, to admit that I'm a bit messed up, to tell him I didn't actually want him to go, to ask him to take his sweater off again and get back into bed and spoon me for one more night. To give me the chance to tell him I loved him, because I thought I did—just not enough to over-power everything else.

But I didn't do any of that. I just waited for him to leave the room, walk down the stairs, and close the front door behind him a little louder than he normally would.

Day 1,397

Thursday, May 16, 2019

"Hello." Tom beams at me from behind dark sunglasses. "It's a beautiful day."

"Hello. Yes, it is." I smile back at him. I'm in a good mood after a productive morning. I cleaned the house from top to bottom, baked two layers of vanilla sponge, and finally finished the Manhattan skyline. The heat from outside feels good on my face, but Tom is waiting to come in. I step away from the sunshine reluctantly.

"Want to help me finish my cake?"

"Ooh, yes, please." Tom pushes his sunglasses onto the top of his head. "Only if I can get a piece, obviously."

"I think I can manage that." The truth is, I'll probably give him half the cake to take home. I hate throwing out cake, but I don't want to eat it day after day. I give away as much as I can—to Sadie and the kids, to Tom, to Jacob, to Neighbor Jackie for taking my garbage cans out every week. I leave it on the kitchen windowsill in a Tupperware box, which she washes and puts back when it's empty. Sometimes, she leaves me a review of sorts inside the box. Like "very tasty" or "I preferred the chocolate muffins."

Tom knows he's guaranteed plenty of cake, but he likes to tease me.

"I've never made a cake," he confesses.

"We just need to do the buttercream and jam filling. But we could do it from scratch next week, if you like? It's easy, I swear."

"Easy for you maybe. My culinary skills don't stretch much further than a stir-fry."

"So you can chop vegetables and push them around in a wok?" This time it's my turn to tease.

"Hey, smarty-pants. Sometimes I add noodles." Tom nudges me with his elbow.

It was only a split second of contact, but as soon as it's over I'm acutely aware of the absence of his arm. Even through my sleeve I could feel the warmth of his bare skin. I concentrate on gathering ingredients: double cream, white sugar, vanilla extract, strawberry jam.

"What can I do?" When I turn round, he's sitting on the worktop, swinging his long legs like a teenager.

"You can get down from there, for a start," I scold him. "We need a big mixing bowl and a fork. A wooden spoon and a sieve."

He jumps down. "OK. Let's see how long it takes me to find those." He starts opening drawers and cupboards, looking in all the wrong places. It feels strangely intimate, letting him rummage around in my utensils. It's also funny. Who would keep a sieve in the same place as baked beans and canned fruit?

"I'm just softening the butter," I tell him, hitting buttons on the microwave.

When I turn round, he's holding up a fork and a bowl, a big smile on his face.

"Sorted?"

"Sorted."

I show Tom how to beat the butter until it's smooth and creamy. We sift the sugar, add vanilla extract, and spread the mixture over the base of one of the sponges. Finally we add a thick layer of strawberry jam on top, then top it off with the other sponge.

We're silent for the most part, but it's not awkward. I think he might be the person I'm most comfortable not saying anything to. I let the weirdness of that sit with me for a moment, then hand him the icing sugar.

"Just one more thing. I'll let you do the honors. Sprinkle it over the top. A light dusting."

"Well. That looks incredible. Of course, you did the hard part." Tom steps back to admire our creation.

I smile. "Team effort. Now for the best part—we get to taste it."

I cut two generous slices and Tom gets side plates from the corner cupboard. Having gone on an exploratory mission half an hour ago, he now appears to be entirely au fait with the contents of my kitchen.

"We can't have cake without tea," he says. "I'll make it."

I sit at the kitchen table and wait for him. "It's named after Queen Victoria, you know. Apparently she had a slice with afternoon tea every single day." I run my finger along the filling and lick it clean.

"I'm no royalist, but she's my favorite queen." Tom joins me with two mugs of tea. "She was ahead of her time. Did you know she proposed to Prince Albert?"

I shook my head. "I like Mary, Queen of Scots."

"Ooh, controversial choice. This cake is amazing, by the way."

"Yes. Yes, it is."

"You'd better make me a salad next time. I'm going to get fat if you keep this up."

I raise my eyebrows at him over my mug. "There's not an ounce of fat on you."

"Can I tell you something?"

"Always."

"I'm lonely."

I stare at him. I wasn't expecting that.

"I often think about how different things would be if I still had Laura, if we had our babies. If things had gone another way, I'd have a family."

I picture the other Tom, the one in the park with the gurgling baby strapped to his chest, and I feel a pang of sadness.

"I get lonely too sometimes," I admit. "But at least you're out there in the world. You could meet your soul mate tomorrow, just walking down the street."

"Do you believe in soul mates?"

I think about it. "I don't know, actually."

"You could meet someone too, Meredith."

I roll my eyes at him.

"It will happen. If you want it to."

I shrug. "Maybe I'll find another hermit and he'll move in here and we can be hermits together."

"You could have lots of little hermit babies together."

"A hermit house."

We laugh.

"You know you're not a hermit really?"

"You don't think?"

He grins. "A hermit is a religious recluse. You're just a regular, non-believing recluse."

We have easy banter over more cake. He tells me he's started running and that he'll find it too hard to stick to his healthy eating plan if I keep feeding him cake. I tell him I'll start making healthy treats without butter or sugar. When he leaves, he takes me by surprise with a tight hug.

I turn to my jigsaw after Tom leaves, but I can't concentrate. My knees stiffen up, locked in position after too long at the coffee table. I stand up and look outside. It's slightly overcast but dry. I check the time and keep looking. It's seven minutes before someone walks past my house.

Meredith, Alone

I move through the rooms slowly, finding my shoes, a sweater. I'm thinking of Tom as I take my steps down the garden path. I don't want him to be lonely. I have the seed of a thought in my mind, too negligible to make any sense of yet. I make it to the end of the path again, and it's starting to feel quite normal.

1991

It was a quiet Sunday. We were cutting out paper dolls at the kitchen table while Mama baked bread. She hummed along with the radio, lost in a world of stirring and mixing and kneading. Occasionally she looked over our shoulders to check that we weren't cutting anything we shouldn't be. Fee once cut all her dolls' heads off, which didn't go down well.

"We're too old for this," Fee whispered to me. I glanced at Mama, but she was focused on her bread, the muscles in her forearms tightening as she pressed the heels of her hands into the dough. Over and over again she did it, for what seemed like hours. I liked to watch—it was quite hypnotic.

Fee was right—we were too old for paper dolls. But Mama didn't want us to grow old before our time. Besides, I enjoyed slicing the scissors through the thick paper. I took my time, making sure I followed the lines. I was creating the girl I'd never look like—she had thick blonde hair, a neat nose, and a big smile. I dressed her in a turquoise dress with white polka dots, carefully pressing the tabs around her flat body.

The doorbell rang. Mama tutted. "Who turns up unannounced on a Sunday afternoon?" She turned on the tap with her elbow, started rinsing the oil and flour off her hands. "Will one of you get the door, please?"

Fee jumped to her feet. "I'll go." Anything to get away from the paper dolls.

I kept cutting in silence, while Mama dried her hands, checked her reflection in the oven door, and smoothed down her hair.

Fee's head appeared round the edge of the door. Her eyes were wide. "Our aunt is here," she said.

"Auntie Linda?" I felt excited. She sometimes brought fish and chips and cans of fizzy juice over on the weekend. Maybe we wouldn't have to eat Mama's bread after all.

"She says she's Auntie Anna."

"Fuck," Mama said.

"Is she a friend of yours?" The auntie-but-not-auntie thing was weird.

"Not exactly." Mama put her hand on my shoulder. "Best behavior, girls. Don't cause a scene."

The lady who said she was Auntie Anna sat on the chair in the living room, the three of us opposite her on the couch, Mama in the middle of her two girls. Her hand was warm and floury over mine and her fingers tightened whenever Auntie Anna asked me a question. Giving me a warning, without saying a word.

Auntie Anna told us that she was our father's older sister, that she hadn't seen us since we were babies, that she'd missed us. She told us she was only in Glasgow for a few days, visiting from Ireland. I wanted to ask her if our father was in Ireland. I wanted to ask her everything, but my voice didn't seem to be working.

Fee had no such difficulty. "Where's our dad?"

I felt Mama's body stiffen. I wished she'd let go of my hand and give me some space. My throat felt tight, as if her fingers were squeezing there too. I held my breath and waited for Auntie Anna to speak.

She was small and soft, with a friendly face and curly dark hair skimming her shoulders. "He's in Liverpool just now. He'd love to see you."

Liverpool. I didn't know where that was—I hoped it wasn't

too far away. I stared at Fee, my eyes begging for a reaction, but she wasn't giving anything away.

"Did he give you any money for us?" Mama asked.

"Well...no, but..."

"Well. There you go. Good fathers provide for their children." Mama stood up, pulling us to our feet. "Come on, girls, let's go and make tea for our guest."

I wanted to stay and talk to Auntie Anna. I had so many questions. But Mama wouldn't let go. She dragged Fee and me into the kitchen.

"Our dad's in Liverpool?" Fee demanded as soon as the door was closed. "You told us he was abroad."

"Fiona, I have no idea where your father's been all these years. He could have been in Australia for all I know." Mama kept her back to us as she filled the kettle and arranged cups and saucers on a tray.

"Whereabouts is Liverpool?" I whispered to Fee.

She shrugged. "Not far? It's where the Beatles came from. The yellow submarine song."

"Can we go to Liverpool?" I asked Mama.

She laughed. "Of course you can, angelface. When you're old enough to get there yourself. Your father knows exactly where you are. He can come and see you anytime." She yanked open the cutlery drawer.

"But...but..."

"But, but. You sound like a robot. Get the milk out of the fridge, will you? I'm going to go and have a cup of tea with Auntie Anna in peace." She pointed to our abandoned paper dolls. "You two get back to your little game. You can say good-bye to her before she goes."

I looked at Fee desperately, but she was staring at the floor. She had a bright pink spot on each cheek. I grabbed the milk bottle and slammed the fridge door shut. Either Mama didn't notice, or she didn't care. She took the milk out of my hand and swept out of the kitchen, closing the door firmly behind her.

Before she left, Auntie Anna gave Fee and me a crisp five-pound note and a small chocolate bar each.

"Thank you," we said in unison. I took a hesitant step toward her just as Mama looped her arm through mine and slowly pulled me back. As soon as the front door closed behind Auntie Anna, Mama stormed back into the kitchen. Fee and I ran into the living room and rested our hands on the windowsill, and watched Auntie Anna get into her small red car.

She sat for so long before driving off I wondered if she was plucking up the courage to come back in. Or could we squeeze out of the window, jump into her car, and drive to Liverpool? Finally she looked at the house and saw us at the window. She smiled and waved. We waved back enthusiastically as she drove away. Fee squeezed my shoulder and ran upstairs.

I stayed at the window, my hands pressed against the glass until the red car had disappeared.

I ate my chocolate bar in the bathroom, then slipped my five-pound note down the side of my mattress. I didn't know how far it would take me, but I was going to go to Liverpool.

I've dreamed about Auntie Anna over the years. Sometimes, she's chasing me along a beach, and I'm stumbling, and she catches me just as I wake up. Other times I'm the one doing the chasing, but she's too fast for me. She grows smaller and smaller and smaller until she's a tiny speck, but I don't stop chasing her. Both versions are equally disturbing.

In the weeks after Auntie Anna's visit, I thought about how different things could be if I'd been a little braver. If I hadn't let Mama's fingers squeeze me into silence. The burden of missed opportunity weighed constantly on my shoulders. I couldn't stop thinking about going to Liverpool. Whenever Fiona and I were alone, it was all I wanted to talk about.

"Don't you want to go? Don't you want to see him? Maybe we could stay there," I added casually, "in Liverpool," as if there was any doubt what I was talking about. Like I would be returning to its familiar streets, a girl who had never ventured beyond the outskirts of Glasgow.

"Life wouldn't be easier in Liverpool." Fiona crossed her arms behind her head and stretched out on the grass. It was a sunny day. Mama had started a new job at the local pub last month and was working all day. She'd left us a list of chores to do and strict instructions to complete them before she returned *or else*. But she underestimated us. We were efficient and quick, and worked well as a team if I followed Fiona's orders. Our final chore was to hang the clean washing on the line. I watched the bottom edges of the yellowed pillowcases rise and fall in the slight breeze.

"You don't know that," I grumbled. "You don't know what it's like to be anywhere else."

"I know more than you. You're not Annie and there's no Daddy Walton waiting to rescue you."

"I know I'm not Annie, and it's Daddy Warbucks." I rolled onto my side and stared at my sister's profile. I always envied her snub nose. Mama said I had a pointy nose, like a witch. Fiona's snub nose had just the right amount of freckles, not too many. *Kisses from the sun*, Mama called them.

"She's had us for years," I grumbled. "It's his turn."

"Meredith, she'd never let us go."

I shrugged. "We could just go anyway. We could go right now. Let's be brave."

Fiona squinted at me. "We are brave. That's why we're still here."

I fell onto my back and stared at the sun until my eyes hurt.

"I bet Liverpool is massive," she said. "Much bigger than Glasgow. How would we find him?"

She was right. She was always right. I hated her for it. I felt something harden in my chest. It might have been my heart, turning to stone.

"I want to rip all the washing off the line and stomp all over it," I said. "I want to smash the whole place to bits. Burn all her clothes."

"That would be pretty stupid," my sister said gently. "Why don't I give you a manicure instead? You can pick the color."

She jumped up and held her hand out to me. I let her pull me to my feet. She was still taller than me, but I was catching up. I followed her into the house, wondering if I'd ever be the boss. If I'd ever get the chance to make decisions for myself.

My sister looped her arm round my shoulders. "I guess he might come back for us." Neither of us believed her, but we were good at pretending.

Day 1,405

Friday, May 24, 2019

Barbara tells me I'm in control of this conversation, but I don't want to be. She seems like a lovely woman, with big brown eyes that look a little bit sad, even when she's smiling. She's wearing skinny jeans and a white shirt buttoned right up to the neck, a chunky cardigan in blocks of bright colors and fabulous white shoes with a thick sole. Her hair is gray with slices of silver, cropped close to her head.

When she arrived, she bent down to scratch Fred under his outstretched chin and told me she grew up with cats but now shares her home with a Dalmatian called Doris. This helped, a little. I've always felt an affinity with people who talk about their pets as if they're close family members.

"You've taken a huge step, Meredith, getting in touch with our rape support center," Barbara says gently. "I know you're probably feeling overwhelmed, maybe a little scared. Please remember that however you're feeling right now is totally normal. If you'd like to talk about something else, that's fine. Or we can just sit for a while. We don't need to talk about anything. Whatever feels comfortable to you. I'm not on the clock. I'm here for as long as you need me to be."

Some of the tightness in my chest eases. "What's Doris like?"

Barbara smiles. "Doris is a character. I got her from a rescue center when she was a puppy. She'd been left behind in a flat when tenants were evicted. Tied to a bedpost with a rope, she was. I don't know what her early months were like, but I don't think she got much affection—or food. She was a skinny wee thing when I took her in. She's about five years old now, and she's big. She's my best friend."

"She sounds amazing."

"She is. Except when she's sleeping at the end of my bed, farting like a trooper all through the night."

We both laugh.

"I got Fred six months after I was raped," I say. The word sounds strange coming out of my mouth, like I'm trying to speak a foreign language for the first time, unsure of the pronunciation.

"And how did you and Fred find each other?"

"My friend Sadie got him for me. I had no idea. She thought he would help. Turned up one day with him in a shoebox. He was tiny."

"Did he help?"

"I'm not sure. I mean, he's been great company. But he hasn't exactly helped me leave the house. It's not as if he needs to be walked or anything."

I suddenly realize how grateful I am for Sadie's choice of pet for me. Her gesture was simply a kind one, not motivated by frustration or impatience. She wasn't trying to force me to do anything I wasn't able to do. She just wanted to make me feel a little better. She wanted to bring love into my home.

"Actually, he has helped. Enormously," I tell Barbara tearfully.

"I'm glad to hear it. Animals can be so therapeutic."

We sit in comfortable silence for a moment, sipping our tea. The kitchen clock ticks, the washing machine hums.

"How do you do what you do?" I ask Barbara between cups of tea. I keep forgetting to drink mine. It goes cold and a film settles over the top, like algae on a pond. I get up to make more; I'm glad of the distraction. I know how to make tea. And hers is easy: no milk, no sugar.

"What do you mean?" Her voice remains soft, but something changes in her eyes. She wants to keep the focus on me.

"Don't you find it hard? Talking about stuff like this all the time?"

"Of course I do. But however hard it can be for me at times, it's nothing compared to how difficult it is for you, and all the other brave women and men who share their stories."

"You must hear some awful things. Like, really awful."

"Meredith, what happened to you was awful."

"Not compared to some people. I wasn't beaten. I wasn't dragged down a dark alleyway in the middle of the night. I wasn't left for dead. You must have spoken to people who went through those things."

"You can't compare yourself to anyone else. What happened to you was awful. End of story. There's no hierarchy of abuse. Trauma is complex, and very personal. I'm here to support you through your individual experience—whatever that is."

I sit back down beside her with fresh mugs of tea. "I should have stopped him. I let it happen to me. I should have screamed or pushed him away. I didn't try hard enough."

"Meredith, you're not alone in feeling like that. Many sexual assault victims blame themselves, particularly when they know the abuser. Lucas raped you. There's absolutely no doubt about that."

Suddenly embarrassed, my cheeks are burning. I want to be anywhere but here, sitting with this woman I don't know any-thing about other than the fact she has a Dalmatian called Doris and doesn't take milk or sugar in her tea.

I try to send a telepathic message to Fred, who is no doubt stretched out on my bed having a lovely nap. I want him to weave between my ankles or jump onto my lap, an interaction

I take for granted several times a day. Right now, I'm craving it. I need something to take me out of this moment and away from the past.

"It's normal to doubt yourself. It's normal to blame yourself. A long time has passed since the assault. A long time to invest in feelings of guilt and self-recrimination."

I'm tired. I want to crawl up the stairs and slide under my duvet.

"He forced himself inside me. Held a dish towel over my mouth. It didn't last long."

I feel like I'm sitting beside myself. It's a little like jet lag. I've only had it once, after I came back from a trip to Canada in my early twenties. I remember slight nausea, dense waves of exhaustion, and feeling as if I had cotton wool inside my head. I'm spent.

"Did you think about reporting him to the police?" I'm grateful when Barbara moves the conversation on.

I shake my head. "He was—is—my sister's husband. I know I should have done. It's difficult to explain my thought process. I'm sorry."

"Don't apologize, Meredith," Barbara says, not for the first time since she first sat down in my kitchen, almost three hours ago. "Again, your reaction was perfectly normal. Many rape victims don't report the crime. They're even more unlikely to tell the police if they know the perpetrator. In your case I can completely understand why you didn't."

"You can?"

"Yes. Absolutely. Did you tell anyone what happened?"

"Sadie—my friend who brought me Fred."

"When did you tell her?"

"The next morning. We were supposed to meet for lunch that day. I phoned her to cancel, and it just came out. I wasn't intending to tell her. I still couldn't believe it had actually happened."

"And what did Sadie do?"

"She came over, straightaway. She brought me the morning-after pill—she's a nurse. She took photos of the bruises on my arms, tried to talk me into phoning the police."

"But you didn't."

I shake my head. "I told my mother and my sister a couple of weeks later."

"How did they react?"

"They didn't believe me."

My words hang in the space between us. Barbara's eyes cloud over.

"Fee—my sister—she does now. It's complicated. He's a bad man."

"You're a brave woman, Meredith."

I want to believe her. Maybe one day I will.

"It's actually because of Fee that you're here now," I tell her. "He beat her up, and she reported him to the police, and they gave us a bunch of leaflets. Yours was in there."

"Meredith, it's not too late." The tone of her voice has changed. "Rape crimes can be reported no matter how much time has passed. Our service would provide you with someone to support you throughout the entire criminal justice process."

"I'll think about it," I tell her. "I really will."

The sky is dark when she leaves, but there's a lightness in the air, teasing summertime. I can hear cars in the distance and a baby crying somewhere close by. Apart from that it's quiet. There's nothing scary about tonight.

"I'll walk you to your car," I say suddenly.

"Thank you," she says.

It feels right to take her arm, so I do. Looped together at the elbow, we walk slowly down my garden path. I can feel a slight breeze at the back of my neck, exposed where my hair is scraped up into a ponytail. We've taken a few steps when I realize I don't have shoes on, and my socks are damp. Barbara hasn't noticed—or if she has, she doesn't care about such minor details; I am, after all, a grown woman who can walk outside in socks whenever I wish—so I keep going.

"Will you be OK, Meredith?"

"Yes," I tell her. "My friend Celeste is coming over tomorrow morning. We're going to do some calligraphy together."

"What a lovely way to spend a Saturday," Barbara says. She gives my arm a squeeze before carefully extracting her own. I watch her unlock her car and put her big bag on the back seat. I'm standing on two wet feet, on the pavement outside my house, and my breathing is even, my heart rate steady.

"Take care of yourself, Meredith. You know where we are if you need us. You can call the helpline anytime. And you'll take a look through the information I've left with you? There are lots of resources there for you: counseling, group therapy… Have a think about it."

I nod, and I will think about it. I realize I'll probably never see Barbara and her sad eyes and quirky hair and chunky cardigan again. Our paths might cross in the supermarket, although I don't think I'm ready to give up online shopping just yet. We certainly won't share another moment like the one we shared today. She has a piece of my heart, a piece nobody else has, and I trust her with it. I know she'll look after it for me.

She pauses before getting into her car. "Meredith, if you want to involve the police, you'll get all the support you need. It will be investigated as thoroughly as if it had happened yesterday."

"I know," I say. I also know that it would be highly unlikely that it would go anywhere. There's no forensic evidence, no witnesses. It would be my word against his. Right now, I'm not sure I have room in my life for his words. I'm starting to elevate my own world again, and I don't want him to squash it back down.

"I'm very proud of you," Barbara says, as if she can read my mind.

"I'm proud of me too," I say, and we both laugh. It's time to say goodbye, but shaking hands seems amiss. We both reach that conclusion at the same time and open our arms wide.

After Barbara's car disappears, I stand on the wet pavement for a long time, searching for the moon behind the clouds.

Day 1,406

Saturday, May 25, 2019

I wake up before the day begins in that slippery time when darkness is still clinging on. My body is sweaty, my duvet bunched up between my legs. The dream comes back to me before I can stop it. I'm at Celeste's party, but I can't find her. I walk around the room, searching for her shiny bob and gap-toothed grin, then I move faster to try to keep up with my racing heart. I'm running, and people are laughing, and then a large shoe appears in front of me and I go flying across the floor. The shoe belongs to Lucas, who bears down on me, laughing more loudly than everybody else.

I open my bedroom windows wide, breathing in the fresh air. Then I call Fee, but I don't tell her about my dream. He's given her enough nightmares. Instead, we talk about the time we spray-dyed each other's hair and I had purple ears for a week.

Day 1,408

Monday, May 27, 2019

I'm standing at my kitchen window, looking into the garden and thinking about nothing in particular, when I spot them. It's not unusual to see little birds hopping along the fence. But I've never seen one with bright green feathers and a peach face, let alone two. Not outside a zoo, at least.

I can't take my eyes off them. I watch them lead a dainty dance, staying close to each other. Their colors remind me of those hard candies you buy by the tin.

I read somewhere that swans mate for life. I'm not sure about other bird species, but these two look like they're pretty inseparable. Whenever one of them hops away, the other follows. I wait until they're facing me, then take a photo of them huddled together—it's not the clearest image but the colors are still vivid. I can't decide whether Tom or Celeste would appreciate it the most, so I send it to them both.

Celeste replies within seconds: Awwwww!! Are they lovebirds?

I smile. That's so Celeste.

I drink two mugs of tea and watch the birds until Fred curls round my ankles, looking for food. I fill his bowls and put a pan of water on the stove to boil. I've spent so long looking at the birds, I've not made the risotto I'd planned for dinner. Pasta it is then. I grab a jar of pesto out of the cupboard, slice some mushrooms. Every few minutes I glance outside, checking that the birds are still there. I'm worried that if I don't watch them, they'll fly away.

I'm eating my pasta, back in front of the window, when my phone buzzes.

It's Tom: They look like lovebirds!

Celeste said the same thing, I think.

A quick internet search tells me that a lovebird is a small type of parrot. I get excited when I click on an image—it looks exactly like the birds on my fence. Maybe I should buy a bird feeder and some seed, give them a reason to stick around.

I tear myself away from the birds to start work. An hour later, when I'm back in the kitchen to make another mug of tea, they've disappeared.

When I'm getting ready for bed, another message comes through from Tom.

You'll never guess what I've found.

I'm about to reply to tell him it's far too late for guessing games, when he sends me a link to a news website.

EXOTIC PARROTS BRING LOVE TO GLASGOW

11 March 2018

Scottish birdwatchers are scanning the skies even more avidly than usual, after bright green lovebirds with peach faces have been spotted in several gardens in the East End of Glasgow.

The parrots are believed to be escaped pets, but they've managed to survive outdoors thanks to food from residents' bird feeders. Experts are now trying to track the movements of the exotic birds.

Denise Prentice, a spokesperson for the Scottish Ornithologists' Club, said they believe the first sighting of the birds was in September 2017—and that there may be as many as six of them.

"It's so exciting that the lovebirds are rearing young here in the west of Scotland," Prentice said. "Very few species of parrot have been able to breed in the wild in the UK, and it's never happened north of the border before."

The lovebirds, which feed on berries, seeds, and tree buds, can live for up to fifteen years in captivity. They get their name from their strong monogamous pair bonding, plus the long periods that paired birds spend sitting together.

I feel special! I text back to Tom, before forwarding the article link to Celeste.

You are special, he replies.

Wow, Mer—you're special! Celeste writes.

I laugh so loudly that Fred lifts his head from his paws and stares at me.

"You wouldn't get it," I tell him as I get into bed.

WEEJAN: How are you all this morning?

RESCUEMEPLZ: Been better, to be honest ☹

JIGSAWGIRL: What's wrong, Gary?

RESCUEMEPLZ: I saw my brother yesterday. We went for burgers.

JIGSAWGIRL: And it didn't go well?

RESCUEMEPLZ: Not really. He asked me if I was still taking my happy pills. I said yeah. Then he laughed.

WEEJAN: Sounds like my ex-husband.

RESCUEMEPLZ: I just want him to understand. But he won't even try. My whole family thinks I'm a joke.

JIGSAWGIRL: Well, we don't think you're a joke.

WEEJAN: I don't even think you're funny.

JIGSAWGIRL: I hate it when people call them happy pills. Like they're some magical cure. If only…

WEEJAN: I know, right?

RESCUEMEPLZ: *If you're happy and you know it clap your hands*

JIGSAWGIRL: I'm clapping!

WEEJAN: LOL! Me too.

RESCUEMEPLZ: *If you're happy and you know it stamp your feet*

JIGSAWGIRL: Stamp, stamp!

WEEJAN: I can't be bothered stamping my feet. Can I clap my hands again?

RESCUEMEPLZ: Oh, trust you.

JIGSAWGIRL: What comes after feet?

WEEJAN: Nod your head?

JIGSAWGIRL: Hmm, I don't think so. I'll google it.

RESCUEMEPLZ: *rolls eyes*

JIGSAWGIRL: *If you're happy and you know it shout hooray!*

WEEJAN: Hooray.

RESCUEMEPLZ: Hooray.

JIGSAWGIRL: You can do better than that!

WEEJAN: HOORAY!!!!

RESCUEMEPLZ: HOORAY!

JIGSAWGIRL: Gary, do you feel better now?

RESCUEMEPLZ: I do. But only because you two are absolutely bonkers.

JIGSAWGIRL: Well, you started it.

RESCUEMEPLZ: Touché. Anyway, thanks.

WEEJAN: Glad to be of service.

JIGSAWGIRL: Any time. ☺

Day 1,413

Saturday, June 1, 2019

I make my list first. Preparation is key.

Onions
Oat milk
Peaches / nectarines
Toilet paper
Dish soap

Two days ago, I walked to the end of my street. I stopped at the corner and looked around. My eyes scanned the line of houses: similar to mine but all slightly different in size and shape. I grouped parked cars into colors—four black, two white, one silver, three red, one blue—until distance made it too difficult to differentiate. I didn't pass anyone on the way to the corner, but on the way back I saw a man with a small dog walking toward me. I felt something in my chest, but I told myself it was excitement, not panic, and breathed through it like Diane tells me to.

I slowed down a little but didn't stop—that would make me look ridiculous. I moved to the inside of the pavement to give him space to pass. I was relieved he had a dog—it gave me something to look at. It had red curly hair and floppy ears.

"Afternoon," he said.

I looked up, just in time to catch his face. He had salt-and-pepper hair and a long chin. He was smiling.

"Hello," I said.

"Have a nice day," he said.

"You too," I said.

I'd forgotten how kind people can be. For the rest of the day I couldn't concentrate on anything. I kept thinking about the man with the salt-and-pepper hair and the dog with the floppy ears.

Yesterday, I walked a little farther. I walked until I could see the spot where the houses end and the small row of shops begins. There's a newsagent's, a grocer, a hair salon, and a dog-grooming place. I could see some people milling around outside them, but from where I stood they were faceless, fluid shapes.

It was a warm day. I tilted my face toward the sky, enjoying the warmth on my skin. It felt the same as it does on my doorstep or at the end of my garden path, but also different.

On the way back home I passed two teenagers—a boy and a girl. They were looking at a phone screen, laughing. The girl elbowed the boy in the side of his body and he bent double, mocking her. She pointed out something else on the phone. I glanced at their faces, but neither of them looked at me. I let out my breath.

Today is the big one. I do a quick visualization exercise before I leave the house, like Diane suggested, but I get confused thinking about how the shop will be laid out and decide I just have to do it. If I can't find the onions, it's not the end of the world. My shopping list is, in fact, something of a prop. As always, I have enough food in my kitchen to keep me alive for weeks.

Careful planning went into my outfit. Black leggings and trainers for comfort. A white T-shirt—loose and breathable. I thought about wearing my hoodie on top, but it's a warm day and the risk of sweating is already high. Even though the option of putting a hood up is appealing, I think it would actually draw more attention to me. People always look suspiciously at people in hoodies, for some reason. So I opt for my denim jacket, which has ample pocket space for my shopping list, bank card, phone, and keys. I don't want to have to rummage through a bag.

I brush my hair in front of the hall mirror until it goes a bit static. I check I have no food between my teeth—unlikely, as I had soup for lunch, but you never know—and put on lip balm. It's mint flavor, and it tingles a little.

I turn and I walk and I open my front door.

A journey of a thousand miles begins with a single step, Diane wrote in an email to me last night. I'm not sure if she knows where the saying comes from—I'm hoping she wasn't trying to pass it off as her own. Admittedly, I had to google it to remind myself—I thought it was Confucius but it was his contemporary Lao Tzu.

My journey is not of a thousand miles. It's probably only half a mile there and back.

I have a knot in the pit of my stomach, which I'm used to. But it feels different today. I sometimes think of it as a large ball of elastic bands wound tightly together. If one band stretches too tight and snaps, the whole thing will fall apart. But today it feels secure. It might even be helping to weigh me down, keeping my feet on this pavement.

It's Saturday, probably the busiest shopping day of the week. When I told Diane this was when I was going to do it, she put her serious face on.

"Are you sure that's a good idea? Perhaps a quieter day of the week would be a good starting point?"

"It's not a busy department store," I told her. "I think I'll cope."

I had no idea whether I would cope. But I didn't want the decision to be Diane's.

"You have my number," she said. "I'll be by my phone. Call me if you need to talk to someone. Or I can talk, and you can just listen."

"Thank you," I said.

I slip my hand into my pocket and press my fingers against my phone.

A couple walk on the other side of the road, arm in arm. Ahead of me, I see a woman pushing a stroller. She's walking fairly quickly, from what I can tell. If I stay at my current pace, I won't catch up with her. Apart from her the street ahead of me is empty. I wonder how many of the houses are empty too. What do other people do on Saturday afternoons? They meet friends for coffee, they take their kids swimming, they go to the movies. They moan about having nothing to do when they have the whole world within reach.

I sneak a look at the nearest house. It has a blue front door and a small pot of orange flowers on either end of the step. The next one has a tiny stone birdbath on the stones in front of the bay window. I wonder where the lovebirds with the peach faces are now.

I look at ten more houses, trying to figure out who sleeps in their beds, who cooks in their kitchens, who draws their curtains and locks their doors at night. A couple of times I catch a glimpse of someone in the room at the front of the house and look away quickly. I don't want to get a reputation as someone who stares into people's windows.

I'm almost at the house with the black door. It has fairy lights around the upstairs windows—I'm not sure if they're left over from Christmas or if they're a year-round decoration, but I like them.

The house with the black door and the fairy lights is the last house on the street. I take a deep breath and press a hand against the base of my belly. The knot is still there but it's intact. It's time to go shopping.

The young woman behind the counter doesn't even look up as I push open the door with a palm that's definitely clammier than it was a few minutes ago. I walk quickly to the back of the shop and take my list out of my pocket.

Onions
Oat milk
Peaches / nectarines
Toilet paper
Dish soap

I happen to be standing right next to the toilet paper, so I grab a packet. A few more steps and I'm at the dish soap. I should have picked up a basket. The thought of dropping peaches all over the floor makes me feel nauseous. I look back at my list. One thing at a time.

There's someone else standing at the small fruit section—a tall man wearing a cap and baggy jeans. I approach slowly, clutching my toilet paper and dish soap to my chest.

He chooses a banana, and the sight of it in his hand makes me think of something Fee used to say. *Is that a banana in your pocket, or are you just pleased to see me?*

I wonder what she's doing right now. I might call her later.

"All right?" The man with the banana doesn't wait for an answer and walks away.

"All right," I say back.

There are no fresh peaches or nectarines. I could buy canned ones, but I pick up a banana instead. I can eat it on the way home. I'm hungry, I realize. This required more than soup for lunch.

It feels adventurous to deviate from my list. I look around to see what else catches my eye. There's a fresh doughnut stand that wasn't here the last time I was, and a whole "allergens" section. I grab a fudge doughnut and a granola I've never seen on the grocery website. I need an onion for the stir-fry I'm planning to make for dinner. Luckily they're in plentiful supply, unlike peaches. I choose two that are relatively blemish-free, then replace one. When I need more, I'll come back.

I wasn't aware of the young woman making her way toward me from behind the counter until she's right beside me.

"Need any help?" She has long blonde hair scraped into a bun on the top of her head and a metal bar through her eyebrow.

I stare at her, then look at my list. "Do you have oat milk?"

"Hmmm, I don't think so," she says. "Let me check."

I wait beside the onions for her to come back. A woman and a little boy clutching a large toy dinosaur come into the shop.

She sees me looking and smiles. "He takes it everywhere with him."

I smile back. "I like it."

The woman with the bun is back. She waves a carton at me. "Will almond milk do? Don't have any oat milk, but we should get a delivery on Tuesday. If you like, I can put some aside for you."

"Almond milk is perfect." I breathe a sigh of relief and take it from her. "Thanks."

"No bother." She goes off to speak to the woman with the boy.

I walk around the shop one more time, finding out where everything is. I pick up mushrooms and a packet of dried cranberries, then walk to the counter. The woman and the boy have gone. It's just me and the woman with the bun.

"You up to anything today?"

"Um, I'm not sure," I tell her honestly. "I might do some baking."

"Cool," she says. "Do you have a bag?"

I look at her blankly. "Um...no."

"It's five pence for a plastic bag," she says.

"Sure," I say quickly. "Of course."

I watch her pack my five-pence bag. At the last minute I grab a chocolate bar I've never seen before and hand it over. When it's time, I put my card in the machine the wrong way and get a bit flustered, but then I get it right. I tell her no, thanks, I don't need my receipt.

"Have a nice day," I tell her before I leave. We make eye contact and I realize she has beautiful hazel eyes flecked with yellow.

"Cheers. You too," she says.

I walk out of the shop with my bag and think about phoning someone—Sadie or Tom or Celeste or even Diane—but I decide to wait until I get home. I want to keep this moment to myself for a little longer.

I put my bag down on the pavement while I peel my banana. It's perfectly ripe—much better than the bananas I get with my online delivery that need four days in the fruit bowl before I can eat them.

"Meredith—is that you?"

I hear her before I see her, because I'm not looking at anything apart from my banana. I have no idea who she is, this elderly woman in a smart red coat.

"It is you! I haven't seen you in forever!"

I smile, holding my banana awkwardly because it's peeled now and I can't put it back in my bag. "Hi...how are you?"

"It's Marie—Marie Rossiter. Mrs. Rossiter."

Third-year history. "Mrs. Rossiter...wow. I'm sorry, I didn't recognize you."

"Oh, that's all right, dear. I'm a lot older than I used to be!" She laughs. "Mind you, so are you. How are you? You haven't changed a bit."

"I'm good," I tell her.

"I'm glad to hear it, dear. What are you up to these days?"

"I'm a writer. I live just along the street."

"Wow, a writer? Well, that doesn't surprise me. Your essays

always were of a very high standard. Anyway, I'd better go and get my hair sorted out." She laughs again. "We're having people over for dinner tonight."

"Have a nice time," I tell her.

"Thank you, dear. You take care."

I'm halfway home before I realize that Mrs. Rossiter doesn't know anything about me other than what I've just told her. She doesn't know what she doesn't know. She might go home and tell her husband, "I bumped into one of my old pupils today. She's a writer now." And that will be it.

Day 1,414

Fiona looks different. She has chunky white-blonde streaks in her hair and a flush of color on her cheeks. Her eyes look brighter— is she wearing eyeshadow? I can't tell, but if she is, it's working. She looks ten years younger than she did the last time she stood on my doorstep.

"I've brought cake," she says, handing me a white box.

"Thanks."

She follows me into the kitchen, drops her bag on the floor, and peels off her jacket.

"How did you get on with the Rape Crisis woman?"

"Barbara. She was nice." I open the box and smile. Carrot cake. My favorite. I busy myself getting plates, a knife, forks, boiling the kettle.

"Want to talk about it?"

"I'm not sure. Maybe. Not yet, though."

"Well, whenever you like. I'm proud of you, Mer."

"I'm proud of *us*," I say. "What about you? Are you OK?" I haven't told her that I often lie awake at night, worrying about her. We've fallen into the habit of texting each other last thing, but even then I can't completely relax. The shadow of Lucas looms large in my mind.

"I am actually. He's gone to stay with his uncle in Dundee."

"You've heard from him?" I stare at her.

"No, no." She shakes her head. "I saw his mum at the post office."

287

"Karen." I remember the small meek woman at the barbecue at Mama's, when Lucas proposed, then at their wedding.

"She apologized. Said she's mortified, that she doesn't know what came over him."

"*She doesn't know what came over him?*" I grip the handle of the kettle and focus on pouring the boiling water into our mugs.

"I know, I know." She moves closer to me. Her fingers graze the base of my spine; the lightest touch, letting me know she's with me in the way that counts.

"I might need to do what you did—with Barbara, or someone else," she says, and maybe it's for me, or her, or for both of us.

"I think it will help," I say.

"In time," she says quickly. "When I'm ready."

"Of course," I say, because I know everything about being ready. And on that note—"I walked to the shop yesterday."

"Fuck! Really? Meredith, that's huge. I'm double proud of you."

"Thanks." We sit down and I take a mouthful of cake. "Wow. This is amazing. Where did you get it?"

"I made it." My sister beams at me.

"I don't believe you. It's too good."

She laughs. "I swear to God. I've been baking a lot, the past couple of years. It's my escape."

I stare at her. "I've been baking a lot too. But I'm not as good as you. You should go into business—this is actually incredible."

"I've made a few birthday cakes for friends. There might be something in it—who knows? Maybe I'll finally get out of that supermarket."

"If you're going to be coming round more often, I'm going to get really fat."

My words hang in the air between us. "I'd like that," she says. "Not the fat part, the coming round part."

"Remember how you used to call me fat, when we were kids?" I can't help myself.

"I was a stupid kid. I was jealous of you. You had this thick dark hair, beautiful big eyes. You were...mysterious."

I stare at her. "I had no idea. I was jealous of you. I wanted your blonde hair and your freckles."

"Kisses from the sun," we say simultaneously.

I eat my cake, watch Fiona drink her tea, look at her freckles, her snub nose, her blue eyes. As familiar to me as the features on my own face, even after everything. *Mysterious.* I whisper the word in my mind, trying it on for size. Maybe it wasn't too late to consider a different version of myself from the one Mama had strapped me into, like a too-tight coat.

"She was awful to me too, you know," Fee says.

I take our empty plates to the sink and turn on the tap. There's a tiny brown bird hopping along the back-garden fence. I watch him perform his carefree, one-legged dance.

"Meredith," she says.

"It's not a contest, Fee."

"I'm not trying to turn it into one. I just want you to know that you weren't the only one. I mean, she didn't hate you more than me, or anything like that." She joins me at the sink and grabs the dish towel. "Here, let me dry."

I hand her a wet plate. "I don't remember her being that bad to you."

"She was worse when you weren't there."

"That makes sense." I turn off the tap and look at her. "I'm sorry, for what it's worth."

"You've got nothing to be sorry about. What could you have done about it?"

"I don't know. But you could have told me."

"I didn't want you to know. I wanted you to think that at least one of us had some power over her." She reaches out to touch my arm—briefly, lightly. "When I think about it now, I should have told you. I guess I was trying to protect you. It was stupid."

"We were young. You were young. It wasn't up to us to figure things out."

We give my words time to settle, to unite us in my kitchen after decades of those unsaid.

"I know. But still..." She looks out of the window, her mouth set in a firm line. I look out too. The tiny brown bird is gone. There's not a breath of life out there.

We stand there for what feels like the longest time. We hold hands; I'm not sure who instigates it.

"I don't know what to say, Mer."

"Neither do I. More cake?" I let go of her fingers and reach across the worktop to turn the radio on. Happy pop music fills my kitchen.

We sit down and eat our cake to the sound of the Beatles. I think about my childhood dream to go to Liverpool and find our father. It fizzled out as soon as I was old enough to realize it would be years before I had the money or the freedom to go anywhere. And by that time he'd been gone for so long I almost doubted he ever existed.

An hour later, I wave goodbye to my sister from the end of my garden path. We've had three years apart but it might as well have been a lifetime. We were both going through the same thing but following parallel paths rather than walking the same one. Over tea and cake we dipped into parts of our pasts, but we've only scratched the surface. I don't know how deep we'll ever go. But for now, this is enough.

Day 1,420

Saturday, June 8, 2019

My party jumpsuit is lying on the bed. I stand in the doorway of my room and look at it. It has a high neck but a low back, so I'll need to go braless. I feel a shiver of something in my body. Excitement? Trepidation? Baring my back to the world—or Celeste's closest friends and family, at least—is one of many big steps I'll need to take. But I'm feeling brave.

I had a choice of black, dark green, or purple. My instinct was to go for black, but I decided to live on the edge and switched to purple at the last minute. It's a beautiful shade, more blue than red, like a plum that's not quite ripe. It has long sleeves and tiny satin buttons at the cuffs. Gently flared legs, long enough to wear heels but not so long that the bottoms drag along the floor. I tried it on as soon as it arrived, testing it with my new strappy sandals. Fred followed me around the house, up and down the stairs, sitting down, then standing up, reaching high and bending low. He kept a safe distance, as if he understood that cat hair on the new jumpsuit wouldn't be appreciated.

"This is important," I told him. "I need to make sure I don't have any wardrobe malfunctions on the night. That would be embarrassing."

It's still too early to get ready, so I focus on Celeste's gift. I've bought her a calligraphy set: a pen with a smooth marble-like finish, a wooden pen holder, interchangeable nibs of different widths, and eight little pots of ink in shimmery colors.

I wrap the box in blue paper the color of a summer

sky, then finish it off with wide organza ribbon tied in a large bow.

None of the thirtieth-birthday cards, with explosions of glitter and shiny balloons and champagne bubbles, felt right. After much scrolling, I found it. A small square in thick card stock, with a simple message encased inside the outline of a heart: "One Friend Can Change Your Whole Life."

I don't want to belabor the point, so I keep the inside brief:

Dear Celeste,
Have a wonderful birthday!
Much love,
Mer

I put the wrapped calligraphy set and card into a stiff gift bag and sit it on the little table in the hall next to my keys. I check my phone. Finally, it's time.

I can do many things on my own, but applying fake tan to my back would definitely have been easier with another pair of hands. I did it last night, sitting on the floor of my bedroom in front of my tall mirror, twisting my head round to try to see what I was doing. I wanted to do it ahead of time just to make sure I didn't end up looking like a mahogany sideboard, and it's turned out OK—from what I can see. The website promised a "natural, sun-kissed glow"—I'll settle for not looking like someone who's had very little UV radiation for the last three years.

A bath would make me too relaxed, so I shower, wash and condition my hair, shave my legs and under my arms. Then I stand under the hot water for six minutes and try not to think beyond the next half hour.

I never do anything interesting with my hair, so I'm going to curl it tonight. I've been practicing in front of YouTube videos all week and I'm pretty pleased with my efforts, although the first few attempts were laughable. I sent Sadie a photo of two of them, pulling a funny face. She sent back a row of crying-laughter emojis and two words: Shirley Temple.

When my hair is curled in a non-child-star-from-the-1930s-type way, I clip the sides loosely back from my face and kneel on a cushion in front of my tall mirror to do my makeup. I've practiced some different looks, but none of them felt like me. I play it safe with my usual tinted moisturizer, mascara, and pink lip gloss, but I want to do more—it's a party, after all.

I unearth an old makeup bag from the deep recesses of the bathroom cabinet and find what I'm looking for—eyeliner and bronzer. The last time I used them was two months before I withdrew from the world. A last-minute week in Tenerife with Sadie. We drank warm white wine on the plane, we fell asleep on our sun loungers after lunch every day, we laughed at our respective holiday book choices—she read the latest installment in the Fifty Shades series; I read Madeleine Thien's *Do Not Say We Have Nothing*. We floated on ridiculous inflatables in the pool: she had a flamingo; I had a giant pizza slice. I came back with a red nose and peeling shoulders; she came back with the phone number of a guy she'd got chatting to on the plane when I was asleep.

"You'll never call him." I laughed as she pointed him out to me in the passport control line. "He lives in Edinburgh." Our lives were so small that forty miles constituted a long-distance relationship, but we liked it that way.

I had no idea that my life was about to become even smaller.

I think of Sadie as I add eyeliner flicks and dust bronzer over my cheekbones. I haven't told her what I'm doing tonight, but I don't know what she's doing either. I might call her from the party and make a big announcement: "You'll never guess where I am!"

She'll love that. She'll say "fuck" a lot. In a good way.

I unclip my hair, fasten my strappy sandals round my ankles, and look at my reflection.

I'm ready, but I still have over half an hour before my taxi arrives. I pre-booked it this afternoon, because I don't really know how busy taxi companies are these days, and I don't want to be late.

A thought dances through my mind. I don't have to go. I can cancel the taxi, take the jumpsuit off, scrape back my hair, and put my pajamas on.

"No," I say, making eye contact with the woman with her arms folded on my wall. "I'm doing this."

I decide to go downstairs and have a cup of tea, maybe do a bit more of my jigsaw to calm my nerves. Freshen Fred's water bowl and check the back doors are locked. I know they are, but there's no harm in making sure. Better to be safe than sorry.

I stare at the pieces of Van Gogh's *Café Terrace at Night*, strewn across my coffee table. I have twenty minutes. *If I can find all the edges, I'll make it to the party*, I tell myself.

When the text comes, I have only a handful of edges.

Your taxi, a Volkswagen Passat, is en route and should be at your property in approximately 6 minutes.

I abandon Van Gogh and stand at the front window, checking the time every ten seconds. I'm starting to get a little warm. I pull at the neck of my jumpsuit. Maybe I should have gone for the dress after all. But then I would have had to fake-tan my legs as well as my back.

A car slows down outside my house and my heart jumps. It drives on.

I check the time again.

I think I need some water. Or maybe a lot of it. Maybe I should lie down for a few minutes.

I know Celeste will enjoy her party whether I'm there or not.

It's not like I'm a VIP guest. I've only known her for five minutes. I'm having second thoughts about the card. It's too much; I should have gone for a standard glittery 30.

With shaky fingers I go to my call history and jab at the taxi company's number.

A cheery woman tells me it's on its way. "Sorry, love. Traffic's murder tonight."

A few minutes pass, as slow as death. A man walks past my house with a tiny dog on a lead, followed closely by a little blonde girl on a scooter. The man looks behind him and says something to the girl. He spots me at the window and smiles. I smile back. I try to put myself in his shoes, walking a dog and a little girl around the neighborhood. Maybe popping into a shop or two, picking up Saturday-night treats.

I can't do it. I can walk to the shop for onions and almond milk but I can't go to a party. I can't. I can't. I can't. I've been so focused on getting out of the house that I haven't thought about what I'll be faced with when I get there. A room full of people I don't know. Small talk and dancing and worrying that I'm too old to go without a bra. I probably won't even get to speak to Celeste. It's like a wedding—you can get to the last dance without exchanging more than a few words with the bride and groom.

There's a car outside my house. I take a deep breath, pick up my bag, and walk to the front door.

It takes a moment to get the taxi driver's attention. When he realizes I'm not just acknowledging him, he gets out of the car.

"Need some help, hen?" He walks up the path.

"Yes," I tell him. I rummage in my bag, retrieve two folded twenty-pound notes.

"Take this. And this." I hand him Celeste's gift bag. "Please can you take this to the bowling club? I can't go anymore. It's a birthday party. You can just hand it to anyone and ask them to pass it to Celeste."

"Celeste?"

"Her name's on the card."

He takes the bag. "You're not going?" He looks confused, but he has kind eyes. And I've paid him double.

"No. I'm not feeling well all of a sudden."

"Aye, you don't look too good, hen. Maybe you should get some rest."

"Thanks for doing this."

"No bother, hen. You take care."

I watch him walk back to his car, holding the gift bag tightly in his right hand. Before he drives off, he waves to me.

I wave back, then slowly shut my door on Saturday night.

1989

"You can't wear that." Fiona stood in front of me, hands on her hips. She was eleven but thought she was twenty-one.

"What's wrong with it?" I demanded. I twirled in front of her, liking the way my pink skirt billowed out. It was a little tight on me, but it would be fine if I didn't eat too much party food.

"You look like a baby." Fiona opened her wardrobe door and started rummaging. "Here, try these on." She threw a pair of jeans at me.

"I'm not wearing jeans to a birthday party."

"Are you five years old?"

"No," I admitted, but I ignored the jeans. I picked at a loose thread on the hem of my skirt. I hadn't worn it for a year, since we went to the ballet with Auntie Linda. She'd got free tickets from her boss and Mama was supposed to come too, but she changed her mind at the last minute. It was one of the best nights of my life. I decided the pink skirt definitely deserved another outing. Why shouldn't it be to Sarah Little's birthday party?

"Meredith, none of your friends will be wearing stuff like this."

"I don't care. I like it," I said, trying to sound more confident than I felt.

"Just try the jeans on." Fiona turned back to her wardrobe. "I'll find you a top that goes."

I was torn between showing my sister who was boss and not wanting my friends to think I was a baby. Reluctantly I decided Fiona would always think she was the boss anyway.

I wriggled out of the skirt and pulled on the jeans. They were actually OK—the denim was soft and stretchy, so they fitted well.

Fiona was forever telling me I was bigger than her, but not in these jeans.

By the time I was dressed, with a white T-shirt tucked into the jeans and a cropped blue cardigan on top, I got my sister's seal of approval.

"Perfect," she said.

"Are you sure?" I looked at my reflection in the mirror.

"Trust me," she said.

I quickly wrapped Sarah's present, a trio of sparkly nail polishes I had bought at the pharmacy when I was picking up Mama's cough medicine. Then I wrote the card, which had a big rainbow number ten on the front and said "Happy birthday, special girl!" inside. I wished I'd checked inside the card before I'd bought it, because Sarah wasn't really a special girl to me; she was just someone in my class whose mum probably made her invite me to her party to be nice. But there was nothing I could do about that. For today Sarah would have to be my special girl. I wrote *from Meredith* without any kisses—I didn't want her to think I was trying too hard.

Sarah didn't live far from us—two streets down, along from the train station.

"I'll walk you there," Fiona said. "Then I'll come back for you."

"Thanks," I said, like it was no big deal, like I wasn't relieved that Mama wouldn't have the chance to embarrass me in front of my friends.

When we got downstairs, Mama was singing along to the radio in the kitchen, something about respect. She sounded like she was in a good mood. Fiona nudged me, jerked her head in our mother's direction.

"Mama, I'm going to Sarah's party!" I shouted as casually as I could.

The radio was off and she was in front of us within seconds.

"Whose party?"

"Sarah's party. I told you about it ages ago. And I reminded you yesterday. The invitation is on the front of the fridge."

"Stop lying, Meredith. Who would invite you to a party?"

"Sarah Little," I said desperately. "She's in my class. It's just a party in her house. It's not really a party actually. We're getting pizza and watching a movie."

"*Getting pizza and watching a movie,*" she said in a babyish voice. I looked at my sister, who was sitting on the stairs. She shrugged.

"Fiona's taking me and bringing me back. I'll be home by eight thirty."

"Is that right?"

"Mama, please." I was begging, but I didn't care. I'd do anything to spend time in someone else's house for a few hours. A house where people laughed and watched movies and didn't have to worry about making the wrong noise or being in the wrong place or saying the wrong thing.

Mama crossed her arms and looked me up and down. "Did you get dressed in the dark?"

"Fiona styled me," I said, avoiding my sister's eyes.

She tutted loudly. "Your sister's the last person who should be giving fashion advice."

"I'll get changed," I pleaded.

She laughed. "On you go then. Better be quick or you'll miss the party."

I raced upstairs and tore off my clothes. I put my twirly pink skirt back on—Mama would like it, I decided, and I'd never listen to my sister again—and paired it with a cream blouse with a frilly collar. I smoothed my hair down and took a deep breath.

At Sarah Little's party most of the other girls were wearing jeans. But Sarah's cousin Emma wore a long silver skirt that sparkled when she moved. When Sarah's mum put a record on, Emma and I let our skirts twirl a little, sharing a smile.

Day 1,421

Sunday, June 9, 2019

I phone Celeste as soon as I wake up because I know if I don't, I never will.

"I haven't left my house for one thousand four hundred and twenty days," I say in a rush.

"Meredith—is that you? What are you talking about?" She sounds sleepy. Confused, but not angry.

"Sorry...yes, it's me. I haven't left my house for one thousand four hundred and twenty days. Three years and three hundred and twenty-five days. More than two hundred weeks. About forty-seven months. Maybe forty-eight." I take a huge gulp of air. "That's why I couldn't come to your party last night. I tried, I really tried. I was ready to leave and everything. And then...well, I couldn't do it. I'm so sorry, Celeste. I wanted to be there so much."

"What did you have on?"

"What? Um...a jumpsuit."

"What color?"

"Purple."

"That's my favorite color."

"Really? Mine too."

"I bet you looked bloody amazing in it."

I think about the jumpsuit, the strappy sandals, the fake tan, the curled hair, the eyeliner flicks, the bronzer. I feel ridiculous and small. I want to release Celeste from this conversation, but she speaks before I can make an excuse.

"Mer, I love my present. It's perfect."

It's the thing everybody says, but I believe her. And yet—because I'm me—I double-check. "You do?"

"I do. I can't wait to use it. Thank you so much."

I'm pleased, but I wonder what I was thinking. Three years of not going anywhere, and I think I can casually call a taxi, put on a purple jumpsuit, and walk into a party with a shiny gift bag? I slump over the table. I'm exhausted, my head is starting to hurt, and there's a lump forming in my throat.

"I just wasn't ready," I whisper.

"Meredith, it's OK." Her voice is soft. "Really. Listen, I need to wake up properly, have a shower. Can I call you tonight? We'll have a long chat?"

"Yes. But...I don't know where to start."

"We'll start at the beginning and take it from there. You can tell me as much or as little as you like."

It feels good to let Celeste take charge. I go back to bed and sleep for most of the day. At 7 p.m. she calls me, and we talk. I tell her about Lucas, sobbing as I replay the memory out loud. She cries too. She tells me how brave I am, that I can get through this, that she'll be there by my side, that I have so many people in my corner.

Day 1,425

Celeste is right—I do have people in my corner. Tom arrives with a warm sourdough loaf and a box of cherries. "Just because," he says, grinning.

I pour olive oil and balsamic vinegar into two dipping bowls, and we tear off chunks of bread with our fingers. "The simple things are the best," he says, and his words hit me right in my soft spot, and suddenly my own words are tumbling out. I tell him about Celeste's party, down to the jumpsuit and the strappy sandals, and he doesn't interrupt, not once.

"Meredith, what you're doing...the work you're doing... it's all for you," he says, when I've finally finished and go back to stuffing bread in my mouth. "You're not doing this for me, or Sadie, or Celeste, or anyone else. You're doing it for yourself— and you deserve it. Can you see that?"

"I'm trying to."

"Nobody expects you to be perfect, Meredith."

"God. That sounds like another of Diane's affirmations."

He smiles. "Maybe that one will stick?"

"Maybe."

Day 1,426

Friday, June 14, 2019

"I'd like to talk today. No CBT."

"Of course, Meredith. Is there anything in particular you'd like to talk about?" Diane rests her elbows on her desk and moves forward slightly. It strikes me again just how beautiful she is. Auburn hair, alabaster skin, eyes like freshwater pools.

"I'd like to talk about my mother."

"OK. It's been a while since we talked about her. Has there been any contact?"

"She phoned a few weeks ago. It didn't go well."

"I can imagine."

"I always feel sick when she calls. But now...I'm angry. I'm angry at her, and I want to forget about her. I don't know how to deal with all that."

"I'd be surprised if you didn't feel anger toward her."

"I don't think I can forgive her..."

"You've been the victim of abuse for a long time, Meredith. For your entire life, I'd say."

"I'm not a victim," I say quietly but crossly. "Mama always said..."

"What did your mama say, Meredith?"

"She said victims were weak and attention-seeking." I can hear her voice now, the words slicing through plumes of smoke. The weight of her glare sends adrenaline fizzing through my body and makes my guts twist. I have my period. Or tonsillitis. Or a fractured finger after she trapped it in the back door. It doesn't matter. Her message is always the same: I'm melodramatic and selfish.

"Do you think maybe your mother was wrong, Meredith? What if she was here with us now, just listening, not able to hurt you with her words or her actions? What would you say to her?"

"I'd ask her why she treated me the way she did."

"And how do you think she would respond to that?"

"She'd probably laugh."

"OK, what about if she was being honest, if she was asking for your forgiveness? How do you think she would respond if that was the case?"

I try to think of Mama that way—as an honest person. Someone who cares about other people's feelings, who doesn't take pleasure in being cruel, who has the ability to say "I'm sorry." It's impossible. It would be easier to create her from scratch, cell by cell.

I'm not aware that I've drifted away until Diane's voice gets louder. "Meredith." The way she says it, I know it's not the first time.

I focus on her face again. "Sorry."

"I lost you for a moment there. Are you OK? Do you want to take a break? Get a glass of water?"

"I have some." I lift my shiny bottle from the table and take a swig. I hadn't realized how dry my throat was. I drink more, gulping it down.

"Let me frame this in a different way. What would you like to hear your mother say? What do you wish she could say to you, if she had the ability to show her vulnerable side?"

"She doesn't have a vulnerable side."

"We all do, Meredith."

"Well, hers is very well hidden."

"Yes, it sounds like that. Meredith, what I'm trying to do here is help you separate yourself from your mother's actions. Yes, she did cruel things to you. But she didn't do them *because* of you. Can you think of a reason for her behavior?"

A heavy sigh escapes from my body. Diane's questions are exhausting. I'd love her to come up with an answer now and again, even though I know, by now, that's not the point of all this.

"I don't know," I admit. "I guess she was unhappy. I really don't know anything about her childhood, her life before us. To be honest, she was like a stranger most of the time. She had this shield—we couldn't break through it."

"You mentioned earlier that you feel sick when she calls you. What do you think you could do about that?"

"Tell her to stop calling?"

"Hmm...you could. Or you could just stop answering."

"It's not that easy."

"Isn't it?"

I look at everything but Diane. My kitchen wall. The floor. My nails—definitely in need of a manicure. I'm wearing a short-sleeved top today. I look at the mole at the base of my thumb. Turn my arm over, let my fingers find their way into the soft grooves, rest there for a few seconds. Trace my timeline of scars.

Finally I look at her. "I guess."

"You see, you're in control here. You can set those boundaries. You don't have to speak to her. You don't have to see her. And you don't have to justify those decisions to anyone. Not to her, not to your sister—not to anyone."

"OK," I murmur, still rubbing my arms. *I'm sorry*, I say inwardly, to my younger self: my four-year-old, nine-year-old, twelve-year-old, thirty-six-year-old self.

"That's the first step. The next is to try to let go of what happened in the past. Not because she deserves forgiveness. But because it's stopping you from living your life the way you want to live it. And I'm not just talking about leaving your house."

"You're not?"

She shakes her head. "I'm talking about you taking control, Meredith."

I don't remember her touch. It should be something I don't even have to think about, because it was just there. Something so essential and accessible that it was like I was an extension of her in those early years. But as hard as I try, I can't invoke a memory.

In my dreams I reach out for her. But my arms turn to stone and crumble into fine dust.

Tonight, my dream is different. I dream I'm being held. It's a close grip, and I feel safe and warm. Sleepy. Before my eyes close, I look up. It's not her face—it's a man.

I wake up before I find out what it feels like to wake up in his arms. I close my eyes against the early-morning light and try to slip back into the dream, but it doesn't work. His features float away, and the empty space where his face was haunts my thoughts for the rest of the day.

Day 1,427

It's amazing what you can find when you google "social recluse." And it's not always a good idea. I discover that there's a label for people like me in Japan. If I lived there, I'd be an official hikikomori—defined by the country's Health, Labor, and Welfare Ministry as someone who has remained isolated at home for at least six consecutive months without going to school or work, and rarely interacts with people outside their own immediate family.

Six months? I'll raise you three years, hikikomori of Japan.

I read an article about forty-five-year-old Haru, who lives in Greater Tokyo with his elderly mother. He's been a hikikomori, on and off, for fifteen years. "Most of us are normal people who have been forced into reclusivity," he says. "It's not a choice."

I decide I would like Haru if I met him. He seems like an intelligent sort. The likelihood of an in-person meeting is slim, for obvious reasons. Still, there's always Zoom.

Apparently the term *hikikomori* was coined by a psychiatrist in the late 1990s to describe young people who had withdrawn from society. My affinity with my newfound label wobbles slightly when I learn that hikikomori have a reputation as dangerous sociopaths. One hikikomori was arrested for kidnapping a seven-year-old girl and keeping her hostage in his room for more than five years. Another broke out of his self-imposed isolation to stab two customers at his local convenience store.

The article quotes a Japanese psychologist who says, "People become hikikomori for a wide range of reasons, and it can happen at any age. Often the person has had a bad experience at school or college, has been through a public disaster or personal trauma, or has quit their job to look after an elderly parent and has never returned to the workforce."

Haru's parents divorced when he was six, and he hasn't seen his father since. He struggled at school, always feeling like he was different from his peers. At college he couldn't make deadlines and dropped out of his course. He never felt equipped for the workforce, found it difficult to hold down a job, and eventually stopped trying. When he was thirty-five, he was diagnosed with autism.

"I sleep a lot, and read books," Haru says. "I don't like being in the house, but I'd rather be here than at work, feeling like a failure."

I copy and paste the link to the article into an email to Celeste with a single line—Is this my dream man?—and hit send before I can change my mind.

Day 1,428

Sunday, June 16, 2019

I hear the letter box, but it's Sunday so I assume it's a bundle of leaflets promoting buy-one-get-one-free products at the local shop or some other type of junk mail. I don't check it until I've done my stair workout, showered and deep-conditioned my hair, drunk my blueberry and banana smoothie, and rubbed flea treatment in the little spot between Fred's bony shoulder bones.

It's not a BOGOF leaflet, or a takeout menu, or an invitation to discover God. It's a thick cream envelope with my name on the front in attractive, slightly old-fashioned-looking writing. The "M's" have a subtle curve and the tails of the "g's" curl like Fred's semi-relaxed tail when he sits on the kitchen windowsill.

I pause before opening it, wanting to savor the excitement. I have a little flutter in my belly, and it's the good kind. This is a big deal for me. Apart from the annual postcard from Sadie when she takes the kids to Center Parcs, I never get any mail apart from bills and catalogs I haven't signed up for. Definitely not something with my name looking all fancy on such sophisticated stationery.

Eventually my curiosity gets the better of me. I sit on the third stair from the bottom and slowly open the envelope, taking care not to rip it.

The sheet of paper is also cream and thick—weighty between my fingertips. I know straightaway the four characters are Japanese, but I have no idea what they mean. I stare at the thick black lines and wonder why symbols I don't understand are making me feel so emotional. I turn the sheet of paper over and there, in the bottom right corner, is exactly what I expected to find: a curved capital "C."

Thanks to the wonder of Google, it doesn't take long to understand my Japanese message. If nothing else, three years as a hikikomori has given me stellar research skills.

In Japan the kanji characters for the four iconic trees that flower during springtime (cherry, plum, peach, and apricot) create the concept of *oubaitori*. In Japanese philosophy it's the art of never comparing yourself to others, but recognizing value in your own unique character.

I send Celeste a text—You're the best—and she responds with a single "X." Then I sit at the kitchen table, drink a cup of peppermint tea, and look at my oubaitori. At some point the sky becomes less gray, and a tiny enticing pocket of bright sunlight beams onto the cream paper, making Celeste's calligraphy even glossier.

Day 1,434

"Are you busy?" Fee gets straight to the point.

"I'm just back from the shop."

"That's great. You're becoming quite the regular at that shop."

"It's going slowly," I admit.

"Hey, I'm kidding! You're doing brilliantly. You're my hero."

"Oh, give it a rest," I say, but I'm delighted.

"Can I come over?" Her voice is serious.

"Right now?"

"I'm coming over," she says, and hangs up.

It only takes her twenty minutes to get here, but it feels like hours. I clean the kitchen floor while I'm waiting, moving the mop in large sweeping circles.

"Have you been working out?" she asks me when I open the front door.

I touch my cheek—it's warm and clammy. "Just cleaning," I say.

"No need to clean for my benefit."

"I wasn't." I roll my eyes at her back, follow her into the kitchen. I don't tell her not to walk on the floor, and by the time I remember, it's too late—her trainers have left a faint pattern across the freshly cleaned surface.

"How's it going at Shirley's?" I ask her.

"It's all right," she says. "A bit cramped. I'm looking for some-thing else."

"I haven't seen Mama for weeks," she says as soon as I turn my back to pour the dirty mop water down the sink.

"OK," I tell the tap.

"I just wanted you to know."

"OK."

"She's not happy. She calls a lot."

"Rather you than me."

Fee shrugs. "Fair enough. Anyway, that's not really why I'm here."

"It's not?" I turn to face her.

She pulls a brown envelope out of her pocket. "A couple of months ago, she asked me to sell some of her crap on eBay. Boxes of random stuff she'd been holding on to for years. Anyway, I finally started going through it all last night." Her eyes flash. "And I found this."

I feel a rush in my brain and remind myself that it's excitement. I look at my sister and try to figure out if it's good or bad news. She nods at me.

Inside the envelope is a small newspaper cutting, yellow with age. Only four lines, framed by a black rectangle:

Michael Young, 36, of Glasgow, passed away at home on
August 12, 1993. He is survived by his daughters Fiona, 16,
and Meredith, 14. A service will be held at 2 p.m. at Blackstone
Chapel on Thursday, August 19. Family only. No flowers please.

I start crying for a man I never knew. Fiona leaves the room and comes back with a handful of toilet paper. I sob into it.

"He was so young," I say when I can control my voice.

"I know."

"Michael. His name was Michael. That's a nice name. A good name."

"Meredith, he might not have been a nice man. We don't know anything about him."

"I know that," I snap.

I look at the small piece of soft paper, at the simplicity of my father's name in print. Fiona's right. To create a glorified history of him is naive.

"I want to believe he was good," Fiona says. "But the one thing we know about him is that he was never there. He never came for us."

"We have a whole other family we've never met," I say, instead of admitting she's right. "Remember Auntie Anna?"

"I do. She was nice. But I'm not sure I want to try to be her niece. Not now."

I'm not sure I want to either. But I like having the option.

"You know there's one way to find out where they are, how he died?"

She nods. "I called her earlier. She's just angry."

"Maybe it's time for us to get angry."

"Or maybe it's time to let it go."

"I've spent forty years letting things go, Fiona." I remember what Diane said about being in control. "I want to know about him."

"There are websites; we can search records. Do some detective work. You always wanted to be Nancy Drew."

I laugh. "You're right—I did."

She takes her jacket off and stays for an hour. I put the newspaper cutting between us on the table and open the bottle of red wine that's been in my cupboard for years. In the absence of the truth we weave together a story for Michael Young.

"I think he wanted to be a good father," I say.

"Maybe he did. But it's not enough to want something, is it? You have to do the work."

"Some people aren't designed to be nurturers."

She nods. "In lots of different ways."

"I wonder if he would have been good to us, if he'd had the chance?"

Fee shrugs. "I don't know, Meredith. I guess we'll never know. And we have to be OK with that."

Finally we agree that Michael Young was a flawed man with a generous heart who lacked the courage he needed to fight for what he wanted, and fell in love with a woman who couldn't love him back.

Later that evening, Celeste phones to find out how I'm getting on with my "mission." A brief wave of embarrassment sweeps over me. I'm hardly going to live on Mars. But I suppose I am on a mission of sorts.

"You're doing so well," she says. "Who knows—in a few weeks you might be ready to go to the movies, go clubbing, go out to a fancy restaurant."

I laugh. "You know, the thought of going to the movies is actually a huge turnoff. Who wants to listen to people crunching popcorn? There's no leg room at all, the seats are really uncomfortable—"

"People don't turn their phones off. That's a big one."

"Exactly! People don't turn their phones off. Why put up with all that—pay for all that—when I can sit in my cozy, calm living room, watch whatever I like, pause the film if I need to go to the toilet or get a snack? And speaking of snacks, I can eat anything I like, not just popcorn and hot dogs and chewy sweets that stick to my teeth. I can also have a nice, warm, purring cat on my lap the whole time. And if I fall asleep, there's nobody around to hear me snore. Except Fred, and he doesn't care."

Celeste laughs. "You make a strong case. But I'd still like to go to the movies with you. We can smuggle Fred in, if you like."

"We'll see. What have you been up to?"

"Oh, not much. I've been redecorating my flat. Oh, and my

brother came over for dinner last night, but he's a pain in the ass. Eats all my food, moans the face off me, then disappears and I don't see him again for weeks."

I laugh. "Families, huh?"

"Honestly, you wouldn't believe him. He's the biggest spoiled brat you'll ever meet. He fell out with his girlfriend at my birthday party and caused a massive scene."

"I guess I'd have seen it, if I'd been there."

"Ah, Meredith, I'm sorry."

"Oh, don't be sorry! It's the truth."

"Well, you're lucky you didn't have to witness it. Seriously, I was mortified. He got her so riled up, she threw a tray of shots at him and stormed out. Just as my mum brought my cake out."

"A birthday to remember," I murmur, feeling ashamed. "I'm sorry I wasn't there. I'm sorry I couldn't be a better friend to you. I hope I will be one day."

She doesn't speak for a few seconds, and when she does, her voice is quiet and shaky. "Meredith, don't say that. It couldn't be further from the truth."

"It was just so nice to get to know you without having to talk about it. I hate it when people feel sorry for me. It's a gut reaction, I know. But I still hate it."

"Meredith, it's fine. I promise."

"Still, I should have told you sooner. It was stupid of me."

"No—I get it. Really, I do."

"You do?"

"Sure. You wanted me to get to know the real you. You're not your environment, Mer. Not leaving your house might affect your life in a million different ways, but it doesn't change the person you are—not at your core. It doesn't at all change how I feel about you. In fact, it makes me love you even more."

I think I'm going to cry. I take a deep breath. "Celeste, has anyone ever told you you're a wise, wise woman?"

She laughs. "It's not something I hear very often, I must admit. But I like it."

"Thank you," I tell her.

"What the hell for?"

"For helping to take a weight off my shoulders that's been there for years."

"I'm only being honest with you, Mer. But you're very welcome."

She tells me what she's planning to do to her flat and how fed up she is with dating apps.

"I'm just not clicking with anyone," she moans.

"You only have to find one person," I tell her. "Actually..."

"What? What were you going to say?"

"Well, I know someone you might be interested in meeting."

"You do? Ooh, how exciting! Tell me more."

I can do better than that, I think. "Come over next week, and I'll fill you in," I tell her. "When are you working?"

"I'm off Thursday and Friday."

"Perfect." I glance at my calendar, at the next purple "T." I try to make my voice casual. "How's Thursday at eleven thirty?"

"I'll be there. Do you want me to bring anything?"

"Just yourself."

"OK. Great. And you'll tell me all about this guy you have in mind for me?"

"Of course."

Day 1,439

My kitchen is always clean, but today it's spotless. While I've been cleaning, I've been planning. I'll make tea, of course. That's what they'll both expect me to do. That's what I always do.

I have no concerns about conversation. Celeste loves to talk, and Tom can be pretty chatty too. I have three plates on the table, ready to be uncovered—ginger loaf with lemon icing, crunchy almond cookies, and a beetroot and chocolate cake I'm particularly proud of.

I'll have a cup of tea with them until Sadie phones. She's a crucial part of my plan. "I love it!" she said last night when I asked her to help me. "What will I say when I call you?"

"It doesn't matter." I laughed. "Your usual nonsense will do."

"I'll come up with something really dramatic."

"OK, whatever. You know they won't hear you, though?"

She's going to call me at 11:45 a.m., and I'll excuse myself and go into the living room, leaving Tom and Celeste to bond over cake.

It's been a long time since more than one person has been inside my house, apart from Sadie and her kids, and little people don't count. I find myself doing stupid things that don't really need to be done, like dusting the radiators and vacuuming the curtains. I'm grateful when the phone rings and I have no choice but to put down the duster and take off my rubber gloves.

It's Celeste. "Meredith, I'm having a nightmare." She sounds stressed.

"What's up?"

"My car broke down on the way into town. AAA came out and had to tow it to a garage. I'm currently sitting next door—in the smallest café in the world—waiting for it to get fixed. They've told me it could take a couple of hours. I'm so sorry...I won't make it over today. Or not until much later, at least."

"Oh, Celeste."

"I know, it's rubbish."

I think about the beetroot and chocolate cake, about Celeste and Tom laughing in my kitchen. I've been excited about bringing them together, but not just for them. I'm longing to hear other people's happy voices in another room of my house. I don't even need to know what they're laughing about. I just want it to be my background noise. I can't remember when I've looked forward to something so much.

"I'll come and wait with you." As soon as I say it, I know it's what I want to do.

"What? Seriously?"

"Yes, of course."

"But...are you ready for that? I mean, I know you've been doing really well. But I'm in the city center. How would you even get here?"

"I'll take the bus," I say. "It's time."

I need to spend a few more minutes persuading Celeste that nothing bad is going to happen to me between my house and Café Retro. When I hang up the phone, I don't have time to think too much about anything because Tom is due to arrive in half an hour. I text him instead of calling to make it easier to dodge his inevitable questions.

Tom, would you like to meet me somewhere else for a change?

Hey! I was just about to leave. Sure…if you're sure?

I'm sure. Can you meet me at Café Retro on Mitchell Grove?

Mitchell Grove? In the city center?

That's the one. It's next to the car garage.

I'll find it. But why the heck do you want to meet there?

I like it. It has surprisingly good coffee.

Meredith, you don't drink coffee. What's going on? Are you OK?

Why are you being weird?

Damn you, Tom, I think. *Always needing an answer.*

I'm always weird.

Meredith, what's going on?

It's part of my CBT work. Can you be there? It's important to me.

Of course I can. What time?

Just ASAP. See you soon! x

I'm a bit grubby from all the housework, but I don't have time to shower so I make do with washing my face and under my arms. Deodorant, hair in a ponytail, some tinted moisturizer, and a change of clothes and I'm ready to go.

As ready as I'll ever be.

I give myself a few minutes to sit on my bed and do my breathing exercises. In through my nose, out through my mouth.

Today definitely isn't going to plan. What would Diane say to me, if she was on my computer screen right now?

She'd say, "Meredith, what's the worst thing that can happen?"

And I'd roll my eyes inwardly because I've heard those words come out of her mouth a thousand times, but I'd say, "I could have a panic attack."

And she'd say something like "Do you know what to do if you have a panic attack?"

And I'd nod, because I do.

And she'd say, "When did you last have a panic attack?"

And I'd say, "Two months ago."

And she'd say, "Would you rather go and meet your friends and have a panic attack and be able to deal with it, or stay at home and not see your friends?"

And I'd say, "I'd rather go and meet my friends."

"I'd rather go and meet my friends," I say out loud. I'm trusting that the world hasn't changed so much that the X19 bus doesn't leave from the end of my street for the city center every twenty minutes.

"I'm going on a bus." I say the words to myself over and over, like a mantra, as I walk along my street. The street that's so familiar to me now. I know the house with the perfectly trimmed lawn always has fresh flowers in a vase at the front window. That the white car halfway down on the other side of the road has had a flat tire for weeks. And I know Jacob's freckled face and chirpy voice.

"Hey, Meredith!"

"Jacob, hi!" I slow down as he walks toward me. "How are you?"

"I'm good, thanks. I've just been to the Science Center with my papa. Just dropped him off at home; he lives up the road."

"The Science Center? Wow. I've not been there for years."

"Have you ever been up the tower?"

"No, Jacob, I can't say that I have."

"It's the height of over thirty double-decker buses. And the tallest freestanding building in Scotland."

"Well, that's pretty high."

"It's more than pretty high, Meredith. And guess what? It moves in the wind! Cool or what?"

"I'm not sure I'd venture up there on a windy day."

"I think you need to push yourself out of your comfort zone,

Meredith. That's what my teacher says to me when I pick the easiest math challenge."

I grin at him. "I think you're right, Jacob. Anyway, I need to go and catch the bus."

"Safe journey, Meredith. See you around."

There are only two other passengers. I sit at the very back, because I want to be able to see everything.

I text Celeste: I'm on my way.

Then Tom: Are you there yet? I'm on the bus!

I look out of the window, relaxing into the rhythm. I have a good vantage point here on the back seat. I can see everything that's happening on the street, all the people of different shapes and sizes and colors. But only for a second, because the bus keeps moving. And they never, ever look into the bus. I can watch them safely, separated by steel and glass and whatever else holds a bus together. I'm going to get on more buses. I might spend an entire day just going around the city on different buses.

My phone buzzes on my lap. It's Celeste: Take care! See you soon xx

I go back to watching people. There are so many of them. I'm going to have to walk the final part of my journey, and it might be on crowded streets—the bus isn't going to stop right outside the café.

One step at a time, I tell myself. *I'll deal with that when I get there.*

The bus stops; one person gets off and a crowd gets on. I watch a dozen or so people flop onto seats and discard their shopping bags. There's a group of five teenagers who don't sit down but stand near the front, their slim fingers grasping the handrails. I wonder if they'd be sitting here, at the back of the bus, if I wasn't. It occurs to me that I've chosen the seat normally claimed by the younger generation; it makes me feel just the tiniest bit rebellious. I never sat at the back of the school bus. It would have been Fee's first choice, but I always insisted that she join me in the safe middle zone.

Nobody on the bus is looking at me. Nobody cares. They're either talking to their travel companions, or looking out of the window, or staring at their screens. I check my own phone— I've missed a call from Tom.

He answers right away. "Meredith, are you OK?"

"I'm fine. I'm on the bus. Where are you?"

"I'm just heading toward Mitchell Grove. Meredith, this is a very strange place to meet. What's going on? Are you sure you're OK?"

"I'm fine, honestly. I'm just leaving my comfort zone."

"You sure are." Tom laughs. I can hear traffic noises in his background. "Couldn't you have chosen somewhere out of your comfort zone, but a little closer to home?"

"I felt like taking a risk," I tell him—and it's not a lie.

"Where the hell is this place anyway? Have you been here before?"

"It's next to a car garage. Just trust me."

"I do trust you. That's why I'm meeting you in the middle of nowhere. How long will you be?"

"I'm not sure. Another couple of stops, then a five-minute walk maybe? Just grab yourself a drink and check out the menu."

"I can see it. I'm not sure if it's a menu place, Meredith. More of a whiteboard-type situation."

I smile. "You're such a snob, Tom."

"I just prefer your kitchen to Café Retro, that's all. Right, I'm here now. Hurry up, will you?"

"I'll tell the bus driver to put his foot down. Is it busy?"

"It's dead. Actually, no…there's one other person here."

"Well, just make yourself comfortable and wait for me."

"Oh, don't worry—I'm not going anywhere. You owe me a huge slice of whatever passes for cake in here."

I end the call and put my phone into my bag. I can't keep the grin off my face.

When I get off the bus, I find the postcode for the café and put it into the map app on my phone. It tells me I'll be there in seven minutes. I think I'll be there in five—I walk faster than most people and the fire in my belly is spurring me on today.

I turn the corner and see the woman about two hundred yards away. She's arguing with a man in a leather jacket, waving her cigarette around in the air, poking the fingers of her other hand into his chest. He squares up to her, and she gets louder. She's drunk. Her hair is white blonde and short. She's wearing a cropped pink jacket, tight black trousers, and open-toed sandals.

I freeze, feeling the tension build in my chest. Faces flash in my mind: Fee, Sadie, Tom, Celeste, Diane—the support system that's come together for me just when I needed it the most. I take a deep breath, then another. They're still arguing, but they're also walking. They're coming toward me, and I can't move.

I don't care about the man in the leather jacket. I can't take my eyes off the woman. I stare at her until she's close enough for me to see her face properly, until I can be sure she's not my mother and that's when my legs crumple and I sit on the ground until the world stops spinning.

The couple kneel beside me, their concerned faces only inches from mine.

"Are you all right, hen?" The woman peers at me. Her breath smells stale, but she's definitely not my mother. In fact, she looks nothing like her. "Do you want a cigarette?"

"No, thanks. I'm OK." I try to stand up, and they both grab one of my arms.

"Do you need help?" the man asks.

"I just felt dizzy for a moment. I'm fine now. But thanks."

"OK, hen. You take care." The woman winks at me. They walk away together but start arguing again. Something about money in the tin underneath the bed and taking, taking, taking and never giving back.

I check my phone and start walking again. My friends are waiting for me.

Café Retro is more neglected than retro. The letters on the sign have faded so much they're barely there, as if they've been washed away by decades of rain. For the avoidance of doubt someone has written "CAFÉ RETRO" in thick black marker on a large piece of paper and taped it to the inside of the door. It works—I can see it from the other side of the street.

I wait for a gap in the traffic and cross over. My phone rings— it's Sadie. Right on time. I forgot to tell her about the change of plan.

She doesn't even give me the chance to say hello. "Meredith, thank God! I'm having a nightmare here. James has the shits and Tilly has drawn all over the kitchen walls."

"Yet you have time to phone me?"

"What? This was the plan, right? My fake emergency?"

"I'm teasing you," I tell her as I approach the café. I see Tom first. He's sitting in the corner nearest the window, reading a magazine. The only other person—apart from a woman in a striped apron sweeping the floor—is Celeste. She's at a table toward the back of the room, scrolling through her phone.

"Meredith, what the fuck is happening?"

"Sorry, Sadie—change of plan. I'll explain later . . . I need to go."

"Hey, lady—not so fast. Where are you? I can hear...Are you on a motorway?"

I laugh. "No. But I'm not far from one."

"Meredith Maggs, tell me what's going on."

"I will. Just give me a few minutes. I'll call you back, I promise."

"You'd better."

"I will. And, Sadie...I fucking love you."

I end the call and push open the door to the café.

They look up at the same time.

"Mer, you're here!" Celeste says at the same time as Tom says, "You've made it—brilliant!"

I smile at them both, suddenly feeling a little nervous. Keep smiling as they look at each other, then back at me, with all the questions in their eyes.

"I'll just order a cup of tea, shall I?" I say brightly. "Anyone need a refill?"

"Meredith, I can't believe you're here—it's amazing." Tom appears at my side. "But what's going on?" He lowers his voice. "Do you know that woman over there?"

"I do, in fact. She's my friend Celeste. I told you about her, remember? The birthday party? Excuse me, could I have a pot of breakfast tea, please? Thanks."

I grab Tom's arm before he can say anything. "Come with me." When we get to Celeste's table, she stands up and wraps her arms round me.

"Mer, this is incredible! I'm so proud of you! Did you get the bus? Was it OK? I'm so in awe of you right now."

I squeeze her back. "Thank you. I'm pretty proud of me too. How's your car?"

She rolls her eyes. "I have no idea. Hopefully on the mend. You're an absolute star for coming to keep me company."

"Celeste, this is my friend Tom. Tom, this is my friend Celeste.

I wanted you to meet." I nudge Tom with my elbow. "Come on, let's sit down."

We end up moving to a bigger table, and for the next hour and a half we drink tea and eat scones and talk about all sorts of things, like our favorite TV shows and what it's like to travel by bus and the most interesting birds we've ever seen. We make a plan to go to the Kelvingrove and look at *Christ of Saint John of the Cross* and then walk around the university buildings and maybe go to one of those cute little places on Great Western Road for afternoon tea. That seems like something I can work toward, rather than something I can only dream of. We agree that we probably won't ever come back to Café Retro but also agree that we'll leave a generous tip for the woman in the striped apron, whose scones are actually very light and fresh with just the right amount of crumble. A couple of times I think I catch something between Tom and Celeste, and I lean back in my chair and sip my tea and give it a chance to develop, but they quickly draw me back in and I wonder if maybe I'm just seeing what I want to see.

Eventually the garage phones Celeste to let her know her car is ready and she insists on driving me home. I accept—I'm exhilarated, but also exhausted. We say goodbye to Tom and I watch Celeste watch him walk to his car until she looks at me and says, "What?" with a little smile on her face.

"Nothing," I say, and we both laugh and I think she knows what's going on but we don't say anything else on the matter. In fact, we don't say much all the way to my house; we listen to the radio and Celeste sings along to any lyrics she knows, her soft, clear voice filling the car, and at one point I close my eyes and think I actually could fall asleep.

Day 1,445

Wednesday, July 3, 2019

"She's ill, Meredith."

"Who?"

"You know who."

She's right. I don't know why I'm acting like our mother isn't always close to the forefront of my mind. She lurks within easy reach, like the school bully who's always three steps behind. If anyone can see through me, it's my sister. Of all the things that have slipped away from us over the last few years, this is not one of them.

"How do you know?"

I sit on the couch, then stand up again. Start to pace.

"Auntie Linda called me. It's cancer. She's dying."

I never thought I'd hear those words. I thought the words would be "she's dead" and they would be the only reason for my sister to call me, ever, for the rest of our lives. Finding out she's dying is worse than finding out she's dead. I have a choice now.

"What are you going to do?"

"No, Mer." Fee's voice is firm. "What are *we* going to do?"

"I have no idea," I admit. "But I need to hang up. I think I'm going to be sick."

Auntie Linda looks the same as she did four years ago and, I realize, the same as she did twenty years ago. The same hair, the same lipstick, possibly the same coat. The same deep-set serious eyes that light up when she sees me.

"Aw, hen. It's good to see you." She wraps her arms round me, squeezes tightly. She's short but sturdy. She smells the same too—roses and soap. I feel like I'm ten years old again.

"Hi, Auntie Linda," I say into her hair. "Thanks for coming over so quickly."

She fusses over me for a moment—I'm too thin apparently, but I haven't aged a bit—then insists on a tour of my house before Fee arrives. She oohs and aahs in all the right places, tells me what a success I must be to own my own house, and all by myself, my goodness, without any help from a man. Auntie Linda went straight from her mother's house to her husband's house, she says (God rest his soul).

I smile and thank her but I can't relax. Auntie Linda was—is—a sweet woman who has more than earned her honorary title, but she's also Mama's friend. I accepted her unique role in our family without question when I was ten. Thirty years later, it doesn't sit so comfortably with me.

My chest floods with relief when the doorbell rings.

"You're late," I hiss at Fiona.

She shrugs. "I'm always late."

Auntie Linda doesn't fuss over Fiona the way she did me, but they have a different relationship. I've barely seen the woman for a decade; Fiona was probably at the pub with her a few months ago.

I make tea while they chat about Auntie Linda's daughter Maggie, who's expecting her third baby. Auntie Linda has been busy knitting a wardrobe in all the colors of the rainbow, because they don't know what they're having and in Auntie Linda's world little girls never wear blue.

"You taught me how to knit," I say as I carry the tray of mugs and biscuits to the table.

"So I did, pet. I'd forgotten about that. You were so patient. I taught you to do it right-handed, not knowing you were a leftie." She laughs and helps herself to a shortbread cookie.

I liked to watch her knit. It relaxed me.

"When did you last see Mama?" Fiona asks, reminding us all why we're here.

"Yesterday. She's in a bad way, hen. Slept almost the whole time I was there."

"What did the doctor say?" I grip the handle of my mug.

"They think she has a couple of months. Maybe not even that."

"I knew those cigarettes would be the end of her." Fee is restless; she's breaking up her biscuit, scattering crumbs all over my table.

Auntie Linda takes a sip of her tea. "She asked for you. Both of you."

Fee and I exchange a look. I notice the imperceptible shrug of my sister's shoulders; I'm not sure whether Auntie Linda does.

The mood in the room has shifted, as if a heavy cloud has blocked the morning sun.

"We need to think about it," I tell Auntie Linda.

She nods. "I get it, hen."

"Why are you friends with her?"

If she's surprised by my question, she doesn't show it. "We grew up together. I'm a lot older, of course. Old enough to remember when she was born. Her mama used to put her in the big stroller out the back door. My brother and I used to climb the fence and sing to her, try to get her to stop crying. Until our mother came and pulled us down by our pants."

"What were her parents like?" I ask. "We never met them."

"Her dad was a quiet sort. Kept himself to himself. Her mama was fierce. We heard her shout a lot through the wall. It was quieter when her brother visited. Your mama's uncle Joe."

We have a great-uncle we didn't know anything about. I look at Auntie Linda expectantly, but she breaks eye contact with me and studies her hands. When she looks at me again, her eyes are wistful.

"Uncle Joe wasn't a good man. Your Mama only spoke about him once or twice. She didn't ever tell me exactly what happened..."

"I can't handle this." Fee pushes her chair back noisily and stands up. "What's the point? We come from a fucked-up family. Our mother had a fucked-up life, and she tried to fuck us up as well. End of story."

I reach out to try to stop her, but my hand grabs onto nothing as she storms out of the room.

"Let her go, pet," Auntie Linda says. "She's upset."

I stare at her. "I'm upset too."

"I know you are, pet. You deal with it in different ways."

"Why are you friends with her?" I ask her again.

She sighs. "I tried my best, pet."

I'm not sure what she means, but I remember the trips to the ballet and the sleepovers and the salt-and-vinegar chips after my swimming lessons, and my body softens a little.

"I know she found it hard to show you she loved you."

"It was a bit more than that, Auntie Linda."

We look at each other across the table. If there was ever a time to go into detail, it's now. But this situation has created enough guilt. I don't want Auntie Linda to feel guilty for what she didn't do. She couldn't have stopped what she didn't know about. What's the point in telling her now?

"I'll make more tea and go and see how Fiona is." I rest my hand on Auntie Linda's shoulder as I stand up from the table. I don't want her to go anywhere, not yet.

I find Fiona in my bedroom, staring at *Woman with Arms Folded*.

"What's this all about?" she demands, pointing. Then she folds her own arms across her chest.

"She reminds me of you," I tell her.

She doesn't laugh. We stand shoulder to shoulder.

"Meredith, I'm sorry." Her voice is thick. "I'm so fucking sorry."

"I know you are." I tug at her arm until it comes loose, grab her hand. "Come on. We can't leave Auntie Linda sitting on her own."

We go back downstairs, hand in hand. Auntie Linda is doing my breakfast dishes, humming softly to herself. She looks up when we walk in. "I've always been so glad you girls have each other."

I squeeze my sister's hand. "Me too."

Fee squeezes back, but I can feel the tension in her body. I know she's struggling. This is harder for her, I realize. I said goodbye to our mother a long time ago.

"You shouldn't be doing my dishes," I say firmly, steering Auntie Linda away from the sink.

"What do you know about our father?" Fee blurts out.

Auntie Linda dries her hands and sits back down at the table.

"They met young—they were only teenagers. On and off for years after that. It was never what you'd call a serious relationship. I always thought that was a shame. He was good for your mama, so he was."

Fiona and I look at each other. She bites her lip; I feel mine start to tremble.

"He was a nice man?" I ask shakily.

"He was, pet. Not that I ever knew him all that well. The last time I saw him, you were only a wee lassie. He was a quiet sort, didn't say too much."

"Unlike her then?" Fiona's arms are folded again.

"Aye, they were like chalk and cheese."

"What happened between them? Why did he leave?" I lean a little farther over the table, trying to temper the impact of my sister's spiky stance. Then I remember Auntie Linda was friends with my mother, so she's clearly not turned off by confrontational women.

Auntie Linda sighs. "Hen, I'm not too sure. Back then, I could go weeks without seeing your mother. It wasn't like it is today, with mobile phones and Facebook and all that nonsense. I was busy myself, bringing up the kids and working full-time. I remember I'd been trying to get hold of her for a wee while. When I finally saw her, she told me he was gone for good. He got a job working offshore."

She takes a gulp of her tea. "As far as she was concerned, it was good riddance. But after that her mood got low. She fell apart. And you two sweethearts were only wee girls."

I glance at Fee. She's biting her top lip.

"Auntie Linda, it was never your job to sort her out," I say firmly.

Auntie Linda's mouth is set in a firm line. "Hindsight is a wonderful thing, pet," she says finally.

She stays for another hour, writing down what she can remember about our father in neat handwriting on the back of my grocery delivery note. I stick it to the front of my fridge—a sparse list of names and places she's not 100 percent sure of.

At the bottom of the list is the name of our mother's doctor and her room number at the hospital.

1987

We cut through the park on our way back from the shop, swinging the shopping bag between us. It sailed perilously high in the air, threatening to shower us with bread rolls and cans of soup—lentil for me, mushroom for Fee, pea and ham for Mama.

A crowd of kids congregated around the swings, sitting at the top of the slide, their long legs hanging loose. I saw them first and picked up my pace. Fee took the opposite approach. She slowed down and returned their stares.

"Fee, don't," I hissed under my breath.

"Don't be such a scaredy-cat," she scoffed, pulling at the bag until I came to a standstill beside her. I had no choice—if I kept walking, the bag would burst. She was in control, as always.

"I need the toilet," I begged.

"No, you don't," she snapped. To the crowd she yelled, "What are you staring at? Do you want a picture? It lasts longer!"

A couple of them laughed. One of the taller boys jumped off the swing, stuffed his hands in his pockets, and sauntered toward us.

I was gripping the handle of the plastic bag so tightly it had formed a hard ridge along the center of my palm. "Let's go." I tried to keep my voice steady. "Seriously. He could have a gun or a knife or anything."

Fiona laughed. "Mer, he's twelve. He doesn't have a gun." She straightened her back and puffed out her chest.

"Give us a picture then." The boy's hair was shaved high on the sides; his face was a canvas of spots. He was tall, almost as tall as a man, but still had the narrow shoulders and scant chest of a child. He stopped a few feet away from us, put a cigarette in his mouth, and lit it without breaking eye contact with me.

I looked at my sister. She screwed her face up at the boy. "What are you talking about?"

"You asked if we wanted a picture, so give us a picture. You must have some crayons in your pocket, wee girl. You can draw me one." He took a long drag then did something weird with his jaw to blow a large, perfectly round smoke ring. I stared at it.

"Fuck off and take your stinking cigarettes with you." Fiona's voice was calm.

The boy laughed. "You've got a right mouth on you. Just like your mother."

Something strange happened in my chest—like my heart missed a beat. I felt like throwing up. I looked at my sister. Her nose twitched, once, but apart from that she was unflappable.

"What do you know about our mother?" she demanded.

"That she's a slut."

"She fucking is not."

"Whatever. You look like her anyway."

It happened so quickly I barely had time to take a breath. I thought I'd dropped the bag, then I realized Fiona had grabbed it from me. I watched it crash to the ground, watched my sister take a can of soup in her hand and aim it at the boy's head.

It didn't hit him—it landed in front of his feet, then started to slowly roll back toward us.

"Good shot," the boy said, a slow smirk spreading across his face.

I really needed the toilet now. I'd fibbed before just to get her to hurry up, but the heaviness in my bladder was real, and it was still a five-minute walk to get home.

"How do you know our mother?" Fiona's voice got louder. The can of soup kept rolling. If we didn't get it back, we'd both get half portions tonight. But I was too scared to move.

"Everyone knows your mother."

"Liar."

The boy shrugged. He was bored with us now. He glanced back at his friends and gave one of them a nod. "Whatever, wee girl. Tell your ma Donnie's lad says hello."

"Who the fuck is Donnie?"

But the boy had turned away from us, and he walked back to his friends, muttering something I couldn't hear.

"Who's Donnie?" I murmured.

"Oh, for fuck's sake, Meredith." Fiona marched to retrieve the dented can of soup. I picked up the bag and held it open, but she stalked past me.

I ran to catch up with her. "I don't know why you're annoyed with me."

"I'm not."

"Fee, don't walk too fast. I need the toilet."

"You're such a baby." She slowed down, but I decided to walk just behind her anyway.

I gave her a few minutes and waited until her shoulders relaxed a little. "What do you think that boy was talking about?"

"Well, we don't know half the stuff she gets up to, do we?"

"What do you mean?"

"The nights she goes out and doesn't come home—where do you think she is?"

"I have no idea," I told her. "With Auntie Linda?"

"She might start off with Auntie Linda, but I don't think she ends up with her."

I didn't really understand what she was saying, and we were almost on our street. All I could think about was getting to the bathroom. I didn't care who Donnie was or how Mama knew him. "Let's just get home and have dinner. She'll be wondering where we are."

As soon as I saw our house, I started running, holding the

bag of shopping tight against my belly. I let it go on the doorstep, not caring about the soup, and grabbed the door handle. It didn't move. I pushed down on it.

"Oh, move over." Fee pushed me out of the way. The handle didn't budge for her either.

"She's locked us out, the mad bitch." She started banging on the door. I looked at the upstairs windows. All the curtains were drawn, even though it wasn't yet 5 p.m. I thought I saw an imperceptible twitch, but I might have imagined it.

I sat down on the step just as I felt the release and scrunched my eyes shut as the warm liquid trickled down the inside of my thigh.

"Come on, let's go round the back." Fee jumped off the step. "I'll smash the bloody kitchen window in with her pea and ham soup if I have to."

I squeezed my knees together, covered my face with my hands, and willed the world to disappear. I didn't know Fee was still there until I felt her hand on my shoulder.

"Don't let her break you," she whispered.

I looked up at her. "I've wet myself."

Her eyes were steady, convincing. "So what? Those sweatpants are ready for the garbage anyway. Let's get you inside and cleaned up."

I shook my head. "I can't."

"OK, Meredith. You asked for it." I watched her kick off her shoes and pull off her jeans. She stuffed them into the shopping bag, then swung it dramatically over one shoulder. Her faded underwear were adorned with the repeat pattern of a cartoon cat with a smiley face.

I burst out laughing.

"Are you laughing at my Skinny Malinky long legs?" Fee swayed her hips from side to side, then knocked her knees together.

"Yes," I told her. "But also…I'm wearing the same underwear."

Day 1,446

Thursday, July 4, 2019

The hospital looms over us, cold steel and glossy glass. There are approximately three million people milling around outside. At least, that's what it looks like.

"I don't think I can do this." I grip the inside of the car door.

"Of course you can." Fee yanks up the handbrake and starts rummaging through her bag. "She'll be on her best behavior. There'll be doctors and nurses there."

"It's not just about her. It's all those people. They're everywhere."

Fee sighs and unfastens her seat belt. "Meredith, none of those people give a crap about you. They probably won't even look at you, unless you get in their way. Come on—let's get this over with."

I look back at the entrance to the hospital, at the sea of bodies moving through the doors. "I don't think I'm ready. It's too much."

"Look at him." She points at a bare-chested middle-aged man waiting at the bus stop. "Do you think that guy cares what people think of him? If he can stand there in all his half-naked glory, you can get out of the car."

"It's not quite the same, Fee."

"So you're just going to sit here? What about Mama?"

"What about her?"

"She's dying, Meredith. If you don't see her today, you might not have another chance. And that's up to you. But I don't want you to regret it."

"Fee, I don't really care about seeing her," I tell her. "I'm here for you."

"Then be here for me. Let's do this together."

I'm getting hot in Fee's car. I press the button to lower the window and try to gulp in the fresh air. A man and two young boys walk past; one of them sees me watching them and sticks his tongue out at me. Without thinking I stick mine out too. The young boy grins.

I tune back in to what my sister is saying, my eyes still on the boy. He's holding the man's hand tightly and skipping rather than walking, the way kids with little legs do.

"Haven't you been out loads now? You've been going for your shopping, right?"

"I've hardly been hanging out at the shopping center," I mutter.

The trio are at the hospital entrance now, and then they're gone, swept in by the revolving door. I wonder why they're here—I hope it's for a good reason. A new baby sister maybe, or bringing someone home after too many nights apart.

"You don't understand," I tell Fee.

"I'm not claiming to." She shrugs, then turns on the engine.

"What are you doing?"

"We're leaving. I'm not sitting in a hospital parking lot all day. I've got stuff to do."

"That's not fair. I'm not stopping you from going in."

She kills the engine again. "OK. It's half past two. Let's sit here for five minutes, then you can decide. Deal?"

"Deal." I relax into the chair. "Thanks for being patient."

She pulls a face at me.

"I've missed people watching," I tell her, my eyes on an elderly woman crossing the road in front of us, an enormous fruit basket in her hands. "That's one thing I couldn't do at home. I used to go to the park sometimes, before...you know. Just sit on a bench and watch people come and go. It relaxed me."

"On your own?" She pulls another face.

"Sure. You should try it sometime. It's quite liberating actually."

"Maybe I will," she says. Then, after a beat: "What else did you miss?"

I think about it. "I missed something I'd lost a long time ago. Us being little girls. Together all the time."

She laughs. "We can't go back to that, Mer."

"I know. But I still miss it. Things were easier then, even though they were so much harder. I know that doesn't make sense."

"Actually, it does. We had hope."

I twist my body around to face her. "Fee—we can still have hope." She looks back at me, and her eyes are shiny. I grab her hand. "Let's go in."

She looks like a tiny bird in the hospital bed. A tiny bird with a rattle in its chest, attached to lots of tubes and wires. Not the woman in the sequin dress and trench coat, barefoot on the pavement outside her house, asking me for money on the loneliest night of my life. I'm overwhelmed by sympathy, faced with a dying woman who lived a life without love. I didn't expect to feel sorry for her. Life is full of surprises.

"She had a bad night," the nurse tells us. "Don't be alarmed by her breathing—it's getting harder for her to clear the fluids from her throat. If she wakes up, you can give her some water."

We nod and wait for the nurse to go.

"She's really dying," Fee whispers.

"I know," I whisper back. I half expected to find her sitting up, cackling at the television, giving the nurses hell about not being able to smoke. Her cackling days are clearly over. Her skin looks paper-thin, and it has a bluish tinge. She's always been thin, but she looks like she could snap in half.

Fee sits on the chair beside the bed, and I stand behind her. For half an hour we watch our mother slide closer toward the end of her life. She doesn't open her eyes. Before we leave, I stare at her face, trying to find a tiny piece of love.

Day 1,449

Sunday, July 7, 2019

Sadie and I walk to the shop together to take my mind off my dying mother. It takes a lot longer than it should because every few steps we take, she grabs me and tells me how amazing it is to be outside with me, that she's so proud of me and she's been so excited thinking about all the places we can go together.

"Let's go to the movies," she says. "There's a new Rebel Wilson film out I really want to see. We could go to that fancy new theater at Princes Square. It's got sofas!"

I laugh at her enthusiasm. "One step at a time. It still feels a little bit weird to be doing this—just walking down my own street."

"When do you think it'll feel normal again?" She says it with interest, no judgment.

"To be honest, I don't know. Some days are easier than others. It's like I'm learning to do stuff all over again. Because everything is different. I'm not the same person I used to be."

She links her arm in mine. "You're still my Mer. You're still the same to me."

We walk arm in arm, like we used to after school.

"Guess who I met in town the other day," she says casually, and I know straightaway who she met in town the other day, because there's only one person it can be. Only one person—in my history, at least—who warranted the buildup.

"You met Gavin?" I try to make my voice equally casual.

She gapes at me. "How did you...? Yes, I met Gavin."

341

"Still tall and more handsome than he'll ever realize?"

"Still tall and more handsome than he'll ever realize," she concedes with a smile.

"Did you speak to him for long?"

"No. I had the kids, and they were climbing up my legs, begging me to take them to Burger King."

I smile, and wait, because I know there's more to this story.

She doesn't keep me hanging. "He's engaged, Mer. Getting married next month to Julia. Whoever she is."

"She's a lucky woman," I tell her.

"You OK?"

"I am. Honestly. Gavin and I... it would never have worked. Maybe it was a case of the right person at the wrong time. Or maybe not even the right person at any time. It wasn't meant to be. I know that sounds so passive. But I believe it."

I'm telling her the truth. I can't picture myself walking down the aisle toward Gavin. Or anyone, for that matter. Maybe one day I will, but it's not on my priority list. Before that happens, I'll take that trip to Tuscany, and I'll raise a glass of the finest Italian red to Gavin and Julia—whoever she is—when I get there.

Sadie insists on buying rolls and sliced sausage and cans of soda. "It's what we used to eat when we went back to mine after school," she tells my raised eyebrows.

"I remember," I say. "I'm just not sure my insides can handle it anymore."

We're waiting to pay for our teenage nostalgia when a group of young men in soccer tops enter. They're buoyant and loud—from a six-pack of beer, possibly. None of them even look in our direction, but I feel my senses become heightened when they stride past us.

"You OK?" she whispers, moving closer to me.

I press my arm against hers, quelling the rush of stress

hormones. Diane's right. Sadie grounds me just by being by my side.

"I'm fine," I whisper back, but I'm still so aware of the group of men, who are at the other end of the shop now. They're laughing and joking around, ribbing each other in restless voices. I keep my eyes on the shop assistant. I tell myself that if she's not worried about them, then I shouldn't be either.

The old woman in front of us takes her bag and shuffles away. Sadie and I step forward, our arms still pressed together, just as there's a loud smash at the back of the shop.

"Fuck's sake." The sales assistant rolls her eyes and walks wearily toward the raucous laughter.

I look at our rolls and sliced sausage and soda, then I become aware of the men walking back toward us, and the next thing I know I'm outside the shop, gulping for breath, trying to stop my body from shaking.

Day 1,453

Thursday, July 11, 2019

I might be leaving my house now and then, but my life hasn't changed all that much. I still have my old routines. I can now run up and down the stairs fifty times in eight minutes forty-seven seconds. Why join a gym when I can work up a sweat like that?

Tom is staying for lunch. He's not with Holding Hands anymore—he's started a course to train as a counselor. We've already established that I won't be a case study. We're friends now—true friends—and anyway, I'd feel bad if I ditched Diane.

But old habits die hard, I guess, and Tom and I have stuck to our Thursday dates. Celeste has a day off from the salon and is joining us. I might suggest taking sandwiches to the park. It's a sunny day, and I feel like stretching my legs. They both claim they're not interested in anything more than friendship, but I've seen the way they look at each other. I remain quietly confident in my matchmaking efforts.

I'm inspecting the contents of my fridge for suitable sandwich fillings when my phone buzzes.

It's Fee. Are you home? I'm coming over.

And I know, without question, that our mother is dead.

Day 1,461

Friday, July 19, 2019

Auntie Linda insists on organizing the funeral, and neither Fee nor I put up much of a fight. Surprisingly, Mama had enough money to pay for everything, with a couple of hundred to spare. We agree to donate it to a local children's charity.

A handful of people we don't recognize turn up on a wet summer's day to say their goodbyes. The minister keeps it brief and generic—there are no touching anecdotes, no accomplishments, no remarkable qualities to speak of. As Fee and I requested, he doesn't mention us by name.

Auntie Linda is the only other person to speak. She stands before the small gathering in her black suit jacket and skirt, and reads a short poem—something about angels that means absolutely nothing to me.

Fee and I don't go with the rest of them to the pub. Instead, we drive to the beach, eat salty fries with our feet buried in the sand, and don't talk about our mother.

When she drops me off, hours later, Tom is sitting on my doorstep.

"Is that the guy you're always talking about?" Fee peers at him through the car window.

"Yeah, that's Tom." I wave to him; he raises his hand in return.

"What's the deal with you two? Have you got the hots for him?"

I laugh. "God, no! He's my friend."

"Your friend?"

"Yes, Fiona. Men and women can be friends, you know."

"You're so progressive, Meredith," she teases.

"I'm teaching him how to swim."

"At this time of night?"

"No, you idiot. I wasn't expecting him tonight. He's here to make sure I'm OK, I guess." I smile at my friend, sitting on my doorstep.

"Well, maybe I'll meet this guy properly sometime."

"Absolutely." I unclip my seat belt. "I'll have you round for dinner one night, with Tom and Celeste."

"Who the fuck is Celeste?"

"Oh, she's another friend. She's at a yoga retreat this week."

Celeste sent me a photo earlier, of a single white gladiolus. *To give you strength today*, she wrote.

"They both offered to come to the funeral," I tell Fee.

"That was nice of them." She understands why I didn't want them there. I've grown fiercely protective of my new life and the people in it.

"Thanks for the fries." I give my sister a quick hug before I get out of the car and walk toward my house.

Day 1,466

Wednesday, July 24, 2019

In Mama's absence, we unearth the secrets of the tiny decrepit house we grew up in. By unspoken agreement I tackle our old bedroom, which is pretty empty, and the living room, and Fee does the rest. Auntie Linda's cousin turns up with a transit van and a couple of friends and they make half a dozen trips to the local dump, getting rid of furniture that was past its best decades ago.

After two days, we're done—our mother's life condensed into four cardboard boxes, the stench of nicotine clinging to our clothes.

"I stink," I grumble as Fee drives me home. "I can't wait to have a shower. I'm meeting Sadie at three." My mind is moving forward, away from the old neglected house and the ugly memories imprinted on every surface.

"I'll come in for a few minutes," Fee says as she pulls up outside my house. "I need to show you something." She reaches into the back seat, lifts the top flap of one of the cardboard boxes, and takes out an old white shoebox held together by a large elastic band.

I gasp. "The photographs?"

"I found the photographs. But this is even better." She clutches it to her chest until we're in my house, then grabs my arm. "Meredith, I really need you to see this."

I let her lead me into the living room, and watch her sit on the floor and open the shoebox. Fred does his signature figure eight round my legs, purring softly. I scoop him up and rest my chin on the top of his head, feeling his heartbeat under my hand.

"Read these." Fee hands me a small brown envelope.

I put Fred back on the floor and take the envelope from her, trying to read her face. It's an unfamiliar expression—excitement maybe. She sits beside me on the couch as I open the envelope and take out sheets of writing paper folded into thirds.

"I didn't want us to do this in her house. It didn't seem right."

Dear Fiona and Meredith,

I hope you are both well. I'm writing to you from Belfast! Do you know where that is? Ask Mama to show you on the map. Everyone is very friendly here, but I'm missing my precious girls.

I hope you're both enjoying school and working hard. I think of you every day. I'll keep writing to you. I would love to get a letter back.

Look after each other.

Love Dad

I unfold the next one.

Dear Fiona and Meredith,

How are you? I'm still in Liverpool. I like it here—the people are very friendly. I'd love you to visit one day. Maybe during the school holidays?

It must be cold in Glasgow just now—I hope you're keeping warm! Do you still like hot chocolate? I used to make it for you after your bath. It seems like yesterday! I can't believe you're both in secondary school now.

I miss you both so much.

Love Dad

"How many are there?" I whisper, tracing the word "Dad" with my finger.

"Hundreds," she whispers back.

I call Sadie and cancel, and Fee and I sit together on my living room floor and read every letter.

Day 1,484

Sunday, August 11, 2019

I've bought a secondhand car, a bright yellow bubble that makes me smile every time I look at it.

"That's so cool!" Jacob yelled from his side of the street, and we agreed that he'll wash it for me once a month for a fiver. He's saving for his mum's Christmas present.

Whenever I can, I drive to my new favorite place—the beach. When you want to get out into the world but still have space from other people, it's the perfect destination. I can drive for half an hour and feel like the city is a world away. In the trunk of my car I have a bag with all the essentials, come rain or shine: flip-flops, rain boots, a towel, a blanket, a floppy straw hat, sunscreen. Everybody's self-care kit is different, Diane told me the last time we spoke. There are no rules.

Today, my kit includes a bucket and spade for Matilda. She loves the beach too. We take off our shoes and run hand in hand along the sand and dance on our tiptoes over the edge of the cold water. We fill the bucket with shells and sticks, dig a hole and bury our treasure, then dig it all up again, doing this another eight or nine times until she gets bored. She's just turned two, and she'll never remember me sitting in my kitchen with sad eyes.

Sometimes, Sadie and James come with us, and I love that too, but I feel like I have time to make up with Matilda. I didn't meet her until she was five days old. She was born by emergency C-section, and Sadie lost so much blood she had an extended stay in hospital. I cry when I think about the things I missed out on and the times I wasn't there for Sadie.

"Don't be ridiculous," she said when I phoned her in tears, because it just seemed to hit me out of nowhere that I'd spent more than three years under self-imposed isolation.

"You *were* there for me," she told me. "Always. I mean, I could always count on you to be home, right?" And she laughed, and I laughed and cried, and I promised her fiercely that I'd be the first person to visit her in the hospital if she has another baby.

"Oh, I'm far too old to have another baby," she said, but then she changed the subject and I knew that maybe part of her was hoping that it wasn't out of the question. If she does have another baby, I'm glad it will be with Colin. He's the kind of loving, loyal, generous guy you want your best friend to end up with, and he's also the kind of guy Sadie needs—funny and patient and great with her kids. It was a little weird meeting him, of course. But he seemed nervous too, and when Sadie went to the bathroom and left us alone in the quietest corner of the pub we could find, he leaned over the table and told me how proud Sadie was of me.

Last week, James and Matilda had a sleepover at my house, and Colin took Sadie to her favorite restaurant and asked her to marry him. She phoned me at midnight, yelling, "Meredith Maggs, you'd better be my fucking bridesmaid!" They're planning a winter wedding, and I've never seen Sadie so excited.

"You can bring a date to the wedding," she said this morning when I picked up Matilda.

"You keep saying that," I said.

"Well, you can."

"We'll see," I said. December seems a long way off.

"Colin has some nice single friends…" she said, winking at me.

"Enough," I told her.

I'm not lying when I tell her that dating is the last thing on my mind right now. People talk all the time about sharing their lives with someone else, but I'm not ready to share mine. And in any case, I *am* sharing my life—with my sister, and my friends, and James. And Matilda, whose tiny sandy fingers squeeze mine as we make our way along the beach, back toward the car.

She stops and holds her arms up to me. "Meh," she says, and I scoop her up and hug her tight. Then I take out my phone and take a selfie of our grinning faces.

Day 1,510

Friday, September 6, 2019

Fee is on time for once. "Maggie had her baby," she tells me as she opens the passenger door for me from the inside.

"Auntie Linda's Maggie?"

"Yeah. A wee boy. All those pink cardigans gone to waste."

I smile. "Tell her congratulations."

"I will. She was asking after you."

"What did you tell her?"

"Nothing really. Just that you're doing well." She waits until I've fastened my seat belt, then pulls onto the road. "You are doing well, right?"

I look out of the car window, at the houses of people I don't know. "Yes, I think I am."

She turns the radio on and floods the car with loud music. I turn the volume down and focus on the road ahead, watching people get on with their lives—alone, in couples, in families. After a few minutes, we drive over the Kingston Bridge, where a 180-degree view brings together majestic Victorian buildings and vivid street art.

"I'm nervous."

"Me too." Fee tightens her grip on the steering wheel. I look at her knuckles, her pale, slim hands.

"OK." I go back to watching the world.

The cemetery is vast, devoid of living people but crowded with graves. "We haven't brought flowers," Fee says, turning off the engine.

"I didn't even think of that," I admit. "I don't think it matters, really."

"How the hell do we find him?"

We go our separate ways and start at opposite ends, under clouds that feel like they're sinking down on us. I hope we find him before it rains; I don't have an umbrella.

I read names and ages and learn what people will be remembered for. Being a loving husband, or a devoted mother, or a true angel, or someone who was *taken too soon*. Some don't get a sentiment, not even an adjective. I think about what that means, why nobody thought it was appropriate to give them an extra word or two, a message of love.

Michael Young's gravestone is small and slim. We learn that his middle name was Angus, that he was a *Son, Brother, Father*. At the bottom of the slab it says:

HE DOES NOT COME INTO JUDGMENT,
BUT HAS PASSED FROM DEATH TO LIFE.
JOHN 5:24

"This can't be him," I say.

"The birth and death dates match." Fee squats in front of the gravestone. "It has to be him."

"He was religious? I find that hard to believe."

"Why? There's lots we don't know about him."

I look at her, looking at the stone. "I guess. I'm surprised, though."

"There's a good chance he didn't decide what would go on his gravestone, Meredith. Maybe whoever bought it was the religious one. Or one of those people who say they believe in God but only go to church on Christmas Eve."

I stare at the words on the stone. *Son, Brother, Father.*

"I don't feel anything," I whisper—only to myself, but Fee hears.

"Me neither," she says, wincing as she stands up. "Ouch. My bones are getting old."

"Normally the final piece of the jigsaw puzzle is so satisfying to place. But it doesn't feel like that."

"Maybe it's not the final piece," she murmurs.

We're quiet for a long time. I think about what she said; I hope she's right.

"I'm four years older than he was when he died. He had no life at all. What would you say to him, if he was here? If he was alive and just turned up one day, out of the blue?"

Fee laughs. "I'd say, 'What the fuck were you thinking, getting involved with her?'"

"Well, if he hadn't..."

"I know."

"There's so much I want to say." I'm talking to Fee, but I'm picturing him. I have a clearer image of him in my mind now, thanks to a couple of old photographs Auntie Linda unearthed.

We stand in silence, shoulder to shoulder, for a few minutes. I'm still acclimatizing to the great outdoors, and it's cold. Apparently I'd forgotten that early September in Scotland can be winter-coat weather. I pull the edges of my cardigan tightly round my ribs and pull my cuffs over my hands. It's a habit I can't break. I edge closer to Fee and nudge her shoulder with mine. "Hey. Are you OK?"

"I'm great," she says.

"Seriously?"

"Seriously. I feel like my life is just starting."

"I hate you." I pull an exaggerated face. "It takes me so long to get over stuff."

We laugh, spontaneously and freely, then remember we're in a graveyard and laugh even more.

"I'm sorry," she says. "I know I'm a pain in the ass."

"We're so different."

She nods. "But the same really."

"I'm going to report Lucas to the police. For what he did to me. It's the right thing to do." I've been building up to those words for days; letting them out feels like cutting myself free of a heavy weight.

Fee hugs me tightly. "I'm so proud of you, Mer."

"I'm proud of you too, Fee."

We stand for a moment, just being together. I'm about to suggest that we leave when she says, "Want to go and get some lunch?"

I loop my arm through hers and we walk away from Michael Angus Young for the first and last time.

Day 1,516

I can't stop laughing.

"You've swallowed half the pool," Tom says.

I can't help it. "This is my happy place," I tell him. I adjust my goggles and take a few deep breaths. "Ready?"

He nods, his fingers positioned over his digital watch. "Ready, set, go!"

I duck my head under the water and propel myself to the bottom. It's only my third visit but I can already feel my shoulder and back muscles getting stronger. I hover near the tiled surface for as long as I can, until my lungs start to feel tight and the urge to breathe builds in my chest. At this point my own voice whispers in my head, *I am lucky to be here*, and I let myself drift to the surface, imagining myself to be as controlled and serene as the synchronized swimmers I used to watch on the television when Mama would let me watch the Olympics.

Tom is grinning.

"Tell me," I demand between gulps of air.

"You've got a PB—seventy-two seconds! That's ten seconds longer than last time."

"Woohoo!" I shout, splashing him. I don't care that people are looking at me. I might even be crying, but hopefully Tom won't notice a dribble of tears down the side of my already wet face.

He laughs and splashes me back. "You look like a seal with your hair all plastered down like that." And so I do a really terrible seal impression, and even more people look at me, but I couldn't care less.

Officially we're here so Tom can practice his backstroke, so we get down to business. He's having actual swimming lessons as well, because I might be able to hold my breath for seventy-two seconds (and counting) under the water, but I'm not a teacher. He reminds me of this regularly.

"Work those legs," I tell him. "Fast backstroke swimmers have strong legs."

"I'm not trying to be a world champion, Meredith," he mutters. "I just want to make it to the other end of the pool without a float."

"Trust the process, Thomas. Eyes up! Keep your body as long as possible. Long and lean and strong."

We're taking a break when I spot her in the viewing gallery. She's reading a book, her head tilted forward, her glossy dark hair skimming her shoulders.

"I was just thinking... I haven't heard from Celeste for a while," I say casually.

Tom doesn't look at me. "Didn't you have coffee with her last week?"

"Oh yeah, that's right. Feels like ages ago. Well, I haven't heard from her since then."

"Hmm. She must be busy."

"Do you think so?" I stare at the side of his face until he looks at me, then nod my head pointedly toward the viewing gallery. He follows my lead and feigns surprise.

"Oh. Well. There she is."

"There she is indeed." I'm not sure if it's the weight of four eyes staring intensely at her, but at that point Celeste looks up from her book. She smiles, gives us a small wave, her expression uncharacteristically shy.

"I don't remember telling Celeste we'd be here this morning," I say casually. "I must have mentioned it when we had coffee last week, the last time I spoke to her. Isn't it nice of her to come and meet us?"

"Yes, I guess it is. Maybe we could all go for lunch when we're finished here?"

"Oh, I have plans," I tell him breezily.

"That's a shame," he says.

I punch him lightly on the arm. "I think you've done enough swimming for today. Top marks, Thomas. I'm going to stay for a bit and do a few more lengths."

He fake-punches me back. "Thanks, Mer. You're a diamond, do you know that?"

"I sure do." I grin at him, and he grins back.

I watch Celeste watch him leave the pool. She looks back at me, and I wink at her. She brings her book up to her face, leaving only her smiling eyes visible. I take a deep breath and glide across the water, my bare arms, scars and all, making ripples. I'm going to the deep end.

Acknowledgments

My mum is an avid reader. Before she joined the ebook uprising, she was known to devote the majority of her luggage allowance to her holiday reading. She introduced me to the world of books and nurtured my love for writing stories from an early age, supplying me with a steady stream of notebooks and pencils.

So she read all the books, and she'd say to me, now and again, perhaps not when I was ten but certainly when I was twenty-five, or thirty-two, or thirty-nine: "You could do this, you know." I didn't believe her until I finally finished writing a novel, decades after I'd started writing anything that had the slightest hope of resembling one.

If I hadn't inherited my mum's love of literature and my dad's relentless work ethic, I wouldn't have got to this point. And so my first and biggest thank-you has to go to Mum and Dad, Elaine and Alan, for always believing in me. For giving me gentle reminders, but letting me get there in my own time.

So much gratitude to the following:

My tour de force agent, Juliet Mushens, who always says exactly what I need to hear (and knows exactly what I need to write), and the incredible Mushens Entertainment team. Huge thanks also to agent Jenny Bent for flying the Meredith flag in North America.

My publisher Jessica Leeke at Penguin Michael Joseph—you made my dream come true. I knew from the first time we spoke that you were The One.

Acknowledgments

Also at Penguin Michael Joseph: Jen Breslin, Sriya Varadharajan, and Ciara Berry. Thanks for being absolute stars, for handling my book with such care and creativity, dedication and drive, and for holding my hand when necessary.

Beth de Guzman at Grand Central Publishing, whose passion for introducing Meredith to North American readers has blown me away.

Lee Motley (UK); Albert Tang and Grace Han (U.S.)—what amazing covers you designed.

GinaMarie Guarino, LMHC, Katie Thomas, and Nicola Williams—for answering my questions about therapy and social services with candor and patience.

My CBC Creative course mates Claire, Katharine, Lisa, Lucy, and John—you believed in Meredith when I didn't yet know who she was or what she'd become.

Gillian Spiller (née Craig), my BFF (bosom friend forever), a constant in my life for so long I've stopped counting the years. We've been friends even longer than Meredith and Sadie. Thank you for reading this book when it had The Title We Shall Not Speak Of (IYKYK), and for championing it despite said title.

Joanna Blackwood (née Craig), my dearest Jo, my kindred spirit. I don't know where I'd be without you (you've rescued me more times than I can remember). I've never laughed with anyone the way I have with you. Let's scale those mountains!

Claire Frances Clark-Medina—where do I even begin? You're my biggest fan, and the feeling is entirely mutual. None of this would be the same without you. Here's to many, many more years of daily voice notes, reciprocal therapy sessions, and extoling the virtues of reality TV.

Acknowledgments

Louise and Robbie, your big sister has written a book! You're within these pages in small but significant ways, because nothing I do is ever really separate from you guys.

Nana Betty, Gran, Nana Bibith, Papa, Uncle Willie, and Uncle Hugh—I know how proud you'd be of me. How I wish you were here.

Benji, Elizabeth, and Alice—here it is. That thing I was doing in notebooks and on my iPad while you slept and learned and swam and danced and played hockey. It's all for you.